Praise for *A Lady's Revenge*

"An intense spy thriller that hooks readers from the first page… Devlyn makes a unique mark on the genre with her powerful prose and a gripping vengeance theme."

—*RT Book Reviews,* 4 Stars

"Devlyn reveals the darkness of the spy game and entices readers with a talented and determined heroine."

—*Publishers Weekly*

"The characters were pure perfection… Tracey Devlyn will be going on my list of must-read authors with Lisa Kleypas, Julia Quinn, J.R. Ward, Elaine Coffman, etc. It's that good."

—*Books Like Breathing,* 5 Stars

"Espionage. Revenge. Romance… it's all wrapped in strong writing, vivid characters, and beautiful sensuality. A must-read for historical romance fans…"

—*Read All Over Reviews*

"Devlyn offers a unique twist the hero-as-tortured-spy theme with a hard-hitting and emotional romance that makes me believe this author is here to stay. The heat between Guy and Cora made me a firm believer in their romance."

—*Romance Novel News*

Checkmate, My Lord

Tracey Devlyn

sourcebooks
casablanca

Published by Sourcebooks Casablanca, an imprint of Sourcebooks, Inc.
P.O. Box 4410, Naperville, Illinois 60567-4410
(630) 961-3900
FAX: (630) 961-2168
www.sourcebooks.com

Printed and bound in the United States of America
VP 10 9 8 7 6 5 4 3 2 1

To Helene Curtin,
my most amazing mother-in-law. I will never forget our
first meeting, with you sitting in a hospital bed. Even
then, you welcomed me into your family with open arms
and a heartwarming smile. Thank you for sharing your
son and for always celebrating my accomplishments,
no matter how small or large, with hugs and kisses.
Love,
Tracey

One

"Please, my lord," Catherine Ashcroft said. "If you would only read my husband's letters." She indicated the small packet she'd placed on the Earl of Somerton's clutter-free desk moments ago, willing him to pick it up. Despite her personal misgivings about her humorless neighbor, she had made this godforsaken trip to the city to beg his assistance, hoping her late husband's friend would know what to do.

With trembling fingers, she pushed the tattered, black beribboned packet across his desk. "These two mention you," she said. "I have more at Winter's Hollow. Could you please read them and tell me if anything feels amiss?"

He cast her a level stare. "Aren't you in a better position to judge such things, Mrs. Ashcroft?"

From the moment she had entered his study ten minutes ago, he had treated her with courtesy and respect, but she had yet to witness a single emotion crease his strong brow or bend his full lips. It had always been so with him. Unlike her late husband, Jeffrey, she had never enjoyed a companionable relationship with the earl. Their acquaintance had always been one of distance and wary glances. A situation she now regretted, for Lord Somerton might be the only one who could help her locate her husband's murderer. A murder she might have been able to prevent had she been home to receive his numerous missives.

Catherine's gaze took in the earl's wide shoulders and six-foot-something frame, both a formidable contrast to Jeffrey's slighter build. Not for the first time, she noted his calm strength and an almost indistinguishable aura of danger penetrating the air around him.

"Indeed, sir." Her fingers curled until her nails dug into the tender flesh of her palm. "I have already determined something's wrong, but what, exactly, I do not know." Had there been any other way of determining Jeffrey's state of mind, she would have gladly followed it. Being in the earl's company made her body hum with restlessness and her mind waver with doubt—a state that likely had her father, a highly decorated naval officer, convulsing in his grave. There had been no getting around this meeting, though. Jeffrey's virtual abandonment three years ago ensured she knew little of her husband's activities and even less of his desires.

Lord Somerton's eyelids lowered a fraction. "What makes these letters different from the rest of Ashcroft's correspondence?"

This was the difficult part. His lordship was known

for his cold logic and his intolerance for theatrics of any sort. How could she explain the tenor of desperation that penetrated Jeffrey's every word? Its subtlety would be easily missed by those unfamiliar with her husband. Most would think her daft to fault her husband's written words of love, but Catherine knew them a farce. Would Jeffrey's friend also read the message beyond the words?

"I'm not sure I can supply you with a satisfactory explanation, my lord," she said. "It's complicated, to say the least."

He tapped his fingertips against the small stack of letters several times and then caught the telling sign of irritation and stopped. "I'll be sure to listen very closely, Mrs. Ashcroft."

Emotion, at last. But it came with a cost. His scrutiny intensified and the space between them turned thick and suffocating. Catherine smoothed her damp palms down her black pelisse, and a sudden urge to flee scraped against her nerves. What if she had been wrong about the character of Jeffrey's letters? Maybe he really did wish to reconcile and happened to be in the wrong place at the wrong time. If that were the case, her entire trip to London was nothing more than a humiliating waste of time.

"Mrs. Ashcroft," he said, "I don't mean to press you, but I have another appointment at the top of the hour."

Catherine parted her lips and pulled in a slow, steadying breath while directing her gaze away from the earl. The austere quality of his lordship's study made her itch to return to Winter's Hollow. Every room in her country manor was decorated with

cheerful colors and warm, inviting furniture to make
her guests feel at ease and welcome. But more than
that, she ached to return to her six-year-old daughter.
Sophie's limitless curiosity and boundless energy
always soothed Catherine's nerves.

London held nothing for her but pain and loneliness and an acute sense of inadequacy.

She forced the tightness from her chest and the
doubts from her mind. She had not been wrong in
her assessment. From the disjointed nature of Jeffrey's
letters, she believed he was either suffering at the time
he wrote them, or he was trying to tell her something.
Both circumstances had kept her up long into the
night until she had finally made the decision to seek
out Lord Somerton's help. That, and the knowledge
that Jeffrey might still be alive if not for her absence.

Meeting the earl's gaze, she said, "I don't know
that I can explain how they're different, my lord." She
nodded toward the stack of letters. "In those words, I
do not recognize the voice of my husband."

When his features flattened, revealing the smallest
hint of skepticism, Catherine knew she had failed.
She closed her eyes briefly in disappointment before
gathering what was left of her pride and then stood.
She would have to find another way to decipher
Jeffrey's final scribblings. "I'm sorry for wasting your
time, sir. I thought my word on the odd nature of
my husband's correspondence would be enough for
you to at least read them, especially since your name
appears more than once. But I can see I was wrong."
She held out her hand. "If you'd be so kind as to
return my property?"

He scooped up the packet and strode around his desk. The closer he came, the smaller, more insignificant she felt. Then he stood before her, and the heat from his body reached through the layers of her clothing to her flesh.

Slowly, almost painfully, she lifted her gaze to meet his, and awareness stabbed through her center, splintering her mask of sophistication. An old weakness, one she had long since conquered, but not forgotten, washed over her. *Oh, dear Lord.*

Catherine's intimate relations with Jeffrey had been sweet and calming, beautiful in their perfection. Not primal or compelling. Not hot and wanting. The earl's big body and his I-can-see-into-your-soul eyes made her yearn for a night of mindless, unrestrained lovemaking.

She tore her attention away from his unusual luminescent eyes and focused on the letters. Always, she had sensed a volatile power lurking behind his cool facade. One that drew her, one that resisted all arguments of morality. Several years without a man's caress had obviously taken a toll on her starving body.

Lord Somerton stepped closer. "Are you unwell?"

Yes. Never had her attraction for this man overwhelmed her senses so completely. Her urge to flee trebled. She gestured again toward the packet. "My lord?"

His hold tautened. "You no longer require my help, Mrs. Ashcroft?"

Catherine's pulse jumped. Something unpredictable and menacing prowled behind his words. Dropping her arm to her side, she said, "Of course I do. But I sense your hesitance and I have no more time to persuade you to my cause."

Her plain speaking caused both his eyebrows to arch high, and his eyes, a light blue mixed with steel gray, appeared to glow and pulse with an inner life. She had never seen such a startling eye color on anyone else and had always thought the uncommon hue haunting and beautiful. And impossible to forget.

"No more time?" he asked. "Why the hurry? Your husband was killed a month ago."

Guilt slammed against her chest. Her love for Jeffrey might have vanished long ago, but she still cared enough to mourn his death, for her loss and for Sophie's. "I know," she said between gritted teeth. "My reasons don't concern you."

His lips thinned. "I am trying to understand the situation. I don't often have a dead man's wife sitting in my study asking me to read her private correspondence." He waved the packet in the air. "So I must ask once again—what makes these letters any different from the others you had received from Ashcroft?" His features returned to their placid position. "I cannot assist you if you refuse to communicate the full extent of your concerns."

"Please, my lord." Not thinking, she gripped his arm. "Won't you read my husband's letters and tell me what you make of them?" She had come prepared to divulge the full scope of Jeffrey's transformation and to confess the appalling circumstances of her marriage before his death, but now an unexpected embarrassment trapped the shameful words in the back of her throat.

He studied her face for several seconds before his gaze shifted to her hand. Catherine freed his arm, discomfited and shocked by her rash action.

Releasing a breath, he waved toward her chair. "Please, won't you sit?"

Not until that moment had Catherine noticed the dark patches beneath his eyes and the deep grooves bracketing his full lips. Fatigue pulled at his handsome features, and Catherine felt an answering tug of empathy.

What would cause the Earl of Somerton to lose sleep? A family crisis? He had no close living relatives, only his two wards. Former wards, for they were both adults now. She found it hard to reconcile that the detached man before her was the same individual who had taken in two young children after their parents were brutally slain by thieves. All in the name of friendship.

"If I've come at an inconvenient time, my lord," she said in a gentler tone, "I apologize. Would you prefer that I return tomorrow?"

"That won't be necessary." He indicated her chair again. "Please."

Catherine resumed her seat, and the earl followed suit.

"I am persuaded to read your husband's letters, madam."

"Thank you—"

"But I must know what about their contents compelled you to travel all the way to London to seek me out."

He was nothing if not persistent. Pulling in a fortifying breath, Catherine said, "Not long after my daughter was born, Jeffrey became involved in several reformation issues that required him to spend a good deal of time away from us." She plucked at the soft fabric of her reticule. "At first, I applauded his passionate belief that he could make a real difference and even encouraged him to build political relationships that would aid his many causes."

The earl nodded. "Ashcroft was well respected among his peers. He had distinguished himself as a man of honor and principle."

"Yes, well," she said, "during the first year, he wrote to us at the end of every week and came home as often as his schedule would allow. By the second year, his correspondence dwindled to once a month and his visits to three or four times a year. After the third year, he no longer bothered to make an appearance, not even for my daughter's birthday or for Christmas, preferring to send gifts instead."

"And his correspondence?"

"Nothing more than beautifully written instructions on estate management."

"I see," he said in a low voice. "Go on."

Catherine forced herself to maintain the earl's gaze. "Until my husband's funeral, my daughter had not seen her father in three years and I hadn't received a personal note from him for the same length of time." She glanced away then, swallowing back the bitterness that rose to the top of her throat. "My husband's silence came to an abrupt end a month before his death."

He glanced at the packet. "Are you saying Ashcroft sent these, and the ones you have at home, all within the last month of his life?"

"Yes, my lord." Her throat closed around the damning words.

"You are only now reading them?"

"When they first arrived," she said, finding it difficult to speak, "I was burying my father, and my staff chose not to forward them. By the time I had a moment to read the letters, I received word that my husband had been stabbed to death by footpads."

"I am sorry for your loss, Mrs. Ashcroft. On both accounts."

"Thank you." Her heart ached, not for her husband or even her father, for both had forsaken their families for their careers, but for her daughter, who would live the rest of her days without a father. "I regret the lengthy delay. However, once you read Jeffrey's odd ramblings, you will see I was right to bring them to your attention." She pressed on, knowing he would indeed think her a featherbrain after her next words. "My husband was in some kind of trouble before he died, sir. I can feel it in the depths of my soul. I no longer believe a random criminal killed Jeffrey. This situation has the stamp of something far more deliberate."

Her declaration did nothing to disrupt the earl's pensive expression. What was he thinking? Was he devising ways to get her out of his study? Was he measuring her words and wondering if he could trust her judgment? Or did he worry he was dealing with the illogical thought patterns of a woman scorned? Her knee began to bounce beneath her skirts.

"A rather sensational view of the matter, Mrs. Ashcroft."

Catherine clenched her teeth against a sharp retort. She had prepared herself for his mockery, but that did not stop the sting of his words. "Read the letters and see if you still think so."

He studied her for an interminable amount of time before he finally asked, "How long will you be in London?"

"Not long," she said. "I must get back to my daughter."

Nodding, he rose to his full height, and Catherine experienced the same sensation of smallness—no, delicacy—when his large frame towered over her. On one level, his presence was disconcerting, but on another, he calmed her, made her feel safe and secure.

"I have another pressing matter I must attend first, Mrs. Ashcroft." His crystalline gaze roamed her face with a thoroughness that sucked the breath from her lungs. "Go home to your daughter. I will join you in a few days to review the rest of Ashcroft's correspondence."

Her limbs sagged, heavy with relief. "Thank you, my lord. I appreciate your assistance. Grayson and Mrs. Fox will be happy to hear of your return."

"Do not bother informing my staff of my imminent arrival," he said. "I do not plan on staying long."

༄

August 7

"Chief, we need the other letters."

The Earl of Helsford's pronouncement pulled Sebastian Danvers, Lord Somerton, out of his dark musings, which had occupied more of his time of late.

Sebastian shifted his attention from the black ribbon wound around his finger to his agent, Guy Trevelyan, Lord Helsford, who stood near the library window. "You're sure?"

"As sure as one can be when deciphering the words of what appears to be a desperate man."

If anyone could piece together Ashcroft's message, Helsford could. As a master cryptographer, the earl's talent at cracking complex codes was unmatched. A talent Sebastian had used well over the years to thwart Napoleon Bonaparte's hunger for domination.

"Perhaps Ashcroft's widow held the others back to lure you away," Ethan deBeau, Viscount Danforth, interjected with his normal lack of finesse. He sank farther into the cushioned chair, propping his booted foot over the opposite knee. "After the failed attempt on your life, we must rule out nothing."

As they were wont to do since yesterday afternoon, Sebastian's thoughts turned to the widow, and his thumb pressed into the black ribbon. She had changed little in the last four years. Her blond hair, creamy complexion, and petite body were as lovely as ever. She wore the same conservative attire that proclaimed her English to the bone and of the country. But her confident tone and direct gaze were new. No longer did she hover behind a man's protective shoulder or avoid lengthy eye contact. The woman he spoke to yesterday exuded confidence and vibrated with purpose and conviction.

She had come to him for answers, alone and unprotected. What would it feel like to have such a champion? To have a woman brave the city in order to beg the assistance of a virtual stranger on his behalf?

Sebastian pulled in a shallow breath. Dark, unproductive musings, indeed.

"He's right," Helsford said into the silence. "You

are a direct threat to Napoleon's success. We cannot be too cautious."

Sebastian nodded, recalling the recent assassination plot Helsford had uncovered in time to save his life. A plot Lord Latymer, his friend and superior, had helped concoct. "I will keep your words of warning in mind."

During his time with the Nexus, an elite group of international spies sworn to stop Napoleon Bonaparte's conquering tempest across Europe, he had learned many things, often the hard way. But the one lesson he would never forget was that one can never know another's true heart. A beautiful face could be a mask for the blackest soul, and the most horrific mien could provide protection for the purest heart. Worst of all, most people were not wholly evil or wholly good, but something infinitely more dangerous—a little of both.

Sebastian glanced between the two men who had been friends since childhood, men he had helped raise, train, mold. Helsford, silent and thoughtful; Danforth, a volatile mix of passions. Both lethal when the moment called for such actions. The only one missing from this reunion was Cora deBeau, Danforth's sister and one of Sebastian's best intelligence gatherers.

Over the years, he had wondered what their lives would have been like had Ethan and Cora's parents not been murdered. The incident had set off a chain of events that turned the trio of friends into the brilliant spies they were today. Many thought Lord and Lady Danforth's deaths resulted from an interrupted theft, but those close to the family knew otherwise.

Predicting the coming storm between England and

France, his mentor, Roland deBeau, the late Viscount Danforth, had begun introducing unusual skill-sets to his two children to test their interest and aptitude. Of the deBeau children, Cora had always been the most focused, the most levelheaded. Those qualities, and many more, had made her an excellent pupil.

During one of their pickpocket training sessions, his mentor had asked Sebastian to evaluate his children's progress. It was then the elder Danforth had extracted a promise from twenty-three-year-old Sebastian to watch over his children should something happen to him. Three weeks later, Danforth and his wife were brutally murdered by a French assassin and Sebastian became the guardian of two grieving children, Cora ten and Ethan fourteen.

Although he had little experience with children, he had been overseeing his vast estates since the age of twelve—which made him a perfect guardian for Ethan. He understood the young man's grief and fear and lack of confidence. His resentment and his restlessness. For it was Sebastian's restlessness and determination that had caught the attention of Roland deBeau, the former chief of the Nexus.

So Sebastian followed his mentor's wishes and became Ethan and Cora's guardian. To take their minds off their terrible loss, he continued their father's unique training, shaping them into instruments of the Crown.

"Shall I pay Mrs. Ashcroft a visit?" Danforth asked in a low, silky tone, a voice he'd used to great effect in boudoirs across two continents.

"No."

The viscount raised a dark brow, sharing a glance with Helsford.

Sebastian understood their confusion; he was rather surprised by his quick response, too. Any other time, he would have ordered Danforth to employ his special skills. Women loved him. They happily revealed their husbands' or lovers' secrets for a few hours in his bed, where he made them feel special and desirable.

A vision of the widow surrendering to the agent's well-honed touch tightened around Sebastian's chest. Mrs. Ashcroft's gentle beauty had always drawn his eye, and for that reason alone, he had kept her at a distance. He never dallied with his agents' women. So the sharp swell of jealousy he suffered in reaction to Danforth's query both surprised and confused him.

He shoved the ribbon into his coat pocket and discarded the disturbing image of Danforth and the widow. The task of removing the image from his mind took far longer than it should. He forced his thoughts toward a conversation he'd had earlier that morning with the Superintendent of Aliens. "According to Reeves, the Alien Office is investigating my part in Latymer's deception."

Danforth shot up from his chair and Helsford turned his back on the window.

"Are they mad?" Danforth demanded.

"What's this?" Helsford asked.

Sebastian rose to refill his glass from the sideboard. He took a healthy, fortifying swallow of the brandy. "It is nothing I would not do if I were in his place."

"That's absurd and you know it, Chief," Danforth said. "You nearly lost your life because of Latymer's scheme. Besides, no one is more loyal to our mission than you."

Sebastian stared into his now empty glass, debating whether to replenish it or not. "Ah, but it was my friend and my watch."

"Latymer was also your superior. You can't be expected to know his every move." Danforth strode the length of the library. "Bloody nonsense, if you ask me."

"What now?" Helsford's calm question was a stark contrast to the viscount's fierceness.

"Now I retire to Bellamere Park while the office determines the extent of my commitment."

The viscount stopped pacing. "They're exiling you?"

Sebastian resumed his spot at the sideboard. "Reeves suggested a holiday away from the city."

"Who the hell does Reeves think he is banishing the chief of the Nexus?" Danforth continued his defense. "The man's been in charge of the Alien Office scarcely a year."

"Precisely," Sebastian said. "Reeves has not been in his position long enough to develop a solid opinion of me one way or another. And who knows what nonsense Latymer might have been spewing in his ear." He had intended to stop pouring at the two-finger mark, but the amber liquid kept rising. "I am inclined to follow his suggestion. It's long past time I visit my country estate."

"By removing you, he's putting England at risk."

Sebastian studied Danforth, growing more worried for the viscount's peace of mind by the day. In the last year or so, his temper and volatility had grown. "I will not be gone so long as that." He kept his voice calm and even. To Helsford, he said, "Did Ashcroft divulge anything else besides whispers of a faction seeking to destroy the Nexus?"

"Only a personal message to you, sir."

Dread stirred in Sebastian's gut. "Go on."

"He asked that you look after his family."

Anything but that. Sebastian tossed back half the glass's contents.

"Doesn't Ashcroft's property abut Bellamere?" asked the ever-sensible Earl of Helsford.

"Yes."

A new light entered Danforth's eyes. "Brilliant," he said, oblivious to Sebastian's mental turmoil.

Helsford understood, though. Empathy softened the man's normally fathomless black eyes.

Danforth continued, "You can see to your estate, retrieve the other letters, and watch over Ashcroft's family." He smacked Helsford's shoulder. "We'll keep an eye on Reeves and his Inquisition from here."

Such a neat bow tied around an untidy package. "Yes, brilliant."

"What are you going to tell Mrs. Ashcroft about her husband?" Helsford's soft query reminded him that the worst was yet to come. "We are still investigating the situation."

Danforth's expression flattened as understanding dawned. "I'll do it."

Sebastian sent him a grateful yet pained smile. "Thank you, but no."

"There is no reason for you to deal with this alone, Chief," Helsford said.

"My watch, remember?" Sebastian's stomach

churned unpleasantly. "You can help by finishing those ciphers and keeping me informed of Reeves's activities." He glanced from one man to the next. "There can be no announcement as of yet. Our men need more time to find those responsible."

They all fell silent. The younger men were no doubt reflecting on the scarcity of information they had collected since finding Ashcroft in a filthy alley, lying in a pool of his own blood. Sebastian's thoughts, however, had turned toward the future, toward Ashcroft's widow and the truth about her husband.

August 7

The moment Catherine exited Grillon's Hotel, a fierce midday sun stabbed her already burning eyes. She paused in the shade of the building until the white spots overwhelming her vision disappeared. She had hoped to be quit of the city well before now, but a putrid stomach had demanded she stay near a chamber pot all morning. Which gave her plenty of time to review her conversation with Lord Somerton, when she wasn't scrambling for the pot.

Even now, a faint roiling deep in her midsection made her question the wisdom of embarking on a long carriage ride. But her parental instinct pushed her onward, despite the potential consequences to her pride. It was just her bad luck to have selected the pork instead of the fish.

"Excuse me, ma'am." A young man motioned to the door behind her.

Her normal vision restored, Catherine gave up her shadowed spot. "My apologies, sir." She continued on to where her maid, Mary, watched over her trunks while waiting for the carriage to arrive.

Lord Somerton's delay continued to chafe her nerves. So much of her life had been wrapped around the act of waiting. Waiting for her father, waiting for her husband, and waiting for the denizens of Showbury to lower their pompous noses. And now she must anticipate Lord Somerton's arrival and pray he could help assuage her terrible guilt by tracking down Jeffrey's killer.

Then she could begin anew with her daughter and hope her conscience would ease its hold on her in time.

A large cat with matted fur darted across Albemarle Street, chasing a smaller scruffy black dog, whose short legs were nothing more than a dark blur.

"Oh!" Mary exclaimed, scurrying out of the way when the two creatures streaked by, ruffling Catherine's skirts.

Catherine followed their zigzag path, hoping the little dog would make it to safety. She glanced at Mary and they shared a smile. But the disappearing animals made Catherine consider her own departure. Was she doing the right thing by leaving the city? The restless energy thrumming through her veins begged her to stay and search for clues. Whatever they might be.

"Good day, Mrs. Ashcroft," a man called from the street.

She turned to find a blond-haired gentleman dismounting from a rather expensive piece of horseflesh. He handed the reins to a young hostler and approached her with a sure stride.

"Yes, sir?"

He removed his beaver hat, revealing an array of handsome curls, then bowed. "I am so glad to have caught you," he said. "Allow me to introduce myself. My name is Frederick Cochran." Sorrowful blue eyes gazed at her. "A good friend to your husband, or was, I should say."

Mary backed away to a discreet distance.

Cochran, Cochran, Cochran. The name was so familiar, but she had never seen this gentleman before. Her mind scoured her memories for some mention of him, but nothing surfaced. Then, her eyes widened as a vague recollection danced on the periphery of her vision. No, surely she could not be so fortunate. In one of Jeffrey's last letters, amidst his incoherent scribblings, was the mention of someone called Cochran. Or was it Corbin? Collins? If only she had brought all the letters, rather than a sampling, she could verify the name.

"Mr. Cochran? Your name is somewhat familiar, sir."

"Indeed? Did your husband speak of me?"

"To be honest, I'm not sure how I recognize your name," she said. "You were looking for me?"

He inclined his head. "Due to circumstances beyond my control, I was unable to attend your husband's services. When I heard you were in the area, I rushed over to offer my condolences."

"I had not thought my arrival was widely known."

"When one works at the Foreign Office, one hears all sorts of chatter."

"Foreign Office?"

"Why, yes," he said in a curious tone. "That's how I came to know your husband."

Catherine's world narrowed to a small circle of vision, one that centered on Cochran's mouth. She stared hard, waiting for more words to emerge. Words that would clarify his ridiculous statement. None arrived.

"Pardon, sir? Are you implying my husband was also employed by the Foreign Office?"

He searched her face. "You didn't know."

Time slowed, and Catherine's heart slammed once, twice, three times against her rib cage. The crowd, the carriages, the squabbling vendors disappeared. Only silence remained. Punishing, unrelenting silence. Deafening, suffocating silence. "How long?"

He glanced around. "Is this your carriage approaching?"

She nodded, not removing her gaze from his face.

Taking in her small cache of luggage stacked behind her, he asked, "You are returning home?"

"Yes, Mr. Cochran," she said with growing impatience. "Please answer my question."

The carriage rocked to a halt, and Cochran motioned her inside. "Let me explain in a more private setting."

Catherine considered the propriety of allowing a stranger into her carriage, especially while in mourning. But this was London, not Showbury. No one knew her here, and she had learned long ago to take matters into her own hands if she wished for a particular result.

"Very well, Mr. Cochran. Mary," she called.

"Yes, ma'am?" The maid eyed Cochran.

"Would you mind riding with the driver for a short time?" Catherine asked.

"No, ma'am."

While the hotel staff busied themselves loading her trunks, Cochran assisted her into the carriage and made arrangements to have his horse tied to the back. When Mary was seated and all was in readiness, he bounded inside and settled across from her.

They rumbled down the street in silence for what felt like hours. Her pulse pounded hard within her ears and sweat trickled down her right side. "Please do not torture me with this suspense any longer, Mr. Cochran. How long was my husband with the government and in what capacity?"

"I believe Lord Somerton brought him into the fold about four years ago."

Catherine ignored the sharp clenching pain around her heart. "And his capacity?"

He brushed a few specks of dust from his coat sleeve. "Since Ashcroft is gone, I suppose telling you won't do any harm. But I must ask you to keep what I'm about to impart to yourself. Discussing Foreign Office affairs—even old affairs—could have an ill-effect on current initiatives."

"You have my word." She would promise him anything at the moment. "I will not repeat your confidence."

"Ashcroft was in the business of collecting sensitive information."

"What sort of information?"

"I can't go so far as to tell you specifics," he said, "but he sought any type of intelligence that would protect England's shores."

"Do you mean he was a spy?"

He paused a moment. "The preferable term is agent."

Jeffrey was a spy. For four years. Under Lord Somerton's tutelage. *Dear God.* How could she be ignorant of something so important and dangerous? Could Jeffrey's work for the government be the reason he all but abandoned his family to the country?

"He wasn't always an agent, mind you," Mr. Cochran said. "Somerton started him out as a messenger. Your husband made many forays across the Channel retrieving vital intelligence on Napoleon's movements."

Gut-churning dread washed over her, not only for the danger her husband faced but also for the role Lord Somerton had played in Jeffrey's activities and his decision to keep this knowledge from her. How amused he must have been yesterday. "Are you aware of the details surrounding my husband's death?"

"He was set upon by footpads, as I recall."

"That is what was reported to me." She studied him. "However, I have reason to believe something far more nefarious occurred."

"What do you mean?"

"Based upon what you've disclosed and the nature of the letters I delivered to Lord Somerton, I can't imagine any other outcome at the moment."

"Letters?" A new intensity entered his tone.

"My husband's," she said. "Jeffrey sent me several pieces of correspondence before he died. They made little sense to me, but a few of them mentioned Lord Somerton, so I thought they might be of use to him."

"Interesting, to be sure." He stared out the carriage

window. "Did your husband mention anyone else in his correspondence?"

Catherine hesitated, still unable to recall where she'd come across the man's name, though the letters seemed the most likely source. "I'm afraid I don't recall offhand," she said. "Once I receive the letters back from his lordship, I'll review them again and let you know."

"Very well," he said. "Since we are developing a temporary partnership, I will say that I share your view on Ashcroft's means of death."

"You think he was executed, too?"

"Not at all." His face scrunched in a look of disgust. "The French execute their citizens. The English perform more civilized forms of removal."

"What possible method of killing countrymen could be considered civilized?"

"One that is quiet and effective and not for the public's delectation."

Catherine stared at him, uncomprehending.

"Assassination, Mrs. Ashcroft," he said. "Although I cannot confirm it for a certainty, my sources revealed that your husband sustained a knife wound to the underarm."

An image of Jeffrey's naked torso lying across a sheet-covered table in the parlor at Winter's Hollow surfaced. "My husband endured a great many stab wounds, sir."

"A ruse, no doubt," he said. "Few but the most highly trained men are aware of the fatal location or of the technique used."

"What technique did the murderer use?"

"The full answer would be difficult to hear," he said. "Let me say only that the killer did more than merely stab your husband. He made sure to sever a vital artery."

Catherine closed her eyes and drew in a deep breath. When she had her stomach under control again, she asked, "Why did Lord Somerton not explain this to me as you are?"

"It is difficult to say why his lordship does anything. However, in this instance, I suspect he was more concerned about the investigation."

"Investigation?"

Cochran grimaced, as if realizing he'd said too much. "The Foreign Office is investigating a few of its staff for aiding the French, and I'm afraid Lord Somerton has not escaped their notice."

She thought back to her brief audience with the earl and recalled the dark circles beneath his disturbing eyes. "That is unwelcome news, sir."

"Indeed, it is for all of us, ma'am," he said. "Lord Somerton is known for his loyalty and willingness to defend those under his command to the death. If Lord Somerton is found guilty and that trust is broken, the Foreign Office shall never be the same."

"Well, let us hope the investigation proves Lord Somerton's innocence rather than his guilt." Why she hoped so after the earl's subterfuge she couldn't be sure. But her husband believed him to be a man of honor and so would she—for now.

"Yes, yes, let us hope." He cocked his head to the side. "Am I correct in that you share a border with Lord Somerton's country estate?"

Something about the way he asked the question made her sour stomach take a turn for the worse. "Yes."

"Very good," he said. "Superintendent Reeves is a cautious man and will require Lord Somerton to leave the city while the investigation is under way. No undue influence, you understand?"

"Of course," she said. "But why is it good that we share a border?"

"Because you can help us keep watch over Somerton while he's away from the city."

"Pardon?" she asked, incredulous. "Are you asking me to spy on his lordship?"

"Goodness, no, dear lady," he said. "I would not put you and Sophie into such a dangerous position. All I ask is that you share with me any unusual activity you might witness and, in exchange, I will keep you apprised of our inquiry into your husband's murder."

Catherine stilled. "You know of my daughter?"

He nodded. "Ashcroft spoke of his *redheaded moppet* often. So much so, that I think of her as a treasured niece." He rubbed the side of his forefinger along his full, bottom lip. Thoughtful, silent. His blue gaze conveyed a secret message she could not decipher. "Perhaps one day I shall meet her."

Redheaded? Jeffrey hated his red hair and often bemoaned the fact that Sophie's blond curls were interlaced with the atrocious color. This conversation had ventured down a path that made Catherine unaccountably ill at ease, but she couldn't for sure say why. She strove for a noncommittal answer. "Yes, perhaps."

"Splendid." He rapped on the small sliding door

behind his head. The carriage slowed. "I shall call on you in a few days. It will be a most productive visit."

Her fingers tightened around her reticule, the black jet beads digging into her flesh. "Productive for whom, Mr. Cochran?"

He hopped down from the carriage and then turned to give her a knowing smile. "For us both, of course." He shut the door but held her gaze as he accepted the reins of his horse. "*Adieu*, Mrs. Ashcroft."

The carriage jerked forward, jostling Catherine as it regained a more even rhythm. She hardly noticed. Her mind spun so fast it felt like the large terrestrial globe that used to take up a good deal of space in her father's study.

Around and around, her thoughts revolved, but they failed to land on anything that would help her understand the events of the last few days. What she'd hoped would be a sleuth-like bid for justice had manifested into an immersion of spies and intrigue.

One thing was for certain, though. Her rather mundane country existence was about to become a good deal more interesting.

Two

SEBASTIAN'S CHEST ROSE HIGH UPON SEEING THE GRAY stone walls of his childhood home. Unlike him, Bellamere Park, with its clusters of square chimneys and expansive gardens, had changed little in the four years he had been away.

Closing his eyes, he inhaled the earthy scent of newly shorn grass and crisp air, never realizing until that moment how much he had missed spending time in the country, where a man concerned himself with putting food on his table, rather than preventing the next attempt on his life.

The last few months had challenged his intellect, his endurance, and his long-held beliefs on a level that frightened even him, a man jaded by intrigue and ruthless when it came to the pursuit of his objectives. Never before had he wondered if all his sacrifices, and those of his men, had been worth the price.

Not until recently.

Sebastian tried to hold on to the unusual tranquility

pouring over him, but he was unsurprised when it dissipated into the biting afternoon breeze. Shrugging off his disappointment, he opened his eyes and kicked Reaper into a trot for the final quarter mile of their journey.

As he descended the low rise, he glanced to the east, toward the Ashcroft estate, and felt a sense of foreboding. Dealing with death, in all its many forms, had become part of his life. Although he could still experience remorse, pity, and sympathy, he never allowed himself to linger in the emotions for long. He could not afford to.

But the Ashcroft situation was different, more complex. More gray than black or white. His duty, first and foremost, was to England, to the security of its borders, and to the safety of its people. The needs of one woman and one little girl were secondary. They could not factor into his actions. He released a steadying breath. Not at all.

Reaper tossed his big black head and broke into a gallop. The powerful thrust forward pulled Sebastian out of his ruminations, and he tightened his grip on the reins again and loosened his thighs. His mount obeyed instantly and slowed his gait back into a trot.

He could wring Jeffrey Ashcroft's neck for sending those letters to his wife rather than to him. He understood his caution, and the agent's plan had been ingenious. Who would ever suspect a man of sending his wife coded messages intended for another? Ashcroft had known his wife well. Had known it was only a matter of time before she brought the letters, dotted with Sebastian's title, to him.

The too-intelligent fool's only mistake had been in not keeping abreast of his wife's activities, or he would have realized she wasn't at Winter's Hollow to receive his correspondence. The delay had likely cost the young agent his life. Another secret to keep.

But as Jeffrey had known she would, his Catherine had traveled to London with the damned letters, and Sebastian had been forced to pretend nothing was amiss. It was a role he had played a hundred times before, though this time proved more difficult.

Every instant she turned those big brown eyes on him, he had come close to telling her everything. She had always had a disturbing effect on his control. When her husband was alive, he had found the wherewithal to fight her pull. Now that Ashcroft was dead, no more physical obstacles stood in his way. Only a ghost.

Sebastian shoved aside his pointless musings and halted Reaper outside of Bellamere's wide double doors. An instant later, a liveried footman emerged to hold his master's exhausted mount. After several hours in the saddle, Sebastian's endurance had also waned. He wished now that he had sent word ahead to warn his staff of his arrival. Waiting for his chambers to be aired and linens to be laid seemed like an eternity to his crumbling strength.

By the time his foot hit the top step, though, his aging butler materialized. "Good afternoon, my lord."

"Grayson." Sebastian smiled at his former accomplice to unspoken crimes, taking in the stooped quality of his shoulders and the deep grooves in his forehead. The man appeared to have aged a score of years since his last visit. "You don't seem surprised to see me."

"Indeed not, sir. Rucker sent word ahead."

"Of course he did." Sebastian must remember to give his London butler an extra day off for his welcome, albeit insubordinate, forethought. "Then you know Parker is following behind with my luggage."

"Indeed, sir. We'll be on the watch for your valet." Grayson waved his age-spotted hand toward the open door. "Per your preference, my lord, I did not assemble the staff." His butler did an admirable job of keeping his displeasure out of his tone. "However, they are ready to serve you as needed."

Nodding, Sebastian said, "Well done, Grayson." He had never favored the custom of pulling the servants from their duties to line up in neat rows to bow and dip toward their employer as he majestically strolled down their center. A bunch of useless rot, as Danforth would say.

Entering the spacious Great Hall, Sebastian found it as much unchanged as the exterior of the manor. Built during the virgin queen's reign, the Great Hall was designed to leave its visitors speechless. And it did. Whether in awe or horror depended on one's fondness for ostentatious trimmings.

Even though he'd spent much of his childhood here, his gaze still roamed over the twin marble columns stretching three stories high. Wide Flemish tapestries lined both sides of the room, covering the upper portion of the walls, and a twenty-foot trellis table sat center-stage before a fireplace large enough to harbor an average-sized man.

His ancestors had a flair for the extravagant—not really to his taste, but he held fond memories of

Bellamere Park and would always consider this his true home. He'd been away far too long, he realized with some regret.

Raised, muffled voices down the corridor drew his attention.

"That would be Mr. Blake, my lord," Grayson said.

"In my study?"

"Yes, sir."

"Is he with a tenant?"

"No, my lord." Grayson's pale blue gaze shifted to the distant closed door. "Mr. Blake is speaking with your neighbor."

Sebastian's heart jolted. "Jeffrey Ashcroft's widow?"

"Yes, sir."

Removing his gloves, Sebastian strove for calm. Thoughts of his fatigue evaporated. He hadn't expected to see her this soon, and he certainly hadn't wanted to be covered in road dust at their first meeting. "What business does Mrs. Ashcroft have with my steward?"

"More of the same, I suspect."

He stared at his butler, wondering how he was supposed to decipher the man's remark when he hadn't set foot on his estate in years. Pulling in a fortifying breath, he turned to find out and did his damnedest to keep his pace even, unhurried. "Thank you, Grayson. That will be all."

As he neared his study, he noted the door was ajar. The agitated conversation from within wafted through the opening, reaching him.

"The railing is completely missing, Mr. Blake," a female voice said. "Garry Lucas came close to tumbling through the small opening and falling into the river."

"But he didn't, Mrs. Ashcroft," the steward said. "Had Garry's mother kept a better eye on her son, we would not be having this conversation."

"Mr. Blake, you know as well as I that the northern bridge is a favorite thoroughfare to the village for the children."

Sebastian recognized Mrs. Ashcroft's voice. He leaned closer to the opening.

"Mmm–hmm."

"You said the bridge railing would be fixed a fortnight ago."

"Mmm–hmm."

"When might we expect its repair, Mr. Blake?"

"Mmm… soon."

"Could you please put down your brush and honor me with your full attention, sir?" Her voice held a warning edge.

The steward answered with a deep sigh, followed by the clattering sound of wood against wood. "I have heard your every word, Mrs. Ashcroft, and have responded accordingly. What else do you want from me?"

"Action, Mr. Blake. I want you to care for his lordship's tenants as is your responsibility."

"I know my responsibility."

"Then why do you ignore it?"

Sebastian's eyebrows rose. The side of his cheek pressed against the door frame, bringing his ear closer to the conversation. He hoped Grayson or one of the other servants didn't happen by and see him eavesdropping in his own home.

"I do not ignore my duties, but I refuse to cater to the tenants' every complaint."

"Is that not for his lordship to determine?"

"Lord Somerton is not here. In his absence, he trusts me to do what's best for the estate."

"Broken bridges are best for the estate?" Incredulity sharpened her tone.

"Of course not—"

Sebastian pushed open the door, having heard enough of the steward's feeble explanation. The moment he entered the study, his nostrils flared, assaulted by the thick, cloying smell of linseed oil and turpentine. His gaze swept across the room, taking in the dozens of amateurish oil paintings leaning against every viable surface. And some not so viable surfaces, like his mother's two-hundred-and-fifty-year-old Cassone chest.

Then he found her, standing five feet away from his steward, wearing all black as custom dictated, her blond hair knotted at the back of her head. But today, her appearance seemed more somber, more severe than when she had visited him in London. Instead of repelling him, however, her look drew forth several questions, intriguing his analytical side and capturing his attention much longer than was proper.

"Excuse me, sir." Indignation lined the steward's brow. "What do you do here? We are in the middle of an important meeting."

Sebastian tensed at the younger man's tone until he realized Blake had no idea that he was speaking to his employer. Two years ago, he had hired the steward, sight unseen, on the recommendation of an acquaintance. Even though they had never met, Sebastian had corresponded frequently with the gentleman and never had cause to be concerned about his management of Bellamere.

Sparing Mrs. Ashcroft another long look, Sebastian caught the glint of righteousness sparkling in her eyes. When she noticed his attention, the sparkle brightened a moment and then dimmed until it extinguished altogether.

An odd pang of disappointment gripped his chest.

"Sir? I must insist on an answer."

Mr. Blake's shrill command interrupted his contemplations of the widow. "A better question is," Sebastian's attention slowly settled on his steward, "what are you doing here? The last I recall, this was my study, not your studio."

The steward's face lost all color. "Lord Somerton?"

Sebastian gave him a mocking bow. "At your service." His gaze cut back to the widow. "Mrs. Ashcroft."

"My lord," she said with a curtsy. "Welcome back."

The neutral tone of her voice gave Sebastian pause. What had he expected upon seeing her for the first time? A bright smile? A glimmer of warmth? Another slow perusal of his body, as she had done in London?

The answer did not come to mind. Whatever he had expected, it wasn't impassivity.

"My apologies for the mess, my lord." The steward jumped off his high stool. "Had I known you were coming, I would have removed my collection."

"Perhaps you might do so now while I speak to Mrs. Ashcroft."

"Of course." The steward began scurrying about the room, gathering as many canvases and frames as he could carry. "Right away. I'll call for a footman to fetch the rest."

"I'm afraid that won't be possible." Sebastian moved to the door and held it open. "The staff are busy preparing my rooms." He had no intention of making this easy for the man.

Mr. Blake attempted an awkward bow. "As you wish, my lord."

"Mrs. Ashcroft, please join me."

She pulled her reticule close and glanced away as if bolstering her courage. The action was reminiscent of how she used to respond to his presence years ago. Where had the confident and determined woman from London gone? Then he recalled the conversation he had overheard between her and Mr. Blake, where she had defended the safety of Showbury's children.

Sebastian set aside the widow's bewildering behavior for now. To the steward, he said, "Open the windows once you've cleared out your possessions. Then I should like to speak with you in the library."

Mr. Blake knocked over a jar of brushes. "Yes, sir."

Sebastian closed the door against the steward's fumbling attempts to clean up his mess. Of all the places the man could have set up his studio, why had he picked Sebastian's study? It would take weeks to rid the room of such strong odors.

He set the problem from his mind and guided the widow down the corridor. "Do you have a moment? I thought perhaps we could step outside to clear our heads."

"Certainly," she said.

He glanced down at her profile, trying to divine her thoughts, but it was no use. Somewhere along the way she had crafted an elegant mask, one with perfect neutral symmetry. It was a tactic he knew all too well.

They strode through the Great Hall and exited one of the double doors leading out to a large terrace at the rear of the house. Sebastian guided her to the stone balustrade that separated the small table and chairs from the formal gardens and parkland beyond. His lungs expanded with a deep, purifying inhalation while he studied the area for potential threats, an act as natural to him as breathing. When he finished his search, he took in his first glimpse of Bellamere's gardens in years.

Row after row of flawlessly groomed hedges and precisely placed flowers greeted his eye. Winding gravel paths connected each unique section to the last. Statuary, ponds, and iron trellises dotted the landscape, providing secluded nooks to soothe one's soul.

The sunken garden was a particular favorite of his. Many times as a boy, he would take refuge in the far corner of the deep-set rectangle, where a small fountain gurgled and splattered water over its low basin. There, he had dreamed of a different life, filled with laughter and family... filled with love.

Even then, his responsibilities had threatened to overwhelm him. As heir to a thriving earldom, he'd had much to learn. Which meant long days of study with his tutor and intense sessions on estate management with his father, who was more concerned with creating a replica of himself than nurturing a motherless boy.

His rigid schedule left little time for being a child, and when he became the seventh Earl of Somerton at the age of twelve, his childhood disappeared. Not until years later had Sebastian understood his father's obsessive need to ready him for the management of his inheritance. His father's obsession was fed by his fear and the knowledge that he was dying and Sebastian would be left all alone. It was Sebastian's first lesson in sacrifice. His father had forfeited a close relationship with his son for a greater good.

Movement to his right pulled him from his bitter-sweet contemplations. He transferred his attention to the widow and found her studying him. For the first time, he noticed the fatigue pulling at her pretty eyes and wondered what, besides Mr. Blake's oils, might be plaguing her.

Ashcroft. The muscles in his neck clenched tight. Of course, she would be worried about the circumstances surrounding her husband's death. Sebastian regretted not being able to set her mind at ease—though learning the truth behind her husband's brutal murder might have the opposite effect.

Ignoring her evident signs of strain, he focused on a matter he could control. "Better?"

She blinked two times in quick succession. "Pardon?"

"You are rubbing your temple," he said. "Did Mr. Blake's painting supplies leave you with a headache?"

"I've never understood how he stays cooped up in that room for hours." She lowered her arm. "Every time I meet with him, my head begins to pound within minutes."

"Shall I have Mrs. Fox bring you something for the pain?"

"Thank you, no. The fresh air will do." A few seconds later, she asked, "You needed to speak with me, my lord?"

"Yes," he said. "May I call on you Sunday, after services? I thought we could further discuss the letters Ashcroft sent. Given what I just witnessed inside, I fear tomorrow will prove too busy a day."

Her mask slipped then, just the smallest bit. But he saw disappointment flash across her face as clearly as he could see the single freckle marking the right side of her slender neck.

Again, she leveled her dark gaze on him. Intent. Probing. And somehow, seductive as hell. "Have you nothing to share with me now, my lord?"

"I believe it might be best to discuss the matter once I've had an opportunity to wash the road off and rest for a few hours." Talking to her now, with exhaustion beating against his mind, could open the door for mistakes, and that was something he must guard against when near this observant widow.

"Yes, of course," she said, drawing her reticule close once more. "I will leave you to it."

He stepped closer, resting his hand on the balustrade near her hip. Before he knew what he was doing, he pulled in an exploratory breath, searching for her scent and finding only a subtle essence that identified her as a female. Nothing artificial, no expensive perfumes or aromatic soaps. No, this was pure woman.

Sebastian's chest expanded and he had to swallow hard before he could speak again. "I take it Mr. Blake's antics are the reason Grayson urged me to return in his last update."

She nodded. "He did not want to bother you, knowing you were needed in London. But, after Mr. Blake attended a local art exhibit last autumn, his disinterest in managing your estate affairs has magnified at an alarming rate."

He waved his arm toward Bellamere's vast gardens. "Everything here seems to be in order."

She peered over the grounds below. "Yes, your steward likes his comforts."

"And the tenants? How have they fared?" He suspected he knew the answer already, given the conversation he had overheard.

"They grow increasingly disgruntled, my lord."

"Why do I get the feeling I've placed you in an untenable situation?"

"I don't mind confronting Mr. Blake," she said. "I actually look forward to our tête-à-têtes. My household all but runs itself these days, so addressing your tenants' concerns has given me something else to focus my mind on."

"How do I respond to such a statement?" he asked. "*You're welcome* doesn't seem quite right."

"What I have done is of little concern," she said. "Grayson, on the other hand, has to work with the man and try to keep the peace within the household."

Sebastian had a deep affection for the old retainer and did not like hearing about the butler's undue frustration. "I take it Mr. Blake not only absconded with my study but a suite of rooms as well."

"How did you know?"

"It's obvious the steward's cottage would not be sufficient for his needs." He released a sigh. "It appears I have much to rectify in my short visit."

"A man in your position should be able to trust those in his employ to see to his interests."

Her defense caught him off guard, and his grip tightened on the balustrade. "You are much too kind, I assure you, Mrs. Ashcroft. We both know I have a duty to the sound management of this estate, one of which is placing qualified individuals into positions of importance." He paused a moment. "But I thank you for the encouragement, all the same. And I appreciate your intervention with Mr. Blake."

"You're welcome, my lord."

She took a step back, and that's when Sebastian realized the gap between their bodies was achingly small. He straightened.

"I've been keeping a list of items needing your steward's attention." She retrieved a folded piece of paper from the depths of her beaded reticule. "You might find this of use as you move forward."

Taken aback, Sebastian peered at her offering with a mix of wariness and wonder.

"My lord?"

He reached for the list. "Thank you."

He studied her neat writing and counted twenty-seven items. "You are quite organized, Mrs. Ashcroft. An admirable trait." She had structured the information into a series of columns, noting the item in need of repair, the tenant's name, when Mr. Blake was notified, dates she'd checked on the projects' progress—

His gaze narrowed on the last column labeled *Date Completed*. The column that held not a single date. "Mr. Blake has failed to address all of these repairs?"

"I'm afraid so, my lord."

"Some of these date back to a year ago."

She held his gaze, her silence ringing louder than

a death knell. Then she said, "Thankfully the older repairs are more aesthetic in nature. As you can see, the bridge repair occupies the first slot. The farther you go down the list, the less priority the repairs hold."

Frustration coiled inside his muscles. Damn his steward's incompetence. The relaxation he'd experienced upon seeing his estate was nothing more than a vague memory. "I'm grateful for your attention to my tenants' needs, Mrs. Ashcroft. Is there anything I might do for you in return?"

A look of bewilderment crossed her face. "N-no, sir. Attending to those items is more than enough."

"You are rather easy to please, Mrs. Ashcroft."

She chuckled low, but the sound held little humor. "On the contrary, my lord. I'm told I'm quite difficult to please."

"Then it is their failure, not yours, madam." Sebastian experienced an ungovernable need to ask for the name of anyone who had made such a callous statement, so he could drag him back here by the scruff of his miserable neck to apologize.

She sent him an appreciative smile before fixing her gaze on the horizon, toward her home. "I must be off. I promised my daughter a stroll to the lake before dinner."

Mention of her daughter had the same effect as sleet rolling down his spine. Somehow he had to find a way to honor Ashcroft's request of watching over his family without becoming personally involved. For their safety and his sanity.

"She fares well, too, I hope."

"More than well, my lord." The somber edges of

her features transformed into glowing angles. "Sophie is a sweet-hearted girl, full of life, and rather horse-mad, I'm afraid. She turns seven next Saturday."

"From the sound of it, your daughter is keeping you busy."

"Indeed, she does. Her old nurse, too. The poor woman can do little more than watch her flit from one distraction to the next."

"No matter how hard they might be, enjoy these years while you can. Children grow up all too soon."

The widow studied him with a peculiar look that made heat gather around his neckcloth. He broke eye contact and took the opportunity to scan the gardens and treeline again. "I should not keep you any longer. May I escort you home?"

"Is anything amiss, sir?"

Sebastian jerked his attention back to his companion. Her gaze flicked up from his hands, where he toyed with his signet ring. "No, why?"

"You appear distracted." She waved toward the area he had been searching. "Searching for something?"

Surprised by her perception and irritated by his lack of finesse, he emptied his expression of all emotion, stopped twirling his ring, and forced his voice into an equally bland tone. "I am merely enjoying the view, madam."

"Ah, I see."

But Sebastian could perceive that she had not been fooled. He cursed again. His transition from protective agent to bored aristocrat had been too abrupt, too jarring. This mess with Latymer and Reeves was affecting him more than he realized.

He settled what he hoped was a pleasant smile on his lips. "May I provide an escort, Mrs. Ashcroft?"

"No need, my lord." She sent him a thin smile. "I have navigated the path connecting our two properties many times. If you have nothing more for me, I shall retrieve my horse and head back to Winter's Hollow."

Sebastian gritted his teeth, bowing. "Thank you again for your assistance. I shall see you Sunday."

She curtsied, and set off for the stables.

He tapped the folded list against the stone ledge while he followed the widow's route through the garden until she disappeared behind the small maze of tall green hedges.

Despite his blunder with the surveillance, the sensual awareness that had been present during their meeting in London was all but nonexistent today. In fact, she seemed a wholly different woman. Her wardrobe, her hair, her openness—it was all… suppressed. So what had changed in the last four days?

He caught a small glimpse of her again when she turned toward the stables. One thing that had remained the same from their previous meeting was the layer of underlying loneliness he sensed in her. This she could not mask. At least not from him, a man who had lived in emotional isolation for years. Too many years for him to change now, but the widow made him yearn for something closer, something more meaningful.

His gaze roamed over the gardens, and paper crackled between his stiff fingers. Once again, his responsibilities had closed in on him. What he had viewed as a sanctuary a mere half hour ago now felt like another beautiful, unwanted burden.

Three

CATHERINE DID HER BEST TO RETREAT FROM LORD Somerton's presence in a calm, there's-nothing-wrong-with-me manner. But there was something wrong. Something very wrong. It was all she could do not to run, not to flee from the chaos crowding her mind and the unholy sensations invading her body.

How does one run from oneself? She closed her eyes and allowed her lungs to expand on a long breath. The exercise didn't help. Nothing would at the moment. She was too far gone into self-recrimination. Squaring her shoulders, she refocused on the path.

The man she had spoken with today was vastly different from the one she had encountered in London. Today's Lord Somerton was compelling. His anger over Mr. Blake's inaction, his concern for his butler, and his appreciation of her efforts were the reactions of a man who cared. Not someone who could not be bothered with a grieving widow's request.

His eyes—a piercing blue-gray flecked with an unholy silver—were perhaps what disturbed Catherine the most. The combination of striking colors bore right through to her soul, laying open all the raw pain she tried to hide from the world.

She felt wary around him. Exposed. Drawn to the strength chiseled into his lean features.

That strength had not faltered once. At least not until she'd defended his decision to leave Bellamere in the hands of his steward. A flash of surprise, maybe even gratitude, had lit those amazing eyes.

Catherine veered toward the stables. While making her way down a small hill, she allowed her thoughts to circle back to his stunned reaction. One would believe he was unaccustomed to such defense. Much like she was unprepared for his offer to return a favor. In her experience, few men offered such things without an ulterior motive. But, in his expression, she saw only sincerity and gratitude.

She shook her head, unwilling to contemplate the earl's motivations any longer. She couldn't allow herself to be swayed by a few kindnesses. For all she knew, he had staged everything for her benefit.

Why he would go to such lengths, she didn't know. All she knew in that moment was she had given him an opportunity to tell her the truth about Jeffrey's murder, and he'd chosen yet again to remain silent. Not one flicker of regret had crossed his handsome face.

She had been watching.

Closely.

"Good afternoon, Mrs. Ashcroft."

Catherine halted mid-stride, startled by the grooms-man's greeting. "Hello, Jasper. Could I trouble you to bring out Gypsy?"

"Ain't no trouble at all, ma'am." He leaned the

pitchfork against the side of Lord Somerton's enormous barn before disappearing into its depths. Two minutes later, he led Gypsy to the mounting block and rubbed the mare's nose until Catherine was settled onto the saddle.

Jasper handed the reins up to her. "Did you see his lordship, ma'am?"

She patted Gypsy's neck. "Indeed I did, Jasper."

"Do you think his lordship will see to things?"

Known for his gentle nature, the groomsman rarely spoke his mind. That he did so now confirmed the deplorable state of Mr. Blake's management. "Yes," she said. "I think Lord Somerton will see to many things."

He nodded. "Some folks have it in their heads that his lordship agreed with Mr. Blake's way of taking care of concerns."

"But you know better. Isn't that correct, Jasper?"

"Aye, ma'am." He scratched the back of his head, making his hat go askew. "Though some folks wonder why it took his lordship so long to return."

Damn men and their infernal habit of being absent. "Lord Somerton is a busy man, with many responsibilities. If he had known what was happening here, I'm certain he would have returned posthaste. His lordship hires individuals, like yourself, to care for his properties, because he cannot be in more than one place. Unfortunately, not every member of his staff has the same love of their job as you do."

The barrage of words had barely left her lips before Catherine cursed her wayward tongue. If she could have done so without an excessive amount of blood, she would have bit the troublesome appendage off.

What on earth was she doing defending the earl yet again? She did not even know if he deserved such support. For all she knew, the man was an excellent candidate for a cell in Newgate.

The groomsman smiled. "I knew it had to be something like that, ma'am. My uncle used to be his lordship's head gardener. You'd never meet a more surlier, hard-to-please man than Uncle Henry, but he often spoke well of his lordship." He tipped his hat in her direction. "Thank you for setting my mind at ease. I'll let the others know."

Catherine nearly groaned. The earl had better have been sincere in his outrage over Mr. Blake's lack of attention. If he wasn't, she'd have a lot of explaining to do. "Be sure to say hello to your wife."

He released Gypsy and stepped back. "That I will, Mrs. Ashcroft."

The ride back to Winter's Hollow gave Catherine time to wrestle her tumultuous thoughts back into their proper place. She rather liked Mr. Cochran's idea of keeping an eye on Lord Somerton, even though the process was clearly spying. But her mind seemed willing to overlook that fact for two simple reasons. One, if the earl was found innocent of treason, he—along with Cochran—might be able to solve the mystery of her husband's death; and two, just being near Lord Somerton made her feel sensations she hadn't felt in a long time. And God forgive her, she didn't want to give that up yet.

To think Lord Somerton would be the one to awaken her body came as a surprise, considering his penchant for isolation and avoidance of finer feelings.

But it had always been so with him. Even while Jeffrey was still alive, much to her shame. She had never acted on the deep yearnings of her body, nor had she given the earl reason to suspect she carried them.

They had felt wrong, all the same.

Her first opportunity to observe him would be in two days, when they discussed Jeffrey's correspondence. A thrill of anticipation brightened her mood.

She reined in Gypsy outside her much smaller barn. Her toes had barely touched the ground before a small body plowed into her skirts and long, thin arms encircled her waist. "Mama, you're home!"

Catherine laughed, as she always did when around her precocious daughter. She twisted around to smooth her hand over Sophie's soft red-blond curls. "What's all this? Surely I was not gone long enough to warrant such an enthusiastic welcome."

Big, sorrowful blue eyes peered up at her. "You were gone foreeever. I thought that mean Mr. Blake gobbled you up."

In her nine and twenty years, Catherine had few things she could boast about, her daughter being the one exception. Sophie amazed her each and every day with her infectious laugh, insatiable curiosity, and uncanny ability to recall the smallest of details.

She pried open her daughter's clasped hands and found one held a wooden warrior brandishing a sword. From her earliest days, Sophie had been fascinated with anything that had to do with knights, castles, war, and horses. Catherine suspected part of her interest had to do with her desire to hold her father's attention.

Every time Jeffrey had visited, he and Sophie would add a new figure, weapon, animal, or piece of furniture to her miniature castle. In recent years, it had been left to Catherine to continue their tradition of bringing Castle Dragonthorpe to life. She knew the experience was not the same for Sophie, but her sweet daughter had been careful not to show it.

"Don't be silly, young lady," Catherine said. "If anyone was going to do the gobbling, it was I." She emphasized her pronouncement by tickling her daughter's middle, underarms, and neck.

The girl's laughter echoed through the stableyard. The joyous sound delighted Catherine's aching heart.

"Stop, Mama! Stop." Another wave of uncontrollable giggles followed.

A boy emerged from the barn, and Sophie's laughter broke off, replaced by a sunbeam smile. "Teddy, we're going to the lake. Want to come?"

He glanced at Catherine and then into the stables. "Can't, Miss Sophie. I've chores to finish."

Her daughter's face fell. "Can't they wait until later?"

"No, Miss Sophie," he said. "I'm still trying to catch up from this morning. Mama wasn't feeling well and—" He swallowed hard. "Maybe tomorrow."

When her daughter started to protest, Catherine set a hand on the girl's narrow shoulder. "Teddy, sounds like your mother could use a big bowl of Cook's chicken soup. I'll drop some off later this afternoon."

"Thank you, ma'am." He shuffled his feet. "She'll take to Cook's soup much better than what Papa and I have been fixing." His gaze shifted to Sophie, then back to Catherine. "Should I see to Gypsy now?"

Catherine nodded. "Thank you, Teddy."

He tugged on the mare's reins. "Come on, girl. I've a nice big carrot waiting for you." Gypsy's ears perked up, and she followed him inside with a bit more prance to her step.

Sophie sighed and leaned into Catherine's hip. "He never wants to play with me."

Catherine kissed the top of her daughter's head and nudged her toward the house. "We've talked about this."

"I know," she said in a beleaguered voice. "He's working to help his family. But boys need to play, too."

Smiling, Catherine said, "Yes, they do. Let me see if Carson can spare Teddy for a few hours tomorrow."

Her daughter spun around, her hands clasped together in a prayer-like fashion. "Truly, Mama?"

Catherine tapped her daughter's nose. "I'm making no promises. Carson has the final say."

Sophie jumped. "Oh, thank you, thank you."

Catherine laughed. She hoped her daughter would always be this easy to please. "You're welcome. Now let's collect our poles and see if we can catch some fish for dinner."

Hand in hand, they set off. "Can I go with you to see Teddy's mama? She's always nice to me at church."

"Of course, dear," Catherine said. "But I want you to wait in the gig until I know what's ailing Mrs. Taylor. I don't want you getting sick."

"What about you?"

"I'll be fine, pumpkin. There's no need to worry about me."

Her daughter nodded, having no reason to doubt Catherine's word. "Grandmama said I must 'temper my enthusiasm' on Saturday. Does that mean I can't have fun on my birthday?"

Catherine knew her mother was being cautious about appearances. Society observed a strict set of customs when it came to mourning one's father and grandfather. However, Catherine would be damned if she allowed Jeffrey's absence—even in death—to cast a black cloud over another of her daughter's birthdays.

"Normally, I would agree with your grandmother," Catherine said. "But I have taken special care to invite only our closest friends and relatives." She tweaked one of her daughter's curls. "We can laugh until our bellies hurt."

Sophie eyes twinkled. "And dance until our feet fall off."

Catherine laughed. "And sing until the dogs howl."

"And eat sweets until we cast up our accounts."

"What are you two going on about?" a new voice demanded.

Swiping the tears from her cheeks, Catherine smiled at the newcomer. "Good afternoon, Mother." The same height as her daughter, Evelyn Shaw commanded attention wherever she went. Her slender beauty, keen wit, and approachable nature made her a much sought after companion in any social gathering. However, few would recognize her mother in all her current disheveled and dirt-dusted glory.

Sophie bolted forward. "Grandmama, we're going to have such a grand time on Saturday."

The older woman transferred her basket of cut flowers to her opposite arm and hugged her grand-daughter to her middle. "From the sound of it, the festivities have already begun." She peered up at Catherine. "Do you think that's a good idea?"

Catherine winked at her daughter. "What is a party without laughter?"

Giggling, Sophie asked, "Will you dance with us, Grandmama?"

"Certainly not." Grandmama looked aghast. "I will be much too busy using my fan to beat back all the young men who will be vying for your attention."

"Young men? I do not want to dance with *men*."

"Then I'll turn my fan onto the grubby boys who will no doubt be scampering about."

Frowning, Sophie asked, "Who will be left to dance with me?"

"Don't you have any female friends?"

Sophie chortled. "No, Grandmama. You can't be serious."

"Indeed, I am, young lady."

"But I'll be seven."

"So you will."

Sophie rounded on Catherine. "Mama, tell her I'm much too old to pair up with girls."

Turning her hands up in a helpless gesture, Catherine said, "Sorry, sweetheart. I have yet to sway your grandmama to my side once she has her mind set."

Sophie glanced at her grandmama and then back to Catherine. Her eyes narrowed, suspicion making her scowl. "Grandmama, is this another one of your *inducements*?"

Her grandmama sniffed. "You make the notion sound positively criminal."

Shifting her weight to one foot, Sophie propped

her little hands on her hips. "What must I do for you not to scare off my dance partners?"

"The rose bushes could use a bit of snipping."

Sophie started to protest until she saw her grand-mama's eyebrow arch. "Perhaps, you would rather weed the herb garden?"

Her daughter's curls jounced with a violent shake of her head. "No, ma'am. I love snipping off dead things."

"It's settled then." Catherine placed her hands on Sophie's shoulders and kissed the back of her head. "Run along and locate our fishing gear. I have some-thing I need to discuss with your grandmama."

With her shoulders bent forward and her head hanging low, Sophie trudged up the path as if she towed a great load.

"I shall see you at seven tomorrow morning, young lady."

Sophie's mouth dropped open, but she quickly closed it again. Instead of protesting, she made for the garden gate and released her frustration with a solid stomp of her foot and a low growl from her throat.

As soon as she was out of hearing range, Evelyn Shaw chuckled. "Such a little spitfire. Not unlike you at that age."

Catherine stared at the garden's arched entrance long after her daughter had disappeared around the corner. "She will not be pleasant company at the lake now, thanks to you."

"Nonsense," her mother said. "One bite from a fish and her sunny disposition will resurface. You know as well as I do that Sophie does not sulk for long."

"True." Catherine's response ended on a long sigh.

"What's wrong, daughter?" Warm fingers closed over Catherine's arm.

The simple touch replenished Catherine's faltering courage and, at the same time, splayed open her terrified heart. "Lord Somerton has returned."

Her mother's hold tightened. "Did you speak with him?"

"Yes. He came upon me at Bellamere while I was admonishing Mr. Blake about the bridge repair."

"What did he do?"

"He threw the steward out of his study."

"No." Her mother's eyes rounded. "You jest."

"Not at all," Catherine said. "I wouldn't be surprised if Mr. Blake finds himself searching for employment elsewhere. Quite soon, in fact."

"I do like a decisive man," her mother said. "Months of turmoil resolved in a single afternoon. Makes you wonder why wars are fought."

"Greed causes wars, Mother. Not broken bridges."

"Enough about that now." Her mother waved the subject away as one would a pesky insect. "Did he say anything about Ashcroft's letters?"

"No," Catherine said. "He did ask to call on me after Sunday services, though."

"Why not tomorrow?"

Catherine recalled his haggard features, even more pronounced than when she had seen him in London. "He has much to attend to at Bellamere."

"Indeed," her mother said. "Given his current coil, I suspect Lord Somerton will want to confirm the contents of your husband's letters. Probably wants to make sure Ashcroft did not implicate him in any way."

"Implicate him in what?"

"I have no notion," her mother said. "This situation has grown so complicated that I wouldn't be surprised if a French spy were to appear before this was all over."

"Oh, Mother," Catherine said. "Do not let that active mind of yours run amok. As much as I hate to consider this, I suspect Jeffrey attached himself to the wrong woman and Mr. Cochran and Lord Somerton are somehow involved."

"I must say I like my theory better," her mother said. "Yours is just so… common."

"Indeed, it is."

They stared at the garden gate, both steeped in their own musings, then Catherine shattered the silence. "I am thinking of offering Lord Somerton my help."

"Help with what, dear?"

Swallowing back her apprehension, Catherine said, "He's been away for a long while. It will take him days to meet with the tenants, hear their grievances, locate the appropriate craftsmen, and monitor their work. All while he searches for a new steward."

"Don't you have a list of what needs to be done?"

"Yes," Catherine said. "I gave what I had to him, but I'm sure he will wish to visit each site."

"What are you thinking, daughter? Why this?"

Catherine braced herself. "Working with the earl on the repairs will give me an opportunity to observe his activities."

Her mother's lips thinned into a firm line. "I do not understand what this Mr. Cochran thinks you will see. It's not likely that his lordship will reveal anything of value. One does not carry on about one's treasonous exploits in front of a neighbor."

"You are no doubt right." Catherine found herself unable to confess that she had another reason for spending time in the earl's presence. "However, according to Mr. Cochran, Lord Somerton knew more about Jeffrey's death than he let on during our conversation. Perhaps I will see or hear something of relevance."

"I can't be comfortable with this situation," her mother said. "Lord Somerton is no fool."

"Nor am I," Catherine said. "I will remain vigilant."

"Promise me, you will cease this charade the moment you detect danger."

"Promise." Catherine kissed her mother's forehead, then sighed. "Even in death, my husband keeps us in a constant state of anticipation. Always waiting for some sign of him—a letter, a gift, a visit. Why did I not put an end to this half-life three years ago after he missed Sophie's fourth birthday?"

"What would you have done, Catherine?" her mother asked. "Gone to London and dragged your husband home?"

"Why not? It's what a husband would have done to a wife in similar circumstances."

"I can think of two reasons." She anchored the basket around both her forearms. "One, if you had managed to force your husband home—and that's a rather large if—society would have labeled you a termagant and your husband a gelding."

"Mother, I don't think—"

"And two, any man who must be led home by his ear would not have made a happy addition to this household." Her lips pursed. "I daresay if you had not been moved to stick a knitting needle in his eye, I would have."

Catherine's lips twitched. Wouldn't the infamous Isaac Cruikshank have had a jolly time drawing a continuity scene with Catherine dragging her husband home by his oversized ears in one drawing and her mother chasing after her wayward son-in-law with a sharp, gleaming knitting needle in another? She could even see the title of the caricature: *The Gelding*.

The humorous Cruikshank scene faded to the back of her mind and an image of her daughter's hopeful, yet guarded expression surfaced. An expression she had seen so many times over the years, one that diminished into disappointment and then resignation.

"A daughter should know the security and strength of her father."

"Yes," her mother said. "But so few do when competing with the *ton*'s entertainments or the Crown's business."

Catherine's throat clenched at the note of regret tingeing her mother's voice. For years, she had resented her mother's passive attitude toward her father's long absences while an officer in His Majesty's Royal Navy. Not until she found herself standing in her mother's shoes had she been able to put aside old resentments—and exchange them for new ones.

"Sophie will survive the void left behind by her father," her mother said. "She will come out of it stronger, more self-reliant, and more considerate of others' feelings." She paused, her determined gaze boring into Catherine's. "As you did."

Catherine lifted the older woman's hands to her mouth and kissed the backs of each. "As *we* did, Mother."

Her mother's fingers squeezed Catherine's. "Yes. As *we* did."

They stayed that way for several seconds until her mother pulled away, wiping moisture from her cheeks. "We cannot let this business with Lord Somerton and Mr. Cochran carry on too long. Not only is it dangerous, you and Sophie must move on with your lives. No more wallowing around in this senseless guilt."

"Mother, I—"

Voices from within the garden interrupted Catherine's rebuttal. A young girl's high-pitched voice intermingled with a man's low baritone. Before long, Sophie and their manservant, Edward, passed beneath the arch, toting rods, creel baskets, and a container full of worms.

"I'm ready, Mama." Sophie ran the short distance, her creel sliding off her shoulder. She displayed none of her earlier ill humors.

Catherine ignored her mother's gloating look. "Here, let me help you with that, dear." She lifted the long strap supporting the creel and hooked it around her daughter's neck, so that it rested diagonally across her small body. Made for adults, the basket still bounced low against the girl's knee. "Is that better?"

"Oh, yes," Sophie said. "Now I won't have to worry about losing my fish."

Catherine gestured to the rods Edward held. "I'll take those."

"You sure, ma'am? I can carry them down to the lake so you don't soil your fine dress."

She glanced down at her black merino riding habit. "Thank you, Edward. You're right, of course." To Sophie, she said, "Run along to the lake while I change into something more appropriate."

"Yes, Mama." Her small frame nearly vibrated with its need to run free.

"Listen to Edward," Catherine warned. "Do not go into the water and be careful with the hook."

"Yes, Mama." Her acknowledgment came faster this time, more impatient.

"Don't you worry none about us, ma'am," Edward said. "I'll take good care of Miss Sophie until you arrive."

"I know you will, Edward. I'll see you both in a little while."

"Come, Miss Sophie," the manservant said. "Have you ever played Ducks and Drakes?"

"No," Sophie said, beaming. "But I'm sure I'd like to."

"Oh, you'll love this game," he said. "You take a nice flat rock, you see, and throw it across the lake's surface…"

While the two gabbled on about the best angle for skipping rocks, Catherine strode to the house, with her mother at her side. "He's always so patient with her."

"You probably worry about her antics more than the rest of us," her mother said. "It's a mother's lot, but try not to stifle her exuberance too much, daughter. I always feel much younger when in her presence."

"This coming from the woman who told my daughter to 'temper her enthusiasm' on Saturday?"

Her mother sent her a cross look. "Most of our guests understand the situation here, but I thought she needed a gentle reminder about appearances."

"You were quite right, as always." Catherine patted her mother's arm. "I must go change."

"Enjoy your time at the lake, dear."

Catherine climbed the stairs to her bedchamber, but instead of ringing for a maid to assist her with her dress, she went to her writing box, one of the few presents hand-delivered by her husband. He had taken great delight in showing her the box's hidden compartment, thinking it a clever contraption. She thought back to when she had shown Sophie how the mechanism worked. Her daughter had been spell-bound for an entire week, constantly asking Catherine to open the secret compartment. When this business with Cochran and Lord Somerton was behind them, she would present the writing box to Sophie. Her daughter would cherish it far more than Catherine.

She tapped the edge of one panel and another clicked open. Lifting the panel wider, she retrieved a stack of five letters. Although no one else knew of her hiding spot, she wanted to make sure the letters were where she left them, knowing she would have to deliver them to the earl on Sunday.

The moment she had returned home from London, she had sifted through her final stash of missives for any mention of a Mr. Cochran. She didn't come across his name until she had reached the final letter. Even though she knew it would be fruitless, she pulled the folded missive from the beribboned packet and attempted to decipher Jeffrey's words. But like the last hundred times, chunks of legible phrases were broken up by a series of meaningless words.

With impatient fingers, she refolded the note and jammed it on top of the others. She tossed the packet into the secret compartment and moved to close it.

"Mama, are you ready?"

Catherine pivoted to find Sophie standing in her bedchamber's doorway, flushed and unkempt.

"Not yet, dear," she said. "I thought you were headed down to the lake with Edward."

"I wanted to bring my little wooden boat." She held up one of the first figures Jeffrey had carved for Castle Dragonthorpe.

"Be careful not to lose it."

"Yes, Mama." Sophie's blue eyes settled on the writing box briefly. "I'll see you at the lake."

"I won't be but ten minutes behind you."

Sophie smiled. "Enough time for me to catch the biggest fish." Then she was gone.

Catherine laughed and turned to close the secret compartment on the writing desk. She smoothed her fingers over the fine grain, contemplating her meeting with the earl after Sunday services. Once she handed the letters over to Lord Somerton, she hoped he would soon be able to answer all of her questions.

An exhilarating trepidation coursed through her blood. And God help her, she looked forward to seeing the earl again. She became *aware* while near him. Aware of her heartbeat, aware of her flushed cheeks. And aware of the ache between her legs. All of these sensations had been denied her for so long, she had nearly forgotten they existed.

Her fingers found the buttons on her riding jacket, and she began unfastening them. Jeffrey might not have desired her, but she hadn't mistaken the glimmer of interest in the earl's eyes.

Remembrance alone was enough to send a pulse of heat through her body. She would hold onto the heat and the memory of the earl's silvery eyes until Sunday, the day she would become a spy.

Four

SEBASTIAN DANVERS TIPPED BACK THE LAST OF HIS brandy, his mood blacker than the cheerless moon outside his library window. Alone with his own thoughts, his mind had inevitably focused on Lord Latymer's scheme with the French to have him assassinated. From the moment he'd learned of his friend's treachery, Sebastian's well-crafted plans to put an end to Napoleon's dictatorship had splintered into a thousand useless fragments.

Latymer's deception had come close to crippling the Nexus beyond redemption. Had the French succeeded in killing him a fortnight ago, his agents would have been operating blind, placing them and England in jeopardy. The safeguards he'd put in place long ago would have bought them all a little time, but not much.

All his attention to detail had still not protected his wards, and as a result, both had come close to losing their lives in a recent skirmish with a depraved

Frenchman. Sebastian had never married and had no intention of doing so; therefore, Cora and Ethan were the closest he would ever come to being a father. Even with them, his role was more mentor than parent.

Unfortunately, Latymer's treachery was not the worst complication of Sebastian's last mission. The former under-superintendent's subsequent, and rather convenient, escape forced the Alien Office to turn its suspicious eye on Sebastian. He was officially *unofficially* placed on leave. Relegated to the country like some recalcitrant child while the new Superintendent of Aliens sifted through his confidential files for signs of sedition.

Gritting his teeth, he strolled back to the brandy decanter and poured another healthy measure into his glass. A man in his position did not surrender over a decade's worth of clandestine operation files without experiencing a degree of gut-churning dread.

Sebastian turned to stare at the single sheet of paper resting on the small writing desk. The damned thing had kept him pacing long into the night. Before he'd left London, Superintendent Reeves had demanded a list of names, precious names. His agents' names. Sebastian had protected his operatives for years by never revealing their identities. Not to his superiors, nor to other operatives. Everyone used code names to protect them and their families.

Thank God for his foresight. Had he shared their identities and current locations with Latymer, they would all likely be dead now. But the combination of Reeves's request and Sebastian's brush with death gnawed at his conscience. For the first time, he began to question his decision to not share his agents' information with a select few at the Alien Office.

What if his safeguards failed? What would become of those he had protected with his silence? Who would take command of the Nexus and lead his agents safely through their next mission?

He had only to recall Cora's captivity in an enemy dungeon for that particular point to be driven home. If the madman who had kidnapped her hadn't carried a distorted version of love for her, Sebastian suspected she would have left the dungeon in pieces, rather than sustaining horrid bruises, cuts, and burn marks.

Still, he hesitated. If the request had come from his previous superintendent, William Wickham, Sebastian would have had fewer qualms about handing over such deadly information to a man he knew and trusted.

In the year since Reeves's appointment, he had allowed Sebastian to run the Nexus as he saw fit. Sebastian was certain a gentleman with Reeves's credentials—Oxford education, learned lawyer, King's Printer—would look into the backgrounds of those closest to him. The same as Sebastian had done when Reeves accepted the appointment. If Latymer had whispered lies into Reeves's ear, Sebastian would have to trust that the superintendent would use that clever mind of his to untangle the lies from the truth.

Tearing his gaze away from the blank sheet of paper, he strode to the window and pressed his forehead against a cool pane, savoring the contrast to his heated skin. He looked to the east, toward the widow's estate. From this vantage point, he could just make out… nothing. With a new moon riding high in the sky, he could barely see the large urn-shaped flowerpots marking the entrance to the sunken garden.

Thoughts of the widow brought him back to his blunder on the terrace earlier in the day. Unobtrusively scanning an area for potential threats was one of the first tasks he'd mastered after joining the Alien Office. So, how was it that a widow from the country noticed his preoccupation, but skilled international spies could not?

From what little he had gleaned from his butler, Mrs. Ashcroft made a habit of detecting people's failures. His steward's in particular, and now his. Her keen observation skills weren't the only reason for him to remain vigilant in her presence. While speaking with her earlier in the day, he'd had an annoying tendency to compare her honey-colored hair to that of a soft winter's sun and her petite, yet perfectly proportioned figure to sculptures he'd seen of the Roman goddess Venus.

With Superintendent Reeves searching his private files and the widow distracting his thoughts, it was no wonder he'd bungled his surveillance of the garden and the shadowed tree line beyond. Sebastian closed his eyes and forced the tension from his neck, shoulders, and arms. He worked his way down his body until his knees unlocked, and he leaned his weight fully against the windowsill.

Damnation, he was tired. Intrigue had ruled his thoughts for so long that he could not recall a time when the Realm's safety hadn't commanded his daily schedule. Long hours, sleepless nights, and extended trips away from home. Add in a liberal dose of lies, deceptions, and countermeasures, and one had a recipe for growing older far faster than the body was designed to handle. His three and a half decades suddenly held the weight of a man twenty years his senior.

Pushing away from the window, he liberated his glass of its amber contents. The expensive liquor slid down his throat with practiced ease but refused to dull his disquieting thoughts. He grabbed the decanter and sat down at his desk with an uncharacteristic *plop*.

A glass in one hand and the decanter in the other, he rested his forearms on his desk, framing the sheet of paper. The emptiness mocked him. Burned his eyes with its challenging glare. Why hadn't he thrown the bothersome thing back in the drawer and said to hell with Reeves and his debilitating demands? Because he couldn't answer one simple question: *Should he?*

His heart began the familiar, painful tattoo while he watched ghostly vowels and consonants weave together to create forbidden links. Links that could one day force a power-driven ruler to his conquering knees.

Sebastian had sworn never to write down such valuable intelligence. If the information fell into the wrong hands, dozens of lives he was responsible for would be forfeited, and by extension, hundreds would perish. *Should he?*

Dear God, he didn't know. Never in his life had he been so indecisive. But this decision could have ramifications far beyond his comprehension. And yet, if he did not give Reeves the list of secret service agents and something happened to him *and* his safeguards collapsed, the Nexus would suffer. England would suffer.

He tipped the heavy crystal decanter toward his

glass again, not stopping until the liquid threatened to spill over the side. He stared at the trembling contents for a long contemplative moment before raising the drink to his lips and indulging in an uncivilized gulp, and waited.

Ah, there it was. Finally.

The first stirrings of numbness penetrated the deep recesses of his mind like a slow, thick fog pushing through the streets of London. Sebastian inhaled a cooling breath, silently encouraging the numbness to greater depths. He took another sip for good measure before exchanging his half-empty tumbler for an ink-dipped quill and then steeled himself against the inevitable bout of sickness. Because no matter how potent the spirit, Sebastian would never feel at ease with what he was about to do.

Dabbing the pen's nib against the inkwell, Sebastian considered his first entry. None of them would be easy, but the first—the first name would start an unpredictable series of events that frankly scared the hell out of him. He tightened his hold on the pen. Who would be his first sacrifice?

Images flashed before his eyes with blinding speed, making his head spin and his world tilt to the left. That's when he saw it.

A missive propped against the table lamp. He recalled Grayson handing it to him hours ago, but he had paid it no mind for he had already crossed the threshold into the darkness that engulfed him more and more these days. Why he noticed it now, he couldn't be sure. But he welcomed the distraction.

Replacing the quill, Sebastian picked up the missive

and regarded the neat script. Beautifully formed letters
made by a confident hand. He lifted the parchment
to his nose and detected a faint feminine scent that
managed to calm his raging imagination in a way the
alcohol hadn't.

Breaking the seal, he pressed open the folds and
skimmed the contents. Warmth flooded his chest.

Dear Lord Somerton,

*I do hope you are settling in at Bellamere Park.
After giving your situation additional consideration,
I would like to extend an offer of my services. I have
come to know the craftsmen in the area quite well and
can make recommendations based on that knowledge.*

*Should you wish to go it alone; however, I have
taken the top three pressing issues from my previous
list and indicated an appropriate craftsman for the
task. Grayson will know how to contact them. This
abbreviated list will get you started while you are
sorting through the circumstances at Bellamere.*

Please let me know if I can be of further assistance.

Your faithful neighbor,
Catherine Ashcroft

Catherine. His thumb traced over the widow's signature. Like her handwriting, her name exuded quiet
confidence, warmth, and invitation. The room shifted
again, righting itself, and the darkness surrounding him
began to ebb away.

She wanted to help him.

Sebastian could not recall the last time someone wanted to be of service to him without an outstretched hand in return or, in less favorable circumstances, using the service as a mask for something a great deal more diabolical. He supposed the widow could be pandering to him in the hopes of snagging a new husband.

But that scheme did not ring true. With a difficult marriage behind her, she would not be keen on taking vows again. Unlike the aristocracy, Ashcroft had no qualms about investing his money in the Stock Exchange. As a result, his widow and daughter were set for the foreseeable future. However, she was nothing if not practical and would want what was best for her daughter. Which meant she might be father-shopping rather than husband-hunting.

He pressed the tips of his fingers into the flesh covering his pounding temple. Agents shackled with families could be compromised by the enemy and distracted from their purpose. He had known this when recruiting Ashcroft. But the young man had shown such promise that Sebastian had ignored the greatest—and last—lesson his murdered mentor had ever taught: Families don't survive the spy business.

And Sebastian would have to live with the knowledge that, given the same situation, he would have recruited Ashcroft all over again. Because England had needed the clever young man as much as, if not more than, his family did.

Sebastian blew out a harsh breath. The sight of Jeffrey Ashcroft slouched against the side of a soot-covered building, blood spreading across his filched peasant's shirt, surfaced with aching clarity. Slamming his eyes shut, he squeezed the bridge of his nose in a feeble attempt to block the memories of that disastrous night. When pressure failed to provide the desired results, he retrieved his glass and belted back the last dregs of his drink.

Once he retrieved the rest of Ashcroft's letters, and Helsford deciphered them, Sebastian would come up with a believable story for the widow. One that would identify a murderer and provide Catherine and her daughter with a measure of justice.

From the tone of Ashcroft's previous correspondence, Sebastian suspected the agent had stumbled across something significant. Something he hadn't wanted to reveal through their normal channels of communication. Which meant they could be dealing with one or more prominent figures in the government or the *ton*.

Again.

They were still trying to assess the damage done by Latymer's scheming. If the Foreign Office was housing another high-level double spy, the repercussions could be disastrous. Sebastian prayed Ashcroft's last batch of correspondence held the vital clue they needed in order to circumvent another threat.

Sebastian stared hard at Catherine's signature. All thoughts of Ashcroft, danger, and missives faded to the background. The widow, with her generous heart, staunch support, and perfect English body, sliced through his troubled musings.

What would it be like to share the company of an attractive woman who wished him no ill will? Just a few stolen hours. Hours in which he debated nothing more complicated than overseeing a series of repairs. And where he might steal a kiss or deliver a caress.

Could he spend time with Catherine and keep the details of her husband's death a secret? Could he watch over his agent's family and plot ways to entice the widow into his bed? He released a cynical half-snort. Of course he could. It was what he did best.

Deception, lies, and secrets.

Five

THE INTRUDER STARED AT THE SLEEPING FORM WELL into the pre-dawn hours for the simple pleasure of knowing he could. The widow's locking mechanisms were good, but they were no deterrent for a man who had spent years accessing forbidden places.

The bed creaked and its inhabitant shifted onto her side, facing him. Feminine perfection. Innocence personified. A weapon of destruction.

All she had to do was open those long-lashed eyelids and the serenity of the moment would be lost, transformed into precipitous violence. But her eyes remained shut and her soft, even breaths pierced the air with their gentleness.

Disappointment settled in his chest. Even though he enjoyed the power of undetected observation, he loved the thrill of discovery more. Loved witnessing his victim's first moment of awareness, that paralyzing second when she senses danger lurking within her haven of safety. The ensuing gasping, pleading, and crying for mercy all added to his pleasure. The longer his victim lived in a world of anticipatory terror, the greater his excitement.

Fear stimulated him in a way no other sentiment could. He craved its power, sought its bliss. He looked forward to the moment when he could blend his secret passion with his driving ambition.

Soon. Everything was falling into place. Before long, he alone would hold the power of the greatest minds in England, and beyond. Lions taken down by their beloved lambs.

Bored by his companion's idleness, he bent at the waist and smoothed back a lock of hair from her pale, unlined forehead. Her skin was warm against his lips, her scent fresh, exciting. *Soon.*

Straightening, he pivoted to leave and his boot landed on something small and hard. He waited for the ensuing crack, the telltale sound that would signal his presence.

But nothing cracked or shattered or snapped beneath the pressure of his weight. He carefully lifted his boot and knelt down to retrieve the object. Holding it up to the faint light filtering in from the window, he made out the wooden shape of a kilted man holding a long two-handed claymore.

He glanced back at the sleeping form and smiled.

Dropping the warrior into his coat pocket, he slipped out the nursery door.

Six

August 11

SEBASTIAN MADE HIS WAY DOWN THE GRAND STAIRCASE with a crushing headache and burning eyes. If he had not had a full day planned, he would have shot Parker for disturbing his sleep. Instead of murdering his valet, he had scraped his body off the sweat-cooled sheets and made his way downstairs.

Within seconds of gaining the entrance hall, Grayson appeared. "My lord, there is something you should know—"

"In a moment, Grayson," he said. "Please bring a strong pot of coffee to my study and then we can discuss what's troubling you."

"But sir—"

"Coffee, then talk." Sebastian headed toward his study, hoping the noxious fumes caused by Blake's singular passion had dissipated. The last thing his aching head needed was an immersion in turpentine and linseed oil. Turning the handle, he braced himself against an olfactory assault; however, only the merest of fumes reached his nose. He drew a deeper breath and received the same pleasant result.

A sound from the opposite end of the room drew his attention. He nearly groaned at the pleasure-pain of finding the widow in his sanctuary. The sight did much to improve his sour mood, but he now regretted not allowing Grayson to perform his duties. If he had, Sebastian would have detoured to the kitchen for a restorative cup of coffee and another splash of cold water over his face. Perhaps then he would have been prepared for this keen-witted woman.

Nothing for it, he closed the door and braced himself. "Mrs. Ashcroft."

She jerked into an upright position, her cheeks a deep, becoming red, whether from bending over the metal bucket on the floor or from being startled, Sebastian wasn't certain.

"Good morning, my lord."

Feeling disoriented, he nodded toward the bucket. "What have you there?"

"An old family recipe for neutralizing unwanted aromas." Her flush deepened. "I decided to make myself useful while awaiting your arrival."

Sebastian glanced around, finding three more buckets. "Your family appears to be very wise, Mrs. Ashcroft. I can barely detect Mr. Blake's oils."

"Yes, it is amazing what charcoal, soda ash, and dampened cloths will do."

"Have you been waiting long?"

Confusion clouded her pretty brown eyes. "I arrived a few minutes before the appointed time."

Caution gripped his stomach. Habit forced his gaze

to make a thorough sweep of the room, looking for anything peculiar, out of place, or that didn't belong. If anything, the room appeared a good deal tidier than it had yesterday. But Sebastian could not shake the feeling that he was missing something vital.

He returned his attention to the widow—*Catherine*. "Forgive me, Mrs. Ashcroft, but I seem to have forgotten our appointment."

She stilled. "Shall I come back at a more convenient time?"

The room became blistering hot, and he tried to loosen his too-tight cravat. A vague recollection hovered at the periphery of his mind. "That won't be necessary. Perhaps you could remind me of the nature of our meeting."

She strode toward a small octagonal table and picked up her reticule. Digging inside, she produced a note and offered it to him. "This might jar your memory, sir. I received your summons quite early this morning."

Even from this distance, he could see her name scrawled across the outside of the dispatch, the writing both familiar and somehow wrong. What had he done in his inebriated state last night? The churning mass in his stomach curdled and swept into the back of his throat with unexpected vigor. He raised his fist to his mouth, fighting back the foul taste. What had possessed him to send a dispatch to her at such an absurd hour?

Once he had his body under control, he said, "Last night, I was… not myself and fear I might have written that note at an awkward moment." He flicked his fingers toward the missive. "Would you be so kind?"

She peered at him with wide, owlish eyes. "You want me to read your note to you?"

"Yes."

Her gaze flicked down to where his fingers toyed with his signet ring. Sebastian locked his jaw and clasped his hands behind his back. "Please?"

"This is rather awkward, my lord. Are you certain you do not wish to look at it yourself?"

"Quite, madam."

The command in his tone caused her lips to compress and then she smoothed her fingers over the creases and began reading.

My dear Catherine,

I accept your kind offer of assistance. Please attend me at ten tomorrow morning.

Your forever grateful neighbor,
Sebastian

She hesitated over his Christian name, a subtle confirmation of the message's too-familiar address. Although not appropriate, the contents weren't as bad as he'd feared. Snippets of last night began to crystallize and take shape. Much to his shame, the volatile mix of fatigue, frustration, and doubt that had become harder for him to master had spilled onto the paper in the form of a dangerous yearning.

Even now, hours later, he craved the companion-ship of this woman. Why? There were hundreds of widows in London who would provide such solace and would come to him with far fewer complications. Knowing all of this did not stop him from wanting to sink his hands into the mass of gold silk piled atop her head.

But she had done so much for him already, during a time when she should have been concentrating on her own difficult circumstances. How could he ask for more? "I am sorry to have inconvenienced you, Mrs. Ashcroft. My summons was a regrettable mistake."

"Mistake?" A shot of dismay skittered across her features. "You have not inconvenienced me, sir. I would be grateful for the opportunity to help."

The tendons in Sebastian's neck pulled tight. "You have already provided more assistance than I deserve, madam."

"The process would go much more smoothly and quickly with my aid." She tilted her head to the side. "I assure you, this task would be a welcome diversion. You do recall that I offered to help?"

"Yes, I recall," he said. "But I also know you likely did so because it is in your nature to set things aright."

She started to protest, but he held up a staying finger. "Within the last three months, you have lost your father, your husband, and you have dueled with my steward. I will not add to your burden."

Dropping her gaze, she said nothing for several seconds. He followed her line of sight, to where her hands clutched the drawstrings of her reticule with crushing force.

Finally, she lifted her chin and straightened her back. "Very well, my lord," she said. "Please feel free to call upon me should you change your mind."

"Do not fret, Mrs. Ashcroft," he said, driving the point home. "If I find myself in need of counsel, Grayson is more than up for the task."

Nodding, she regarded the door behind him. "Grayson would make an admirable attempt at seeing to your needs."

Against his will, he asked, "Attempt?"

He could see the topic made her ill at ease, but she eventually answered. "When Mr. Blake began refusing to meet with your tenants, Grayson tried to resolve their issues without the steward's knowledge, but then his knee started bothering him and he could no longer move about the estate."

Sebastian had noticed a subtle limp in his butler's gait. "Go on."

"Unfortunately, Mr. Blake became aware of what was going on and made a terrible scene, embarrassing Grayson and infuriating some of your tenants." Indignation strengthened her voice, her gaze steadied. "This is the main reason why I became involved in your estate affairs. Not only did I keep the issues in front of Mr. Blake, I relayed information between Grayson and your tenants."

Few people distinguished themselves enough to warrant Sebastian's notice or garner his admiration. Somehow the widow had managed to do both. "How unfortunate that I did not know any of this before releasing the man." The sideboard, with its stoppered decanters of various colored liquors, drew his attention.

He glanced outside and noted the narrow shadows around the hedges. Lifting his watch-fob, he confirmed the hour. Bare minutes before eleven. *Eleven*. Much too early to indulge and much too late to have lingered for an absentee earl.

Had she really waited an hour for him to arrive? If any of his agents learned he had been late for a meeting that he'd set, they would never let him live it down. At least those who dared to tease him wouldn't. Most didn't.

Unlike many members of the *ton*, he never slept past seven, even when he stayed up into the wee hours of the morning. His body did not need much sleep to function properly. Or, at least, it hadn't.

"It would take me no time to turn the list of repairs I gave you into an actual work schedule," she pressed.

If she were a man, Sebastian would swear that God had finally thrown a kindness his way. But she was a woman. An intelligent and tempting woman. Therefore, God was not involved. Only the Devil, and he had his trident pointing straight at Sebastian's heart.

Sebastian wasn't certain why he felt compelled to resist her generous offer. The reason might have had something to do with his continuous and overwhelming desire to feel her bare body wrapped around his, to tangle his fingers in the loose skeins of her silken hair. To free his mind of everything but her.

Or the reason might have had something to do with Ashcroft asking him to watch over his wife, and making love to a woman he was supposed to protect felt wrong. Even to a ruthless bastard like him.

Whatever his motivation, at that precise moment, his decision to resist seemed vitally important. Stepping toward the bell-pull, he gave it two hard yanks. "Mrs.

Ashcroft," he said, "I can see that you have a genuine need to set things to rights around here. However, I have managed my family's affairs for over twenty years. Fear not, I will remedy this situation."

As rebuffs go, it wasn't the harshest he'd ever delivered, but it was by far the hardest. Especially when she turned those expressive brown eyes on him, and he saw them flicker with hurt.

"Yes," she said at last. "Yes, of course, you can. How silly of me to have thought otherwise." She waved her hand toward the buckets. "You will have no further need of those by tomorrow." She dropped into a curtsy. "When you are ready to discuss Jeffrey's letters, please send for me. Good day, my lord."

The finality of her farewell cut into the steel surrounding his heart. But he did not try to stop her. Instead, he bowed. "Again, my apologies for the disruption—"

The click of the door closing cut off his apology. He didn't blame her. Not one bit. Although he had spent a lifetime perfecting the art of lying, nothing felt perfect about this situation. In fact, a sense of wrongness elbowed him in the gut with a pugilist's precision.

❦

August 11

"No, m'lord," the farmer said, propping his shovel against the back wall of a small lean-to. "I explained what needs to be done to Mrs. Ashcroft. Haven't the time to go into it again."

Sebastian clenched his teeth around a curse. He

had met with the same resistance all afternoon. Most of his tenants weren't as vocal about their displeasure as Mr. Hayton, but all made sure Sebastian understood he would get nowhere without Mrs. Ashcroft's assistance. The effects of Blake's mismanagement ran deep in their minds, and they were not ready to forgive Sebastian.

"Mr. Hayton," he tried again. "I mean to have men working on the repairs as early as next week. If you would take a few minutes to show me what needs attending, I'll be able to provide a detailed list."

The last time Sebastian had seen Hayton, a few strands of gray had striped the area above the old man's ears. But he had always tackled each day with admirable enthusiasm, putting many men younger than he to shame. Now, Hayton sported a full head of gray hair and his normally square shoulders slumped forward as if they were too heavy for his frail body.

"The roof needs fixing now." Mr. Hayton retrieved his pitchfork. "Rain's coming. Waiting till next week'll do me no good."

Sebastian gathered Reaper's reins. "I'll do what I can to get someone here sooner."

"Mrs. Ashcroft knows who to contact," Mr. Hayton said, combing the pitchfork through a pile of soiled straw.

Sebastian set his jaw, not used to such willfulness and in no mood to hear yet another tenant touting the widow's accomplishments. Mounting Reaper, he set off for home. He'd had enough for one day. He knew he had let them down by not ensuring the steward was performing his duties. However, flogging him in the face at every turn would not make him regret his inaction any more, or remedy the damage already done.

Over the course of the next fortnight, he would show them that he remembered how to be a competent landlord and pray they would allow him to repair the many wrongs done by Blake. As he rounded the farmer's small cottage, Sebastian observed the thinning thatch on the northeast corner of the roof. At least he'd persuaded the stubborn old goat to mention that much.

"Good afternoon, Lord Somerton," a man's voice hailed from the road.

Sebastian turned to find Showbury's vicar sitting astride a large chestnut, a welcoming smile on his face. "Mr. Foster." He joined the other man on the rutted drive, making note of the deep tracks and adding them to his growing list of tasks. "What brings you out this far?"

"I'm meeting Mrs. Ashcroft at the McCarthys to check on the eldest daughter." The vicar guided his horse around a large hole in the middle of the road. "All of sixteen and on her way to becoming a new mother." He shook his head. "And the father nowhere to be found."

Sebastian's lips thinned at the mention of the widow. "Does the girl have anyone to help when the babe arrives?"

The vicar sent him an approving smile. "Indeed, my lord. Despite her current predicament, Meghan's a fine young lady and the McCarthys are good people."

"Do you and Mrs. Ashcroft work together often?"

"Oh, yes, my lord," the vicar said. "I find Mrs. Ashcroft's assistance and practical nature invaluable. And Showbury's residents admire and respect her, which makes visits like today's go much smoother."

Something about the vicar's praise of the widow unsettled Sebastian. He eyed his riding companion, who appeared a few years younger than he and sported masculine features some women might find attractive.

"Are you married, Mr. Foster?" Sebastian heard himself ask.

"No, sir. Not at present," the vicar answered. "But I have been thinking on the subject of late."

Rather than calming the odd swirling sensation in Sebastian's stomach, the vicar's answer made the feeling grow stronger. Before Sebastian could decide whether to inquire further, Mr. Foster waved toward a cottage.

"Ah, here we are, my lord."

Sebastian's gaze swept over the homestead. He expected to find the same age-worn buildings and unkempt prospects that he had encountered on his other inspections. Instead, the cottage and outbuildings appeared well-maintained, plucked free of weeds and devoid of clutter. Yellow and white flowers lined the footpath leading up to the cottage.

The vicar pulled his mount to a halt. "Declan McCarthy moved his family here a little over a year ago. He's hardworking and a skilled carpenter, but I'm afraid the residents of Showbury have never welcomed the family as they should."

"Irish?" Sebastian asked.

"Yes, sir." The vicar's lips firmed, his back straightening. "They're honest folks and don't deserve suspicious treatment. If not for Mrs. Ashcroft, I fear the family would've been forced to move on by now."

For the love of God. Did the woman have her hands in everything? "How did Mrs. Ashcroft help the family?"

A flush spread across the younger man's cheeks. "Well, she, um—" The vicar's eyes widened, then he waved at someone behind Sebastian. "Hello, Mr. McCarthy."

Sebastian eyed the vicar, waiting for the man to finish his sentence. But the vicar dismounted, avoiding his gaze.

With no other choice, Sebastian followed suit.

Declan McCarthy held out his hand. "Good day, Vicar."

"It is that, Mr. McCarthy." The vicar shook the man's hand and then turned to Sebastian. "I'd like you to meet Lord Somerton. Just returned from London."

The carpenter's friendly mien leeched away. "M'lord."

"McCarthy."

The Irishman turned to the vicar. "Are you here to see my Meghan?"

"Yes, sir, I am." Mr. Foster glanced around, frowning. "Has Mrs. Ashcroft not arrived?"

McCarthy rubbed the stubble across his chin. "Not yet. I expect her any minute."

"I've never known Mrs. Ashcroft to be late for an appointment," the vicar mused after checking his timepiece.

"I'm visiting with each of my tenants, McCarthy," Sebastian said. "Is there anything you need?"

Declan McCarthy's thick eyebrows drew together. He looked to the vicar, who gave him an encouraging smile. "The gate leading into the south paddock needs some mending," he said. "I was going to take care of it myself once I finished repairing the molding on the door leading to your gallery."

"My gallery?"

"Declan," the vicar said in a rush. "Is Mrs. McCarthy inside?"

The carpenter nodded, his gaze shooting between Sebastian and Mr. Foster.

Sebastian studied the vicar's flushed face. "Mrs. Ashcroft, I presume?"

"At the request of Grayson, I believe." Mr. Foster swallowed hard. "Declan, I'll go pay my respects to your wife before checking on Meghan. Perhaps Mrs. Ashcroft will have arrived by then."

Catherine had mentioned that she'd operated as Grayson's liaison, but he hadn't imagined her assistance extended to Bellamere.

"Would you care for a refreshment, m'lord?" McCarthy asked.

He glanced at the McCarthy cottage and found three curious faces in a window. A young boy and girl craned their neck, this way and that to see the stranger outside, and a pretty brunette, who looked to be on the verge of womanhood, stood sentinel behind them, watchful and unmoving. Sebastian guessed the eldest of the three to be the enceinte Meghan.

Wanting no part in the upcoming discussion, Sebastian turned back to the carpenter. "Thank you, no. I must be on my way."

After mounting Reaper, Sebastian turned to the carpenter. "When you've repaired the molding, come see me. I have additional work, if you're interested."

McCarthy's eyes widened in surprise. "Thank you, m'lord."

Sebastian nodded to both men before wheeling Reaper about. "Gentlemen."

As he left the McCarthy residence, Sebastian found himself scanning the country lane for a blond head. Mr. Foster's concern for her absence replayed through his mind for nearly two miles before he shut out the vicar's voice. A decade of deciphering men's words and their true intent had him imagining calamity where none existed.

Showbury wasn't London. Men did not go around terrorizing innocent women in this sleepy village. He had to let his mind rest, to suppress the uneasy feeling eating at his stomach. His special talents weren't needed here. He would save those for when he returned to the city.

While in Showbury, he would need to employ patience and charm. Patience to break through layers of mistrust erected by his tenants and charm to convince the widow he needed her help after all. Because without her, making the necessary repairs around his estate would be a study in frustration and inefficiency.

He kicked Reaper into a faster pace, one to match the anticipation thundering through his blood.

Seven

CATHERINE MADE HER WAY DOWN THE STAIRCASE, going over what she would say to Meghan McCarthy. Such an inauspicious beginning for a shy young girl, especially since she refused to reveal the identity of her babe's father. The vicar was an optimist, though, and had asked Catherine to join him one more time at the McCarthy cottage to see if they could coax a name from her.

This venture would no doubt be as unsuccessful as the last. Every time someone broached the subject with Meghan, she became agitated and withdrawn. At first, Catherine thought the girl protected the father because of some misplaced loyalty. But during their last unfruitful conversation, Catherine began to suspect the girl feared her beau.

For this reason, Catherine had agreed to accompany Mr. Foster for another visit. This time, she would find an opportunity to speak with Meghan alone. See if the girl would confide in her. Reveal her secret. Deep in her own thoughts, Catherine missed the low exchange of voices at the entry door.

"Good day, Mrs. Ashcroft," the newcomer said.

She glanced up to find the gentleman she'd met in London handing his hat and gloves to her butler. "Mr. Cochran," she said, at a loss for words. "This is quite unexpected. What brings you to Showbury?"

"Why, you, of course." He combed his fingers through his hair. "Do you not recall my promise to see you in a few days?"

"Indeed, I do." The stiffness in her muscles relaxed from their initial shock. "You simply caught me by surprise."

"Shall I return at a more convenient time?" he asked. "You appear to be on your way out."

"I have only a few minutes to spare, then I must be off to an important meeting." She motioned toward the drawing room. "Shall we?"

"By all means."

Still stinging from Lord Somerton's rebuff, she had a difficult time piecing together information she could share. "If you've come for a report on my observations, Mr. Cochran, I'm afraid I have little to convey." She sat on the edge of the high-back chair, leaving the lemon and mint striped sofa for her visitor.

He eased himself onto the sofa with a languidness that bespoke of someone settling in for a nice long chat. Folding one leg over the other, he asked, "Why is that, Mrs. Ashcroft?" The smoothness of his voice cut through the air like a saber slicing through its victim.

"His lordship returned only yesterday, sir," she said. "I was fortunate to gain a short audience with him. If I hadn't been meeting with his steward when he arrived, I would not have had even that yet."

"Yes, I see what you mean." He drummed his fingers on the cushion beside him. "How did Lord Somerton appear?"

Catherine searched her memory. "Tired. Somewhat preoccupied." *Incredibly compelling, satisfyingly disgusted with his steward. Achingly grateful.* "But his condition might have had more to do with his long journey from London and the disturbing news he received about his estate than with his troubles in the city."

"Disturbing news, you say?"

Conscious of time ticking away, she said, "Yes, a steward who took advantage of his position." She rose. "I'm sorry, but I really must go if I'm to make my appointment."

Instead of following suit, he merely smiled and indicated her seat. "Another moment of your time, please."

Catherine hesitated. She had nothing more to share and she refused to keep Meghan and the vicar waiting. Their audience with the young mother would be difficult enough without the delay.

"I cannot," she said. "I would be happy to meet with you afterward."

"I, myself, am under time constraints." His smile turned brittle. "Please. Sit."

Gritting her teeth, she sat.

"Thank you." His blue eyes bore into hers. "Have you ever heard of the Alien Office, madam?"

"No, sir."

"I'm not surprised. Few have," he said. "The Alien Office operates under the auspice of the Home Office, although some members of the office report directly to the Foreign Office."

He paused, seeming to wait for her acknowledgment. "I'm listening," she said dutifully.

"Simply put, the Alien Office's sole mission is to gather intelligence, both at home and abroad, of any potential threat against England."

"I suspect they have their hands full at the moment." She noticed her knee bouncing, a sign her patience was coming to an end. "Interesting, but I don't understand what this has to do with me."

"You soon will. It's important that you understand the full scope of the situation in which we find ourselves."

"Very well. Go on."

"As I mentioned, a small number of the agents in the Alien Office report their activities to the Foreign Office. These individuals comprise an even lesser-known group called the Nexus. The Nexus's reach spans many countries—England, Germany, Austria, Italy, America, and more—and the agents' identities are a carefully guarded secret, even within the Alien Office."

Dread settled over Catherine. "Perhaps I've heard enough of this secret organization."

"It's not so easy as that," he said. "You and I, we have an agreement. One I shared with my superior, who now has certain expectations."

"Why did you do such a thing? We were just talking, sharing confidences."

"You thought participating in the Foreign Office's investigation a lark, madam?"

"No! No," she said in a calmer voice. "I merely agreed to observe Lord Somerton during his stay at Bellamere in exchange for news about my husband's murder investigation."

"This is true," he said. "But we have come by new information. Information that raises the stakes."

Catherine made a valiant effort to close off her hearing. All she had wanted was for someone to help her confirm her husband's means of death. By doing so, those who killed him would be brought to justice and Catherine might be able to begin the process of forgiveness—of Jeffrey and of herself. She had been certain that a jealous husband or lover had killed Jeffrey, so she had not thought beyond that one possibility. Good Lord, why would she have ever considered her husband was a spy?

"As it turns out, Somerton commands this elite group of international agents."

"Lord Somerton? You're sure?"

"Oh, yes."

Relieved by the news, she said, "That's good then, even heroic." The earl didn't appear the dashing type, nor could she see him gallivanting about as a footman or gardener or whatever disguises a spy uses.

"Somerton's actions were quite heroic, madam. For several years." He glanced out the window, revealing the line of his jaw where a muscle beat. "But he became greedy, as many men do in his position."

"Surely you are mistaken. He's an earl, for goodness sake."

"Greed afflicts all men, no matter their rank, wealth, or personal convictions."

She did not believe such rubbish. Over the years, she had witnessed many acts of kindness from individuals who had little to spare. Not all men were greedy, just the bad ones.

So which was Lord Somerton? "What immoral path has greed led him down?"

"Espionage."

"Yes, we've already established that he is a spy."

Cochran's features hardened. "Against his country."

"A double spy, you mean?"

"Correct," he said. "The Foreign Office has reason to suspect that he is using intelligence received from his agents to aid Napoleon's bid to become emperor of Europe, of all the world, if left unrestrained."

The idea was so fantastical to be ludicrous. "If you believe his lordship to be guilty of seditious behavior, why not arrest him?" Her eyes narrowed. "You did say you worked for the Foreign Office, did you not?"

"Indeed, Mrs. Ashcroft," he said. "However, this situation takes a little more finesse than slapping him in irons. Somerton might not be the only agent in the Nexus involved in this unfortunate scheme."

She clasped her hands together in her lap to stop their trembling. "I assume you have some reason for telling me all of this?"

"You are correct," he said. "I do have a reason for revealing the sensitive nature of this issue. We cannot arrest Lord Somerton, because he alone knows the identities of the agents comprising the Nexus. The moment we apprehend him, they will disappear, and we cannot allow that to happen. Until we confirm the guilt or innocence of each person, we must be careful not to draw attention to our suspicions."

"Because you fear a French invasion and believe the traitorous members of the Nexus will continue their efforts, with or without their leader?"

"Bravo, Mrs. Ashcroft. You have summed up our concerns precisely."

Rather than preen for having gained his admiration, Catherine felt sick to her stomach. "So what is it you would have me do?"

"The Foreign Office has directed Somerton to compile a list of his agents while in the country."

"After protecting them for so long, will he comply? Especially in light of your accusations?"

"Hard to say with any certainty," he said. "Knowing Somerton, I wouldn't doubt that he'd create the list and then conveniently misplace it."

"I'll be interested in seeing how his lordship faces this challenge."

"Glad to hear it, Mrs. Ashcroft, because this is where we need your assistance." His gaze caught hers, held her immobile with feral claws. "I want you to copy the list of names and deliver them to me within the next sennight."

"*What?*" She bolted from her chair and paced the confines of the drawing room. "You cannot be serious. What you're asking me to do goes far beyond our arrangement of reporting suspicious activities."

He didn't flinch at her outburst, simply followed her about the room. "Indeed, it does."

"What if his lordship catches me? If he's as ruthless as you say, I'm putting not only myself in danger but also my daughter."

"That is an unfortunate side effect to this request, but my superiors are concerned about Somerton's ability to complete his task."

"Unfortunate side effect?"

"You do understand now that the Nexus might be the ones responsible for your husband's death, don't you?"

She strove for calm. "I surmised as much."

"Then you also realize that the letters Ashcroft sent you were likely coded messages, warning the intended recipient of Somerton's perfidy. Are you certain Ashcroft did not mention my name anywhere in his correspondence?"

Catherine felt every drop of blood drain from her face. "This can't be happening."

"Ashcroft did mention me."

She nodded. "It's how I recognized your name."

"You lied to me," he said. "This revelation complicates matters."

"How so?" she asked. "If the letters were meant for you, shouldn't that knowledge clarify, rather than complicate?"

He waved off her comment. "I must think on this more. In the meantime, keep an eye out for a list of names. It will bring you one step closer to the justice you so desperately seek."

Catherine's jaw tightened. "How on earth do you expect me to locate something so important?" Especially after Lord Somerton rebuffed her earlier. "If he compiles it at all, he'll likely keep it in a secure spot in the family wing."

"Mama, are you still here?"

At the sound of her daughter's muffled voice, terror ripped through Catherine. She glanced at Cochran, whose gaze slithered from the closed door back to Catherine. She did not like the calculating gleam pulsing in his eyes.

"In whatever manner you deem necessary and expedient, madam." He nodded toward the door. "Let her in."

"I would rather not," she said. "Are we finished? I am late for my appointment."

He stood, the action so abrupt that Catherine stepped back, even though several feet separated them.

"Indeed, we are." Before she could stop him, he strode to the door and opened it.

Her daughter, who obviously had her ear plastered to the wood panel, tumbled inside. She popped up with the speed of a rabbit, looking from Cochran to Catherine with wide-eyed curiosity. "Hello," she said.

"Miss Sophie," he said. "It is nice to finally meet you."

"It is?" her daughter asked.

Catherine angled her body between them. "Sophie, run along. I believe you have lessons to finish."

"I heard your voices." She didn't budge. "Aren't you going to see Meghan McCarthy?"

"Yes," Catherine said, disturbed by the way Cochran continued to stare at her daughter. "I'm leaving for the McCarthys now."

In a stage whisper to Cochran, Sophie said, "She's insane."

"Sophie, we do not discuss such things in front of visitors."

Cochran glanced at Catherine.

"She means enceinte. In the family-way," she provided.

"McCarthy," he said. "This Meghan is Irish?"

Her daughter nodded. "Mama's going to try to find out who the father is."

"Sophia Adele, enough gossip," Catherine said. "Back to the nursery. Now."

Her daughter, not used to Catherine's sharp tone, dropped her head. "Sorry, Mama." She ran from the room.

With her daughter no longer under Cochran's sharp gaze, Catherine was finally able to take a full breath. "My apologies, sir. Sophie does not meet many strangers."

"Like her mother, she has made this a most productive visit."

She stared at him in confusion until she recalled his comment in London about wanting to meet Jeffrey's daughter.

"Now I will leave you to your appointment," he said. "Sounds like you have a challenge ahead of you—in more ways than one, to be sure."

Catherine did not need the reminder of the terrible task ahead of her. How had she become entrenched in espionage? She prayed Lord Somerton cooperated with the Foreign Office's edict, and soon.

After collecting Cochran's hat and gloves, Catherine led the official to his sleek black curricle. "If I locate the item, how will I notify you?"

He settled onto the high bench and accepted the reins from Teddy. "You won't. I'll be in touch. Good day, Mrs. Ashcroft."

She followed his curricle's breakneck progress down the lane, while smoothing her fingers over her aching throat.

"Gypsy's saddled and ready for a nice trot, Mrs. Ashcroft."

"Thank you, Teddy." Using the mounting block, she settled onto the saddle and arranged her skirts before taking the reins. "I'll be back in a few hours."

"Aye, ma'am."

Catherine kicked Gypsy into motion, her mind a constant stream of *ifs*, *buts*, *hows*, and *whens*. She must set aside this issue of Lord Somerton's list of agents for the next couple hours and focus on Meghan McCarthy. The girl's situation needed her full attention.

But her good intentions ground to a halt the moment her gaze swept westward. On a low rise separating their two properties, the earl sat astride a monstrous black horse. Apprehension stiffened her spine. She peered down the lane and was relieved to find it empty.

However, her perceptive mare sensed her rider's anxiety and became agitated, forcing Catherine's attention away. Once she had regained control of Gypsy, she squinted up at the hill. Nothing but undulating grass met her gaze.

A breeze whipped by, ruffling Gypsy's mane and chilling Catherine's heated flesh.

She shivered.

Eight

"Mama, I have to go."

Sophie's indelicate comment took a moment to penetrate the dark layer of Catherine's thoughts. She had not been able to focus on anything since her disturbing discussion with Cochran yesterday and Lord Somerton's unexpected—although brief—appearance at Winter's Hollow. As a result, her talk with Meghan McCarthy had the same dismal results as previous attempts they'd made to discover her lover's identity.

"Mama?" Sophie squirmed at her side.

"Five more minutes, dear."

"*You shall love your neighbor as yourself,*" the vicar quoted. "Jesus went on to say that we should love one another as he loves us."

Catherine's brows rose, and she wondered if Mr. Foster's sermon had anything to do with Lord Somerton's return or Mr. Blake's mismanagement.

Sophie crowded into Catherine's side and tugged at her sleeve. "Mama, I can't wait."

Catherine caught the note of panic in her daughter's voice. She glanced down and saw Sophie's big blue eyes round with alarm. She sighed and started collecting their personal belongings. In her severest voice, she whispered a warning in her daughter's ear. "You will follow me from the church like a civilized young lady. Is that understood?"

Her six-year-old nodded and scooted to the edge of her seat. "Yes, Mama."

They marched toward the open entrance door, and Catherine smiled apologetically to the other parishioners as they passed. When she neared the last pew, the Earl of Somerton's penetrating gaze caught hers. He neither smiled nor nodded, simply followed her approach with gray eyes that glowed with a moonlit iridescence.

Her determined stride faltered, and an embarrassing staccato of anticipation vibrated through her veins, warming her skin. He was dressed in his London finery, and the earl's tailored coat and dazzling white neckcloth stood out in stark contrast to the more loose-fitting and somber-colored garments of most of Showbury's denizens. Why Lord Somerton chose to sit on a hard wooden pew in the back of the church when his family's cushioned seat sat empty at the front, Catherine didn't know.

She would have to mull over his lordship's seating arrangements another time. Because at that precise moment, her daughter's small hand pressed against Catherine's lower back, propelling her forward in a frantic attempt to get outside. Catherine's toe stubbed against the doorsill, causing her to stumble down the two front steps. In a drunken dance of cartwheeling arms and churning feet, Catherine somehow regained her footing at the last minute and skidded to an undignified halt.

For several disbelieving seconds, Catherine heard nothing except the thundering of her heart. She pulled in a calming breath and tapped her hand against her chest in a feeble attempt to soothe her nerves. Even though she had saved her backside, the same could not be said of her pride.

"Sorry, Mama," Sophie yelled over her shoulder. Her little feet tore across the churchyard until she reached the privy, the door slamming shut behind her.

If Catherine didn't know her daughter any better, she would be tempted to thrash the little vixen for breaking her promise. Her temper did not last long, though. It never did when it came to her wild child. Although rash at times, Sophie had a heart that was sweet and pure, especially when compared to other children her age. Rather than pull the legs off a grasshopper, Sophie would rather place the creature in Castle Dragonthorpe, replete with turrets, drawbridge, and a straw bed.

"Are you injured, madam?"

Catherine closed her eyes against Lord Somerton's soft inquiry, her reluctant smile disappearing in an instant. It had been too much to hope that he would have turned a blind eye to her ignoble exit. Given his obvious desire to be quit of her presence the previous day, Catherine was rather surprised by his current solicitude. With reluctance, she turned to greet him, her gaze going first to the church's entrance before settling on his handsome face.

"Do not fret, Mrs. Ashcroft," Lord Somerton said. "No one else observed your near mishap."

The news should have cheered her, it really should. But all she could think about was that *he* had observed her. "That is good to know, my lord. I'm sorry to have disturbed you."

"You didn't." He glanced back at the church. "In fact, you saved me from Mr. Foster's well-intended but rather pointed sermon."

His comment confirmed what she had already suspected. "You think the vicar was trying to mend the rift of Mr. Blake's neglect?"

The right side of the earl's mouth curled into a self-deprecating smile. "Without a doubt."

She considered asking him to expound, but his expression hardened before her eyes.

"Your daughter's hasty departure has proven fortuitous, however."

A shot of chagrin heated Catherine's cheeks. "My daughter is lively—"

"There's no need to explain," he said. "I'm sure neither one of us has forgotten what it was like to sit through church at such a restless age."

His understanding acted as a balm, and the pressure around Catherine's chest relented. So few days passed by that didn't challenge her belief in her ability to raise her daughter without the anchoring presence of a husband. Was she being too strict about Sophie's studies? Not strict enough? Was she giving her enough guidance? Too much? The questions revolved around her mind in limitless patterns, often painful, and generally without answers.

"Indeed, I have not, sir." Catherine regarded the privy, wondering what was taking her daughter so long. Had she missed Sophie's exit? She scanned the area for a mop of blond and red curls.

With most of Showbury attending Mr. Foster's peacemaking sermon, the road and footpaths were deserted. Even the shops were closed up tight, the anomalies being Mr. Littleton, the general store owner, and Mr. Baggert, the butcher. Both men claimed to have their own connection to God, and didn't need to sit through the vicar's ramblings to know right from wrong. At times, Catherine agreed with them. And other times, she simply needed to hear Mr. Foster's reassuring words.

Her search produced no little girl and the privy door remained closed.

Catherine's stomach quivered with a familiar uneasiness. Ever since Cochran's revelations about double spies and coded messages, she had experienced a strange compulsion to glance over her shoulder at odd moments. She also had difficulty letting Sophie out of her sight for any length of time—much to her daughter's dismay.

Over the last year, she had often prayed for deliverance from her boring, well-ordered life. Had she known a perilous game of espionage would be the answer to her request, she would have kept her yearnings to herself. Her gaze bore into the privy's weather-worn door. Sophie was safe, she told herself. The girl's needs were simply taking longer than normal.

"Mrs. Ashcroft?" Lord Somerton prodded.

Startled from her introspection, she shot a quick glance at the earl. "Yes, my lord?"

"Is something wrong?" He looked toward the small outbuilding, where her daughter was taking her merry-sweet time.

She forced a nervous laugh. "I'm sure everything's fine, sir. I fear my daughter might be delaying a tongue-lashing."

"I found this on one of the church steps." He held out a carved image of a destrier, a knight's warhorse. "Does it belong to your daughter?"

"Yes, thank you." She made to reach for it, but a movement on the opposite side of the street snagged her attention. Between the millinery and butcher shops, half-hidden by the building's shadow, stood a man. A short man with a skeletal build eating something tucked inside wrapping used by Mr. Baggert.

Bile bubbled up inside her throat. There were few things that came out of the butcher's shop that could be eaten right from the package. However, at that moment, Catherine could not think of a single one of them.

When the stranger noticed her scrutiny, he stopped chewing. His gaze locked with hers for a tension-filled moment. Then he began the slow mastication of whatever he had tucked inside the butcher's wrapping.

The pressure in her chest returned.

"Do you know him?" the earl asked, his fingertips touching the center of her back, a featherlight connection from which she drew much-needed strength.

Catherine moved toward the small outbuilding sheltering her daughter. The disgusting little man was far too close, and Catherine couldn't stop the niggling suspicion that something was wrong. "I've never seen him before," she said over her shoulder. "Please excuse me. I must check on my daughter."

"Mrs. Ashcroft, allow me to assist."

She hastened across the churchyard, the earl's voice growing more distant. She couldn't respond, nor could she motion for him to follow. Something propelled her forward with an inexplicable drive to put her body between that of her daughter's and the terrible little man.

Please be in the privy, please be in the privy. I swear if you're not I'm going to lash your behind.

The fact she had never laid a disciplining hand on her daughter was immaterial. Simply making the threat gave her overactive mind something to center on besides the horrifying images that it kept dredging up.

"Sophie," she called from a carriage length away.

No answer.

"Sophie—"

A large hand clamped around her elbow. She whirled about, her reticule arcing out to bash her assailant's head.

Lord Somerton blocked her swing with his forearm. "Easy," he said in a calm, not-the-least-bit-perturbed voice.

"My lord, release me." She pulled at her arm, her gaze returning to the small outbuilding. She felt mild embarrassment for her overreaction, but she didn't have time to beg his forgiveness. "Something's amiss with my daughter."

"Stay here." He marched ahead of her and tested the door. Locked. "Miss Sophie." His voice held authority, a note many would not dare ignore.

Catherine, never one to take orders where her daughter was concerned, joined him at the privy's entrance, garnering her a sharp look. Why hadn't Sophie answered his call? Why hadn't she opened the door? She glanced at his profile, taking some solace in his presence, especially after noting the determined set to his masculine features.

"Allow me, my lord." She made to yank on the bolted door.

He caught her hand, and his thumb smoothed over the backs of her fingers. "A moment, Mrs. Ashcroft."

He knocked again, louder this time. "Miss Sophie, this is your neighbor, Lord Somerton, and I'm here with your mother. If you do not come out in five seconds, I'll be forced to kick down the door."

Nothing but an unearthly silence met his warning.

"Five. Four…"

"Sophie dear, please come out," Catherine pleaded. Each number tightened the fist clutching her heart. "I'm not hurt or upset, so you needn't hide in there."

"Two. One." The earl grabbed the latch. "I'm coming in, Miss Sophie."

"No!" shrieked a strangled voice from within.

Catherine shared a quick look with the earl. "Sophie, are you well?"

"No," her daughter cried. Muffled sobs penetrated the privy's oak-planked door.

"Ask if she's injured," the earl quietly demanded.

"Sweetheart, are you injured?"

"No." Her voice sounded small, defeated.

The oppressive tension diminished to a trickle of apprehension. Catherine heard the earl release a breath.

He stepped back several feet. "Perhaps she needs her mother."

Catherine nodded. "Unlatch the door, dear."

She heard the telltale slide of wood against wood. A moment later, Catherine slid through the small opening, holding her breath against the stench of a well-used facility. It took a second or two for her eyes to adjust to the gloom. When they did, she found her daughter backed into a corner, her face wet with tears. "What's wrong?" She worried she already knew why her daughter refused to leave.

Her normally brave little girl bit her bottom lip and cast her gaze to the floor.

Catherine moved closer, wanting to get out of this stinking building that was the size of a broom closet, but knew she must first coax her daughter into confiding in her. She bent at the knees until they stood face-to-face, and Catherine knew immediately why her daughter had refused to leave.

Tears stung the backs of her eyes. "Sweetheart, did you have an accident?"

A small nod. "I'm sorry, Mama."

Catherine cradled her daughter's small chin and forced her head around until their watery gazes met. "No need to apologize, pumpkin. You tried tell me."

"How am I to leave here without all my friends knowing what I've done?"

"Let me worry about that." Catherine rose. "Stay here a moment."

Sophie grasped Catherine's sleeve. "Mama, don't leave me."

"Have I ever broken a promise to you?"

"No."

Catherine kissed her daughter's forehead. "I promise to return in two minutes."

Her daughter swallowed, glancing between the door and the pit sitting in the middle of the building. "Two minutes?"

"Two minutes." Catherine stepped outside and drew in a cleansing breath. She was surprised to find Lord Somerton hadn't moved.

"How does she fare?" he asked in a low voice.

"She had an accident, my lord." She matched his quiet tone. "With such fine weather, we walked to church today, so I must request use of Mr. Foster's carriage."

"There's no need." He motioned to someone behind her. "Mine's waiting."

She peered over her shoulder and found his driver steering a well-matched team of horses. "Oh, no, my lord, we couldn't."

"Why not?"

Catherine lowered her voice. "She might soil your seats."

"No need to worry." He threw open the carriage door. To the coachman, he said, "Miggs, hand me one of the carriage blankets, then lay out another on the bench."

"Yes, m'lord."

Without another word, the earl accepted the proffered item and strode into the privy, eliciting a startled shriek from within. Everything happened so fast that Catherine barely had time to widen her eyes before the earl marched back outside with a blanket-covered bundle in his arms.

As he passed, Catherine caught a glimpse of her daughter's watery blue eyes peering out, her small fingers wrapped around the warhorse she'd dropped on the church steps. Catherine's throat closed, grateful for his thoughtful gesture. How long had it been since a man had carried her daughter in such a protective way? When an answer did not readily come to mind, Catherine fought back her tears.

He placed Sophie inside his carriage and then turned to offer his hand to Catherine. "Mrs. Ashcroft."

She glanced from his hand to his strategically placed carriage to the church beyond. No one milling around outside could have seen past his conveyance and restless horses. Had the earl known before she had ever stepped foot inside the privy what she would find? Could he have arranged such a masterful escape in the short time she was inside? Better yet—would a murderous traitor go out of his way to protect the feelings of one small girl?

"Madam?" he said, with an encouraging flick of his fingers. "Shall we go?"

She glanced at her daughter, who sat bundled in his carriage, enduring a bout of embarrassment but oddly content inside her thick blanket. What if Cochran was telling the truth about the earl's involvement with the French? Placing herself in danger was one thing, but allowing Sophie to come in contact with a potential murderer—possibly her father's killer—smacked of foolhardy behavior.

Speaking of foolhardy, she searched the area near the butcher's shop for the skeletal man. She wanted very much to avoid remembering how she'd charged

across the churchyard, with her reticule aloft, determined to save her daughter from the scary stranger.
All in front of a man she was supposed to somehow
impress long enough to obtain his list. So much for her
motherly instincts.

"He disappeared while we were trying to coax
your daughter outside," Lord Somerton said, his arm
returning to his side.

Surprised, she shifted her attention back to the earl
and immediately felt the effects of his probing gaze.

"Are you sure you don't know him from somewhere?"

"Quite sure. One does not forget such a face."

"True." He held out his hand again. "Ready?"

"Mrs. Ashcroft," a new voice called.

Turning, Catherine sent the vicar a welcoming
smile and then glanced beyond his shoulder to see
parishioners milling around the church. "Mr. Foster.
I see services are over." Behind her, she heard a
muffled yelp and a scuffling noise and then a more
masculine sigh.

"Indeed, they are, ma'am." The vicar stopped a few
feet away and bowed. "Lord Somerton."

"Vicar."

Catherine's gaze slid to the earl, expecting to find
an expression of annoyance, given his curt greeting.
Instead, she found him looking as serious and sophisticated as ever. If not for the small cleft in his chin, one
might liken him to one of the somber marble statues
in the British Museum. But the cleft saved him from
being too unapproachable.

"My apologies for missing the end of your sermon,"
she said.

"I'm sure you had a good reason." The vicar glanced at the earl's carriage. "Are you off so soon?"

Nodding toward the now empty carriage window, Catherine said, "I'm afraid Sophie's not feeling well."

"I am sorry to hear that," Mr. Foster said. "Shall we postpone our ride?"

"That won't be necessary," she said. "I'll have Sophie back to rights in no time. Besides, I'm rather looking forward to our visit."

"Vicar," Lord Somerton said. "It is past time we get the child home."

"Of course," Mr. Foster said. "Forgive me for keeping you. I'll see you later, then, Mrs. Ashcroft."

"Until later, Mr. Foster."

This time, when Lord Somerton held out his hand, Catherine experienced no compunction to accept his escort. With the vicar seeing them off and expecting her to accompany him later, she doubted the earl would indulge in any villainous behavior. Once again, she had allowed her imagination to run amok. Unless Lord Somerton knew about the content of her meeting with Cochran, he would have no reason to harm her or her daughter.

"Thank you, my lord." She laid her fingers in his palm as she ascended the carriage steps. Heat tingled its way up her arm and across her shoulder, spreading until her ears felt like they were on fire. Her hand trembled, and she plopped onto the cushioned bench next to a lump of squirming blanket.

She released his hand, and he shut the door behind her.

Catherine sat forward. "You're not joining us, my lord?"

He glanced at Sophie. "No. I think it best if I ride up top with Miggs."

Catherine reached to open the door. "Please ride inside with us, where you'll be more comfortable. I don't like that we're dislocating you from your own carriage."

Shaking his head, he said, "I don't mind. I rather like riding with old Miggs and his flamboyant stories." He stepped away. "Pull the curtain, Mrs. Ashcroft."

Then he was gone. Catherine stared out the window for several seconds, pondering his considerate actions with those Cochran had described of the Nexus's leader. How could a man show so much care for one small girl and then turn around and conspire against his country? An act that could kill hundreds?

The carriage rocked to the side with the earl's weight, the movement snapping her out of her musings. She closed the curtain and sat back as they lurched into motion. A few seconds later, her intrepid daughter emerged from her cocoon of wool.

Blowing a gold-red curl out of her eye, Sophie asked, "Do you think anyone saw me, Mama?"

Catherine wrapped her arm around the girl's narrow shoulders. "No, pumpkin. Lord Somerton provided a clever disguise."

"Not even Mr. Foster?"

"Not even Mr. Foster," Catherine confirmed. "Lord Somerton made sure of it."

"The earl smelled nice."

Any other day, Catherine would have corrected Sophie's form of address. "Did he?"

Sophie nodded. "Like a tree."

Catherine smiled. "Lord Somerton smelled like a tree? Was it a beech?"

"More like an oak," her daughter said. "Sprinkled with spice."

She pulled her daughter's head toward her and kissed her mop of curls. "Sounds lovely, dear." She adored the innocence of Sophie's imagination. Her daughter was amazing, and somehow she had been born from Catherine's less-than-perfect womb.

Sophie galloped her destrier across Catherine's lap. "Do you think the earl will come on Saturday?"

Catherine's pulse quickened. "Why do you ask, sweetheart?"

Her daughter shrugged. "I don't know."

"Are you sure you don't?" She smoothed her hand over her daughter's curls. "You can tell me."

Sophie picked at the black ribbon on her dress. "I know we're supposed to keep my birthday to just family and close friends, because we're mourning Papa and Grandpapa. But I thought the earl could help me add a piece to Castle Dragonthorpe."

Tears stung the backs of Catherine's eyes and her vision blurred. More and more of late, her daughter craved the attention of a masculine figure. Edward, the vicar, the Walkers' father—it didn't matter, as long as the man showed an interest in her. And now, she wanted to share their special castle-building custom with the Earl of Somerton.

"Mama, please don't cry," Sophie said, her voice cracking. "You can still help. No one decorates the chambers better than you."

"Thank you, pumpkin." Catherine hugged her

daughter to her side. "I'm sorry your father can't be here to celebrate with you."

Sophie shrugged her shoulders again and then cast Catherine an agonized, sidelong look. "Mama, please don't be cross."

"What's this?" Catherine lifted her daughter's chin. "Sophie, you can ask whomever you wish to help build your castle. I would never be upset with you for such a thing."

Her daughter swiped her skinny arm underneath her nose, leaving a liquid trail behind. "I thought the earl could help me set up the torture devices Edward carved for me. I know how you dislike blood and violence." Watery rivulets streaked down her smooth cheeks. "But that's not what I meant."

"Tell me, Sophie," Catherine said with growing concern. "I promise not to be upset."

"Papa's face. I don't see it anymore."

Like the ends of a knot being pulled swiftly in opposite directions, Catherine's throat closed again, swiftly and without warning. The air from her lungs was cut off from the rest of her body. Her head swam, her heart broke. "Oh, sweet pumpkin. You do not have to see your papa's face to love him with your heart." Catherine laid her hand over her daughter's thundering chest. "He lives here. Always will."

Sophie snuggled against Catherine's breast, clutching her wooden horse and sniffing back her sadness. They both said nothing for a long while, simply sat immersed in their own thoughts. Then, in a low voice, her daughter asked, "Will you invite the earl, Mama?"

Catherine closed her eyes. "Yes, sweetheart."

Crisis averted, Sophie soon began chattering on about teaching her pony a new command when they returned home. Catherine listened with half an ear, for her mind had settled back onto the earl. Somehow she would find a way to learn more about his lordship. Perhaps she could invent an excuse to visit him at Bellamere. The contrivance made her cringe. He would likely see through her desperation and think she had designs on his person. If she wasn't in mourning, she might be able to pull off such a scheme—at least for a while.

Her eyes widened. Hadn't the earl mentioned something about her departure being fortuitous before her worry for Sophie overrode their conversation? What had he meant by that statement? She searched her mind for possible reasons. Maybe he had a question about the repairs or about a particular craftsman. Yes, that would make sense.

Now she had to figure out a way to regain their former discussion without seeming too eager. Although she hated the pretense, anticipation vibrated along every nerve and muscle in her body. If she could somehow burrow her way into his good graces, she could play a small part in fixing Mr. Blake's disastrous stewardship while tracking down Cochran's information, plus bring an end to the mystery of her husband's death.

And for a short period of time, she wouldn't be alone.

"Can we open the curtain now, Mama?"

Catherine drew back the heavy material, only to find towering black clouds in the distance.

"Looks like rain, Mama."

"Indeed it does, pumpkin." Catherine tilted her

head back to rest against the carriage seat. She stared at the dark panel above her and tried to ignore the dread seeping into her bones.

❧

Sebastian studied the small collection of books in the widow's library, his impatience growing with each passing minute. He had escaped the vicar's pointed sermon about forgiving one's neighbor only to be met with Mrs. Ashcroft's domestic issue.

He didn't know what was worse—the vicar publicly challenging the residents of Showbury not to cast judgment on their landlord for hiring Blake, or getting himself involved in the welfare of yet another child.

A girl, no less.

He gritted his teeth against the pain of remembrance, of Cora's imprisonment. Of the helplessness that followed. But he did not dwell there for long. Recriminations about the past were useless in the present. The decisions he made today, this minute, were all that mattered. If previous mistakes helped guide him down a better path now, all the better.

Shrugging off images of dungeons and pain-filled eyes, Sebastian stared at the door. Where the hell was she? The longer he idled in the widow's library, the more restless he became.

She had implored him to stay before shuffling her blanket-draped daughter upstairs and issuing a full gamut of orders to her staff. He had thought she was going upstairs to retrieve the letters, but too much time had elapsed for so simple a task.

Why hadn't he disappeared when he'd had the

chance? Their discussion regarding Ashcroft's letters would be better held at Bellamere, away from the distracting presence of a child. He needed to concentrate and he couldn't afford to care. Not again. *Dammit.* Why had he allowed the widow's beseeching brown eyes to win out against his better judgment?

Disgusted with his weakness, he released a harsh breath. Through all the bustle, Sebastian had admired Catherine's ability to direct her household with a firm, yet gentle hand. Her staff anticipated her needs, and when they hadn't, she'd remind them with soft commands followed by genuine gratitude. All signs of a good mistress.

He focused on her bookshelves again. They, too, carried her stamp of authority. Every shelf contained its own category, and every category was alphabetized. Only in the finest libraries had he ever seen such an exacting system.

With her delicate beauty as a distraction, one could easily underestimate the widow's fortitude. His gaze surveyed the room at large. Took in the aged, yet comfortable leather chairs, the purple and yellow flowers on the side table, the colorful draperies protecting the room from draughts. She'd made a home here, despite her husband's preoccupation in London. If Sebastian wasn't so anxious to leave, this would be a room where he could spend many comfortable hours reading in front of the fireplace.

A disturbance in the air drew his attention to the doorway. With pink cheeks, tamed hair, and a radiant smile, the widow's daughter entered the room on limbs more buoyant than a mere quarter hour ago.

The muscles in his neck tautened.

"Thank you for waiting, my lord," Mrs. Ashcroft said. "Sophie has something she'd like to say."

Her daughter dipped into a commendable curtsy. "Thank you for bringing me home, my lord."

She reminded him so thoroughly of Cora, who had also suffered a similar loss as a child. Sebastian inclined his head, ignoring the clenching pain in his throat. "You're most welcome."

"Sophie," Mrs. Ashcroft said, "run down to the stables now and ask Carson to saddle Guinevere and Gypsy. I'll be there in a few minutes."

The girl didn't budge. "Is the earl joining us?" Sophie asked.

"Lord Somerton," her mother corrected. "No, dear. His lordship has attended us long enough."

Relief spread through his limbs at the possibility of escape, but the imp's crestfallen expression wreaked havoc on his conscience.

Glancing at his timepiece, he said, "I must be on my way, I'm afraid."

The widow nudged her daughter toward the door, but Sophie wheeled around after only a few feet. "Can we ask him now, Mama?"

"No. Now is not the time."

Sebastian noticed the widow kept her gaze averted.

Unperturbed, the girl tried a different tactic. "Do you have horses, sir?"

"I have a great many horses."

"A white one?" she asked.

"Yes."

"A black one?"

"Of course," he said, amused despite his best efforts.

"A brown one?"

"Sophie," her mother scolded, eyeing him.

"Well, Mama," the girl said. "If the earl has a black and white horse, he must have a brown one."

Mrs. Ashcroft turned her daughter toward the door. "No, *Lord Somerton* mustn't."

"May I come see your horses, sir?" the girl asked over her shoulder while being ushered out of the room.

Sebastian said nothing. The last thing he needed was a curious girl running around his estate, no matter how enchanting.

"Sophie, I told you," the widow said in exasperation. "Lord Somerton's a busy man. He can't set his duties aside to play nursemaid to you. Now run along."

"But Mama—"

The widow's glare cut her daughter's complaint short.

Sophie dipped into a hurried curtsy. "Good day to you, Earl."

"Lord Somerton," her mother corrected again.

The vixen smiled, and Sebastian knew she cared not a whit about such formalities.

"Good day, Lord Somerton."

He inclined his head. "Enjoy your ride with the vicar."

Once the sound of her daughter's running feet faded, the widow turned to him. "I'm sorry, my lord. Sophie's horse-obsessed and begs an introduction wherever we go."

"Quite understandable."

"I believe you wanted to see these." She held out a packet of letters, tied together with a black ribbon. The ribbon trembled.

"Thank you." He studied her face as he accepted the bundle, but her even features gave nothing away. "I know how hard it must be to share your private correspondence."

"Yes, but worth it if they help you find my husband's murderer." She swallowed. "Did you learn anything from the others I gave you?" She turned the full force of those beautiful eyes on him.

"Unfortunately, no." He held up the new stash. "We need to decipher these in order to fully understand Ashcroft's message."

"I see."

"Tell me, Mrs. Ashcroft." He stepped closer, his gaze sliding over the delicate contours of her face. "What will you do if it's decided that your husband's death was an unfortunate case of being in the wrong place at the wrong time?"

Her eyes widened a fraction, but her answer came swift and determined. "I'll take the letters to someone else."

Sebastian's body went hard. Desire like nothing he had ever felt before rushed through his veins. Not for the first time, he wondered what it would be like to have such a fierce champion. "Are you this loyal to everyone you care about?"

"What can you mean, sir?" she asked. "Would you not do the same for a wife?"

"I have never been married, madam. Therefore, I cannot answer your question." Closer now, he drew in a long, slow breath until her scent drenched his senses. Tantalizing and fresh. Understated, yet feminine. His chest expanded around another deep inhalation. "But I find I like the idea of a wife defending my cause. No matter the obstacles placed in her path."

"You make me sound heroic." She folded her hands in front of her. "I assure you, I am not. Merely practical."

He studied the pulse point on her slender throat, noted its frantic rhythm. Blood streamed into his extremities. "I don't believe you. My tenants provided several testimonials yesterday that would make you eligible for sainthood."

"Don't be ridiculous," she said in a breathless voice. "Unlike your tenants, I had nothing to lose by holding Mr. Blake accountable for his actions."

"Yes, Mrs. Ashcroft." He raised his hand and brushed the backs of his fingers along the curve of her neck. "Unlike *you*, not everyone would have bothered to right the injustice."

"M-my, lord, what are you doing?"

He settled a hand on her waist, bringing their bodies closer together. His gaze transfixed on her lush full lips. Lips that would mold to his in an exquisite embrace. His insides curled into a tight knot of antici-pation. He shouldn't want her, his agent's widow, but he did, with staggering force. Ashcroft's final request faded behind his fevered desire.

It was then he knew she was in danger. And perhaps so was he.

"I'm going to kiss you now."

"My lord—"

Soft flesh, luscious warmth, and an inexplicable rightness assailed his senses the moment he covered her mouth with his. He deepened the kiss and pulled her unresisting body into the cradle of his arms. Her delicate frame was a flawless fit, made for him alone.

The small hands resting on his chest inched their

way around his torso and squeezed with a force that verged on desperation. He cradled her sweet face with unsteady hands. His breaths came more rapidly and his body sought a closer contact. He was losing control, and the realization cut through the fog of desire clouding his mind. Ending the kiss, he buried his face in the crook of her neck and fought to temper his erratic heartbeat.

Think, Somerton! Catherine was under his protection and in mourning. Two inviolable conditions. Until a year and a day, her marriage vows still breathed life, a condition he knew she would honor even though her marriage died years ago. That she had accepted his kiss was unexpected and more than a little stirring.

"I believe it best if you release me now, my lord."

Removing his arms and backing away proved surprisingly difficult. She took a moment to smooth out the creases in her dress and tuck a few stray hairs back in place. Sebastian watched it all with a resignation that lay heavily on his chest. He did not want to lose this. Not yet. His honor be damned.

He couldn't remember the last time he had gone against his better judgment, or the last time a woman had compelled him to lose control. Both situations would normally cause him to pause, to step away and not look back. Maintaining control kept those around him safe.

But he couldn't turn away. His attraction to the widow was tangible and invigorating. Could he do it? Could he pretend to live a normal life in Showbury? For a few short days?

He had to try. For a period of time, he wanted to

submerse himself in raw, unadulterated pleasure. Then, and only then, would he go back to his cold, passionless existence. If he did not seize this rare opportunity, he would regret it always. And he was damned tired of regrets. He would deal with the guilt later.

"Should I apologize?" he asked.

She sent him a sad smile. "No more so than I, my lord."

"Good," he said. "Because I'm not sure I could have managed any real sincerity."

"You do not mince words, do you?"

"On the contrary," he said. "I have done so on many occasions, but with you I do not think it necessary. Or was I wrong?"

"No."

Her quiet confirmation seared his blood. "I have need of your services, after all."

"E-excuse me?"

"Thanks to Mr. Blake, my tenants have become rather suspicious of my commitment."

"In time, they will see the truth of the matter."

"I agree," he said. "With your help."

"Rest assured," she said, "I will do what I can to spread the word of your steward's perfidy. A casual word in Mrs. Walker's ear should set things into motion."

"If you are willing, I should like more from you than a whispered word to Showbury's most dedicated gossip."

Pink crept into her cheeks, and her lips thinned. "I'm not sure what else I can offer, my lord. You were not interested in my knowledge of the local craftsmen."

He slid the letters into an inner pocket of his coat.

Using the back of his forefinger, he caressed the line of her jaw. "That was not a lack of interest you witnessed."

The color in her cheeks deepened, and her uneven breaths peppered his wrist. "What was it, then?"

"Pride." A sin in which he had an overabundance.

"Pride?"

He removed his hand. "Yes." The admission was not an easy one, nor was his motive for revealing his secret. "I did not think I needed your help. However, my tenants have shown me the error in my logic."

"What would you have me do?"

"Everyone I spoke to yesterday was rather content to continue working with you."

She frowned. "You must be mistaken."

"I am not." He canted his head to the side. "I'm interested in learning why you think so, though."

"It's of no importance." She waved his comment aside. "You would have me act as your steward?"

"Only until I hire a replacement," he said. "If you are willing, I could use your help in creating a schedule of repairs."

Her eyes brightened at the suggestion, and Sebastian was struck again by her conventional beauty. Beauty that became less common every time he spoke to her.

"Of course," she said. "But what of Grayson?"

"He has offered his assistance, should you need it."

"You do not wish him to take on the responsibility?"

"No," he said. "I already gave Grayson the short list of repairs you provided. He's content to assist rather than direct."

She considered him for a moment. "You appear quite capable of organizing the tenants' complaints yourself."

"Capable, yes. Willing, no." His callous answer caused her eyes to narrow. "I have other issues requiring my attention while in Showbury."

Her gaze dulled, and Sebastian wondered at its source.

"When might you begin preparing a schedule?" he asked.

"I'll start on it tonight."

"You're certain?"

"Yes, my lord," she said. "The less time I spend on the schedule, the faster the repairs can commence."

Again, her thoughtfulness had a warming effect on his starving emotions. Gratitude manifested into a ball of heat; heat spiraled into desire. Of its own accord, his voice dropped. "Are you an early riser, Mrs. Ashcroft?"

Her feminine instincts could not miss the latent need underlining his words. Instead of retreating, she met his challenge. Her gaze dipped to his lips. "Generally, my lord."

An image of her lithe body, aching for release and tangled in his sheets, flashed before his eyes, sharp and clear. His cock hardened, pulsed with near painful intensity.

A whoop of girlish laughter outside penetrated the intimate confines of the library. Familiar reality iced his heated blood. His spine straightened. "I'll send my carriage around to collect you at nine, then. You can show me what you have over breakfast."

Her perceptive gaze flicked to the window, to where her daughter chased something too small to be seen from this distance. Sebastian watched the widow's cautious enthusiasm for her new project leech away.

The upturned crinkles around her eyes fell into joyless slants and her lips thinned into a line of resignation.

"No need to bother your staff, sir. As I mentioned before, my horse knows the way, as do my feet."

"Very well." He bowed a farewell. "If you'll excuse me, Mrs. Ashcroft? I really must be going."

"Yes, of course."

She guided him through the house, out the front door, and then stopped to await his approaching carriage. A heavy silence hovered between them as they watched his restless team of horses advance. The black geldings tossed back their sleek heads and dug their massive hooves into the ground until his driver Miggs drew them to a halt a short distance away.

Sebastian had an unnerving need to throw back his own head to release the tension thrumming through his body.

"Thank you again for seeing to my daughter's welfare," she said. "Sophie will be retelling the tale of her rescue to the servants for days. I would not have been as successful in keeping her secret." She glanced up at him, revealing a feminine vulnerability few men could ignore.

As it happened, he was one of the few.

He hadn't earned a reputation as a cold bastard for no reason. The brutal slaying of his mentor over a decade ago served as a constant reminder of how one's enemies will use every tool at their disposal to get what they want. Even murdering a man's wife. And torturing a spymaster's ward.

"Excuse me, my lord?" A footman appeared at his side, holding out Sebastian's hat and gloves. He welcomed the distraction and accepted the servant's offering.

He needed to establish a few boundaries for their new partnership, though. The last thing he wanted was her daughter skipping around Bellamere Park, getting into God knew what and reminding him of everything he had set aside for the welfare of his country.

"Mrs. Ashcroft, it's been a long time since I had a child in the house. I find that I work best in a less spirited atmosphere."

Her chin lifted a notch. "I hadn't considered bringing my daughter along, my lord, but I thank you for the warning."

Her chiding retort bit into his conscience. Before he did something ridiculous like apologize or kiss her again, he tipped his hat in her direction. "Good day, madam."

She produced an abbreviated curtsy. "My lord."

Sebastian settled against the carriage bench, calling upon his notorious control not to acknowledge the intriguing widow as he rumbled by. No matter what occurred between Catherine and him, he could not allow sentiment to enter the picture.

Because emotion was a weakness, and weakness killed loved ones.

Nine

SEBASTIAN STOOD AT THE WINDOW OF THE SUNNY breakfast room, holding a steaming cup of coffee while awaiting Catherine's arrival. Yesterday's kiss fired through his mind at unexpected intervals, tying his stomach into an uncomfortable mass of need.

Squeezing his eyes shut, he tried once again to block out the succulent aromas of sausage, bacon, and poached eggs coming from the sideboard. He tried not to recall their texture and taste, their slow glide down his throat. Because if he did, all would be lost. A floodgate would open and last night's indulgence would push to the fore. The coffee helped a little. When the scent of food threatened to overwhelm him, he would bury his nose in the pungent steam of his morning brew.

After forcing himself to eat a late evening meal, he had closeted himself off in the study until the wee hours of the morning. In that time, he'd added only one more name to his list of agents. His progress was slow, painful. No matter how much he reasoned this was the right course of action, each consonant and vowel ripped through him like a stab of betrayal.

Adding each agent's code name and current location would come next, although the thought of having such damaging information in one place nauseated him all over again. But the more he thought about it, the more he wanted to see a visual map of everyone's whereabouts. He might be missing a potential ally or an opportunity to redirect his enemy's efforts.

If nothing else, he could transfer everything he knew to paper, study it, and then burn the record, rather than hand it over to Reeves. The strategy steadied his stomach, somewhat. Having an alternative plan—an escape route, of sorts—removed some of the pressure he'd been carrying around since receiving Reeves's demand.

A low rumbling disturbance near the entry hall caught his attention.

"Lord Somerton can finish his damned breakfast while I speak my mind," a man said. "Stand aside, Grayson, or I shall have to…" The intruder's voice lowered to a conspiratorial whisper, no doubt promising all sorts of retribution.

Sebastian's former ward, Viscount Danforth, was a master of collecting secrets—of the personal variety. Even poor Grayson would not be immune to Ethan deBeau's machinations.

Taking his seat at the table, Sebastian snapped open a copy of the *Times* and waited for the oncoming storm. He didn't have long to wait.

Within seconds, heavy footsteps pounded down the

corridor, and then a tall, disheveled rascal entered the breakfast room. "Somerton."

"Danforth." Sebastian continued scanning the newspaper, waiting. Ethan's restless energy reminded him of a warship's 32-pounder long gun, with its dark, cavernous muzzle staring out a square gun port, primed and ready for ignition.

"What brings you to Bellamere? I thought you were tracking down your mystery savior."

"Trail went cold," Danforth grumbled, making himself a plate from the sideboard.

"Your savior is going to great pains to avoid discovery." He paused. "I wonder why."

He felt, more than saw, Danforth's aggrieved glance. "When I find the hooded bastard, I'll be sure to pose your question." His plate clattered against the table. "How are you doing?"

Sebastian raised a brow. "Well enough. And you?"

"I spent four and a half hours in Superintendent Reeves's office, answering questions about our last mission." Danforth leveled his gaze on Sebastian. "He was inordinately interested in your role."

Sebastian settled back in his chair, projecting a calm he did not feel. "We discussed this in London. I'm here so the Foreign Office can conduct a thorough investigation into the matter without my interference." He rubbed his fingertips over the newspaper. "Latymer's scheming ran deep in the organization. Reeves is no doubt wondering why I did not detect the man's treachery. I certainly would in his shoes." The question of why he hadn't discerned Latymer's double spying had weighed on his thoughts since the day they discovered Danforth's sister, Cora—also known as the Raven—in the man's cellar.

"That's all well and good," Danforth said. "But I've already given them an accounting of those events. To have to relive it a second time was not how I had hoped to spend yesterday afternoon."

"No, I suspect not," he said. "Did you come here only to inform me of your deposition?"

"No," he said. "Helsford's busy with the Littleton case. So Cora asked me to retrieve Ashcroft's remaining letters. Did the widow hand them over?"

"Yes, four more."

"All is well in that regard, I take it."

"She is nothing more than a wife trying to make sense of a heinous crime," Sebastian said. "I detect no ill intent."

"Finally a piece of good news."

"Where's Cora?"

"With Helsford, of course." The viscount lifted a fork full of sausage to his mouth, pausing. "After surviving their recent nightmare, I doubt Helsford's going to allow my sister to stray more than a dozen feet from his side ever again."

Not that anyone could prevent Cora from doing anything she set her mind to. However, they had all underestimated her gaoler. A condition Sebastian had no desire to repeat. "A day or two more, and I would have delivered the letters myself," Sebastian said. "There was no reason to make a special trip."

"That's what I said, but my sister had other ideas."

"Falling into bad habits again?"

"Cora's been through so much," Danforth muttered.

"Directing me and Helsford around takes her mind off other things."

Like being tortured for a fortnight. Sebastian pushed the thought away. He had already spent hours punishing himself. Right now, he needed to focus on the restless man in front of him.

"Helsford asked me to deliver this." He tossed a sealed missive onto the table. "So I can't blame my presence entirely on Cora." A corner of his mouth quirked up. "Although it's a great deal more fun making the runt take responsibility."

Sebastian smiled, his gaze sliding over the nondescript black seal. It was good to hear Danforth's aggrieved tone. He knew when Ethan and Cora were forecasting doom upon one another that the world had somehow righted itself.

No matter how hard he'd tried to keep an emotional distance between him and his two former wards, they paid no attention. They did not fear his quelling looks or stony silence, nor his sharp rebukes. That was not to say they didn't respect him, or give him a wide berth at times. They simply kept coming around, invading his home at unexpected times—like now—and spoke to him as they would any intimate colleague. It was maddening and, if he were honest, comforting.

"Danforth," Sebastian said, "there is no need for you to stay. I have a few ends to tie up here over the next sennight and then I'll be returning to London."

"What of the Foreign Office's investigation?"

"What of it?" he asked. "I've nothing to hide. It's my agents' identities I'm most concerned about, but I'm starting to question my decision on that score."

A stunned expression crossed Danforth's face. "You can't allow them access to our identities, Chief." The viscount reverted to the form of address most of the Nexus agents used. "It would make us all vulnerable."

"Yes," Sebastian agreed. "But it might be even more dangerous to have all the knowledge stored in one man's memory."

Danforth's eyes narrowed. "Nothing's going to happen to you."

"That's a naive perspective, Danforth, and you know it."

The younger man stared down at his plate, his hands gripping his utensils with bruising force. "Everything is changing."

"Yes."

"Well, I don't bloody like it."

"Few of us do."

The viscount crammed half a piece of toast into his mouth, chewing with such vigor that Sebastian was certain the man's jaw would ache later.

"What now, sir?"

Sebastian toyed with the stem of his glass. "Return to London and continue to keep an eye on Reeves. Let me know if you perceive a significant shift in the superintendent's intentions." He dropped the sealed missive on the table. "I have the letters for Helsford, too."

The tension visibly eased from Danforth's shoulders. "Consider it done, Chief." He began stuffing his mouth full of Cook's famous hot cakes.

"Pardon, my lord," Grayson said from the breakfast room doorway. "Mrs. Ashcroft has arrived."

Danforth slowly transferred his attention from the

hot cakes to Grayson, a rogue's grin spreading across his handsome face.

Sebastian's muscles stiffened at the sight, and he fought to keep his features neutral. "Behave."

The bastard's smile grew brighter.

"Grayson, show her into the study. I'll be there in a few minutes."

The butler bowed. "Yes, sir."

"Having breakfast with Ashcroft's widow," Danforth said. "No wonder you wanted me to rush back to London." His expression turned serious. "Have you told her yet?"

Sliding back his chair, Sebastian said, "Concentrate on Reeves and Ashcroft's messages. I'll take care of the rest."

"I hope you know what you're doing," the viscount said, rising.

"Godspeed, Danforth."

Danforth's brows rose. "At least introduce me."

"No." Sebastian set off for his study, his pulse picking up speed with every step. "Go away."

"Come now, Chief," Danforth said. "Not even a quick hello?"

Sebastian grasped the study's door handle. "There would be nothing *quick* about your greeting. Now, off with you." He opened the door, saw the widow leaning against the far side of his desk, and felt a frisson of warmth settle into his chest.

A low whistle sounded from behind him. Sebastian stepped inside and shut the door in Danforth's face.

The abrupt noise startled her, and she jumped back. "My lord?"

"Forgive me, a draught caught the door." She looked even lovelier today than yesterday. Wisps of blond hair curled against her flushed cheeks, and her graceful neck rose above a round neckline that hinted at a full bosom any man would admire.

"Good morning." She walked over to the edge of his desk and tapped her finger against a sheet of a paper. "Here is the schedule."

He joined her at the desk, his chest inches from her shoulder while he studied her well-organized itinerary. The moment he caught her delicate fragrance, the page blurred and the room dimmed. Heat raced across his flesh, and his muscles contracted with the strength of his need.

He turned his head a fraction. "Did you sleep well, Mrs. Ashcroft?"

She did not look up from the schedule. "W-well—" she cleared her throat. "Well enough."

"I did not." Instead of focusing on his task for Reeves and solving the mystery of Ashcroft's death, he had created inventive ways to entice the fair widow into his bed. When he had finally managed to fall asleep, he awoke not long after, sweating and aching and cock in hand.

She was dangerous—to his peace of mind and to his mission. And he didn't bloody well care. For the first time since becoming chief of the Nexus, he would put his own selfish needs before England's and damn the consequences.

He caressed her cheek, needing the contact and yearning for the connection that could only be had while looking into another's eyes. She met his gaze then with fathomless brown eyes, soft with budding desire and an enchanting trepidation. The need to possess burned through his veins. He wanted this woman like none other.

"Perhaps tonight, I might enjoy a more pleasurable slumber."

Her eyes flared wide. She might not have a courtesan's polish, but she was experienced enough in the ways of men to glean his invitation.

A sharp rap at the door shattered the moment. "Chief, I believe you had something you wanted me to deliver."

Sebastian cursed beneath his breath and thought of the many ways in which he would make Danforth pay for this intrusion.

"Chief?" she asked.

He waved off the viscount's careless comment. "Lord Danforth's humor. Ignore it. Or at least, try." He bent and placed a kiss where his finger had lingered. "I'll be back in a moment to take you to breakfast. Make yourself comfortable."

Catherine followed the earl's determined strides, fighting the violent urge to halt his retreat and beg him to continue with his gentle assault on her senses. She released a low, shuddering breath. Like the day before, his touch awakened stirrings that had lain dormant for years. Years where her blood had moved through her veins with boring efficiency.

But not yesterday and not a few minutes ago. She smoothed her hand over her tight chest, recalling their passionate kiss. Never had she been so consumed by the press of a man's lips. Had he not pulled away, Catherine was ashamed to think of what might have happened in the library. In the light of day. With her daughter playing just outside.

No, Lord Somerton made her blood sing with life. But why? From the moment she had visited him in London, he had treated her with cool reserve. Where had the warmth come from? The passion? The need?

The earl jerked the study door open, and Catherine saw the attractive visage of a gentleman in his late twenties. He flashed her an appreciative smile.

"Good morning, Mrs. Ashcroft." He pushed his way past a scowling Lord Somerton and bowed before her, lifting her hand to his mouth. Then he paused to raise an inquiring brow toward the earl.

Lord Somerton sighed. "Viscount Danforth, may I present Mrs. Ashcroft."

The gentleman smiled and kissed the back of her fingers. Catherine needed no introduction, though. The few times Lord Danforth had graced Bellamere's corridors he'd set off a feminine hum of excitement all over Showbury. Although she had only seen him from afar, he was as startlingly handsome as she remembered. With his charm and striking features, he was assured a spot in every young girl's heart. Even Catherine found herself grinning at his antics. "A pleasure to meet you, Lord Danforth."

He released her hand and glanced around. "What brings you to Somerton's lair this morning?"

"None of your business." Lord Somerton indicated the door. "Don't you have somewhere you need to be?"

Danforth glanced between her and the earl, a devilish look in his eye. "But the company is so much more pleasant here."

"A situation easily remedied."

Catherine glanced up at the earl, unsure if the threatening note in his words were made in jest or in warning. His crystalline eyes were fixed on the viscount; they glowed with an unearthly foreboding. She transferred her attention to Lord Danforth and found his face wiped clean of all humor and the slightest bit of wariness dampening his features.

A moment later, Danforth blew out a beleaguered breath. "The package?"

The tension in Lord Somerton's shoulders eased but did not go away. Their silent battle of wills confused Catherine. The earl's reaction to the viscount's playfulness seemed cold, even for him.

To Catherine, the earl said, "I will return in a few minutes. With any luck, your breakfast will still be warm."

Danforth bowed. "My apologies, dear lady. I did not mean to keep you from your morning meal. I look forward to the time when our paths cross again."

Catherine curtsied. "As do I."

"Come, Danforth." Lord Somerton did not wait to see if the viscount would do as commanded. He simply turned and left the room.

Danforth winked at her and followed the earl at a more languid pace. And then, through the closed door, she heard the first notes of a merry whistle.

Catherine's smile faded, wondering about the package Lord Somerton was so keen on sending to

London. And why had Lord Danforth referred to the earl as "chief"? Her mind cast about for something familiar and solid. Something safe. The schedule of repairs she had developed lay in the center of his desk. *Desk.*

The reddish-brown grains gleamed invitingly, tauntingly. They seemed to eddy down toward the nearest drawer handle, tempting her. Fear seared her heart. Dare she peek into the desk drawers of England's spymaster?

She glanced at the closed study door. Would he really keep sensitive information in such an accessible location? Surely, he would not be so trusting, even in the country. Doubtful, but passing up a rare opportunity like this would be foolhardy. Cochran would return soon, and he would expect something tangible to pass on to his superior.

She rushed to open the first drawer. A stack of pristine paper, with his family's seal emblazoned at the top, sticks of red sealing wax, and several uncut quill nibs met her hurried inspection. Pulling the drawer out farther, she groped blindly behind the mound of paper for anything unusual and came up with nothing but dusty fingers.

Even as she tried the second drawer, her conscience screamed with guilt. She couldn't stop wondering at the veracity of Cochran's assertions about the earl. Leading a secret group of agents did not make him a murderer, or even a double spy. There could be any number of reasons why the viscount called Lord Somerton by that unusual epithet, although none came to mind.

But more importantly, the more she spoke to Cochran, the more her suspicions were aroused. Something about the tenor of their last discussion made her feel unclean and off-centered. Cochran's demeanor seemed more predatory during their second meeting, far less congenial than their first. But maybe her insistence they postpone their conversation simply put him in a foul mood.

Despite her concerns, Catherine pressed on. If she could find one thing that would either prove the earl's innocence or point to those responsible for Jeffrey's death, all this subterfuge would be worth the risk.

A noise from the far end of the corridor caught her attention. She angled her head, listening. Then came the distinctive sound of a man's heavy tread. She quickly shut the drawers and straightened his desk. The footsteps grew louder, closer.

She leaned forward to grab a quill and the ink blotter shifted, sliding to the right a few inches and nearly knocking off a stack of ledgers. She scooted the books back in place and made to do the same with the blotter when she noticed a sheet of paper beneath. Could this be the list? The footsteps stopped outside the door. *Out of time.*

Her heart pushed into her throat, and she hurried to straighten the blotter and dip the pen into the inkwell. She scribbled a word into one of the columns, praying the frantic beating of her heart was noticeable only to her ears.

The study door swung open, and Lord Somerton filled the frame. Once again, his big body held her spellbound and made her feel achingly feminine. She followed the path of his penetrating gaze—over her body, the desk, and the surrounding area. A flush burned its way up her neck and fanned out over her cheeks.

Setting the pen aside, she rose. "I hope you don't mind, my lord. You did say to make myself comfortable, and I had an overwhelming urge to sit behind this massive desk."

"My grandfather had it commissioned years ago. It's a great heap of wood that takes up far too much space."

She stepped away to give the desk a better look. "The craftsmanship is quite stunning."

"So it is."

When Catherine glanced back at him, she found his attention was no longer on his grandfather's desk, but on her. The hunger in his gaze was both compelling and oddly bleak. She parted her lips to release a low, shuddering breath, then looked away.

He moved farther into the room, motioning for her to join him. He must have sensed her struggle, for his face was now devoid of expression; no trace of his sensual yearning remained.

"Shall we discuss your schedule while working our way through a cold plate of food?"

"By all means." She scooped up the schedule. "I'm ready."

While they strode toward the breakfast room, Catherine considered the hidden sheet of paper. Could it contain the information Mr. Cochran sought? A list of traitors that would somehow implicate Lord Somerton as their leader?

She still didn't know how the list would be useful for her cause. Would he somehow be able to identify

Jeffrey's killer? So many questions with too few answers. All this subterfuge made her head hurt.

"Another headache?"

Catherine stopped the circular motion of her fingers against her temple and gripped the schedule with both hands. "No, my lord. I simply have much on my mind."

He held out a chair for her. "Would you care to share?"

"N-no, thank you," she said, startled by his question. "You have enough to worry about without adding my concerns."

At the sideboard, he lifted silver domes and began filling their plates. The sight struck Catherine as odd. Never had she expected to be served breakfast by an earl.

"It would relieve my mind to think on something else for a while, Mrs. Ashcroft." He placed a mounding plateful of food in front of her. "What taxes you so?"

Telling him the truth was out of the question, so she settled on a topic close to her heart. One in which he could find little fault. She spooned a dollop of jam onto her toast. "Jeffrey's letters, my lord. I confess I am more than anxious to hear of your assessment."

Silence. Under the cover of her lashes, Catherine chanced a peek at the earl. He appeared inordinately focused on cutting up his food—all of his food—into bite-size pieces.

Finally, he said, "You were right."

She raised an eyebrow. "About what?"

"As you said in London, there was something peculiar about his messages." He stabbed several pieces of mutilated sausage with his fork. "Now that I have the rest of Ashcroft's correspondence, I'm hoping some of the questions that arose in the first batch will be answered in the second."

"What if they're not?"

He didn't bother looking up. "It's best not to speculate. Allow me to analyze the lot and we shall go from there."

He was keeping something from her. Anger coiled in her heart like an asp getting ready to strike. She knew the emotion was ridiculous, especially after all that Cochran had conveyed about him. But she had revealed details about her marriage to this man that she had never discussed with another. Not even her mother.

In the same carefully modulated tone he'd used on her, she said, "Perhaps it is time for me to journey back to London."

"Why is that?" His utensils clattered against his plate.

She ignored the undercurrent of danger lurking beneath his words. "Sitting idle, waiting for news, goes against my nature. I must do something. Maybe I can call upon Jeffrey's friend from the city to escort me to my husband's various haunts. Someone must have seen something of note the night he was murdered." The thought of calling upon Cochran made her stomach quiver.

"Is this the same gentleman I saw leaving your home the other morning?"

For some inexplicable reason, Catherine felt a modicum of relief that the earl hadn't been able to identify his colleague from such a distance.

She nodded, barely able to hold his gaze. "Yes."

"His name, Mrs. Ashcroft?"

Every question he threw at her carried the sting of

authority. Even though his features revealed nothing of his thoughts, his watchful eyes sharpened while awaiting her answer. Catherine's inexperience with prevarication left her indecisive. However, everything inside her rebelled against revealing Cochran's name to this man.

"John Chambers," she said, relying on her instincts. "Do you know him?"

"I'm afraid not."

Catherine's bravado returned enough for her to prod him. "He mentioned something about my husband working with the Foreign Office. Have you heard anything of the sort, my lord?"

His blue-gray eyes flared for an instant before he severed the connection long enough to drain the last of his coffee. "Mrs. Ashcroft, we do not yet know what we are up against regarding your husband's death. Any sleuthing on your part will only redirect our attention and slow the process down."

She dropped her untouched toast onto her plate and rubbed the bread crumbs between her fingers. "I am sorry to hear that, because I must do something besides this incessant waiting."

He indicated her schedule. "You will be."

"It's not the same, my lord, and you know it."

"You are set on this course, I see."

"Yes."

Using a serviette, he wiped his mouth. Catherine could almost hear his keen mind searching for a way to stop her.

"Then there is something I must tell you."

Apprehension cut through her anger. Would he

finally reveal all? In a show of nonchalance, Catherine followed the earl's lead and dabbed her mouth. "Oh?"

"Danforth brought some disturbing news from London."

Her pulse pounded so hard, she could actually feel her flesh lifting at her neck. "Does this have something to do with my husband?"

"I'm afraid so."

With uncharacteristic fervor, she bent forward and placed her fingers on the back of his hand. "Please tell me, my lord. No matter how difficult. Not knowing is worse than any news you could deliver."

He stared at her hand for a long time and then the bones of his fingers curled into a fist, and his lips thinned into a hard line. He shifted his arm, breaking their contact. The room's temperature plummeted, as did Catherine's hopes.

"With any luck, Mrs. Ashcroft," he gathered his utensils again, "you will be spared from ever experiencing the innocence of your statement." He layered food onto the tines of his fork, his movements careful, precise. "As to your husband, I've received word that he was being followed, which might explain some of the comments he made in his correspondence."

For several agonizing seconds, Catherine waited for him to expound, but he seemed disinclined to further discussion. In fact, he appeared the portrait of a man who often dined alone and was quite content with his state.

Except for his glowing eyes. Although he did an admirable job keeping them downcast, disconnected, Catherine caught brief glimpses of the fire burning in their frigid depths. She shivered, unsure what to make of this complicated man.

"Why would anyone be following Jeffrey?" she asked. "Do you think it has something to do with his Foreign Office connection?"

"I have told you all I know, madam."

"Why would I not make the trip then? The answers lie in London, not Showbury."

He stabbed his fork into a slice of bacon and conveniently stuffed it into his stubborn mouth. "As are Ashcroft's pursuers, madam."

"So your reticence is due to your fear for my safety."

He carefully lowered his utensils and leaned back in his chair, directing those incredible eyes—no longer glowing—at her. "Did you trust your husband, Mrs. Ashcroft?"

"Pardon?"

"Your husband," he repeated. "Did you trust him?"

Before the last few years, Catherine could have answered the earl with an unequivocal "yes." Now, however, she was less certain of her answer. Trust had as many facets as a superbly cut diamond. Depending on the light, the gemstone's aspect either sparkled and gleamed or appeared gray and almost colorless.

Catherine saw a lot of gray in Jeffrey's actions. He had provided for them, making sure they had wanted for nothing. But emotionally, her husband had long ago left their world colorless and empty. How does one trust a spouse capable of such callous disregard?

"There was a time when I trusted him implicitly, my lord."

He studied her with an intensity that rattled her

nerves. "During that time, did Ashcroft ever mention me?" When she raised her eyebrows, he clarified. "Or more specifically, my character?"

Yes, numerous times, in fact. Her husband's fascination with the earl was one of those areas Catherine never comprehended. Lord Somerton had always been cordial and pleasant to her at gatherings, but no one she knew besides Jeffrey had ever penetrated the thick, immovable barrier that surrounded him.

"My husband held great admiration for you."

His gaze became even more piercing. "Try to hold on to that knowledge as we maneuver through the next several days."

Catherine was torn. She wanted to bring about a resolution to this whole intolerable affair. Yet the earl's request carried a note of calming sincerity she couldn't ignore. "You know more about my husband's death than you're willing to share, don't you, my lord?"

His gaze did not flicker, nor did he answer her question.

"How much longer do you need to sort out whatever it is that needs sorting?"

"A few days."

A few days. They would be the most interminable of her life.

"Perhaps your daughter might like a tour of my stables."

Shock made her stare at him like an addled resident of Bedlam. "You are inviting Sophie into *your* stables?"

"Consider it a birthday gift."

Her eyes narrowed. "A rather generous one, given your aversion to children."

"I do not dislike children. I simply prefer them

not to be underfoot." He tossed his serviette onto the table. "I'll make an exception for Sophie's birthday."

Catherine was not convinced. "This feels like a rather masterful bit of redirection, my lord."

"Not so masterful if you saw through my ploy."

"For my daughter's happiness," she said, "I'm inclined to allow it. But only for *a few days*."

He nodded, accepting her challenge.

She recalled the request Sophie had made on the way home from church. "This might be a good time to extend my daughter's invitation."

He straightened. "To what?"

"To her birthday celebration," she said. "Your daring rescue the other day has secured you an introduction to Castle Dragonthorpe."

His eyebrow rose in inquiry. "Castle Dragonthorpe?"

"A project she started with her father," she said around a lump in her throat. "All you have to do is dutifully place any new pieces—warriors, farm animals, torture devices—where she points. The furniture, I'm told, is my responsibility."

His features softened, and Catherine wondered about his insistence to keep Sophie away from his estate.

"I thank you and Sophie for the kind invitation." He indicated the schedule. "Shall we?"

Not exactly a refusal or acceptance. He was rather adept at avoidance and redirection. "Of course." She spent the next ten minutes detailing her recommendations and offering possible solutions. Every once in a while, she would send the earl a sideways glance to gauge his reaction. He remained as impassive as ever, but attentive.

"Well done, Mrs. Ashcroft." He folded the sheet of paper and slid it into his coat pocket.

"Once you meet with the craftsmen and discuss time frames and repair costs, I can fill in those columns," she said.

"Then all that would be left is the Date Completed column."

"Thus ending our partnership."

His eyelids lowered. "Would you accompany me to meet with the men?"

There was no dearth of surprises when she was around this man. "I'm not opposed to doing so, but may I ask why?"

"A good question." His lips tilted into a faint, self-deprecating smile. "Two reasons come to mind. The first—the denizens of Showbury respect and trust you. If I arrive on their doorstep with you in tow, my reception will be much more pleasant than my last attempt to mend relations."

His cutthroat logic made the situation feel mechanical, rather than a genuine wish to win over the craftsmen. And then there was her role in the matter. He had relegated her to an adornment, there to bring respect-ability to his visit. "It is good to be useful, I suppose."

"I have offended you."

"No." She searched for the appropriate words. "Your logic is sound, as always."

"But?"

"Showbury's residents are a hard-working, some-what suspicious, and always prideful bunch," she said. "If you approach them as Lord of the Manor, my presence will have no effect."

"What do you suggest I do, Mrs. Ashcroft?"

"Act as though you care, my lord."

"You think I don't?"

His swift dealings with Mr. Blake indicated, if not a care for his tenants, a belief in doing his duty by them. He had also saved Sophie from a great embarrassment. However, this issue of keeping vital information about her husband from her pointed to a more calculating side of his character. "I really couldn't say. You have a way of muddling one's perception of you."

"Do I?"

Fire trailed up the back of her neck as she cleared her throat. "And your second reason?"

"One I should probably not share with you, given our previous discussion." His elbow rested on the arm of the chair, his fingers idly rubbed along his lower lip. "But I will. It is best if you understand."

A tremor started way down deep in the center of her body and slowly worked its way to the very tips of her extremities. She curled her fingers and waited. "Understand what?"

"The danger you're in."

Ten

SEBASTIAN TOOK A CERTAIN AMOUNT OF PLEASURE IN watching Catherine's shock transform into wariness. The woman was twisting his insides into an inconvenient mass of wanting. And her daughter's invitation sparked a powerful yearning that nearly suffocated all his good intentions.

The widow squared her shoulders. "What sort of danger?"

He rose from his seat and moved to stand behind her chair. For a brief second, he considered sparing her. But the man inside him, the one who had given up moments like this to ensure England's safety, bent forward until his lips were but a hairsbreadth from her ear and whispered, "Me."

Her lips parted on a quivering breath. "I've never shared a bed with any man but my husband."

He brushed his fingers along the line of her hair, where it lifted away from her nape. "Are you amenable now?"

"You would not think me uncaring?"

Sebastian knelt at her side, one hand gripping the

back of her chair, the other resting on the table before her. "I suspect you finished mourning your husband long ago."

She bit her full bottom lip and averted her gaze, blinking in quick succession. Empathy twisted his heart. He covered her clenched hands with his. "Was I wrong?"

Her attention remained fixed upon the floor. "No."

Placing his finger on her chin, he urged her gaze around to his. "Why the sorrow?"

"I don't know," she said in a broken whisper. "So many years wasted."

A sentiment he knew well. He could have spent the last score of years cherishing a wife and producing a bevy of children who would comfort him in his old age. Instead, his elder days would be spent haunting the corridors of Bellamere Park alone… and reliving a fortnight of stimulating interludes with his beautiful neighbor.

He splayed his fingers, cradling her cheek. "Then we shall waste no more." Until the moment their lips met, he'd had their *affaire* carefully planned from beginning to end. But he hadn't counted on her degree of passion, her skillful mouth.

She trembled beneath his touch. Pulsed with a pent-up need that fed his barely controlled desire. His hand shook.

In one fluid movement, he drew her up and deposited her on the dining room table. The fine china clattered, the crystal tinkled.

The widow squeaked.

"My lord." She glanced about the room. "What of the servants?"

"They have been instructed to make themselves useful elsewhere." He discarded his coat and leaned one hip against the edge of the table. Unable to resist, he caressed the delicate curve of her jaw and the smooth skin along her throat. Her pulse pounded, his need grew. He nuzzled the sensitive hollow hidden behind her earlobe. "Brace yourself."

Eyes wide with wariness stared up at him while she planted her palms on the white table cover. Her vulnerable expression sent a surge of liquid power through his veins.

He pushed away from the table and slid his hand over the soft leather of her boot-covered ankle, beneath the folds of her riding habit, along the soft profile of her slender leg. Leaning closer, he captured her earlobe between his lips and gently suckled. A seductive rasp of pleasure erupted from her arched throat, compelling Sebastian to linger, to kiss his way down her slender neck until he felt the gentle swell of her breast.

"Oh, dear Lord."

Lifting his head, he watched the play of emotions streak across her face. Desire suited her far more than worry or wariness. Desire transformed her into unadulterated temptation. And Sebastian was tempted. His conquering instincts clamored for control. Screamed for release. Ached for surcease. All of which made his next action nearly unbearable.

He waited for her to acknowledge his lack of attention. When she finally opened her lids, he said, "Second thoughts?"

She blinked hard twice, as if to cast off a deep fog. "God, yes."

Sebastian's muscles hardened, instantly regretting his decision. Of all the cork-brained things to do—

"But not enough to stop," she whispered.

He stilled. Flames licked through his veins, his chest grew taut. "Be very sure, Catherine."

From the way her eyes widened, he knew he'd been unsuccessful in keeping the rough edge from his voice. He also knew the moment he slid into her welcoming body that the devil himself would not be able to rip him from the warmth of her embrace until he'd had his fill.

She trailed her fingers along his cheek and eased back onto the table. The leg he'd bared with his roaming hand rose to an inviting angle, and she hooked her dainty black boot around his backside.

Her acceptance nearly unmanned him. Unable to ignore her encouragement, Sebastian shifted his attention to her breasts, desperate to swirl his tongue around the hard nubs hiding beneath layers of cloth and corset. But he hadn't the patience to unfasten the contraption.

Instead, he slid hungry kisses up her throat and along the delicate ridge of her jaw. The faint scent of a lavender-filled meadow reached his nose. He wanted to pause for a deeper inhalation, wanted to draw her essence into his very center. But the craving to taste her lips one more time won out.

She must have sensed his need, for in the next instant she turned her head until their mouths touched. The dam broke, and Sebastian felt himself sinking into a watery abyss for which there were no handholds.

Catherine could not breathe, and she didn't care. The earl's demanding mouth angled first one way and then the other, stealing her breath and rattling her wits. Never before had she been *overwhelmed* by her lover. Jeffrey had always taken his time and ensured her comfort. She did not even know one could make love on a table.

She loved this mindless seeking of pleasure, this chaotic grasping for gratification. This demonstration of their mutual desire. How long had it been since she'd experienced the simple joy of being wanted by a man? She clasped his head tighter and arched her back, needing to feel the weight of him along every inch of her body.

Cool air swirled around her other calf, her knee, and then her naked thigh. With her voluminous skirts now bunched around her waist, the lower half of her body was exposed for the household's delectation. She prayed his staff followed his instructions and stayed away. Knowing what they were doing was one thing; catching them doing it was quite another.

Ending their kiss, he straightened away, curving his palms over her breasts and stomach, up her raised legs, and down her inner thighs. He didn't stop until both thumbs reached her aching cleft. She groaned and thrust her hips, sending sharp needles of pleasure-pain up her spine.

His thumbs never moved from the crest of her opening, tantalizingly close, frustratingly far away.

She lifted her head. "My lord, please."

"I can feel your heat," he said in a low, rough voice. "See your need."

Her inner muscles clenched, and he moaned like a man on the brink of salvation.

In that moment, she would be whatever he wanted her to be. *If only*—she lifted her hips—*he would*—she grasped the tablecloth—*relieve her*—she tilted her head back and squeezed her eyes shut—*agony*. "Pleeease."

Instead of touching her, he attacked the fall of his trousers. Unfastening the placard with inhuman speed.

As he took his member into his hand and pressed the thick head against her silky cleft, he said, "Need to feel you. Now."

"Yes. *Now.*"

He entered her slick passage. The heated friction more delicious than anything she had ever experienced. Even with her shoulder blades digging into the table, she was swimming in decadence and thrilling at her boldness. But at the halfway point, Catherine's muscles tensed and the exquisite contact transformed into a dull, intrusive pain.

She grimaced, and he stopped. When she opened her eyes, she found his luminescent gaze—now filled with concern—raking her features.

"Did I hurt you with my impatience?"

Catherine's heart slammed into her chest. If she confirmed their lovemaking had caused her some discomfort, he would become considerate and gentle. Boring.

She wanted to live his every emotion, thought, and hunger in full, vivid detail. Now that she had tasted the Bordeaux, she would never settle for the ratafia again.

Cradling his face, she gave him a reassuring kiss. "No, you did not hurt me." A different kind of heat spread across her cheeks. "It's been a long time, is all."

He covered one of her hands, lifting it enough to kiss

her palm. "You needn't be brave. Allow me to share your burden, so that we may both enjoy the moment."

The ache in her throat returned. But not for long. He transferred those decadent lips to hers while he eased his shaft back a few inches. Then he pushed forward until her muscles tautened around him again.

Lifting his head, he locked his gaze with hers, repeating the action of his lower body over and over until finally he settled fully between her hips. "Ready?" he whispered.

She nodded, wrapping her arms around him. The first three long strokes were more exploratory than passionate. By the sixth stroke, Catherine couldn't breathe. The twelfth stroke started an avalanche of sensations that had them both burying their faces in the other's shoulder to muffle their cries of pleasure.

For several heart-pounding seconds, they stayed locked in each other's embrace, enjoying the after-shocks of their lovemaking. And then he lifted his head, kissed her with a reverence that surprised her, and drew away, protecting her modesty with an expert flick of her skirts and pressing a clean handkerchief into her palm.

Giving her some privacy, he swiveled away to refasten his trousers.

"Thank you," she said.

Without a word, he held out his hand to assist her off the table and waited until her legs regained their strength. The process took much longer than it should have. "Perhaps I should sit for a minute."

He did not leave her side, and she found it impossible to meet his eyes as she settled into a nearby chair. She stared down at the wrinkles in her black skirts, at what both represented—the wrinkles and the color—and experienced a moment of conscience. What was she doing having intimate relations with the man who might have ordered her husband's death? What wickedness had invaded her soul to make her crave the ecstasy of his caress?

If word got out about their indiscretion, she would be ruined and her daughter would be mocked. The home they'd made for themselves at Winter's Hollow would be destroyed by a single act of idiocy.

He traced a finger down her cheek. "How do you fare?"

She made to cover his hand and lean into his caress, but stopped herself. Even now, her body hungered for his touch again. But she could not allow herself to fall under this man's spell. Not now. Maybe not ever. From this point forward, she had to consider how her actions would affect her daughter. No more mindless pleasure.

Smiling up at him, she said, "I'm very well."

He kissed her again, and Catherine closed her eyes. She would be strong next time.

When he finally pulled away, he tapped her nose. "I did warn you."

His arrogant comment penetrated the mist of pleasure he'd cast around her. She eyed him with displeasure a moment before she raked her chair back and clipped his toe. He grunted, his leather Hessians providing little protection against a stout oak leg. Rising, she glanced at his injured foot. "Pardon, my lord. I should have warned you."

His grimace turned to an appreciative grin. "*Touché*,

madam." He waved his hand toward the door. "Shall we go meet with your army of craftsmen? I vow to *act* like I care."

"See that you do, my lord." As she rounded the chair, she ground the heel of her walking boot into his injured toe. In a flash, he grabbed her waist, twirled her around, and kissed her hard before setting her away.

Indicating the door again, he said, "After you, my dear."

She stared, surprised by his playfulness. Then her eyes narrowed.

"Your retribution shall have to wait," he said. "We have repairs to see to. You don't want Mr. Hayton's cottage to flood again, do you?"

The tenants. She had to focus on the tenants, but not before imparting her own warning. "I have a long memory, my lord. You would do well to remember that fact."

Catherine tucked a stray hair behind her ear and strode from the room, wishing for a looking glass and delighting in the earl's uneven gait.

Eleven

"YOU HAD AN URGENT MATTER YOU WISHED TO discuss, my lord?" Frederick Cochran eyed his companion with thinly veiled hatred. The man's negligent facade masked a cunning mind and a merciless soul, not unlike Cochran's, but Lord Latymer was a desperate man, one he would not underestimate, even while he exploited the source of the baron's misery.

Summoning Cochran to this wretched gin shop in the middle of St. Giles, rather than communicating by messenger, spoke volumes of Latymer's daring and of his desire to be quit of this situation. The authorities rarely entered the rookery, which made it an ideal location for a high-level fugitive to have a meeting. A bit of dirt on one's face and a layer of tattered peasant's clothing provided a believable cover in this den of despair.

"Lose the formal address," Latymer commanded, accepting a mug from a scrawny barmaid but making no move to drink from it. "You have not reported in for several days, a condition not to my liking. What progress have you made?"

As always, when in the baron's presence, a dark shadow drifted through Cochran's consciousness like the silent, inevitable approach of death. "I paid the lovely widow a visit a few days ago and impressed upon her the importance of obtaining the earl's list." He recalled the widow's initial confusion and then her dawning wariness. He'd achieved the right balance between conveying the severity of the situation and not completely losing her trust. Not everyone could have achieved such a delicate task. "If Somerton has compiled the list, I have no doubt the widow will deliver it before week's end."

"No doubt." Latymer stared at him over his steepled fingers. "Tell me, on the small chance your abilities have missed their mark and the widow fails in her task, what is your plan?"

His neckcloth became too tight and the room too warm. "She's an intelligent woman. I am confident she will do as she's told."

"Of course, you are." The baron's expression did not alter. "But what if she does not?"

The retribution Cochran had planned for the widow if she failed him glided through his mind in vivid detail. A familiar, exciting fever simmered beneath his skin, causing beads of sweat to form on his brow. He shifted in his seat, becoming more uncomfortable with each pulse of his heartbeat. "I assure you, sir. She is not without weaknesses."

"Do not wait long," Latymer said, rising. "Every second I don't have that list is another second lost to your dream. Our destinies are entwined. You would do well to remember that fact."

Cochran watched the baron stride from the overcrowded room, knocking into prostitutes and footpads and defending his person against pickpocket after pickpocket.

After a fair bit of digging, he now knew why Latymer wanted the list so badly. The French were of course involved, but the baron had a more personal reason for betraying his country—and his friend. Now Cochran had to figure out how to best exploit the situation, so that the French got what they wanted and so did he. As for Latymer, the man was nothing more than a bothersome extra step that could be struck from the process.

Even in his borrowed clothes and soot-covered face, Latymer could be picked out of this crowd by a discerning eye. Not Cochran, though. He melded with the filth and vermin inhabiting the warren of interconnected buildings and overcrowded houses. Here, no one paid attention to a child's screams from the next chamber or a woman's whimper in a nearby passage.

Because this was a godless lot, and the devil could roam here unheeded. Cochran smiled and grabbed Latymer's untouched drink. He belted back the watered-down brew and then crooked his finger at the scrawny maid.

Twelve

For the hundredth time, Sebastian glanced at Catherine's profile, wondering what machinations cluttered her brilliant mind while she put the finishing touches on The Plan. On their way back from meeting with the craftsmen—a journey completed in relative silence—they had returned to Bellamere so she could assign a workman to each of the repairs and make adjustments to her schedule.

Something about her eagerness to be of service gnawed at him, even knowing he was the one who had requested her assistance. Why was she here? What possible benefit could she derive from this partnership? She had to be aware of his reputation for ruthlessness—it preceded him everywhere he went. So what would lure her to his home? To spend days in his company? Hours coordinating his repairs?

Why would she risk the good opinion of Showbury's residents by sharing his bed?

An image of Catherine spread out on his breakfast

room table, her head tossed back with one leg locked around his waist, materialized with a clarity that astounded him. In that moment, she had been an angel and a temptress. And tight. So tight that he had nearly lost the few wits he had left.

"My lord?"

Sebastian shut his mind to the seductive image and focused his fevered eyes on Catherine. She sat at his mother's writing desk, brought into his study by the servants a quarter hour ago, looking comfortable and intent. His gaze roamed over her oval-shaped face, pert nose, blond eyebrows, and her lightly fringed lashes that blended with the backdrop of her pale skin.

What was it about her that compelled him to want to be with her, when he knew they must part ways in a few short days? Having her nearby brought an unusual contentment to his life, something he did not fully comprehend and, at that particular moment, chose not to analyze.

"Yes," he said finally. The word emerged harsh, uneven.

Her brown eyes searched his features without a hint of the yearning swirling in their depths that he'd witnessed this morning. "Did you make promises to anyone besides Mr. Hayton?"

"Not that I recall." He dropped his gaze to his desk and shuffled papers around. "Why?"

She bent over The Plan again. "Just making sure I'm prioritizing everything correctly."

"When might the men you hired begin the repairs?"

Her quill pen scratched across the paper. "We still

need to speak with Mr. McCarthy. He's a competent carpenter in need of work."

"I've met him."

The scratching stopped. "You have?"

"Yes, Saturday afternoon, when I attempted to catalog all the repairs myself."

"Is that why we circumvented the McCarthy residence?"

He nodded. "You should add a gate repair to your list."

She looked down at her chart, her lips thinned in disapproval. "You might have mentioned that a tad earlier."

"But I only just now recalled the fact."

Her eyes narrowed. "Any others you're only now recollecting?"

She was adorable when annoyed. "Not that I recall."

Pulling a clean piece of paper in front of her, she dipped her pen into the inkwell with a little more force than necessary. "Tomorrow, I will present an individual task list to each of the craftsmen. In the meantime, please do not feel as though you need to entertain me. I'm sure you have more pressing matters to attend."

She had provided him with a perfect opportunity to escape the erotic images he failed to stop. But he remained rooted in his chair, yearning for her in torturous silence.

Did she not think about their time together in the breakfast room? Did she not grow wet with wanting, with imagining them joined again?

Paper crackled, and he looked down to find the report he'd been trying to read in ruins. He had hoped making love to her would soothe the hunger burning in his loins. But one loving wasn't enough. His body felt more starved than ever, depleted of an essential element he could not long go without.

Standing, he strode toward her, keeping a tight rein on the conflicting emotions roiling inside him. He didn't want to want her. A young widow with a small child would come to expect more of him than he could give. Keeping his agents alive and England free from invasion was all he could manage. Getting involved with Catherine could put them all in danger.

So why wasn't his body listening to the arguments of his mind?

Hearing his approach, she turned to look at him, and her eyes grew wide. Was her reaction due to his determined advancement, or had his mask slipped? Sebastian feared the latter, which did nothing to improve his disposition.

She rose and shimmied around her chair, as if that meager piece of furniture would provide adequate protection. He wanted to witness one glimmer of remembrance in those beautiful eyes, one sign she had not forgotten their passionate interlude this morning.

"M-my lord," she said in a shaky voice. "Did I say something to upset you?"

"Hardly, Mrs. Ashcroft," he said. "You've barely said anything at all."

Her brows furrowed in confusion. "I don't under-stand. We discussed Mr. McCarthy at length."

Sebastian pressed beyond the warning bells and physical blockades. "Ah, but I'm not talking about the

Irishman. I refer to this morning." He stopped a few feet in front of her, the chair between them. "You do remember this morning, don't you?"

Trepidation flashed across her face. "Of course."

"Do you not wish to discuss what happened?"

"No." She shook her head. "Not really."

He frowned. "Why not?"

"To what end, my lord?" she asked. "We indulged the demands of our bodies, a circumstance I hope we can repeat before you return to London. But to talk about what happened gives the event more significance than it truly carries." She raised her chin. "Don't you think?"

He could do little more than stare at her. Words, logic, arguments—they all failed him. Because she was right. He had delivered the same reminder countless times to mistresses who had placed too much meaning on their sexual encounters.

Being on the receiving end of such a reminder escalated his frustration, causing him to lash out. "Indeed, Mrs. Ashcroft." He pushed the chair beneath the desk. "Perhaps I did not make my intentions clear enough."

She clasped her empty hands in front of her. "Oh?"

He stepped closer. "Since you are receptive to furthering our morning activities, I propose an *affaire*."

"*Affaire*?" After a moment, the confusion vanished and her features cleared of all expression. "Kind of you, my lord. But I have no need of your money."

The muscles in his neck grew taut and a vein in his temple pounded. "I'm not suggesting that you become my mistress, but rather my lover."

She thought about that for a second. "I see."

Did she? To be sure, he pressed his point home. "A pleasurable interlude with a definite beginning and end, an association without expectation. The only exchange of payment would be the slaking of our mutual desire."

A satisfactory flush blanketed her throat and covered her cheeks. She might be well versed in negotiating domestic affairs, but Sebastian was a master at more intimate arrangements.

"What of my reputation, my lord?" she asked. "Showbury is small and gossip travels quickly. What will become of my daughter and me when you leave?"

"There are a few options," he said. "We do what we can to quell the rumors, or, if you prefer, we can find you and Sophie a nice place away from Showbury. Somewhere you can start fresh, free from unpleasant memories."

"You have given this some thought."

More than you will ever know. "Like you, I prefer to have a plan."

"What if I don't wish to leave our home? What then, my lord?"

"Then I find a way to persuade you, Mrs. Ashcroft."

She took a small step back. "I do not think this is the right time—"

"When would?" he asked more sharply than he intended. "After we find Ashcroft's killer? When you're out of mourning? Once Sophie is older?"

"I don't know," she admitted. "But I don't want my selfish act to hurt Sophie. She deserves better."

"I will protect your daughter from any ill effects of

our *affaire*," he said. "You have my word. I'm offering you a few days of pleasure, something I believe we both need. Trust me to see to Sophie's welfare."

She turned toward the window and stared at something in the distance. Sebastian's hands balled at his side, waiting for her answer. His pulse grew thick in his ears and sweat ran between his shoulder blades.

"Well then," she said quietly, settling her gaze on his. "The business of when the *affaire* is to begin has already been decided, so the only question remaining is when will it end?"

Never. The answer shot through his head with blinding speed, surprising him with its savagery. Ever since he'd witnessed the secretive smile she'd sent Danforth that morning, he'd been hounded by an animalistic need to possess her, along with an over-powering desire to thrash Danforth.

The viscount's talent for charming vital informa-tion from the mistresses and wives of powerful men had been quite useful over the years. But the thought of Danforth employing those skills on Catherine had stirred a primitive need in Sebastian to rip the young rogue's head off.

"I plan on returning to London by the middle of the following week," he said. "Does that suit for an end date?"

An odd mixture of relief and exasperation crossed her face. Sebastian found himself wondering about the reasons for both.

"Yes, my lord," she said. "Quite definitive."

Unable to resist the temptation of their close proximity, he placed his fingers on her cheek and smoothed his thumb over her bottom lip. "Now that we have the business side of our arrangement decided, I propose a sampling of the pleasurable side."

She nodded, sucking in her bottom lip. When it reappeared moist and red from her ministrations, Sebastian's control snapped. He covered her mouth, drawing her lower lip between his teeth to savor its texture, toy with its softness. Tease and test its plumpness.

Desire streamed through his veins, sleek and hot. He wanted her again. A sampling was not enough. "Never enough."

"Pardon?" she asked.

Sebastian stilled.

"What's not enough?"

Unable to free himself of the haze of hunger numbing his mind, his unblinking gaze remained fixed on her swollen mouth. Had he verbalized his thoughts? Had he been so far gone in the sensation of her kiss as to reveal his hidden desires?

"My lord?"

Sebastian swallowed back an unusual stab of agitation and retreated a step. The new position gave him a better vantage point to view her. Somewhere along the way, her quintessentially English features had become so stunning that they haunted his dreams and plagued his waking hours. Even more so with the evidence of his possession glistening on her lips.

To remove the sting of his withdrawal, he lifted her hand and kissed the delicate blue veins running along the inside of her wrist. "Forgive the intrusion. I know you are most eager to get the repairs under way, which cannot happen until the men have their task list." He released her and gripped his hands behind his back. "Are you free for dinner?"

She checked the timepiece hanging around her neck. "I'm afraid not. Mr. Foster will be here any moment."

Every muscle in Sebastian's body locked in place. "The vicar is coming here?"

"Yes," she said. "I hope you don't mind. We are to check on Mrs. Taylor before dinner. Knowing we would have a long day, I suggested that he collect me from here."

"So that's why you walked over today."

"Yes."

"Always planning, aren't you, Mrs. Ashcroft?" When she said nothing, he asked, "Why must you accompany the vicar to check on Mrs. Taylor?"

She cast him a perplexed look. "Because he asked me to and we have things to discuss."

Things to discuss. He did not care for the sound of that, especially after the vicar's comments about marriage. "Did you tell him that we have work to do?"

"I don't understand, my lord," she said. "We have done all that we can do here today."

Sebastian's jaw hardened. He moved to the window, needing a moment to grapple with the sensations pounding through his veins. Where had this need to throttle every man who came within an arm's length of her come from?

He did not want her spending time with the good vicar when she could be having dinner with him. Did she not feel the same yearning that nearly overwhelmed him every second they were in the same room?

He had to regain control of his body. She was nothing

more than a diversion. Sweet and charming. So different from the pampered ladies of the *ton*.

The memory of Catherine splayed out on the breakfast room table resurfaced, and he amended his assessment. Seductive and tempting. Beautiful and thrilling.

His cock stirred and his stomach clenched. He wanted her. In his bed, with her golden tresses fanning over her body like an angel's cape, while she gazed up at him with desire-filled eyes.

He bit back a curse. *Control, Somerton!*

"My lord?" she called softly. "Was there something you needed me to do before I left?"

Sebastian squeezed his eyes shut and forced himself to recall Ashcroft's lifeless body lying in the middle of a dark alley, his clothes soaked with blood and discarded human waste. The awful scene had the desired effect. His erection withered in record time, leaving him with the sour mood of an unfulfilled man.

"I assume I'll have your undivided attention tomorrow, Mrs. Ashcroft?"

Her spine straightened. "Of course."

"No midweek jaunts through the countryside while I'm here dealing with the repairs?"

"What is this about, my lord?"

"We had an agreement, madam."

"True. Your point?"

"For the next several days, you're working for me, and I expect your full attention on the task."

The tips of her ears turned scarlet. "I'm working *with* you, not for you."

Sebastian opened his mouth to argue, but she held up a staying hand.

"After my husband turned his back on us, the residents of Showbury blamed me for Jeffrey's absence." She swallowed hard. "I constantly battled greedy shopkeepers, disapproving matrons, and small-minded men. If the vicar had not stepped in and befriended me, I'm not sure what I would have done."

The tension thrumming through his body drained away.

"I owe much to Mr. Foster," she said, "and will happily accept any of his requests for assistance. Now, if you will excuse me, my lord." She gathered her things, and Sebastian watched it all through a narrow, slightly blurry lens. He felt like a fool, and offering his apology seemed inadequate.

He had no sooner finished the thought when he found himself standing before her, aching to pull her into his arms and kiss away the angry lines scouring her forehead.

Instead, in the softest voice he could manage, he asked, "Will I see you tomorrow?"

She glanced away as if to give the question considerable thought. Sebastian held his breath, afraid to make the slightest move.

"Might you behave yourself?"

"It is my dearest wish to do so."

Pounding feet sounded down the corridor. Within seconds, his butler knocked on the door before sticking his harassed face through the opening. "My lord," Grayson panted. "Mr. Foster to see you."

The vicar squeezed by Grayson. "I'm sorry for barging in, my lord. Mrs. Ashcroft. But I've received some unsettling news about Meghan McCarthy."

Catherine rushed forward and placed her hand on the vicar's sleeve. Sebastian's hands curled at his sides.

"What's happened, sir? Please don't tell me something is wrong with the baby."

"No, ma'am," he said. "Well, yes. I mean—"

She grasped his hand in both of hers. "Take a deep breath, Mr. Foster."

He sent her a sad smile. "You're always so strong." He pulled in a long breath. "Yes, something is wrong. Very wrong. Meghan McCarthy's gone missing."

*

After sending word to her mother at Winter's Hollow, Catherine and Lord Somerton accompanied the vicar to the McCarthys to help search for the missing girl. According to Mr. Foster, Meghan McCarthy went for a walk with a friend after their meeting with her on Saturday and she never returned home. Figuring their daughter had decided to stay the night at her friend's house, something she often did, the family did not begin to worry until she failed to return home the following afternoon.

When they entered the McCarthy cottage, Catherine noted Meghan's younger sister and brother huddled in a corner, watching their father shove items into a satchel. Both Declan and his wife looked as though they hadn't slept in days, and Mrs. McCarthy's eyes were red-rimmed and sunken with grief.

"What is the latest, Declan?" the vicar asked.

"Still no sign," the carpenter said. "We've pounded on every door and traveled down every lane. Sally Porter said she parted ways with my Meghan near the woods about a mile from here. I'll search the wood-land and then the waterfall she liked to visit."

Somerton asked, "Do you think she left with the baby's father?"

Mrs. McCarthy shook her head. "My daughter's refusal to provide the man's name was not because she wanted to protect him, but rather to protect her and the babe."

Catherine recalled her suspicions about Meghan's reticence. "She was afraid of the father?"

Mrs. McCarthy shared a look with her husband. "We believed so, although the stubborn girl would not admit it."

When everyone fell silent, Lord Somerton asked, "Is no one else assisting with the search?"

McCarthy's features hardened. "No."

The earl didn't react, but Catherine sensed his anger. Her own temper and disappointment bubbled to the surface. "No one?"

"The people around here have never welcomed us." Mrs. McCarthy blotted her nose. "If not for your assistance, ma'am, we would have left months ago."

"I did little more than nudge a few customers in your husband's direction," Catherine said. "Mr. McCarthy's work speaks for itself."

"The vicar and I will help search the woodlands." Lord Somerton's pronouncement held an age-old ring of authority that the other two men responded to without question.

"Thank you, m'lord," McCarthy said. "I welcome the extra eyes."

Mr. Foster nodded. "I'm ready."

"As am I," Catherine said.

Lord Somerton turned to her, his gaze assessing. "Your skills would be better employed elsewhere, madam."

Her spine stiffened. "Do not think to exclude me. Meghan is my friend, and I will not leave until she is found."

"I thought as much," he said.

"Then define 'elsewhere,' if you please."

"Are you up for a few social calls?"

Her brows drew together, not understanding.

"We need more people to assist with the search."

His meaning became clear, and Catherine felt like a fool for her reaction. The one thing she had mastered over the years was the fine art of prodding people to do what they would not otherwise do if left to their own devices. "Of course." To the vicar, she asked, "May I borrow your gig, sir?"

"By all means, Mrs. Ashcroft."

"What of me, m'lord?" Mrs. McCarthy asked. "How can I help?"

Somerton laid his hand on her shoulder. "Let us prepare for the worst, ma'am. Do you have clean linens you can tear into strips?"

She nodded.

"Good," he said. "Have several ready along with hot water and whatever medical supplies you have. Also, keep an eye out for any recruits Mrs. Ashcroft sends our way. Let them know where to find us. Can you manage it all?"

"Yes, m'lord," she said. "I prefer to stay busy."

"Very well." He pointed at Declan's bag. "Do you have any weapons stashed in there?"

The carpenter hesitated a moment, his lips firming into a grim line. "Yes."

"Good," the earl said. "Shall we go?"

Declan glanced at the vicar, who smiled.

They left the McCarthys' cottage en masse. Catherine made her way to the vicar's gig, while the men set off for the wooded area. When she prepared to climb into the conveyance, Lord Somerton's hand materialized in front of her.

Startled, she glanced at him, accepting his assistance. "Did you need something, my lord?"

"See if you can locate a cart." He unraveled his cravat and shrugged out of his coat. "And do something with these, if you will."

Without thought, she draped his garments over her lap as if she'd performed the same act a hundred times before. The mindless deed gave her a brief opportunity to admire the bit of flesh revealed by his open neckline—until his words sank in. "A cart? Do you think Meghan's injured?"

"I don't know," he said. "As I mentioned to Mrs. McCarthy, it is best to prepare for the worst."

"Be careful," she said.

His attention dropped to her mouth, brushed it softly with a single sweep of his gaze before lifting again.

The visual kiss had nearly the same impact as the stunning press of his lips. Catherine's stomach clenched around a surge of longing so powerful she came close to reaching for him.

He stepped back. Had he sensed her temptation? Had he shared it?

"Coerce as many as you can to come, Mrs. Ashcroft. Promise them whatever you must."

The gravity of his tone told her he was more concerned with Meghan's welfare than he cared to share.

A fresh wave of anger washed over her. How could Showbury's residents turn their backs on the McCarthys at a time like this? To do so was simply unthinkable.

She would enjoy this opportunity to remind her neighbors of the many times Mr. and Mrs. McCarthy had set aside their own duties to harvest a crop or protect a home from high waters. She narrowed her eyes on the lane ahead. Yes, indeed.

"Promises will not be necessary, my lord." She flicked the reins. "Be prepared for my return."

Two hours later, Catherine led a large group of chagrined neighbors to the small meadow near the woods. Not long after their arrival, Lord Somerton emerged from the treeline, looking disheveled but no less determined.

Mr. Baggert helped her from the gig, and Catherine rushed to greet the earl.

He glanced over her shoulder, appreciation lighting his blue-gray eyes. "You did well."

"Some had already come to their senses and were making their way here," she said with unexpected shyness. "Others came around with a few not so subtle reminders. No sign of Meghan yet?"

He shook his head. "We've combed the wooded area as best we can with the three of us. I'll have your troops sweep through again, while McCarthy, Foster, you, and I search the streambed that leads to her waterfall."

McCarthy and the vicar joined them, and the earl explained his plan. The carpenter nodded his understanding, but his gaze was on the assembly behind Catherine.

"They want to help," Catherine said.

"Why now?"

"I think they had time to consider what they would do if their circumstances were reversed."

Lord Somerton placed his hand on McCarthy's shoulder. "Allow me to set up a search line and provide the group with some instructions and then we can set upon the stream."

Catherine could tell the carpenter wanted nothing more than to continue his sweep of the area. But in a short period of time, the earl had won McCarthy's respect to the point of deferral.

"Your wife said you have not eaten anything since yesterday," Catherine said. "She sent a small basket of foodstuff along, as did many of the women from the village."

"Thank you, ma'am," he said. "But I'm not hungry."

"You soon will be and probably at a most inconvenient time." She motioned him toward the gig. "Eat, please. Keep up your strength until we find Meghan. You, too, Mr. Foster."

"Did the ladies by chance send refreshment?" Mr. Foster asked.

"Yes," she said. "We have water and ale in the back."

The carpenter pulled a sandwich from an overflowing basket. "I should never have let her out of my sight. She was always so trusting of strangers."

"Meghan's disappearance was not your fault, Declan," the vicar said. "You cannot always know another's mind, no matter how much you love them."

"Ready?" The earl strode toward them and did not stop. He simply wrapped his long fingers around her elbow and pulled her gently, yet firmly, along. "Mrs. Ashcroft and I will head north a quarter mile and work our way down. You two gentlemen head upstream from the south. We will meet in the middle, or until we find Meghan. Agreed?

"Yes, my lord," came their reply.

"Good luck, gentlemen."

They walked in tense silence until the men were out of earshot.

"You think something has happened to Meghan, don't you?" she asked.

"I cannot be sure."

"What do your instincts tell you?"

"That this day is going to end badly."

Catherine bit her lip, trapping the grief welling up in the back of her throat. "Who would want to harm such a sweet girl?"

"Bad people do bad things," he said. "Sometimes for personal gratification, other times out of fear."

She sent him a sideways glance. "You sound as if you know firsthand, my lord."

"I do."

"Did my husband also know?"

His fingers tightened around her arm. "Yes."

"You won't share his travails with me?"

He released her arm to grasp her hand, guiding her through a thicket of shrubbery. "Start scanning for anything out of the ordinary. Discarded clothing, a disturbed area… anything."

His mention of discarded clothing had the desired

effect, for Catherine's line of thought quickly reverted back to Meghan. They traipsed through the thicket for several more minutes until the underbrush gave way to a twenty-foot bluff overlooking a stream.

Under different circumstances, she would have stopped to enjoy the gently rolling hill, the fluttering leaves, and the twittering birds. But the earl paused only long enough to determine the best path downward. Every unsteady step they made toward the stream increased her trepidation, her certainty that they would find Meghan in an unwelcome situation.

She shrugged off the vile images. Meghan was alive. This business with the unnamed father had everyone suspicious and on edge. Perhaps the girl ran away with her lover, knowing her parents wouldn't approve of the match.

Then again, Meghan could have taken a nasty tumble and now she lay injured somewhere, awaiting rescue. So many possibilities. So many unknowns. She glanced around. So much ground to cover.

"Hold on." The earl did his best to keep their descent steady and sure, but the steepness and decaying leaf litter made it impossible. Every few steps, her foothold would give way and she would slide several inches until he steadied her again. Three-quarters of the way down, they gave up the fight and barreled down the hill.

The moment they hit firm, even ground, he turned south. "We will stay to this side. The stream is wide enough and deep enough here that it's unlikely the girl crossed over." He scanned in front of them. "Are you able to keep to within five feet of the water without my assistance? I would like to increase our efforts by moving up the hill a bit."

Because she had walked to the earl's, rather than take Gypsy, she had her sturdy boots on. "I'll manage quite well."

He rested his hand on her cheek. "You're being very brave, Catherine."

She nodded, unable to speak. His unexpected gentleness and praise threw her off balance. "Thank you for not insisting I keep Mrs. McCarthy company."

He cradled her other cheek, studying every nuance of her face. Before her eyes, his features grew stormy, almost savage in their intensity. "Be careful," he said in a rough whisper.

Then he kissed her. Not a quick, hard, possessive kiss. But a hot, I'm-fighting-against-my-natural-instincts kiss. The pads of her fingers had barely grazed his back when he pulled away, almost as if he feared her touch.

"Remember," he said, "do not discount anything you see, no matter how small."

"I won't."

They continued in a southerly direction, often in concentrated silence and sometimes stopping to investigate. As they closed in on the small waterfall, Catherine couldn't decide if she was relieved or disappointed. She mentioned as much to the earl as they picked their way along a rocky edge that led down to a small pool of water.

"If she's not here," he said, "we will continue until we find her."

His calm assurance amazed her. "Have you even met Meghan?"

"I caught a glimpse of her once." He eyed her. "Why do you ask?"

"Simply trying to understand your willingness to help the McCarthys, when others who knew them were not."

He held out his hand to help her around a particularly difficult area. "Despite my absence these last few years, I take my responsibility to my estate and those who care for it seriously."

"Yes, I can see that you do." She hopped from one rock to the next. "But that does not account for your insistence that I do whatever it took to bring additional help."

"Perhaps I can empathize with the McCarthys on some level."

She halted. "Did you lose someone, my lord?"

He set his hands on his hips, staring out over the area below. He nodded to someone, and Catherine saw the vicar and Mr. McCarthy meandering their way toward their location.

"Lord Somerton?"

"Yes, Mrs. Ashcroft," he said through tight lips. "I lost someone quite dear to me. It is not a feeling I would wish on anyone else."

She stepped closer. "Did you find him or her?"

"Her." He swallowed hard. "Yes, I found her. She will never fully recover from the trials of her ordeal."

"I am sorry to hear that."

"As am I, madam. Come." He grasped her hand again. "Let us join the others. I fear the weather has taken a turn."

It was then Catherine noticed the two men below

were cast in deep shadows. She chanced a glance to the west, above the treetops, and found a line of dark clouds rolling their way. The sight was so ominous that Catherine could not stop the thought that Mother Nature was sending them a sign.

Once they reached the other men, Declan McCarthy asked, "Any sign of my Meghan?"

"No," Lord Somerton said. "Not even a set of tracks. Let us do a thorough search of this area before the storm hits."

The temperature dropped and the air grew thick with moisture. Catherine shivered, wishing she had worn her warm wool cape, rather than her nankeen pelisse.

A man's coat enfolded her in blessed warmth. She opened her mouth to thank the earl, but found the vicar's smiling face. "You looked chilled."

"Thank you, Mr. Foster," she said. "I'm afraid I wasn't prepared for such a drastic shift in the weather."

"Nor could you have been," he assured her. "None of us expected all of this."

"Vicar," the earl said. "Perhaps you should take Mrs. Ashcroft back to the gig and see her home. McCarthy and I will finish up here. Once the storm passes, we can resume our efforts."

Catherine wanted to argue, but she knew the men would be concentrating on her comfort, rather than on looking for signs of Meghan. "Thank you. I will check on things at Winter's Hollow and then return to sit with Mrs. McCarthy."

"And I will see how the other search progresses," the vicar said.

The wind picked up, freeing locks of her hair and

whipping them into her eyes. She trapped her escaped tresses with one hand at her temple, gazing back at the earl. A sudden reluctance to leave him behind kept her rooted in place.

Standing in his shirtsleeves and waistcoat, he resembled a gentleman pirate with the wind molding fabric over his muscles, outlining the hidden strength beneath.

He nodded toward the woodland behind her. "Go."

His soft command carried a note of tenderness that tangled with Catherine's heart. What would she do if she found out this man was responsible for Jeffrey's murder? She feared the answer became more complicated with every minute she spent in his presence.

She turned and followed the vicar from the clearing. Within seconds, the rain fell. Sharp, driving nails of water stabbed her face. She tucked in her chin and squinted her eyes. As she stepped under the canopy of trees, the rain eased but the wind kept up its relentless pace.

Unable to ignore the nagging voice in her head, she peered over her shoulder to check on the earl while keeping apace with the vicar. The earl stood alone, with his hand shielding his eyes, watching her.

She stumbled over a rut, propelling her forward. Her shin connected with something hard, and her world tilted downward. She braced herself for the impact. Rather than hitting hard soil, her hands sank into rich, pungent earth made soupy by the downpour.

Everything happened so fast, she didn't think to call out or even shriek her alarm. She glanced up to see the vicar had veered to the left to avoid a low-hanging branch. Had she not been preoccupied with Lord Somerton, she would have followed him on the safer route.

As it was, she was literally elbow deep in mud. "Mr. Foster, I need your assistance."

She clambered to her knees, or at least tried to. Her hands plunged deeper and deeper into the wet soil. And then her hand connected with something firm and round. A log, perhaps. When she made to push off, she realized it couldn't be a log. The surface beneath her hand was too pliable. Too smooth.

Too familiar.

She stared down at her arm, where it disappeared inside a mound of too-fresh earth. "Oh, God." Water rolled down her temples and streamed into her eyes. She blinked to clear her vision, only to have them fill up again.

"Mrs. Ashcroft, are you injured?"

Catherine heard the vicar's voice, but her full concentration resided on her exploratory fingers. She didn't speak. She daren't breathe. Her fingers and her heart were the only things that moved.

When she came across an object that had the distinctive features of a hand, she screamed.

Sebastian was already racing through the relentless sheet of rain when he heard Catherine's scream. He knew what it meant. Had heard that type of scream too many times to count. But once was enough to have it seared onto one's brain like a brand scorching one's flesh. Painful. Memorable. Permanent.

It was the sound of horror.

A sound dredged up from one's most primitive core, when the sight before one is so heinous, so unexpected as to terrify one's soul.

Catherine had found death in those woods.

"Mrs. Ashcroft, what are you doing?" the vicar cried.

"Help me!" she commanded.

Sebastian broke through the underbrush and took in the macabre scene with one glance. Catherine and the vicar were bent over a mound, scooping up handfuls of mud and throwing them to the side. Their frenzied movements told him all he needed to know.

He hauled her up and set her behind him, nudging her toward the meadow. "Do what you can to keep McCarthy away from here. He will likely have heard you." He dropped to his knees and focused on what he hoped was the upper end. "Vicar, start praying."

Neither Catherine nor the girl's father should see death in such a horrendous form. No one should. Sebastian had feared this ending, though he had held out hope for something more palatable like an elopement. But his instincts could not ignore the signs of foul play anymore than a sailor can ignore a red sky in the morning.

A man's roar of pain sounded from behind him. "Faster, Vicar."

No sooner did he give the command than the side of his hand glided over flesh. He stilled, as did the vicar. More carefully, he scraped away the mud. Section by section, they revealed parts of the girl's face. First, her mouth, open and full of wet dirt. Then her nose and cheeks. And finally, her eyes. They stared straight ahead, the rain rinsing them clean to reveal the vacant gray irises of death.

Too late. *Too damned late.*

"Mr. McCarthy, please don't!"

Catherine's entreaty was the only warning Sebastian had before the distraught father pushed him aside.

"Oh, Jesus, no." Declan McCarthy stared down at his dead daughter. Anguish like nothing Sebastian had ever seen crumpled the rugged man's face. "No. Not my Meghan. Not my baby girl." He dropped to his knees and picked up where Sebastian left off, removing great heaps of mud, apologizing and promising retribution in the same heaving breath.

"Catherine, stay back," Sebastian ordered when she made to move to his side. "McCarthy, allow me to do this for you."

The brawny carpenter ignored him, shoveling away layers of mud and dirt until finally his daughter's body was revealed. Meghan lay squeezed inside a shallow grave, with no visible wounds or signs of trauma. Only a small bump on her stomach, marking a second, much smaller grave.

"Sweet Jesus." The scene was so horrific that even Sebastian had to avert his eyes. He looked for Catherine and found her several feet away, her mud-slicked hands covering her silent sobs. He wanted to go to her, wanted to wrap her small frame within the safety of his arms. But he knew in these situations that those involved needed to stay occupied in order to hold back the shock. He noticed she no longer wore the vicar's coat.

"Catherine." He drew her hands from her face, but she continued to stare straight ahead. He bent to peer into her eyes. "Catherine, I need Mr. Foster's coat."

She blinked once, then several more times in quick succession before her gaze cleared.

"Did you hear me?" he asked. "Please find where you dropped the vicar's coat."

"Yes." She nodded and swiveled to find the fallen garment.

"Vicar, please relieve Mrs. Ashcroft of your coat once she finds it and bring it to me."

"Yes, my lord."

McCarthy bent to lift his daughter from her watery grave, and Sebastian laid a hand on the man's shoulder. "I'll help you."

The carpenter nodded and moved to grab Meghan's legs.

Sebastian braced his boot on the opposite side of the hole and then burrowed his hands under the girl's shoulders. "Ready."

Together, they hauled her up, the action creating an awful sucking noise as the pit released the girl from its inky grip. That's when Sebastian noticed the deep purple bruises circling her thin throat.

The vicar appeared at Sebastian's side, using his coat to protect McCarthy's memories as much as possible. They laid her on the ground and everyone stared at her ragged form in appalled silence. Sebastian broke the spell, intending to carry the girl to the cart, but McCarthy shook his head.

"I'll be doing that, m'lord. I failed to protect her as I should. This will be my penance."

Catherine opened her mouth to reassure the grieving father, but Sebastian shook his head. Words would not cut through the man's grief and recriminations; only time would do that. A good deal of time.

He held his hand out to her, needing the contact. She came to him and wrapped her arms around his waist, burrowing her face in his chest. He kissed her sodden head, giving McCarthy time to cradle his daughter in his arms and set off for the meadow, with the vicar leading the way.

Sebastian framed her sweet face, thankful the rain had gentled to a light patter. "I'm sorry you had to witness such evil."

She grasped his wrists, turning tearful eyes up to his. "Who would do such a thing?"

"I don't know, but I vow to find out." He shifted her to his side, though he did not let go. "Come, let us be quit of this place."

Several hours later, Sebastian drew Reaper to a halt outside Bellamere's thick double doors, with Catherine snuggled in his arms. He hadn't the heart to take her home, where her daughter would see her mother in such a disheveled state and would no doubt shower Catherine with difficult questions.

Although the driving rain had rinsed most of the mud off, their skin and clothes were still stained with bits of silt. Catherine's blond hair hung in long, lanky clumps down her back, and her boots carried deep, ruinous gashes.

Grayson and two footmen appeared, rushing to Sebastian's aid. "My lord," Grayson said. "Is Mrs. Ashcroft injured? Should I prepare a room?"

"No and yes," Sebastian said. "Please send word to Winter's Hollow that Mrs. Ashcroft is fine, but will be staying the evening here. Leave two footmen over there as a precaution. And have Mrs. Fox draw us hot baths."

Sebastian could not wait to be rid of his damp, abrasive clothes. He was certain Catherine felt the same, although she hadn't spoken a word since leaving McCarthy's cottage.

"My lord." Catherine stirred, her voice raw. "What are we doing here? I must make sure Sophie and my mother are well."

"I sent two footmen to stay with them," he said. "They will see that clean clothes are sent over." He skimmed the backs of his fingers over her cheek. "It's best you stay here tonight. You're in no condition to see your daughter."

"But the killer—"

"He's accomplished what he wanted and is likely long gone."

The tension in her body drained away, replaced by a racking shiver.

"Here, let us get you out of the elements." With Grayson's support, Sebastian set her down. "Steady."

He dismounted, handing the reins to his butler and offering an arm to the widow. "Grayson, please see what Mrs. Fox can find in the way of food. Mrs. Ashcroft has not eaten all day."

"Nor have you." She snaked her hand into the crook of his arm, leaning on him as they made their way inside. "Bath first, food later."

Another footman arrived to relieve Grayson of his hostler duties.

"My lord." Grayson entered the entry hall behind them. "I'm told the countess's bedchamber is the only aired room. The maids are working on the rose room."

"No need," Sebastian said. "Mrs. Ashcroft can use the countess's chamber."

"Oh, no," Catherine said. "I am happy to wait for the rose room."

"You would have the maids go through all that extra work for no reason?" Sebastian knew she worried about the impropriety of sleeping in a bedchamber next to his, but he couldn't bring himself to care. He wanted her close.

She glanced from him to Grayson, as if the butler would help plead her case. Grayson, like most seasoned servants, learned long ago not to get involved in his employer's business.

"No, I suppose not," she said.

"Is there a fire in the drawing room?" Sebastian asked.

"Yes, my lord."

"We will wait there while Mrs. Ashcroft's bath-water is drawn."

Grayson bowed. "Very well, sir."

They made their way to the drawing room, and Catherine held her hands out to the fire. Flickering red-gold light reflected off her face, revealing a classic profile but for the dark hollows beneath her eyes.

"What a horrible end to what would otherwise have been a grand day," she said.

Given they had started the day off by making love on his table, he had to agree with her.

"You knew all along, didn't you?"

"Knew what?" he asked.

"That we would find her dead."

"Not with any great certainty."

She snorted. "That's what my husband would have called a clanker."

Sebastian's jaw clenched. How did this woman continually see through his mask? "She could have eloped."

"But you suspected otherwise." She sent him a sidelong glance. "Instinct? Or something else?"

Ice trailed down his spine. "Do you have an accusation you would like to share, madam?"

Her probing gaze lost its courage, and she shifted her attention back to the fire. "Of course not, my lord."

Sebastian grappled with his temper. In his line of work, he was used to being an object of suspicion and the veracity of his words always suspect. But to have her question his integrity, especially over the murder of an enceinte girl, burned every nerve ending in his body.

Outside of explaining her husband's role in the Nexus and the facts around his murder, Sebastian had been careful not to lie to her. Very careful.

"By your own admission," she said, "you have enjoyed an interesting past. One that has more than a passing familiarity to the insidious side of mankind. I thought perhaps this incident reminded you of something that occurred in London."

His nostrils flared around a deep breath. When he released it, a great weight drifted away as well. "Only one other occasion comes close to matching what I saw today. Neither image will lose its grip any time soon." His mouth felt suddenly dry, and his thoughts turned to the decanters in his study. "But you are right in that my past has prepared me for days like today."

"A past involving my husband?"

All the weight came crashing down on him again. "You are nothing if not relentless, madam."

A shadow crossed her face. "I suppose I am," she said. "Without the protection of a husband, it's how I've survived living in Showbury all these years."

Sebastian tried to swallow back the guilt that clawed its way up his throat, but his mouth had gone completely dry. Not a single drop of saliva to soothe the sensation of his throat being ripped apart. He grasped the mantel to hold himself in place.

"Won't you tell me what you know about Jeffrey?" she asked, driving the pain deeper.

"I cannot."

"Why can't you? Do you not think I deserve to know the truth?"

He closed his eyes. "Of course I do."

"Then why, my lord? I don't understand."

"I know you don't." He pushed away from the fireplace and paced the small room. "And I can't enlighten you."

"Can't, my lord?"

He whipped around. No one in the last decade had challenged him in the way this woman dared. Not his subordinates or his superiors. She poked and prodded and pried into places that could get them all killed. Did she not understand his silence protected her? And her daughter?

No, because he could not tell her. Not even that much.

But he could reveal the circumstances surrounding Ashcroft's death. At least some of them. "You win, Mrs. Ashcroft."

"I-I do?"

"Yes," he said. "But I doubt your victory will be as satisfactory as you believe."

"Then again, you might be wrong."

A knock sounded at the door.

The widow's eyes narrowed.

Sebastian sent up a prayer of thanks. "Enter."

"Pardon, my lord," the housekeeper said, peering around the door.

"Yes, Mrs. Fox?"

"Mrs. Ashcroft's bathwater is ready."

He looked to Catherine. "After you."

She stopped in front of him. Fierce brown eyes settled on him. "I intend to hear more about this victory."

Thirteen

CATHERINE SAT ON THE HEARTH RUG IN FRONT OF A low-burning fire, attempting to untangle the mass of knots that was her hair. It wasn't going well.

Each time she tried to pull the tortoiseshell comb through a snarl, her wet tresses slapped against her bare arms and dampened her cotton chemise. Even though the hot bath had warmed her to the bone, the fire still felt heavenly against her now chilled skin.

Thank goodness her dear mother had thought to send along a few items to get her through the evening as well as a change of clothes for tomorrow. Everything she had worn today was beyond salvaging. And even if the maids had managed to clean her tattered dress, she couldn't have borne to wear it again.

Each rip and stain would have been an awful reminder of today's events. God forgive her, all she wanted to do was forget.

Her stomach took that opportunity to remind her of how little she'd eaten. Mrs. Fox had prepared a small tray of cheese and fruit for her to nibble on while in the tub. But instead of filling the hollow in her stomach, Catherine had concentrated on digging the dirt out from beneath her nails and picking the flecks of decaying leaves from her hair.

Abandoning her fruitless effort with the knots, she scrambled to her feet and padded over to the tray. She gobbled down two squares of cheese and four grapes before heading back to her place by the fire.

For what felt like the hundredth time, she flicked a glance at the door connecting her bedchamber to the earl's. She hadn't seen him since he'd nudged her inside the room with a pithy comment not to fall asleep in the tub. As if she could sleep with him lurking in the next chamber.

At times, she thought she heard him pacing back and forth, with intermittent pauses at her door. But the handle never turned and the door never opened. She put two more pieces of cheese in her mouth and willed him to check on her.

She wanted to finish their conversation. He had been about to reveal something important. Something that might put an end to this intolerable anticipation, this constant waiting for resolution. She was so tired of waiting.

Setting the tray down, she grabbed the comb again and attacked her hair with renewed vigor. She would conquer her tangles, finish her food, and climb into bed for some much-needed sleep. She would not think of the earl again.

He could pace his bedchamber until the New Year dawned for all she cared. Whatever bothered him had nothing to do with her. If he was haunted by images of Meghan's broken body, there was nothing she could do to alleviate his burden.

She swallowed. Nothing.

A low knock reached her ears.

Her hand stilled, and she choked down her cheese. Or at least, she tried to. A bit of it stuck to the roof of her mouth, refusing to budge. "Yeth?" Her eyes widened, and she looked around for something to drink.

The connecting door cracked open. "May I come in?"

All she could do was nod, for her attempt to force the cheese down without the aid of a beverage only managed to lodge it deeper in the back of her throat.

A halo of light fanned across the floor, broken only by his large silhouette. Sapphire silk clung to his large frame, outlining every hill and dale of his torso with exotic splendor. His dark hair glistened in the candlelight, revealing his own attempt to be free of the day's tragedy.

Cheese forgotten, she met his eyes. They glowed blue-silver. Even more so after they trailed over her thin chemise, made nearly transparent by her wet hair. Catherine fought the urge to cover herself, unused to such heated scrutiny.

Especially from a man like Lord Somerton, whose passion smoldered beneath the surface like a field of peat gone to flame. Aboveground, all looks normal but for the occasional plume of smoke. However, if one peered below the surface, one would spot the silent advancement of a devastating, all-consuming blaze.

Lifting his gaze from her chest, he held out a glass filled with red liquid. "Care to join me?"

"I would love to."

Six long strides later, he knelt next to her and offered her refreshment. Fragrant, humid air trailed into the chamber after him. Catherine lifted her nose and inhaled.

"Musk," he said. "A special blend."

She hid her mortification behind the rim of her wine glass and was relieved when the bothersome piece of cheese washed away without further incident. "With violets, I believe."

"You have a keen sense of smell, Mrs. Ashcroft." His fingers brushed over an untamed portion of her hair. "Do you need help with the tangles?"

Embarrassed by her dishabille, she said, "Are you applying for the part of lady's maid, my lord?"

"If you will allow it."

Good Lord, he was serious. She stared at him dumb-founded, unsure what to say. *Why, thank you, sir. Most kind.* Or better yet, *Splendid!*

In the end, he took her silence for approval and plucked the comb from her hand. He set his drink on her tray and then moved out of sight, making himself comfortable behind her. A bit of rustling occurred before she felt the first tentative tug on her hair.

After a few experimental strokes, he asked, "Am I hurting you?"

Catherine closed her eyes in ecstasy. "Not in the least."

He started at the bottom and worked his way up with a patience and dedication to the task that surprised her. When he finished one section, he would begin the process all over again. His big hands were so deliciously gentle, always soothing a hurt, rare though they were.

Once he had dispatched all the knots, he replaced the comb with a soft brush. Long, even strokes, followed by long, gentle caresses. The rhythmic action lulled her into a semiconscious state, easing away her tension. Soon, her body sagged into a more natural curve.

He draped her hair over one shoulder, leaving her other one exposed and vulnerable and aching for attention. "Better?" he whispered.

She nodded. "I've never enjoyed a hair brushing more. Thank you, my lord."

He kissed the side of her head and then rested his cheek there while his arms snaked around her middle. The movement brought her back flush against his chest. Warmth, security, and a desire-filled serenity flooded her body. Today, she had walked in the footsteps of evil. Tonight, she sat in a halo of heaven. Heaven suited her so much better.

She rolled her head to one side, as if she could snuggle farther into the cocoon of his embrace. "I've never seen the sunken garden from this vantage point. It's quite stunning."

"Thank you," he breathed against her temple. "Of all Bellamere's gardens, the sunken is my favorite."

"So I've heard," she said.

He tipped his head to the side to see her face. "What exactly did Grayson tell you?"

"Who said I received my information from Grayson?"

His arms tautened.

"*Someone* might have mentioned you would hide in the garden to evade your father."

"Someone should not be telling such tales."

Catherine heard the steel underlying his words. "Please don't be upset. It was an idle comment, nothing more."

His hold loosened. "I'm not angry. Where my father is concerned, I have many conflicting feelings."

"As do I," she said. "Many times as a child, I wondered why my father bothered having a family at all. The Navy seemed to be all he ever needed. Or wanted."

The rhythmic brush of his thumb against her bare arm helped smooth the jagged edges of her memories.

"Mine was bent on turning me into the perfect earl."

"How old were you when your father died?"

"Twelve."

"A child."

"One who grew up rather fast." He released a long breath. "My father knew he was dying and wanted to make sure I was ready to take over the earldom. Had he explained that in the beginning—no matter how difficult—I would have spent far less time in the garden and more time at my desk."

She covered his hand. "He would be proud of the man you are today."

"Perhaps," he said.

"Disappointing my daughter is one of my greatest fears," she whispered.

He tugged her face around to meet his. "You're a good mother. No, a wonderful mother," he said. "Yes, you might get it wrong a few times along the way, but Sophie will never doubt she is loved. That's a mistake you will never make."

She smiled, then leaned in to press her lips against his. He did not push for a more intimate kiss, but seemed to enjoy the slow exploration, the affirmation of their past hurts, as much as she.

Ending the kiss, she said, "Thank you."

His eyes softened. "If that is how you express your gratitude, I will try to come up with nice things to say more often."

Catherine wanted to curse when her cheeks heated. They lapsed into a companionable silence for several long minutes.

Then, he asked, "Are you thinking of Meghan?"

She shook her head. "Not at this precise moment, but she is not long from my thoughts."

"I should have forbidden you to join us on the search. It was no place for a woman."

"Nor a man," she said. "Besides, I am not so easily commanded, my lord."

In a slow, deliberate motion, he smoothed his hand up her stomach and between her breasts, his fingers skimming across her left nipple. Her back arched and she pressed her head against his shoulder. His hand continued its erotic journey, not stopping until his devilish fingers cradled the exposed side of her neck. "I am forewarned."

As was she. His thumb urged her chin up, and Catherine came to the uncomfortable realization that this man could command her with little effort if he set his mind to it.

He took her lips in a full, melting kiss. For the next several minutes, time held no sway, discovery gave no pause. When he lifted his head, he asked, "Did I manage to take your mind off whatever is troubling you?"

"Yes," she whispered. "But not for long, I'm afraid." She made to sit up, though her boneless body refused to cooperate.

Without a word, he supported her next effort. "I suppose you've recalled your earlier victory and wish to collect."

"With some things, my lord, you will find I am not a patient woman." She rolled to her feet and retrieved her rose-colored wrap from the foot of the bed.

He sighed, grabbing their wine glasses as he stood. "Let us move to my bedchamber, where there is a chair that won't crumble beneath my weight."

Catherine glanced at the feminine chairs dotting the room and smiled at the image of the earl perched on the edge of the dainty furniture. "By all means, my lord."

He set their drinks on a small side table separating two large wingback chairs and then strode to the bell-pull, giving it two tugs. "Perhaps now would be a good time to start using my Christian name—Sebastian."

Sebastian. A strong name, yet gentle around the edges. Much like its bearer.

"Thank you," she said. "You may call me Catherine."

He indicated one of the chairs. "Please sit."

After taking the opposite chair, he said, "What I am about to tell you mustn't leave this room."

She clasped her hands together. "I understand."

"Not good enough, Catherine," he said. "I must ask for your word."

Her jaw clenched. "You have it."

"You were right to question the reasons behind your husband's murder."

"So he wasn't killed by footpads?"

"No."

"Who killed him?"

"We don't know," he said. "We're hoping the

correspondence he sent you will shed some light on the killer's identity."

Even though she expected foul play, she still had a hard time understanding. "Why would anyone want to harm Jeffrey?"

"Until we know for sure who killed him, I can't answer that question."

"Who is 'we'?"

A muscle jumped in his right cheek. "The Foreign Office."

"Foreign Office?" On some level, she had hoped Mr. Cochran was wrong about the earl's connection to the government. "Doesn't that branch of the government handle foreign affairs, rather than domestic?"

He began twirling his signet ring. "I believe we have veered off our original topic, madam."

"Madam, is it?" Her spine straightened. "I disagree. Everything we've discussed is intricately woven together. Tell me, my lord," she said, matching his formality. "Are the facts behind my husband's death a recent revelation, or have you known it wasn't footpads all along?" When he remained silent, she prodded harder. "Were you aware of this when I came to London? When I begged you to read his letters?"

The twirling stopped. "Catherine, it's complicated—"

A knock echoed through the room, making Catherine jump. Although his expression did not change, Catherine sensed the earl's relief at the interruption.

He strode to the door and accepted a covered tray from one of the maids. "After you turn back Mrs. Ashcroft's bed, that will be all tonight."

"Yes, m'lord."

Once the maid was gone, he slid the tray onto the table separating their chairs. "I asked Mrs. Fox to prepare something a little more substantial than fruit and cheese once we finished our baths." He lifted the cover and inhaled. "Smoked salmon and steamed asparagus. I hope you don't mind the casual setting."

With the truth of his deception echoing in her ears, food was anathema. One bite of the delicious-smelling meal and she would spew all over his expensive carpet. "Not at all. But I am no longer desirous of eating."

He re-covered Mrs. Fox's hard work and stood staring at the silver dome, silent and contemplative. "Many times over the years, I have held back information that could bring comfort to the recipient." He impaled her with his gaze. "None have preyed upon my conscience. Until now."

Catherine's heart constricted, for she understood the cost of such an admission. The knowledge did little to soothe the sting of her humiliation, but she was heartened to hear he took no pleasure in his deception.

"I don't understand your silence," she said. "Are you trying to protect Jeffrey in some way? Do you fear for my safety? Or is there some other reason?"

"Yes."

She waited for him to expound, to deliver a more satisfying answer. He did not.

Frustrated and suddenly, overwhelmingly tired, Catherine rose. "Since our conversation has all but ground to a halt, I am for bed. I find I don't have the stamina for this kind of verbal swordplay. It's been a long day."

When she made to walk around him, he blocked her path. "Please stay."

"Will you answer my questions?"

"Is it not enough to know the true nature of Ashcroft's death and that we're doing everything we can to locate his killer?"

She rubbed her arms. "Believe me, Sebastian, I wish it was enough. I will be quite happy to have this business behind me."

He laid his palm against her cheek and then kissed her with a sweet reverence that made her eyes prickle. "This won't allay your current disappointment," he whispered against her lips, "but I want you to know, all the same."

During their kiss, she had placed her hand over his chest and could now feel its rhythmic beat against her palm. Too fast, much too fast. "I'm listening."

"If I could tell you more, I would. I swear it."

God help her, she believed him. Believed the struggle he couldn't quite mask behind his carefully controlled appearance. She pressed her lips to his palm but said nothing. Something he said earlier simply didn't make sense. "You work for the Foreign Office in some capacity?"

The muscles beneath both her hands flexed. "Yes."

"Then you know whether my husband worked there?"

"I do."

She arched a brow, waiting.

His chest expanded on a deep breath. "He did."

Closing her eyes, she said, "How could I not know my husband was a spy?"

He grasped her upper arms and set her away. "Who said he was? John Chambers?"

She shrugged. "It seemed a logical occupation

given all that's happened." Cochran's name was on the tip of her tongue, but instinct cautioned her to keep his identity secret for a little while longer.

"Tell me, Sebastian," she said. "Once you find Jeffrey's killer, will you then share the full details?"

He stepped away and picked up his wine. "I cannot."

Her heart plummeted, but she was unsurprised by his answer. She'd held on to the tiniest bit of hope that he would eventually provide her with a sense of resolution. Unfortunately, she was still no closer to understanding his involvement with Jeffrey and this Nexus. For all she knew, everything Cochran had told her was the truth. The earl might have developed an ephemeral *tendre* for her and might wish to convey the circumstances around her husband's death, but that didn't mean he wasn't the one responsible. Hopefully, Cochran would come through for her in a way Lord Somerton was determined not to.

"I see." Because of his bone-chilling honesty, she managed to send him a polite smile. "In that case, I guess there's nothing left to say but good night."

His lips thinned. "I will see you in the morning."

She strode across the room and entered the connecting chamber, closing the door behind her. She leaned against the solid oak panel and tipped her head back, willing the war inside her body to abate.

Part of her wanted to ignore all the warning signs surrounding Sebastian—the danger, the prevarication, the single-mindedness. And another part of her wanted to pack Sophie up and head to the coast for a much-needed holiday. His actions with her daughter, his tenants, and Meghan McCarthy all pointed to a caring and considerate man. Grayson admired him and Mrs. Fox adored him. Lord Danforth had an easy relationship with him, even if a respectful one.

All of this still couldn't account for the secrets he'd kept or the isolation he'd lived under. He guarded his emotions with a small infantry. Any tiny chink to his defenses was swiftly replaced by another shield.

She pushed away from the door. A sudden sense of loss blackened her already somber mood. His reticence to confide in her had now forced her to act in a way not to her liking. She must now find her own answers. And in doing so, she must violate his trust and her moral principles.

Catherine lowered herself into one of the dainty chairs and waited.

Fourteen

WITH ONE HAND ANCHORED ON HIS HIP AND THE other clutched around a near-empty glass, Sebastian paused in the midst of the sunken garden. Where was that blasted bench?

He squinted into the darkness, twisting this way, then that way. No bench. He took another lurching step, his powerful frame listing decidedly to the left. *If only this bloody garden would stop moving.*

The widow was to blame for his current predicament. Had she not harangued him with question after question, he was certain they would be more agreeably engaged. In his bed. Naked and sweaty.

Not in a garden cracking his shins on every earthenware container he owned.

He tipped back the rest of his brandy, and this time the amber liquid slid down his throat like liquid silk. His gaze settled on the second floor, on the long balcony framing two sets of double doors. To the right, the countess's bedchamber sat in forbidding darkness, its occupant fast asleep, making Sebastian's situation all the more laughable.

For nearly two hours, he had tried to find surcease from the image of the McCarthy girl lying in a vat of mud, her mouth agape and her eyes deadened.

He had seen death many times and in various forms. Men, women, sick, poor, elderly, young—no one was immune, all could be sacrificed. Children were the worst. Their innocence made them easy targets, their defenses laughable to predators.

Children were the worst.

Sebastian lifted his glass for another healthy swallow, only to be met with a single drop. He eased his arm back down, the empty glass dangling from his finger-tips. Unbidden, his gaze rose to the countess's chamber again. How he wished he could have confided in her. His jaw actually hurt from the strain of keeping his tongue behind his teeth.

One detailed explanation would have been enough to set her mind at ease until the Nexus located Ashcroft's killer. One detailed explanation would have removed the wariness from her brown eyes and kept her in his bed. One explanation would have exposed an organization whose success depended entirely upon its anonymity.

He rubbed his aching temples, hating his role as chief of the Nexus in a way he never had before. He started to lift his glass again and remembered it was empty. Time for a refill.

Shuffling his feet, he made his way up the four steps that led down to his favorite section of the garden. Once there, he could see well enough that he didn't have to walk like an old man anymore, although his balance continued to favor one side of his body.

He entered through his study door, banging his shoulder into the frame. Someone cursed at the opposite end of the room. Sebastian dropped into a crouch, away from the open door.

His rapid change in position made his head spin, and he took precious seconds to shake off his alcohol-induced fog. Once he regained a modicum of clarity, he peered hard into the gloom, searching for shifting shadows and subtle sprays of light. But all remained eerily still. Too still. The air became rife with the intruder's fear.

Setting his glass down, Sebastian removed the long blade from a hidden sleeve inside his right boot. With more determination than finesse, he slid from one piece of furniture to the next, closing in on the intruder's location.

Or at least, where he hoped the intruder was hiding. With nothing more than a sliver of moon riding high in the sky, he was operating on instinct alone. And his inner guide led him to the darkened corner behind his desk.

Keeping to the shadows, Sebastian peered around his desk and listened for the distinctive sounds of life— shuffling feet, shuddering breaths, shaking furniture— while searching the darkness for movement. Nothing. He mentally retraced his steps to the moment he entered the study.

Had he really heard a harsh exclamation? Or was it perhaps his own noisy entrance that he mistook for another? When the possibility gathered merit in his mind, a flush heated his already dampened skin. He straightened from his concealed position, disgusted by his overreaction.

And that's when he caught a familiar scent. A scent that, only a few hours ago, had drenched his senses and made him yearn for a life not his own. A scent that was hers, and hers alone.

Catherine.

Lowering his blade, he sheathed the weapon and moved toward the gloom-filled corner. What had brought her to his study so late at night? Could she not banish the day's events, same as he, and sought solace elsewhere? His heart slammed against the wall of his chest when he considered another more pleasant reason for coming here. Had she been looking for him? If so, why did she remain quiet?

Then he realized she might not have known it was him. He had stumbled into the room from the outside and then immediately ducked out of sight. Maybe she thought *he* was the intruder.

Stopping a few feet away, he heard her faint rasping breaths. "Care to tell me why you're lurking in the shadows, my dear?"

A cudgel sliced through the space between them, connecting with the side of Sebastian's knee. He went down on all fours and had only enough time to raise his forearm to protect his head. But his assailant wasn't interested in bashing his skull.

The cudgel rammed into his lower back. Pain, sharp and debilitating, shot up his spine, arching his vertebrae and throwing him off-balance. He crashed to the floor, incapacitated.

His assailant shuffled closer but was careful to stay out of reach. A low, raspy voice said, "Why, I'm waiting for you, my lord."

Sebastian tried to scramble away, tried to get to his knife. But exhaustion, alcohol, and excruciating pain made him clumsy and slow. A boot slammed into his head, and Sebastian's face crashed into the rough carpet. His last thought before the night claimed him was of her. *Catherine*. Or, more specifically, her scent.

∞

August 14

Sebastian woke to low murmurings behind him.

"Is he alive, Grayson?"

"I believe so, my lord," his butler said. "The doctor is on his way. I dared not move him with such a head injury."

Sebastian recognized the other man as his former ward. He tried to push himself upright, but his arm would not move and his leg hurt like bloody hell. Then he recalled the brutal attack, and his jaw clenched, unable to believe he'd been caught so unawares.

"Wise decision," Danforth said. "Any idea who did this?"

"None, sir."

"Have you noticed any unusual activity in the area?"

"We did have a peculiar event occur yesterday," Grayson said. "A local girl was killed. Lord Somerton and Mrs. Ashcroft found her in the woodland not far from here."

"How did she die?"

"Strangulation," Grayson said. "The poor thing was also *enceinte*."

Opening his eyes, Sebastian saw nothing save the

bottom of his bookshelf. The more conscious he became, the more aware of his body he became. His right arm was trapped beneath his weight and his neck ached from its twisted position.

"Looks like he's waking, sir."

"Chief." Danforth shook his shoulder. "Can you hear me? Can you get up?"

Sebastian winced at the sudden jarring of his arm. "Yes and no," he croaked. "My arm."

The viscount eased him onto his back, taking care of Sebastian's useless arm. Blood rushed into his fingertips, releasing angry needles of retribution into his flesh. He flexed his hand, the action clunky and awkward, until feeling returned. He nodded his thanks.

"Grayson, can you fetch his lordship some water?"

Said water materialized in front of Danforth's face. He accepted the butler's offering with a wry look. "Thank you, old chap." To Sebastian, he said, "I'm going to lift your head a little so you can drink. If I hurt you, grunt or something."

The cool liquid soothed his parched throat, and Sebastian drank until Danforth forced him to pause for breath. His mouth must have been a big, open, yawning hole while he was unconscious. Not a pleasant image.

"Is everyone else unharmed?" he asked, his thoughts going to Catherine.

"Indeed, sir," Grayson said.

Sebastian tried to sit up, but a sharp pain sliced through his lower back.

"Careful," Danforth warned. "You have a nasty bump on the head."

"Your hand," Sebastian said, ignoring the viscount's warning. Once he was upright, he probed the gash above his temple. Nasty, indeed. "What time is it?"

Danforth checked his timepiece. "A little past eight."

Combing his fingers through his hair, Sebastian asked, "Where's Mrs. Ashcroft?"

"She left about an hour ago, my lord," Grayson said. "She mentioned she knocked on your door to relay her plans for the day. When you did not answer, she thought you were overtired from the previous day's events and insisted I leave you be. Your valet reported you missing not long ago."

Danforth whistled low. "You have packed a good deal of activity in the last twenty-four hours. Did you see who assaulted you?"

"No," he said. "The study was dark, the attack swift." Outside of his assailant's raspy voice, all Sebastian recalled was Catherine's distinctive scent. A pure feminine fragrance he would recognize anywhere. Even inebriated. Had she been meeting with his attacker, or had she been in his study minutes before? If so, why?

Setting aside the disturbing questions, he asked, "When did you arrive?"

"Only just." Danforth handed him the rest of the water. In a level voice, he said, "I have news."

The doctor picked that moment to arrive, and Sebastian spent the next hour enduring his less-than-gentle examination. After the doctor left and the drapes were drawn, Sebastian lowered himself into the chair behind his desk and tried to pretend his head was not splitting in two. "What do you have to report?"

"Helsford's informant made mention of a conversation between two gentlemen yesterday in St. Giles." Danforth poured them both a drink before lowering himself into a chair. "Although both wore disguises, they could not completely 'shuck off the stench of quality,' or so his informant said."

"The rookeries are bulging at the seams, but they're still a close-knit community and would be wary of strangers." Sebastian pressed a hand against his throbbing thigh. "I take it the meeting had some significance to our present situation."

"The informant believes Lord Latymer was one of the gentlemen," Danforth said. "He had the same unusual height, lean build, and straight black hair as the under-superintendent."

Sebastian's jaw tightened at the mention of his former friend and superior at the Alien Office. Latymer had plotted with the French to kill him in order to cripple the Nexus in a desperate attempt to protect Napoleon. He still did not understand why Latymer would turn his back on his countrymen and on such a promising career within the Foreign Office.

"Do we have his location?"

"No," Danforth said. "He put his training to good use and lost his tail within ten minutes."

"And the other gentleman?"

"Identity unknown. We have only a description—English, blond, and a peculiar tendency toward violence. If not for Helsford's informant, the barmaid he took a liking to would no doubt be dead now, or wishing for death."

Sebastian gritted his teeth, sending an arrow of

pain through his skull. Men who preyed upon those weaker than they sank below the level of vermin in his estimation. They were nothing more than scavengers, afraid of their own shadow, though always trying to convince the world they were gods.

"Did the informant hear anything of note?"

The viscount's gaze slid toward the door, his look pensive. When he turned back, he asked, "What do you know of your pretty neighbor?"

Dread slammed into Sebastian's chest. "Little, besides the fact that she was Ashcroft's wife and has a six-year-old daughter." *And she frees my soul with a single touch of her lips.*

"The men spoke in low tones, so the informant was unable to glean the entire conversation," Danforth said. "However, the gentlemen spoke of 'the widow' several times and there appeared to be a sense of urgency in their conversation."

"Do you know how many widows there are in England?" Sebastian couldn't keep the derision from his tone. The pressure inside his skull increased with each passing second, making it hard for him to concentrate and even harder to curb his impatience.

"Quite a few, I imagine," Danforth said, unperturbed. "But not so many associated with you."

"My name was mentioned?"

Danforth nodded, cocking his head to the side. "This is the second time Helsford's informant has come to your rescue. Anything I should know?"

At a critical moment during their last mission, Sebastian had received an anonymous note of caution. If he hadn't received the warning at the precise moment he had, Sebastian would have made a terrible mistake.

"Your question is better put to Helsford," Sebastian said. "I have no notion as to who the informant is or why the individual would want to help me." He considered his next words carefully. "But I am starting to question Superintendent Reeves's sudden interest in our agents and his decision to banish me to the country."

"You think Reeves is in league with Latymer?"

Sebastian shrugged. "Coincidences do occur, but I can't ignore the logic linking the two men together."

"Might explain some of what Helsford deciphered from Ashcroft's letters."

"How so?"

"Ashcroft spoke of his suspicions about a double spy in the superintendent's office," Danforth said. "In the last letter of the second packet you delivered, Ashcroft believed he had isolated the traitor and that the man was a liaison to Latymer."

"Did he provide a name?"

"Not in the letters we have."

Sebastian eyed the viscount. "You think there are more?"

"Possibly," Danforth said. "Or the traitors learned what Ashcroft was up to and killed him before he had the chance to identify the double spy in a final letter."

"Or a combination of both."

"There is that." Danforth angled his neck one way then the other. "Who else at the Foreign Office knew of Reeves's request?"

"No one, as far as I know. Reeves gave me his

word that he would be the only other official to see the list of operatives."

"Damn me." Danforth bolted back a drink.

"Indeed," Sebastian said, rubbing his temple. "Find Latymer and expand your investigation to include Reeves. Be careful, Danforth. Reeves is a spy among spies, dangerous and cunning."

"Yes, sir." The viscount flicked something off his coat sleeve. "Does it not disturb you?"

"A great many things disturb me," Sebastian said. "What exactly are you referring to?"

"Knowing powerful people are plotting your death."

"Of course it does." Sebastian started to lift his own spirits to his lips and then recalled his inability to subdue his enemy last night, with Catherine in the house. He set the drink aside. "But it's a circumstance I've operated under since becoming chief more than a decade ago."

"Allow me to send for a few guards. As a precaution."

The viscount, along with Cora and Helsford, had argued long and hard against Sebastian's refusal to bring guards to Bellamere, but Sebastian wanted to spend his time in the country in relative peace and isolation.

He hadn't counted on Bellamere being in disarray, and he certainly hadn't counted on Catherine.

"No," Sebastian said. "The addition of guards would alert anyone who might be watching that I suspect something's amiss. Get me something to work with—find Latymer, identify his companion, and increase your efforts where Reeves is concerned. Rule nothing out."

Sebastian thought back to the afternoon when he

saw a blond-haired man leaving Winter's Hollow. A friend of Ashcroft's—John Chambers—or so Catherine had said. But something in her tone, possibly the slight hesitation before she answered, made him question the veracity of her answer. What possible reason would she have for lying to him?

"Do me a favor," Sebastian said. "See if you can track down any information on a John Chambers."

"Where does he fit into all this?"

"Unknown, at the moment. He might be somehow acquainted with Ashcroft."

"Anything else?"

Sebastian rubbed his forehead and squeezed the bridge of his nose, not liking what he was about to do but knowing he would do it anyway. "Yes." He clasped his hands together on his desk. "Find out if Mrs. Ashcroft met with anyone while in London and see if you can identify the gentleman who paid her a visit three days ago."

"John Chambers, I take it?" Danforth asked.

"Yes." Sebastian sagged back in his chair, feeling more tired than he could ever remember being. If he could just close his eyes for a few minutes, perhaps the pain in his head would ease. "Notify me once you've learned more."

"Somerton, about you and Mrs. Ashcroft—"

"Don't."

Danforth's lips thinned.

Leaning forward, Sebastian said, "Your concern is appreciated. Let us continue to act, rather than react." He considered Danforth's tendency for rash action. "Keep a level head about this."

The viscount nodded, recalling an instant when he hadn't followed orders and had placed his loved ones in danger. "What if the trail leads back to Ashcroft's widow?"

"Tell me, but leave her to me." Sparks of white light flashed across his vision, and Sebastian fought to clear them away.

Danforth stood. "I'll report back once I have more information." He strode toward the door, but his steps slowed until he finally stopped.

Sebastian knew what the viscount was about before he ever turned around. Danforth never backed down from a fight, especially when the skirmish involved someone he cared for.

"Listen, about the widow—"

"Save it, Danforth. I will keep my wits about me. Now, be gone." Sebastian fought to keep his eyelids open. "And do be careful. I have no wish to feel your sister's wrath."

Danforth stood his ground, revealing a hint of his legendary stubbornness. "Grayson mentioned a dead girl at your doorstep."

"A domestic issue, nothing more," Sebastian lied. "Besides, she was hardly found at my doorstep."

The viscount snorted. "I have never known you to be so blind to your surroundings."

Sebastian pressed a hand against his roiling stomach and shook his head in a vain attempt to focus his blurred vision. "Mind who you are speaking to, Danforth…" His eyes rolled back in his head and he pitched forward.

Fifteen

THE PLEASANT BREEZE BLOWING ACROSS THE LAKE DID nothing to alleviate Catherine's concern for Sebastian. This morning, after failing to rouse him from slumber, she went on to meet with each of the craftsmen, then returned to report her progress. That's when she had received the unwelcome news from Lord Danforth that Sebastian was unwell.

Not considering the impropriety of the request, Catherine had asked to see him. The viscount refused admittance, and her angry reaction ignited a disagreeable argument that continued to ring in her ears, even hours later.

"Mama, you have that funny look again."

Catherine glanced down at her daughter. They sat on a large flat rock at the lake's edge, their bare feet dangling in the murky water below. "What look is that, dear?"

Sophie shrugged. "I don't know. It's the same one Papa used to get when he sat alone in the library."

An image of Jeffrey's faraway expression materialized. Catherine knew it well. In the beginning, she
had wondered about it, had often asked him about its
source. But after so many evasions and insulting quips,
she had stopped wondering and asking.

"I'm sorry, Sophie," she said. "I learned this
morning that Lord Somerton was not feeling well, so
my thoughts had turned toward his progress."

"May we take him some of the biscuits Cook and
I made last night?"

Catherine smiled. How she loved this little girl.
"That's very thoughtful, Sophie. When we return to
the house, I'll send Mrs. Fox a note to inquire about
his lordship's welfare." She kissed the top of her
daughter's head. "I have a surprise for you."

Sophie lit with delight. "A surprise for me?" She
tore off a piece of bread and tossed it into the water.

"Smaller bits, pumpkin. You don't want the fish to
mistake our toes for your bread."

"Yes, Mama." She followed words to action. "Do
I have to wait until Saturday?"

"I'm afraid so."

Her little face fell. "Oh, I wish you hadn't told me.
I will go *mad* thinking about my surprise."

"In that case," Catherine said, "I probably shouldn't
tell you that it has to do with Bellamere's stables." She
still found Sebastian's change of heart amazing. One
day he didn't want her daughter underfoot, and the
next he's inviting Sophie into his inner sanctum.

"The *earl's* stables?" Sophie dropped the whole slice
of bread in the lake and clambered up on her knees to
squeeze Catherine's face between her grubby hands.

"Tell me about the stables, Mama. Please, oh, please, oh, please."

Catherine laughed, hugging her daughter to her, but the horse-crazed girl was having none of it.

"Mama, this is *serious*." Her daughter's breath caught and her eyes widened in excitement. "Am I going inside?"

Nodding, Catherine said, "At Lord Somerton's personal invitation."

"You mean I don't have to sneak in?"

"Have you?"

Sophie shook her head. "No, but Teddy and I have been plotting ways to see the earl's horses."

Catherine bit her lip and forced her features into stern lines. "No, young lady." She gave her daughter a little shake to emphasize her point. "There will be no sneaking in anywhere. Lord Somerton will personally introduce you to his horses."

Sophie whooped as she threw her arms around Catherine's neck and pressed a dozen smacking kisses on her face. "Must I wait until Saturday? I will *die* with antishipation."

"Yes, you do." Catherine tweaked her daughter's nose. "And where is all this drama coming from?"

"What do you mean, 'drama'?"

She settled her daughter more comfortably across her lap and pulled a cucumber sandwich from the nearby basket. "You are experiencing some extreme emotions, my dear. *Mad, serious, die*. Quite unlike you." More than normal, Catherine amended.

"Oh, that," she said around a mouthful. "Eloisa Walker's older sister is very sophishticated. She knows all the important words."

"Well, if you're going to mimic your elders, you must listen carefully. You will die with *anticipation* and Eloisa's older sister is very *sophisticated.*"

She nodded her head. "Yes, exactly."

Catherine's smile was bittersweet. Although the Walkers had a penchant for gossip, they treated Sophie as one of their own. With four girls and three boys, the Walkers provided her daughter something Catherine never could. Brothers and sisters.

She had always wanted a large family, not as large as the Walkers, but three or four children would have brought her immense joy and, when the time came, many grandchildren. Being an only child herself, she knew the challenges Sophie faced.

"Mama, who is that man?"

Catherine jerked her head up, her thoughts going to Sebastian. Even though they had been apart for less than a day, she looked forward to seeing him again and feeling his strong arms wrapped around her. She examined one side of the lake to the other, but saw no familiar—or otherwise—masculine figure. "I don't see anyone, dear."

Sophie pointed her half-eaten sandwich at a cluster of trees and tall bushes to Catherine's right. Pushing her daughter's hand down, she tried to piece together greens and browns and pale yellows into a recognizable form. When she was on the verge of giving up, something stirred, and Catherine realized she was looking too high.

Adjusting her gaze, she concentrated harder until finally a face emerged. Bulbous, watery eyes, wide forehead, thin, greasy hair, and yellow, neglected teeth. Catherine's blood froze in her veins.

The disgusting little man from the butcher's shop had visited her thoughts often since their first encounter. Each time, her uneasiness grew. And now, he was in their private sanctuary, observing them with an unholy gleam in his eyes. But who was he and why was he following her?

With a surreptitious sweep of the area, Catherine considered their options. He had picked his location well. In order to return to the house, she would have to pass his hiding spot. She could take the southern footpath, but that would lead them through a dense woodland before turning back east. The isolated nature of the route troubled her more than walking by the man.

She could head west, to Sebastian's estate, even though that way lay an uncertain welcome. But, like the southern route, the west footpath would still take them past the stranger.

"Do you see him, Mama?"

"Yes, pumpkin." She set her daughter away. "Put on your stockings and shoes, please."

"Must we go? I want to hear more about my surprise."

"Do as I say, and we will discuss it all you want. Up at the house."

Catching the note of authority in Catherine's voice, her daughter ended her protest and did as told. Catherine picked up her own discarded footwear. When they were ready to go, Catherine knelt down in front of Sophie. "Listen closely, sweetheart, but do not be alarmed." She waited for her daughter's nod. "We're going to walk past that man, but I do not want you to speak with him or acknowledge him in anyway. Is that understood?"

"Uh-huh," Sophie said, looking toward the man's location.

"That includes staring."

Sophie's eyes flashed to Catherine's. In a stage whisper, she said, "Is he a bad man? Papa warned me about them."

"I don't know." Why were the men in her life never around when she needed them? "And I don't intend to find out today." She glanced around the area to make sure they had retrieved all of their belongings. "Ready?"

Her daughter tunneled her hand into Catherine's. "Ready."

Catherine kept their pace steady and sure, chatting along the way to help keep Sophie's attention on other things, rather than the man who followed their every move. It didn't help. Curious by nature, her daughter could not stop glancing toward the clump of shrubbery protecting the man from her inquisitive eyes.

"What did I tell you, young lady?" Catherine followed the query with a gentle pull-squeeze of her daughter's hand.

Sophie whipped her head around so fast that Catherine was surprised she didn't hear it snap. "Don't talk to him or gape at him." She angled around to look behind them. "But, Mama, he's following us now."

Catherine halted mid-stride. Her heart plummeted all the way down to her toes. When it started the slow, sluggish ride back up to her chest, a wave of murderous rage licked through her veins. She stashed Sophie behind her and met the man's eerie gaze.

He stood thirty feet away, watchful and patient. He neither spoke, nor indicated chagrin for having been caught. Nor did he move.

"What do you want, sir?" she asked.

His head tilted to the side like a dog's did when considering the best way to pounce on a cat. He didn't respond, only pointed toward her house.

She glanced between Winter's Hollow and the ugly man, trying to understand his unspoken message. The attempt only confused her more.

Grabbing her daughter's hand, Catherine pushed them into a faster pace. She nudged her daughter in front of her, aiming to keep herself between Sophie and the awful man.

He cut them off.

"Stand aside, sir," Catherine said. "We're on our way to meet with Lord Somerton."

Shaking his head, he once again indicated the path leading them to Winter's Hollow.

As Catherine's grip tightened around Sophie's small hand, a keen sense of vulnerability shook her to the core. She had no options. Though he was a small man, Catherine detected a wiry strength about him. If they tried to run, he would catch them.

"Mama," Sophie whispered.

The strange man's eyes narrowed, and he stepped forward.

Making up her mind, she gave her daughter's hand a reassuring squeeze and marched toward Winter's Hollow, praying she hadn't sentenced them to a terrible fate. An image of Meghan McCarthy's broken body surfaced, and Catherine's terror knew no bounds.

Had this man killed her? Was he the elusive father? She shoved aside the repulsive thought.

When they reached the garden, Catherine glanced back and found their tormentor gone. She hurried them through the gate and into the house. Once she clicked the lock in place, she felt a measure of relief until her maid Mary entered and announced that she had a visitor. "A Mr. Cochran to see you, ma'am."

Catherine kissed Sophie's forehead. "All is well now, sweetheart. Run along upstairs and change your clothes while I speak to our guest. I'll be up in a little while to check on you." She turned her daughter around and nudged her toward the servants' staircase.

Her daughter pinched the sides of her frock, looking for splats of dirt and bits of grime. "Mama, there's nothing wrong with this dress."

"No, there's not," she agreed. "But it's your play dress, not your house dress. Up you go."

Sophie groaned, but did as told. Her progress up the narrow stairs had all the signs of a convict headed to the gallows.

"Mary, please see Miss Sophie to the nursery," Catherine said.

"Oh, Mama."

Catherine allowed herself a small smile as she watched the two make their way up to the third floor. Once they turned the corner, Catherine rushed to the window to peer outside. Her gaze slashed from tree to tree, building to building, shadow to shadow. But nothing moved or appeared out of place. Everything seemed oddly untouched, yet frightfully violated.

She checked the lock on the kitchen door again

and made her way to the drawing room. When she entered, she found the Foreign Office official lounging on her sofa, an easy expression on his handsome face. "Mr. Cochran, this is an unexpected surprise." *Again.* After their last meeting, she had not looked forward to their next.

He did not rise to greet her. "Good afternoon, Mrs. Ashcroft. I'm afraid our former timeline has been compromised. Have you the list?"

Catherine strode farther into the room. "There is no list, sir."

"What do you mean?"

"I had occasion last evening to search his lordship's library, study, and even his bedchamber, and none contained a list of secret agents." The only names she found were the two tucked under the earl's ink blotter—Sebastian Danvers and Jeffrey Ashcroft. Hardly a list.

"Yes," he said with a slight curl to his lip. "I heard you spent the night with Somerton."

Catherine clenched her teeth. "Perhaps the intelligence you received regarding Lord Somerton's involvement with the Nexus was wrong."

"I can assure you," Cochran said, "the information I shared with you is quite accurate."

"Then maybe his lordship has not compiled the list yet."

"Could it be that you have not looked well enough?"

His humoring smile made her jaw clench. "Where else would I search, sir? Based on what I have witnessed, Lord Somerton is not a threat to anyone. Quite the contrary, actually. He's been nothing but helpful to those in need. What you are accusing him of simply makes no sense."

"All men, even those with evil intent, have a weakness. It is how governments do business, madam. They find the other's weakness and exploit it." He tapped his two forefingers against his lips, considering her for a moment. "The better question here is which one of the Ashcroft women is Lord Somerton's greatest weakness?"

Cochran's piglet gaze sent a rush of wary tingles down her spine. Why had she never noticed his close-set eyes before? "What can you mean, sir?"

A pregnant pause, then the official's face split into an affable smile. "I mean nothing at all. My mind tends to venture off course at the most inconvenient times."

Drawing in a deep breath, Catherine said, "Sir, I have made a gross miscalculation in my eagerness to bring my husband's killer to justice. I can no longer assist you in this endeavor."

Cochran released a sigh. "That is not good news, my dear. Is there nothing I can do to change your mind?"

Catherine shook her head. "No, nothing, sir. I'm sorry to have wasted your time."

Cochran rose from his chair, pulling at the sleeves of his forest green coat to smooth out the wrinkles. "This exercise wasn't a waste of time, madam," he said, strolling toward the door. "It's always best to attempt the path of least resistance, don't you agree?"

Catherine stared at Cochran, not understanding his cryptic remark. "Excuse me?"

His eyes crinkled at the corners. "Give me but a moment and I'll explain." He turned and disappeared down the corridor.

When Catherine heard the front door open, she made her way to the window overlooking the small circular drive. Outside Cochran's carriage stood a short, wiry man with a balding pate interspersed with clumps of stringy brown hair.

Recognition crashed into her chest like an angry bull trying to breach a fence. Cochran joined the stranger, jabbing a thumb over his shoulder while he spoke. The little man listened intently, lifting his gaze in Catherine's direction before scurrying away.

She stepped back, her throat closing around a string of questions. After a couple seconds, she craned her head around the draperies to see Cochran open the carriage door. He reached inside—

From the direction of the entrance hall, a door slammed, pulling Catherine's attention away. Then the sound of pounding boots running up the stairs stopped her heart cold. Sophie was upstairs.

She flew across the drawing room and into the corridor while her mind frantically attempted to understand what was going on. When Catherine reached the bottom of the staircase, it was empty.

She lifted the hem of her dress, preparing to go after the stranger, when a noise from behind stopped her. She whipped around to find Cochran reentering her house with a pretty mahogany-haired woman on his arm. The errant thought that the woman looked none too happy swept through Catherine's jumbled mind.

"What is going on?" Catherine demanded. Her mind screamed for her to run upstairs, to find the strange man and her daughter. Inching her way up one step, then another, she tried again. "Mr. Cochran, who are these people? Why have you brought them into my home?"

Cochran glanced over her shoulder. "In due time, madam."

Catherine followed his gaze. Nothing.

She returned her attention to the couple below her and then eased up one more stair.

Cochran motioned for her to come down. "Perhaps we'd all be more comfortable in your drawing room."

A feminine screech sounded from above. *Mary*. Her fear—barely controlled—unleashed, and she bolted up the stairs.

"Stop," Cochran ordered. "Silas won't hurt them. No guarantees, though, if you charge up there."

Catherine halted, gasping for air. Every instinct she owned urged her onward, but Cochran's threat kept her pinned in place, helpless in a way she'd never experienced before. Then she heard her daughter's furious voice a moment before the little man—Silas—appeared, dragging her resisting daughter down the corridor.

"*Sophie*." Catherine started after her daughter, but a large hand grasped her arm.

Cochran's cold gaze met hers. "I told you. My man has everything under control."

"Mama!"

Silas slung Sophie over his shoulder. Her small hands pounded against his back, shoulders, head, anything she could reach. "Let me down, you rabbity beast."

Catherine jerked hard on her arm and winced when pain shot up to her shoulder. She clawed at Cochran's restraining grip, and his other hand grasped her throat, forcing her chin into an unnatural angle.

"I said stay."

"Mama!"

Unable to move her head, Catherine's eyes found her daughter. "Be still, Sophie." Her fear for her daughter's safety was as palpable as the hands restraining her. "Mama will take care of everything."

Cochran chuckled, his thumb raking across her lips. "Will you, indeed?"

"Release me at once." Her sight was becoming blurrier by the second.

His nails bit into the tender flesh of her neck and then he pushed her down the stairs.

Sophie yelled.

Catherine scrambled for purchase, her world a whirl of images until she caught the balustrade. Cochran came up behind her, grasping her arm and towing her the rest of the way down, giving her no time to catch her breath. Catherine tried to keep her daughter in sight, but failed.

"Mama!"

She fought back tears. "Be strong, Sophie." She twisted around to meet her daughter's frightened gaze. "It will be all right."

"Do you promise?"

Catherine hesitated a moment too long, for her perceptive daughter began to struggle in earnest, kicking and pounding on her captor.

"Say it, Mama. Say it."

"Quiet," Silas ordered with a smack to Sophie's behind.

"Leave her alone," Catherine demanded, fighting Cochran's grip.

Silas's scold did nothing more than stun her daughter

into speechlessness for a half second. Enough time for Cochran to yank hard on Catherine's arm, making her cry out and forcing her toward the drawing room.

Away from Sophie.

Sixteen

CATHERINE STARED INTO HER DAUGHTER'S WARY brown eyes as her six-year-old scooted her small frame back into the chair's cushioned seat.

"That's a good girl, Sophie. Thank you for joining us." Cochran patted her narrow shoulder, acting as though she had been invited down to the drawing room, rather than packed down like a sack of potatoes.

"Now then, where were we, Mrs. Ashcroft? Oh, yes, I remember. You wished to discontinue your involvement in our little investigation." He smoothed his hand over her daughter's blond curls. "I hope I've provided sufficient inducement for you to press on."

"*Inducement?*" Her daughter spat out the word, no doubt recalling her grandmama's various incentives.

"Not now, Sophie." Catherine's gaze returned to Cochran. "Yes, more than sufficient. Now may my daughter return to the nursery?"

Cochran's hands clamped around her daughter's tiny shoulders, looking more like manacles of death than objects of comfort. "But I'm enjoying her company."

His threat could not have been clearer. Because of

Catherine's moment of conscience, Sophie would now be used as a tool to ensure her mother's good behavior.

"All men, even those with evil intent, have a weakness. It is how governments do business, madam. They find their opponent's weakness and exploit it."

Cochran's prophetic words returned to haunt her. How had she missed the depravity lurking behind the official's piglet eyes? Did he even work for the government? Doubtful. She must consider everything he'd told her up to this moment a lie, including Sebastian's involvement with the French. *Sebastian.*

"I'm eager to hear how you're going to obtain the list, Mrs. Ashcroft," Cochran said. "Spare us no details."

At the use of the term "us," Catherine remembered the others in the room. Her gaze slashed to the mahogany-haired woman hovering near the door to the frightening stranger called Silas keeping vigil next to her chair.

At first glance, Silas appeared to be in his late fifties with his hunched shoulders, unsteady gait, and thinning brown hair. But on closer inspection, Catherine noticed his eyes and mouth did not carry the deep grooves so common of that age. No, this drab little man couldn't be more than a half dozen years beyond her nine and twenty.

Her attention shifted back to Sophie, who squirmed beneath Cochran's hold. "Please allow my daughter to go upstairs," she pleaded once more. Cochran's hulking presence so near to her baby sent a shiver of debilitating dread through her. How in Heaven's name would she get them out of this?

He leaned forward, and his thick lips spoke near Sophie's temple. "Mrs. Ashcroft? We're waiting."

Catherine unlocked her ankles and gripped her knees with shaking hands. What did he want from her? She had already searched every room where she thought Sebastian would keep private papers.

Cochran considered her for a moment, then lowered his mouth to Sophie's ear. "Your mother holds out hope that she has a choice in the matter." He straightened, his gaze flattened. "It's best to clear up such misconceptions at the onset. Mrs. Clarke," he called, "stoke the fire. Our fine summer weather has definitely taken a turn, especially during these cloudless afternoons. I don't want the ladies to catch a chill."

A flush of cold panic coated her palms. She glanced from Mrs. Clarke bending over the fire to Cochran's dispassionate gaze to Sophie's pale face and felt the stabilized world she had erected for her daughter fracture.

She pushed up from her chair, intending to go to Sophie, to offer what comfort she could, but Silas clamped a hand around her neck, forcing her back into her seat.

"It is best you stay seated, Mrs. Ashcroft," Cochran said.

"M-mama?" Sophie's voice cracked.

Catherine winced when Silas's fingers tightened on her neck. As she stared into her daughter's uncertain eyes—a look so uncharacteristic of the imp whose escapades kept everyone in the household on guard—a weighty helplessness held her immobile while her brave girl contorted her body to elude Cochran's despicable touch.

Catherine balled her hands into painful knots as

the weight on her chest grew heavier. She pulled in a calming breath, one that barely registered, then forced a reassuring smile. "Do not fret, pumpkin. Mama will take care of everything. I promise."

Her daughter visibly relaxed, having no reason to believe her mother would fail. She never had before. But Catherine knew this time was different. A palpable evil had entered their home, and Catherine worried she had told her daughter her first lie.

Cochran directed his attention toward the pulsing coals. "You did well with the fire, Mrs. Clarke."

The woman averted her face.

Bending forward, Cochran rubbed the backs of his fingers across Sophie's rounded cheek. "Can you feel the fire's warmth, *pumpkin*?" His lifted his amused gaze to Catherine.

Her eyes welled with tears.

Sophie nodded, scrunching up her pert nose and leaning away from his caress. "It's hot."

"Is it?" His careless tone belied his concern. "Shall we ask your mama?"

"Do you think the fire's hot enough, Mrs. Ashcroft?"

Her throat closed around a useless scream. Besides Mary, who had nowhere to go, the servants had all gone home to spend time with their families, as they did every Tuesday afternoon. It was the only time she truly had Sophie all to herself. Even her mother had gone out to visit with friends. Had Cochran known they would be alone? He seemed to know a great deal about them.

She fought the urge to close her eyes, to wish this nightmare away. If anything happened to Sophie—

Swallowing hard, she cut the thought short and allowed her anger to build. She thought back to all the achingly lonely nights she had spent waiting for Jeffrey, all the times her daughter searched the drive for her father.

She thought about how she would kill these men for threatening her baby.

"I will do what needs to be done," Catherine said.

Cochran's gaze flicked to Silas, though his comment was directed at the woman. "I am not convinced. Mrs. Clarke?"

The mahogany-haired woman stared at the fire, unmoving. "Mrs. Clarke, need I remind you—"

"No, Mr. Cochran." The woman turned bleak eyes to the fire and bent to retrieve the red-tipped poker. She turned toward Sophie.

"No!" Catherine catapulted herself out of the chair.

Clawlike fingernails raked across her skin as Silas lost his grip. His other hand swept around, seizing the coil of hair pinned at the back of her head, yanking her to a painful halt. A cry of shock-pain escaped her throat and her body bowed backward.

"Let me go!" Keeping her burning gaze on the glowing poker, she made mad swipes at the hand entrenched in her hair. A couple of her nails connected with flesh, and her captor jerked hard in retaliation, sending her sprawling back into her seat. He did not release his hold.

"Leave my mama alone!" Sophie cried, fighting against Cochran's restraint. Tears streamed down her terrified face.

Unable to free herself, Catherine tightened her

grip on her captor's wrist while she warned Cochran. "Leave her be, you brute." To her daughter, she said, "Sit still, pumpkin. Mama's fine."

She caught Cochran's eye. "I'll tear apart every room, ask questions, eavesdrop on conversations," she panted. "Revisit his bedchamber. *Whatever* it takes." A mother's determination bolstered her tone. "I swear it."

Silence followed her declaration. Catherine focused on Cochran and awaited his verdict with thundering ears. Her daughter's broken cries sliced through her heart yet strengthened her resolve.

Finally, Cochran nodded, releasing Sophie at the same time Catherine's captor withdrew his painful grip on her hair.

She barely had time to sit up before her daughter launched herself into her arms. Catherine hugged Sophie's small, trembling body, keeping a cautious eye on her uninvited guests.

"It's time I formally introduce you to my lovely assistant." Cochran gestured to the mahogany-haired woman. "Mrs. Clarke will join your household until you have completed your task."

"Whatever for?"

"Insurance, of course."

More like a gaoler. Now that the woman no longer held the hot poker, she appeared stern and uncompromising. "How am I to explain her presence?"

His gaze sketched over her daughter, who now fought Catherine's protective hold to see the other woman. "I'm sure you'll agree that your daughter could use a bit of refinement. Mrs. Clarke will make an excellent governess."

Sophie shook her head. "No, Mama. I don't want her."

A lump formed in Catherine's throat. They expected her to just hand over her daughter to this woman? To this unsmiling creature who would no doubt report her every move and would do God knew what to her daughter?

Who was she? What were her qualifications? No one in her household, or in the village, would believe Catherine would entrust Sophie's care to a stranger.

"I see your apprehension, Mrs. Ashcroft. You've no need to worry. Mrs. Clarke is quite good with children." He smirked at the other woman. "Isn't that right, dear?"

"Yes, Mr. Cochran."

"You see," he said, "there's no call for concern."

Catherine tried to reason with him one more time. "I can do this without your insurance."

"No doubt," he said. "Mrs. Clarke, take the girl to the nursery."

Catherine tightened her hold around Sophie. Now that the immediate danger had passed, she did not want to lose sight of her daughter. As long as she could see Sophie, she could maintain the illusion of control.

Mrs. Clarke approached Catherine's chair and held out her hand. "Miss Sophie, come show me your toys."

Catherine stared at the woman's outstretched fingers, noted their slight tremble. The woman did too, and dropped her arm, fisting her hand.

Interesting.

But her daughter had already shied away, clutching Catherine's face between tiny hands that smelled like dirt and worms. "No, Mama," she pleaded, her blue eyes filling with tears. "I p-promise to behave. I promise."

Catherine could barely speak around the tears clawing at the inside of her throat. She rested her forehead against her daughter's and squeezed her eyes shut.

Lord, give me strength.

Her daughter impatiently pushed against Catherine's cheeks, cutting her prayer short. She bent to capture Catherine's gaze. "Please, Mama. I want to stay with you."

Managing a wobbly smile, Catherine said, "I love you, pumpkin. I love you just the way you are. Never forget it. Now cover your ears." She waited for her daughter to comply before lifting her gaze to Mrs. Clarke. "You harm one hair on my daughter's head and you will come to regret it. Understood?"

The woman slanted a glance toward Cochran, then gave Catherine a swift nod.

Drawing in a bracing breath, Catherine eased her daughter's hands away from her ears. "You must go with Mrs. Clarke."

"No." Sophie wrapped her amazingly strong arms around Catherine's neck. "No, I don't want to go."

Catherine noticed Cochran's patience had come to an end. His message was clear—if she could not control her daughter, he would. And soon.

Catherine knew how to handle her daughter's infrequent tantrums. With a mother's gentle strength, she unwound Sophie's arms and set her back. "Sophia Adele Ashcroft," she said in her sternest voice. "Stop this nonsense at once."

"But, Mama—"

"Enough," she said, her heart breaking with each harsh word. "You will go with Mrs. Clarke now, or you'll be forbidden to ride Guinevere for an entire month."

Her daughter's eyes widened in wounded horror, and the remaining pieces of Catherine's heart shattered.

Sophie adored her pony. The two were caught more than once tearing across the open field near the stables. To her daughter, a month without Guinevere would be like a month without sustenance.

Scrambling off her lap, Sophie stood before her with her arms locked at her side and her nostrils flaring with each angry breath. "You can't do that. Papa gave her to me."

Irritation abraded Catherine's nerves. She had done what she could to preserve Sophie's memory of her father, and to his credit, Jeffrey had never forgotten his daughter's birthday. Lavish gifts arrived on time every year to honor her birth—and to soften the sting of another missed celebration.

As a result, Sophie worshiped her father, and Catherine would have it no other way. But Sophie's choice to invoke her father's so-called wishes against her cut deeper than her husband's abandonment had.

Cochran moved to stand next to Mrs. Clarke.

Catherine hardened her resolve, then sat forward in her chair and pointed toward the door. "Go. Now."

Her smart daughter recognized her I'm-through-talking tone and ran from the room, leaving Mrs. Clarke to follow at a more sedate pace.

When the door closed, Cochran threw something onto her lap. She glanced down and recognized

Sophie's lost figure, a kilted warrior holding a two-handed claymore.

"Finish what you started, Mrs. Ashcroft, or I will slit your daughter's throat."

Seventeen

THE OUTER DOOR TO SEBASTIAN'S BEDCHAMBER CLOSED behind a reluctant Danforth. After watching Sebastian succumb to the effects of a concussion, the viscount had not been keen on leaving. Sebastian had spent the last half hour convincing the agent that his efforts were better spent in London, tracking down their enemy, than playing nursemaid.

Sebastian propped his bare feet atop the sitting room's ottoman, unhappy to realize the laudanum the doctor had prescribed was wearing off. Much to his relief, his nausea had dissipated; however, a dull throb continued to batter his brain, lower back, and behind his left knee.

His assailant had known what he was about. With three swift and violent strikes, he had incapacitated a seasoned agent, who knew a score of ways to kill a man—when not in his cups.

Tilting his head back, he gave in to the bone-deep weariness that had invaded his body. For someone who was rarely sick and never tired, his current condition put him in a sour mood. That Catherine had not bothered to check on him all day had nothing to do with his present foul temper. Nothing at all.

He closed his eyes and the relief was instant. The candlelight glowed bright enough to be a nuisance, and he still had a difficult time focusing. Once the muscles in his face relaxed and the tautness in his shoulders eased, he allowed his mind to wander. Allowed it to seek a source of calm and tranquility. Most times when he performed this exercise, he would find himself standing at the bow of a fast-moving ship, heading toward the sunrise, the rejuvenating buff of a sea breeze sliding along his skin.

But not this time. This time, his mind moved inexorably to Catherine, to her mischievous brown eyes and honey-gold hair. To her full, berry-red lips and her petite, God-blessed figure he had yet to fully explore.

Last night, when he found her sitting on the hearth rug, brushing her hair and eating bits of cheese, a feeling of completion had overcome him. Images of them making love beneath the countess's canopied bed, sharing a steaming tub of water, and idling away hours on the balcony while admiring a moonless night drenched his mind.

He had wanted to make love to her so badly last night, but could not break free of the secrets he was sworn to keep. Caution had been his bedmate for many years. So far, discretion had never let him down.

Even so, he had nearly given in to her plea for information. Had nearly unloaded everything he knew of her husband. How brave he'd been. How he'd saved so many lives. How devastating Ashcroft's death had been for him. But all those confessions would lead her to the Nexus, exposing his agents to unforeseen perils. Something he would never do while chief, and never allow her to do.

He prayed she had not become involved in his war with Latymer. In her single-minded attempt to seek justice for her husband's murder, she might inadvertently have stepped inside Latymer's web. He'd learned long ago that what lies within one's heart is often hidden behind the best defenses. But, as he told Danforth, he would rule nothing out. For all he knew, Latymer could have sent her to him in London. A fraud from day one.

His lungs released a shuddering breath, and the distinctive urge for oblivion returned. He toyed with his drink, his mouth watering. Then he made himself recall his vulnerable state last night and pushed it away. He would not endanger those beneath his charge for a few hours of numbness. He eased up from his chair, stretching his back and testing his injured leg.

With more hobble than stride, he made his way over to the bank of high-ceiling windows and peeled back one of the drapes. He was grateful to see the onset of evening approaching. Swirling hues of pink, orange, and yellow rode low on the horizon, bringing an otherwise dismal day to a gracious end.

He wondered how Catherine's meetings with the craftsmen had gone and if she had stopped by the McCarthys' to offer whatever solace she could. Regret weighed heavily on his mind. He should have been with her. Neither task was hers to bear alone.

Then a more insidious thought crept inside his mind. Had she helped him with estate matters for some reason he had yet to understand? No, she had been dealing with his tenants long before Reeves's request. Sebastian rubbed his aching head.

A low knock sounded at the bedchamber door and then an exchange of words ensued. Seconds later, his valet appeared in the sitting room doorway. "My lord," Parker said in a near whisper. "Mrs. Ashcroft is here to see you."

The mere mention of Catherine's name made his body tense with anticipation. *She came.* Sebastian slowly turned toward his valet, his heart hammering inside his chest. "Show her in."

Parker eyed Sebastian's attire. "Sir, perhaps you'd like to adorn yourself of a neckcloth and trousers first? Stockings, too?"

"No need to whisper around me any longer, Parker," Sebastian said. "The pain is down to a tolerable ache."

"Very well, my lord." He hesitated. "And the other?"

For his valet's sake, Sebastian tightened the sash holding his banyan closed and made sure all his manly parts were discreetly covered. "This will do."

Parker nodded and disappeared. The next several minutes seemed an eternity while he waited for his staff to escort Catherine above stairs. Why had she chosen this moment to check on him? Why not hours ago when her cool palm could have soothed his splitting head?

Sebastian stretched his neck first one way, then the other, and rolled his shoulders. The exercise relieved some of his tension but failed to calm his heart. Then he heard the light tread of feminine feet coming down the corridor.

Seconds ticked by, each holding a decade's worth of time. He longed to see her, yearned to feel her body pressed to his. Through the haze of his need, he recalled his promise to Danforth. *"I will keep my wits about me."*

Notwithstanding his imminent departure back to London, he had to maintain a level of emotional distance until he either absolved her of any involvement with Latymer or confirmed a connection. *Yearning* and *longing* had no place in their dalliance.

The door closed in the other chamber, and Sebastian's chest rose high on a deep inhalation. His jaw ached from the pressure of his clenched teeth. And then he noticed the first hint of a feminine silhouette approaching the open doorway.

Within seconds, Catherine filled the frame. Beautiful, proud, tempting. Cautious.

"My lord." Her voice held a slight quaver. "Mrs. Fox said you were attacked by a thief last night. Is this true?"

He studied her shadowed face, unable to make out her features. "We have yet to determine if the man was a thief. Nothing appears stolen. But yes, I came upon a man unawares in my study."

She moved farther into the sitting room. Something was wrong with her eyes and her features appeared drawn and hesitant. Without thinking, he limped toward her. "What's the matter?"

"You're injured." She rushed into the chamber. "How badly?"

"A bruise, nothing to worry over." He tilted her chin up. "Have you been crying?"

❧

"Of course not." Catherine stepped away. She had hoped her bout of self-pity would not be evident by the time she arrived. Except for some sleepless nights over the last several years, she had done an admirable job not wallowing in the fact that she was alone. Every decision—good or bad—was hers to make. The only thing she hadn't had to worry about was money. With Jeffrey gone, she would have to consider that issue now, too—once she cleaned up this espionage mess he'd left behind.

Since she could not discuss the reason behind her puffy, gritty eyes and her long face, she redirected the conversation back to him. "Besides your leg, where else are you hurt?"

"I am well on the mend, Catherine. No need to concern yourself."

"Did Grayson send for the doctor?"

"Yes."

She scrutinized him more closely. He balanced his weight on his right foot and he seemed to be squinting, almost as if it pained him to look upon her. Beyond those two indicators of discomfort, she could detect nothing else.

"What are you doing here?" he asked.

Saving my daughter. "I came to check on you."

He tilted his head to the side. "Did you not just learn of the attack upon your arrival?"

"No, my lord," she said. "You did not answer my knock this morning. At the time, I thought you needed the rest. However, when I returned later, Lord Danforth said you were unwell and couldn't receive visitors. He said nothing about an attack, though."

"If not now, when did you learn of the attack?"

His tone carried an air of interrogation, making her feel as though she had done something wrong. In truth, she had not planned on coming here tonight. But when she'd received his housekeeper's response to her earlier inquiry, she'd had to come. "I sent a note around to Mrs. Fox, not long ago, asking for news of your recovery. A reply came but thirty minutes ago. Sophie wanted to bring you biscuits to speed up your recovery."

By slow degrees, she watched the hardness in his features soften and the rigid set to his shoulders ease. On some level, she regretted his transformation. Now that she did not have his cold inquisition in which to focus her attention, she became keenly aware of *him*.

With his disheveled hair, scruffy face, and loosely tied banyan, he looked disreputable and wholly desirable. She wished they had met under different circumstances, at a time when they could have explored this attraction they held for each other. But their association was caged within the walls of deception, with no way to break the barrier.

He prowled closer, his unwavering crystalline gaze on hers. She held her breath, unsure of his mood and unable to block the memory of her daughter's screams. She could do this. She could do whatever it took to secure the damned list, protect her daughter, and be rid of her gaolers. She could do this.

No matter how much it broke her heart.

His fingertips skimmed the curve of her cheek. "You have been crying. Why?"

She fought the compulsion to lean into his touch. "Meghan." The lie fell easily, too easily from her lips.

"Catherine. *Cat*." He clasped the back of her head, drawing her forward, into the comfort of his chest. "I'm sorry you had to witness such barbarity. Such things are not for the eyes of innocents."

Her arms wrapped around his middle. "Why kill her? The babe's father could have disappeared and never returned." She burrowed her nose deeper into his silk wrap, absorbing his musky scent and banishing forever the stench of mud and death.

"Perhaps the father could not leave," he said. "Maybe he had a family and was afraid Meghan would reveal their secret. Could be any number of reasons. None of them acceptable."

His embrace tightened, and Catherine reciprocated. Air hissed between his teeth, and he jerked away.

"What's wrong?"

"Nothing," he said through stiff lips.

"Liar." She tugged on the end of his sash, pulling the tie free.

He backed up, securing his wrap. "What are you about?"

"You have another injury you failed to mention."

"The doctor has already seen to it."

"What is *it*?"

She saw him weighing his options, no doubt considering whether to brush off her question with a vague response or put an end to this line of query with the truth. From her perspective, the decision took much longer than it should have.

"A contusion," he said finally.

She frowned, having never heard the term.

"Bruise," he clarified. "A rather unpleasant one."

"Is it the same on your leg?"

He nodded. "Thankfully, my assailant did not shatter my knee."

"Oh, Sebastian." She reached for his hand, and her chest clenched when his fingers grasped hers in return. "Where else?"

He released a long, heavy sigh. "Concussion."

She peered at his head, seeing nothing amiss. "Where?"

"Are you this motherly to everyone?"

"Only to those who insist nothing is wrong. Point, please." When he did nothing but narrow his gaze on her, she said, "Your attempt to stare me into submission will not work. That particular tactic ceased intimidating me many years ago." She waved toward his head. "Where did he bash you?"

Rather than point to the location, he grabbed her wrist and lifted her hand to his hair. He carefully guided her fingers through the soft strands until she reached a large bump three inches above his left ear.

She sucked in an astonished breath. "Goodness, my lord. Why are you not abed?"

He closed his eyes, seeming to take comfort from her caress, although she did not touch the painful lump again.

"Hearing you say my name is so much more preferable than 'my lord.'"

Heat rose into her cheeks. "Why do you always evade my questions?" Recalling his other injuries, she stepped around him, her fingers tracing down his nape.

"For the same reason you're keeping the true source of your tears from me." His luminous gaze followed her progress.

His wide shoulders filled her vision, and she once again experienced a sense of her own delicacy while standing next to him. With a feather-like touch, she skimmed her fingers down his back, circling the lower portion. "Is this where he hurt you?"

She heard him swallow. "Yes."

"May I see?"

Over his shoulder, he said, "You might find more than an ugly patch of skin."

She hoped so. Retracing her path, she memorized each silk-draped sinew before gripping the neckline of his banyan. With her eyes riveted on her hands, she drew the shimmering cloth off his shoulders. Something desperate and raw raked along her every nerve ending, making her hands tremble and her breaths shaky.

Once his upper arms were free, the silken wrap, secured by his sash, drooped over his bottom, revealing a long black bruise that ran perpendicular to his spine. It had to be six inches long and about two inches high. The visual evidence of the violence he'd endured and suffered alone forced her pleasurable thoughts to the wayside. "Sweet Lord."

Further speech was impossible, for her throat had closed around that simple, inconsequential phrase.

"It's nothing," he said in a rough voice. "I hardly know it's there."

Fury replaced the ache in her heart. "Well, I know it's there." She reached around and freed the sash again. The length of cloth released, and his wrap melted in a pool of emerald silk at his feet.

Her heart hammered in her ears, nearly deafening

in its ferocity. He was magnificent. Smooth angles and firm ridges. Taut skin and rippling muscles. Without moving a single inch, he stole her breath.

"Have your look, Catherine." His blue-gray eyes pulsed with fire. "Because in ten seconds, I'm going to show you why that was a dangerous decision."

His masculine perfection befuddled her mind so badly that it took her several precious seconds to work through his warning. When she finally did, she dropped to her knees and bent to inspect yet another injury. He stood with most of his weight on his right leg, his left leg cocked to provide a measure of balance but little else.

Similar to his lower back, a large bruise covered the underside of his knee. This one looked so much worse. Rather than a perfect outline of a geometrical shape, the bruise on his leg spread out in all angles like a slow-moving cancer. Her fingers hovered over the area, but she dared not touch. "What type of weapon causes this kind of damage?"

He shrugged. "Some type of cudgel, I suspect."

She sat back on her heels. "You're rather nonchalant about your attack." Her gaze sharpened. "Does this sort of thing happen often?"

"Nine. Ten," he said, ignoring her question. "Time's up." The rich timbre of his voice held both promise and foreboding.

As he angled his body around, Catherine's eyes grew more and more round with every new inch revealed. *Magnificent.* All the adjectives she'd used to describe his body thus far were like defining the Crown Jewels as a set of pretty baubles.

Pretty did not come close to describing his baubles. He held out his hand. "Come with me."

Catherine glanced from his hand to his smoldering eyes to the pulsing length of his erection. And there her attention remained, fixed on the delicate smoothness of his flesh straining to accommodate his building arousal. Engorged veins lined the underside of his staff, leading to a round, velvety tip that pointed toward his navel. From there, she followed a slender line of dark hair down to his thick base, which led back to pulsing veins and straining flesh.

In all her years of marriage to Jeffrey, he had never been so blatant, so confident with his bare form. Catherine's mouth felt suddenly dry, and that's when she realized her jaw hung open. She closed her mouth so fast that her teeth clicked together.

He crouched down in front of her, the action causing him to wince. "I am inviting you into my bedchamber, Catherine. Do you accept, or must I persuade you?"

She was certain he could hear her heart pounding. What started out as a seduction to save her daughter was progressing into far more dangerous territory. She could no longer feel the guilt or the shame, only the hunger of her body. "Both?"

Bracing his hand on the floor, he leaned forward, sliding his nose alongside hers. The caress of his breath fanned over her lips, compelling hers to part. His kiss was warm and passion-filled, making her body tingle in glorious places and her heart sing with anticipation.

"Are you persuaded now?" His words were low, seductive.

Unable to open her eyes, she nodded. "Oh, yes."

"Look at me."

She blinked her eyes open, surprised by the heavy weight of her lids.

"Do you recall the terms of our *affaire*?"

A sharp ache pierced her chest. "Of course."

"Then you recall that I will be returning to London in a few days."

The ache spread to her throat. "You have nothing to worry about, Sebastian. I understand that our time together is ephemeral."

His eyes hardened for the briefest of seconds, then he blinked and their glowing intensity returned. Catherine accepted his hand, and they strode into his bedchamber, one sporting nothing but the perfection of his bare flesh and the other draped in mournful black linen. The contrast was startling and evocative.

The moment she stepped into his bedchamber, Catherine's senses sharpened. Candles flickered around the room—candles she didn't recall seeing moments ago when Parker had let her in. The air was redolent with Sebastian's special scent.

She gathered in a long breath, savoring the delicate woodsy bouquet. The mix of musk and violet suited him much more than the popular sandalwood or ambergris, known for their bold fragrance.

His thumb smoothed over the backs of her fingers. The tender caress drew her attention to the solid warmth of his hand while he guided her toward his massive curtained bed. Like most things in this house, the earl's bed bespoke privilege, wealth, and an appalling flair for the vulgar. But in this instance, the ceiling-to-floor sapphire hangings, with their silver embroidered cuffs and their plush folds, compelled rather than repulsed.

He stopped near the side of the bed and cradled her flushed cheeks. Bending close, he kissed her forehead and then skimmed his mouth over hers. "I am going to do unspeakable things to you in that bed, Catherine," he breathed against her lips. "If you have thoughts of fleeing, now would be the time."

"The only place I wish to flee is deeper into your arms."

The pressure on her cheeks tightened infinitesimally, and his nostrils flared around a shuddering breath. "Then come, my sweet."

At his urging, she carefully curled her arms around his back, sliding her trembling hands up the satiny planes of his shoulders. He was so large. So solid and strong. Yet his hands explored her body with a gossamer touch, with a skill that left her aching for more.

She pressed closer, delighted and aroused by the evidence of his desire. Every inch pulsing against her stomach was for her, for want of her. The realization was exhilarating. Tormenting.

She shouldn't want him so much. Every act between them was nothing more than a link to a greater betrayal. They both had secrets, underlying motives for igniting their passions. And he would soon be gone.

The knowledge that he would leave her behind, as her father and Jeffrey had done, sent a bolt of realism straight through her heart. That flash of insight was all she needed to start mentally erecting a familiar barrier, one designed to keep her heart intact and her sanity in place.

"Turn around, please," he whispered.

She swiveled around, and he began working on the fastenings of her gown. All the while, she continued building her protective wall, stone by stone. However, this particular barrier proved more challenging than past ones. The brush of his fingers along her back and the warmth of his lips pressed against her nape distracted her from her task.

Her gown sagged and then billowed to the floor. She evaluated her barrier and groaned. Large clumps of mortar dripped from the seams, and stones sat haphazardly within each row, leaving dangerous gaps. Cool air kissed her burning flesh, and Catherine scrambled to hold up her quivering wall.

His hands skimmed down her arms until he laced their fingers together. "Relax," he said against her temple.

From his vantage point, she knew he had full view of her nudity, especially when she tilted her head back to rest on his shoulder and arched her arms around until she could clasp her hands behind his neck. With her breasts jutting forward and her bottom snuggled against his rigid length, she felt both vulnerable and luxuriant. His hands caressed their way over her quavering stomach to her swollen, tender breasts. She closed her eyes and tracked his movements with her sense of touch alone.

"Beautiful." He closed his hand over her aching breast, adding the slightest bit of pressure to her ruched peak. A stab of need sliced through her body, lifting her to her toes.

"So responsive." He squeezed again, this time harder, compounding the torturous move by ravishing her mouth.

His tongue slid inside with a thoroughness that made her legs squeeze together. She wanted to hold on to this moment for as long as possible. She wanted to experience a man's need and have him assuage hers. She wanted to feel alive again.

Breaking the kiss, he threw back the covers and climbed into bed. He reclined against the mound of pillows, lifting one knee and holding out his hand in invitation. A shiver raced along her bare flesh, having nothing to do with her state of undress and everything to do with his sultan-like pose. Rippling muscles, smoldering steel-gray eyes, raw desire. The erotic combination stole her breath.

His hand lowered. "Take your hair down for me."

The breath she had been holding *whooshed* from her body. She wasn't used to such blatant commands. They made her feel uncertain and shy, beautiful and bold.

Straightening her spine, she lifted her hands to her hair and began pulling out pins. He followed the unfurling of every long lock with such intensity that her attempt to appear seductive and unhurried began to fray.

When she finally located the last pin, she breathed a sigh of relief as she swept her mass of blond hair over one shoulder. "Anything else, my lord?"

His nostrils flared. "A good deal more, I assure you, madam."

He lifted his hand again, and Catherine noticed it was no steadier than hers. She swallowed back the last of her trepidation and accepted his assistance. Once she had scaled the high bed, Sebastian guided her into position. She nearly balked when she realized he wanted her to mount him. Never had she assumed such a place of power with Jeffrey.

Perceptive as always, he noted her hesitation. "Do you mind?" he asked. "I'm afraid my knee won't hold up to the traditional way."

He radiated so much power and strength that Catherine momentarily forgot his injuries. "Not at all. What of your head wound?"

"I will be careful."

He tugged on her hand, and Catherine followed his summons. With her knees framing his hips and her hands entwined with his uplifted ones, she knelt above him, taking in the surreal image of Sebastian beneath, gazing up at her as if she were his entire world. Power surged through her, and she lowered her starving cleft until it rested on the warm girth of his erection.

Fire shot up her spine and her muscles clenched tightly. Even though he had not penetrated her yet, her body was on the cusp of a mind-shattering release. She rubbed her slick flesh against his hardness, the exquisite friction making them both moan their approval. She increased the pressure and her pace, nearly flying out of her skin every time her sensitive nub connected with his staff.

"Are you through torturing us, madam?" he asked in a desire-clogged voice. Not waiting for her answer, he said, "Kiss me." Releasing her hands, he let his arms slide around her back, nudging her down.

Their lips met, and Catherine lost herself in their feral kiss. It was wild and exciting and unlike anything she could have imagined. And then she felt him at her entrance, probing, seeking, needing.

She adjusted her position, and he eased inside, filling her with a fullness that made her blood sing and her heart thunder. Bracing her hands on his chest, she had the odd thought of how small they looked against the breadth of him.

He grasped her hips and lifted her high, to the point of nearly releasing him from her channel. Then he encouraged her to sink low once again. On and on it went, their languid pace increasing as the scent of desire flooded their senses.

"Come with me, Cat."

She closed her eyes and searched inward for the tiny spark that would ignite her release. But it remained stubbornly out of reach. Her legs quivered from her exertion, sweat dampened her brow. "I'm t-trying. Can't quite—"

"Hold on," he commanded.

With barely enough time to comply, Catherine clung to his shoulders while her world upended itself and then she was staring up at the sapphire canopy above his bed. "Sebastian, your knee!"

"Forget it," he said. "Prop those beautiful legs up and meet me halfway."

Power surged inside her, and Catherine's hips flexed. She kissed his chest, his neck, his mouth, all the while meeting him with a confidence that surprised her. This is where she belonged, within the cage of his arms, beneath the power of his body. Here, she did not want to be strong, did not want to be in control. At least, not yet.

He hit the spark, and Catherine lifted her hips,

pressing closer and closer. No longer pumping a rhythm, only seeking repletion. Greedy in her purpose and not caring a whit.

The spark ignited, sending Catherine into beloved white light.

Their mingled cries of pleasure echoed through the chamber. Within seconds, an unnatural silence settled around them. Their harsh breaths the only indication life existed after such a fierce loving.

All too soon, he peeled his body off hers, kissed his way down to her breast, and then drew her nipple into his mouth. His actions were languid, not meant to arouse, but simply enjoy. When he'd had his fill, he rolled onto his back, bringing her along.

She stiffened in his arms, afraid she would hurt him. "Perhaps it would be best if I did not crowd you."

"Perhaps," he said, keeping his eyes closed. "But I prefer that you stay right where you are."

Unwilling to argue about something she wanted anyway, she carefully molded her body around his and rested her head against his chest. She listened to the chaotic beating of his heart until it calmed to a normal rhythm.

And that's when the first tears gathered. She came here to seduce the earl for a scrap of paper, while her daughter slept beneath a canopy of evil. There was no way to get through this intolerable situation without someone getting hurt, either physically or emotionally.

However, she tried not to fool herself where Sebastian was involved. *Affaires* were commonplace for him. Pleasurable while they lasted, but he likely gave them little thought once they ended.

After his breathing deepened and his hold slackened, Catherine waited a full twenty minutes before easing out of his bed and dressing. She wended her way down the broad staircase, bracing herself for the appearance of a wide-eyed servant. To appease Cochran, she would search the study again tonight and, tomorrow, the library. She pushed the study door open and held her breath. The room was empty. Dark.

She ran to Sebastian's desk and lifted the ink blotter to see if any more names had been added to the sheet of paper she found there a few days ago. The list was gone. "Blast," she whispered.

The realization that she would need a light to continue her search struck terror in her heart. She took precious minutes to see if her eyes would adjust to the gloom. Although she could see a little better, it wasn't enough.

She located one of those lovely Argand lamps on Sebastian's desk, but discarded the notion of lighting it. From what she'd read, they provided the same amount of illumination as six candles. Catherine only needed the light of one.

Unable to locate a taper anywhere, Catherine swallowed her fear and lit the lamp. Golden light flooded the room, momentarily blinding her. She glanced at the crack beneath the door and rushed to retrieve a throw from the chaise longue to place in front of it.

The clock on the mantel mocked her with its incessant passage of time. Perspiration dampened her skin. She searched his desk, his bookshelves, and any other drawer she could find. Nothing.

Recalling the hidden compartment in her writing

box, she returned to his desk and bookshelves to poke, push, pull anything she could get her hands on. Still nothing.

Frustration seethed beneath layers of fear and desperation. She whirled in a wild circle, seeking some other source for secreting away valuables. Nothing, nothing, nothing.

She drew in a ragged breath, grappling with a sense of defeat and utter relief. Pulling herself together, she extinguished the lamp and replaced the throw on the chaise. She stood in the gloom-filled study, hesitating. Her gaze lifted to the upstairs bedchamber, where a handsome, complicated earl slept in a halo of repletion. Repletion she had given him.

Shrugging off the maudlin thought, Catherine opened the tall paned doors leading out to the garden, closing them behind her. She made her way down to the stables to fetch Gypsy, ignoring the burning sensation in the back of her head. She could not worry about a pair of searing steel-gray eyes watching her, not when she was busy repairing the ruins of her wall.

Eighteen

August 16

"Still no sign of the list, daughter?"

Catherine finished entering the date of Mr. Tucker's repair on her schedule before answering her mother. Once the notation was made, Catherine surveyed the meadow for their two gaolers from beneath the small tent Edward had erected for them. Silas was nowhere to be found, a condition that made her more nervous than if he'd been standing five feet away.

She located Mrs. Clarke kneeling on a blanket out in the middle of the field, instructing Sophie on how to build a kite. With nothing more than a couple of sturdy sticks, yards of string, and silk from an old ball gown, her daughter was well on her way to flying her first kite. Catherine wished the joyful moment weren't tainted by an undercurrent of fear.

"No," Catherine said. "Two evenings of searching, and not a single treasonous note."

Her mother drew a long, red thread through a

square of linen. "Have you searched Lord Somerton's rooms again?"

"Not yet." Catherine dropped her quill pen onto her portable writing box. "Now that I've completed the lower level, his private chambers are next." She hated speaking of such things with her mother. Although the words were never spoken, Evelyn Shaw knew how her daughter spent her evenings. Thankfully, her mother understood the situation well enough not to cast judgment on Catherine's actions. "Last night, I caught a glimpse of a half-composed letter on the writing desk in his bedchamber. From the few sentences I had time to read, the words were disjointed and illogical."

"Disjointed," her mother repeated. "Could it be a coded message, like Ashcroft's letters?"

"Perhaps." Catherine stared at her daughter, standing now with the framework of a kite. "I'll copy it tonight, so that I might study it in more detail on the morrow. If I can't obtain the list of agents, Cochran might be appeased with an important message instead."

They sat in silence for a few minutes until Sophie's laughter broke into their musings.

"My granddaughter seems to be taking to her new governess."

"Yes." After the initial shock of their gaolers' invasion had passed, Sophie had gradually warmed up to her constant companion. Mrs. Clarke's kindness and inventiveness kept Sophie's mind occupied with games and an assortment of crafts, rather than the disastrous way in which they were introduced.

"In many ways, Mrs. Clarke is the perfect governess for Sophie."

Proving Cochran's contemptuous comment true. Why would a woman such as she align herself with so despicable a man? The question piqued her troublesome curiosity.

"I am sorry that you have this to deal with in addition to the loss of your father and husband."

"No need to fret on my account." Catherine clasped her mother's cold hand in hers, forcing a light tone into her voice. "Although I would rather be in Brighton, basking in the sun and listening to the waves, my situation could be far worse. I could be consorting with a man weighing twenty-five stone, thrice my age, with a propensity for greasy foods."

An image of Silas skulking in her entrance hall surfaced. After her first evening with Sebastian, she had returned home before the sun had crested the horizon. Silas had been waiting. He'd emerged from a darkened corner, the play of shadows over his ugly features making him appear more insidious than ever. The sight of him had come close to dropping her in a dead faint. Every night thereafter followed the same routine. His only greeting was a question: "Do you have it?"

And each time, she would shake her head and brace herself for his reprisal. Other than his lips thinning in displeasure, he had not reacted, simply stepped back and nodded toward the staircase. She had wasted no time in complying.

"Given that dreadful image," her mother said, "I shall view this situation in a more positive light, but I still prefer that you were not involved at all."

"Had I not drawn attention to myself and Jeffrey's letters, neither Lord Somerton nor Mr. Cochran would have given me a second's thought."

"Where do we go from here?" her mother asked.

A good question. "I must proceed with my search until I find something of value for Mr. Cochran. With any luck, the indecipherable missive I found will assuage their demands." Catherine squeezed her mother's hand. "Can you continue watching over Sophie?"

"Of course," her mother said, sounding put out that she even had to ask.

"Thank you." Catherine recalled Cochran's parting words. *Finish what you started, Mrs. Ashcroft, or I will slit your daughter's throat.* "Promise you will send for me the moment you believe something has gone amiss."

Her mother patted Catherine's hand. "Be at ease, daughter. I will not let you down in this."

The muscles in Catherine's throat constricted. "I never doubted it, Mother."

She sent Catherine a wan smile, appreciating the small falsehood.

A whoop of laughter broke into their reverie of past failures and future happiness. They looked up to find Sophie tearing across the meadow, her kite flying thirty feet above, Mrs. Clarke running alongside, encouraging her with gentle instruction.

Before she realized what she was about, Catherine was on her feet, clapping. Chagrined, she glanced over at her mother, who stood beside her, wearing the same proud smile, her hands clasped together at her chest. They grinned at each other and then turned as one to cheer on their little girl.

◈

Sebastian cursed his impatience, even while the heel of his boots tore into the graveled path leading to his stables. With hours to go before Catherine made her nightly appearance, he could no longer tolerate the sound of his own interminable pacing. He needed something to take his mind off the widow and her penchant for vacating his bed in the middle of the night.

For the last two evenings, they had indulged their carnal desires, and afterward, she would crawl from his bed and set about searching his home with a thoroughness that would put many of his agents to shame. After their first night together, when he was still suffering the effects of his beating and fell into a deep sleep, she had made the mistake in thinking he was not easily awakened. But sleep was something he needed very little of and, as a result, it took him awhile to fall into slumber. Had she waited a little longer before deserting him, she might have pulled off the deception without his knowledge. But she had not, and he had been forced to follow her about the house as she combed through his personal items.

A movement by the paddock fence caught his eye. His steps slowed as he made out the form of a small child sitting atop the rail and watching his groomsman exercising Sebastian's prized white Arabian.

Sophie Ashcroft. Sebastian closed his eyes and counted to five. He could pretend he hadn't seen her and continue on to the stables, where he intended to muck out stalls, brush down horses, clean tack—anything— that would release the tension strumming through him.

Opening his eyes, he noted her precarious perch

and knew he couldn't walk away. Her mother would never forgive him if he allowed harm to come to the child. He would not analyze why he cared about the feelings of a woman who made passionate love to him one moment and deceived him the next.

Blowing out an exasperated breath, he headed for the horse-hungry imp. Even from this distance, he could make out her rapt expression. What he wouldn't do to feel such unreserved joy for something. Anything.

"Miss Sophie," he called.

She started, grabbing the rail for balance. Once she had recovered, she shoved a piece of paper into the pocket of her red pelisse, then glanced over her shoulder with a guilty expression.

"Do you remember who I am, child?"

She nodded. "You're the Lord Earl."

Leaning his forearms against the fence, he followed Cira's progress. He shared the girl's fascination with the Arabian. The horse's trim lines and graceful maneuvers had been perfected over centuries of solid breeding.

"In a manner of speaking, yes," he said with the same patience as her mother. "I am an earl, but the proper way to address me is by using my title—Lord Somerton."

She wrinkled up her nose. "Lord Somerton."

His lips twitched. "Or you may call me Sebastian."

She perked up, but her gaze never veered from the Arabian. "Bastian."

He smiled, liking her version better. "That's right, Sophie." A few silent minutes passed while they both admired the white beauty.

"Did you know Arabians are the oldest purebred horses in the world?" she asked with wonderment.

He did. But how did she? The child couldn't be more than six or seven. "I had heard something to that effect. What else can you tell me?"

She turned wide, expressive eyes on him. Her father's eyes. "King Sol-lom—"

"King Solomon," he offered.

Her eyes opened wider. "Have you heard this story?"

Suppressing a chuckle, he said, "I'm not sure. Why don't you tell me?"

"King Solomon housed forty thousand Arabians in his stable. Can you imagine? They'd fill your big barn."

Sebastian nodded in agreement. "Indeed, they would. Yours, too."

"Holy horses!"

A laugh burst from Sebastian's chest, alarming Cira and the groomsman and sending young Sophie into a gale of giggles. The intrepid child reminded him so much of Cora at her age that he felt an answering pang of longing for simpler times.

"Ohhhh, no," Sophie whined. The abrupt shift from laughter to a child's pout surprised him. He glanced down and found her staring off into the distance, shrinking behind his shoulder.

He followed her gaze and noticed a feminine form headed their way. His heart stuttered for a moment, thinking Catherine had come to fetch her child. On closer inspection, the woman wore a light gray gown, rather than mourning black, and she had brown hair. Not his Catherine at all.

"Who is she?"

"My new governess, Mrs. Clarke."

"You do not like her?"

She shrugged her shoulders. "She's nice. This morning, she showed me how to build a kite."

"Impressive," he said. "How did it fly?"

"Really high. I ran out of string."

"Well done." Remembering the many times he had attempted to elude his tutor, he asked, "Are you hiding from Mrs. Clarke?"

"Not her." She slanted a glance toward her governess again. "Him."

Sebastian kept his pose casual while he scoured the area. The girl's tone carried a distinctive note of fear that could not be easily invented. "I see no one."

"He's there," she said. "He's always there. In the woods, behind Mrs. Clarke."

He peered beyond the governess, into the dense woodland. Still he saw no one.

"Have you told your mother about him?"

Her eyes widened, as if she remembered something important. "Ahh, I'm going to be in so much trouble."

"Why is that?" He split his attention between the approaching governess and the treeline.

"Because I'm not supposed to tell anyone about him." Her voice lowered and she fidgeted with a ruffle on her dress. "Especially you."

Every muscle in Sebastian's body hardened with fury. "How long have they been following you about?"

With her eyes downcast, she slid her hand into her pocket, and paper crackled.

He nudged her with his shoulder. "We're friends now, are we not?"

Her blond eyebrows squeezed together, considering.

"Did you hear of my invitation to visit my stables?"

She brightened, nodding. "Mama said I had to wait until my birthday on Saturday."

"That's correct," he said. "We must be friends, because I don't let just anyone into my stables."

"I feel the same way about Dragonthorpe," she said. "I asked Mama if I could show it to you, but she cried." Her lips pursed. "Not like that bad man made her cry. I think she misses my papa."

Sebastian stilled, trying to keep up with the girl's thought patterns. He had some experience with this particular malady from when Cora was young, but he was more than a little rusty. He tucked Dragonthorpe away, recalling Catherine's mention of the castle. However, ignoring Sophie's comment about Catherine missing her husband took a good deal more effort. He eventually managed it, as he knew he would.

"You miss your papa, too?"

Paper crackled again. "Sometimes."

"Do you have something there of his?"

Her eyes widened. "Oh, double trouble."

The moment didn't exactly call for humor, but the earnestness in the girl's voice tickled something deep inside. "A letter, perhaps?"

"Yes," she said in a small voice. "But it's all gibberish. You'd think Teddy wrote it instead of my papa."

Could she be carrying another letter of Ashcroft's? Sebastian tried to keep his excitement under control. If Sophie had somehow filched one of her father's coded messages, then Catherine hadn't held anything back. She had given him everything.

He stared down at the child's bent head, and a

different sort of pressure squeezed his heart. Had she taken her father's letter in a bid to be closer to him? Instead of finding reassuring words of love, she had found nothing but a confusing string of nonsense. "After your party, I promise to help you read your papa's letter. How does that sound?" He would make sure Ashcroft's final words were a comfort to his only child.

"Mama might get upset."

"I'll take care of your mama. Agreed?"

"Yes, Bastian."

"Would you mind if I took a peek at it now?"

With obvious reluctance, she pulled a folded missive from her pocket and held it out for him.

"Thank you, Sophie." He scanned the contents, no better able to decipher them than Sophie. But toward the end a name stuck out—Frederick Cochran. The name struck a chord of familiarity, but nothing came immediately to mind.

"Oh, yes," he said, glancing down at Ashcroft's words again. "I shan't have any problems deciphering this tomorrow." Another name stood out in stark contrast to the rest—Abbingale Home. Sebastian frowned, not understanding the reference and having no context in which to figure it out.

"May I keep this until tomorrow?" he asked.

"You won't forget to give it back?"

"No." He slid the missive into his coat pocket. "I won't forget. You have my word."

Sebastian glanced up to find the governess at the outer edge of the paddock. He moved on to the bad man. The one who made Catherine cry. "How long has the man been following you, Sophie?"

"Which one—the bad man or the scary man?"

"Either one."

"Three or four days." She sent him a pleading look. "Please don't tell Mama."

"It is our secret."

"Which man made your mama cry?"

"Mr. Cochran."

Sebastian strove for calm, even though his heart rocked inside his chest. "Is Mr. Cochran the one hiding in the tree, Sophie?"

"No, that's the scary man."

He laid his hand on her arm, wishing he didn't have to interrogate the poor girl, but knowing it was the only way to help them. "What does the bad man look like?"

She shrugged. "Tall. Blond like Mama."

"Miss Sophie," the governess called. "It's time for you to come home now."

The little girl pulled so hard on her flounce that Sebastian heard it separate from her dress.

"I won't allow anyone to harm you, Sophie."

"And Mama?"

His heart contracted. "I'll protect her, too."

The governess' strides quickened.

"Promise?" she whispered.

Sebastian suppressed his own sense of desperation. "You have my word."

She made to climb down the fence. "One more thing," he said, with a touch to her arm. "Your governess. When did she arrive?"

"The bad man brought her."

With that pronouncement, Sophie swung her legs

over to the opposite side of the fence and jumped down, hurrying over to her apparent gaoler.

The woman took Sophie's hand, nodded at him, and returned the same way in which she came.

The bad man brought her.

Sebastian dug his fingers into the railing to prevent himself from going after the little girl. Seeing her pixie face mottled with fear nearly broke his heart. Even now, her head hung low, dispirited.

"Sophie," he called.

She turned to face him. "Yes?"

"Don't forget our appointment on Saturday," he said. "Cira's itching to go for a ride."

Her eyes widened and her mouth dropped open. She looked like a startled fish. "I get to ride her?" She turned wondering eyes on the Arabian.

"Indeed," he said, relieved to see her normal exuberance returned. "But not if you're late."

She shook her head. "I won't be. I'll come early, Bastian."

He smiled. "That's my girl."

Sophie skipped away, leaving her governess to follow along behind. Sebastian's smile faded. Turning away from the stables, he made his way back up to the house, faster, more determined than when he'd descended.

He had a great deal to do—missives to write, a widow to contemplate, and a bad man to kill.

Nineteen

THE BED DIPPED BEHIND HIM AND THEN A SOFT rustling followed, alerting Sebastian to Catherine's midnight escape. He tracked her progress about the room, with nothing more than his sense of hearing. She pulled out a drawer on his writing desk, and he detected the distinct slide of paper against paper. The drawer closed, and she moved away. Into the sitting room.

He maneuvered his naked body out of bed, drawing his banyan over his shoulders. At the entrance to the sitting room, he drew in a steadying breath. From this point forward, their association would change, likely for the worse. Regret sliced through his heart. With Catherine, he had caught a glimpse of what life outside the Nexus could be. And he'd liked it.

Bracing his hand against the door frame, he hesitated far longer than a seasoned intelligence agent should. He didn't want to give her up, but the spy in him clawed at his restraints. No matter her reasons, she was here on behalf of his enemy. Her actions had placed his country—a country he had fought years to protect—at risk.

This he could not allow.

No matter the personal sacrifice.

Fortifying his mind, he swallowed back his deep yearning and leaned against the doorjamb, crossing his arms. Fully dressed, she bent over something he couldn't see. Then he saw her dip the nib of her pen into an inkwell.

"Writing me a farewell letter?" he asked.

A short, high-pitched scream burst from her throat, and she shot to her feet. With her back to her make-shift writing table, she faced him. "Pardon?"

He pushed away, moving toward her with preda-tory intent. "Farewell letter," he repeated. "The last few evenings you've abandoned my bed without so much as a kiss farewell. I thought tonight you might be tarrying long enough to say good-bye." When he saw her eyes widen at his close proximity, he pivoted to stalk around the table, trying to catch a glimpse of what she had been writing. "Of course, I would have preferred a kiss to a missive."

Her color was high, and he could hear the painful rasping of her breathing. Sympathy for what he was about to do tugged at his heart.

"Yes, of course." She snatched up the pages on the table. "How silly of me. I will keep your preference in mind next time."

Afraid she would rip the sheets to shreds, he grabbed her wrist. "No need to waste good paper, madam. Allow me to read what you've written so far."

With surprising strength, she wrenched free of his hold. "Um, no." Her movements became jerky and her gaze slashed across the room, reminding him of a caged animal. "I prefer your method of good-bye to mine."

Dropping all pretense, he asked, "Who sent you, Catherine?"

She sucked in a startled breath. "I have no idea of what you mean, sir."

"I think you do." He nodded toward the papers behind her back. "Give them to me."

Backing away, she shook her head. "It's nothing, really."

"You're not leaving this house until I see what you're hiding." He infused as much menace into his tone as possible. "Unless you would like for me to call the constable."

"Whatever for?"

"To report a theft, of course."

Looking more trapped than ever, she clutched the papers to her chest. "Please don't."

He gentled his voice. "You're giving me little choice."

"You don't understand."

"Then educate me," he said. "Explain to me why a widow with an impeccable reputation would risk an *affaire*. Tell me why you would betray my trust."

"I c-can't."

"Why? Why can't you? Who are you protecting?"

"Please, Sebastian." Tears filled her eyes. "I beg you. Pretend you never saw this. If you do this for me, I swear I'll not grace your doorstep again."

Sebastian's chest heaved with his building anger. On one level, he stood before this beautiful woman, who had somehow woven a spell around his heart, angry and hurt, and on another level, he observed the scene from a great distance. Disconnected and uncaring.

Betrayal, lies, and death were nothing new to him. He had come to expect them all with every new mission. That didn't stop him from struggling with the knowledge that Catherine acted out of desperation and the unfortunate side effect was deceiving him. Although he didn't know the source, he understood her motivation and respected her for having the courage to do what needed doing. But still, Catherine's decision not to confide in him split open a wound that not even stitches could mend.

"Tempting, my dear. But, like you, I cannot." He flicked his fingers toward the papers. "I won't ask for them again. When it comes to physical strength, I win."

Unabated tears streamed down her face. Her silent torment was nearly his undoing. Had she wailed and screamed, he would know how to deal with such theatrics. Mournful silence was another thing altogether. Wanting nothing more than to end both their suffering, he stepped forward to remove the papers from her crushing grip.

"If you take th-these," she said around a sob, "they will kill her."

That stopped him. "Her?"

"Sophie."

"Who would dare threaten to harm your daughter?" When she remained silent, he demanded, "What madness have you embroiled yourself in?"

She clasped her hands over her ears, flattening the papers against her head. "I didn't mean to. Dear God, I would never knowingly place Sophie in danger. Never."

"For what it's worth, I believe you." He stepped

forward, aching to wrap his arms around her trembling body. "Tell me what's going on."

"Do you?" she asked, ignoring his command. "Given our circumstances, I'm not sure I'd believe me."

"I've been at this a long time," he said. "There's little I have not seen or experienced."

Sadness stole around the edges of her fear. "How awful for you."

His throat grew taut, trapping his pithy retort. No one had ever taken the time to consider the personal anguish he'd suffered by way of his position. Most thought him cold and ruthless—and they were right—but not until Catherine had anyone examined the reasons behind those qualities.

"Do you trust me, Cat?"

Her eyes welled. "No one is who they seem to be."

"Do you trust me?" he asked in a harsh, unsteady voice.

New tears slid along the path of the old ones. "I want to."

"But you don't."

She swallowed. "He said you and your band of traitors were responsible for Jeffrey's death."

Band of traitors. Sebastian's fear for Catherine grew tenfold, for she had wandered into the midst of a brutal war. "He?" She said nothing. "Did he provide a name for this group?"

"Nexus."

Fury burned through his veins. His gaze dropped to Catherine's hands. "What is it that you think you have there, Mrs. Ashcroft?"

She shifted back a step. "Something that will save my daughter's life."

"Did you by chance purloin one of those items from the second drawer of my writing desk?"

A mixture of chagrin and alarm tumbled across her face.

"Is the letter written with a strange, indecipherable hand?"

"Yes," she whispered.

He sent her a remorseful smile. "It's nothing more than a decoy."

"What do you mean, 'decoy'?"

"A coded message placed specifically for my enemy's redirection." He lowered his voice. "Who knew my enemy would be so beautiful and clever?"

The blood drained from her face. "This message means nothing, then?"

"Only if you're interested in the eating habits of hedgehogs."

"Oh, God." The pages drifted to the floor. "I have failed."

Sebastian glanced down at the discarded pages and noticed she had been copying the coded missive.

"*Sophie.*" She shot across the chamber.

He hooked his arm around her waist and drew her against his chest. "Where do you go?"

She clawed at his hand and kicked at his shins. "Stop it, Sebastian. I must get Sophie and my mother away from here."

"Catherine, enough." He subdued her flailing arms. "You cannot win a physical battle against me. Tell me who he is, so that I can protect you."

The fight went out of her as abruptly as it began. She sagged against him. "Why would you wish to help me after I seduced my way into your bed, only to betray you?"

That hurt. A piece of him had hoped she'd had more compelling reasons for sharing his bed. "Because I must take responsibility for my part in this debacle."

She swiveled her head around to meet his gaze. "In what way?"

"Promise you won't try to flee?" When she nodded, Sebastian eased his hold and guided her to one of the upholstered chairs. He did not sit, nor did he stand unmoving, as he was prone to do in situations of high tension. Instead, he paced. "I have much to repent for, Catherine. However, given the same set of circumstances, I would act the same."

Even bedding a blond-haired, lonely widow in over her head.

"Then why do you feel the need to repent for your actions?"

He sent her a humorless smile. "Because most noble acts have regrettable consequences."

"Jeffrey was a regrettable consequence?"

Sebastian nodded. "And I suspect Meghan McCarthy was as well."

Her gaze became more intent, her voice little more than a whisper. "A-are you a traitor, Sebastian?"

Given the lengths he had gone to and the plans he had diverted to protect his country from a war-mongering upstart, her question was almost laughable, if it weren't so damn painful.

"Is that what your friend told you?"

"He's not my friend."

"Then tell me his name." He recognized the stubborn set to her features before she ever said a word.

"I will," she said, "as soon as you answer my question."

"No."

She blinked. "Are you refusing to answer, or was that your answer?"

Sebastian felt his lips twitch, despite the seriousness of the situation. "No, I'm not a traitor. Your turn."

Her relief was evident. Her features softened and the tautness of her body loosened.

"Frederick Cochran."

He nodded, expecting as much. However, the name he wanted to hear from her lips was *Latymer*. "Tell me," Sebastian said. "Are Cochran and John Chambers one and the same?"

She winced, averting her gaze. "Yes."

"Why the subterfuge?"

"I honestly don't know." She met his gaze. "Everything was happening so fast. I found myself in the midst of something terrible that I didn't fully comprehend, and I acted on instinct."

"Because you didn't trust me."

"I didn't trust anyone at that point."

He skimmed the backs of his fingers down her upper arm. "Do you trust me now?"

"How do I know you're not lying to me like Mr. Cochran?"

"You don't." Sebastian beat back his frustration. "In this, all I can offer you is my word and a reminder. Ashcroft was my friend. He trusted me." Thinking back to Cochran's threat, he asked, "Have I ever threatened you? Made you or Sophie feel unsafe?"

"No. Never." She swiped the tears from her face. "I'm sorry, Sebastian. It's all just... too much."

He cupped her cheek, and she leaned into his touch. The simple action made him feel powerful in a way he never had before. More powerful than when he had obstructed an attempt on the Prime Minister's life and when he had saved a Russian princess from Napoleon's grasp.

"Trust me, Cat."

Fresh tears welled in her beautiful brown eyes. "Yes," she whispered.

His chest swelled and his gaze dropped to her mouth. He wanted to lap the words from her lips, know the taste of her belief. Instead, he focused on pulling every bit of information from her, because he had promised Sophie he wouldn't tell her mama.

"Thank you," he said. "Can you tell me if Cochran is working alone?"

"I thought so until Tuesday," she said. "Cochran brought a woman to act as Sophie's governess, and the frightening man we saw outside church on Sunday has become my shadow."

Sebastian remembered the skeletal creature. Sophie's scary man, no doubt.

"No one else?"

"No."

If Latymer was involved in this scheme, he was keeping to the background, allowing Cochran to take the lead on this mission. Such an elaborate ruse, for what? Latymer's goal didn't appear to be Sebastian's death this time around. At least, not yet. What would make Latymer go to such lengths? What did Latymer value so much that he would turn his back on everything he believed in?

"At least not that I recall," Catherine clarified. "With Cochran threatening to jab a hot poker into my daughter's eye if I didn't cooperate, I'm afraid my focus was somewhat narrowed."

"Bloody bastard." He saw the scene as clearly as if he were in the room. A precocious girl's smile transforming into a mask of terror. And then he saw Catherine—helpless, frightened, desperate to save her child. Desperate enough to betray her neighbor, whom Cochran accused of seditious behavior and murder. "They will come to regret that act of violence, Catherine. You have my word."

She drew in a deep, audible breath and lifted her head. "Perhaps now would be a good time to divulge the full extent of your relationship with Jeffrey."

Sebastian curled his fingers around her warmth on his palm and lowered his arm. Thanks to Cochran, she already knew more than was good for her about the Nexus. Which meant he would not be breaking any confidences or endangering anyone's life.

The notion lifted an unbearable weight from his shoulders. Protecting his agents had always been a burden he had gladly carried and wholeheartedly accepted. But withholding the truth from Catherine had placed a far greater strain on his forbearance than he had realized.

"Perhaps you are right." His gaze fell on the small corner table crowded with crystal filled with an assortment of amber liquid. "Care for a drink?"

"Would love one, thank you."

Sebastian poured two fingers. "Give it a try. Its numbing properties can be quite beneficial."

"You're not having any?"

He rested his forearms on the back of the opposite chair. "No."

She accepted his offering, gave it a delicate sniff before upending the glass.

"Catherine, I didn't mean—"

Her eyes widened and her nose turned a raspberry red, but she made it through the fiery drink with nothing more than a delicate cough. She handed her empty glass back to him. "Quite bracing."

"Indeed." He cocked his head to the side to assess the damage. "Another?"

She shook her head. "I believe I am sufficiently numbed."

Envy rolled through Sebastian. What he wouldn't give to be relieved of the constant carousel of disturbing thoughts and images. "About five years ago, your husband came to my attention. Many spoke highly of him. Praised his intellect, ambition, and sense of morality. I spent the next year gathering intelligence on him, checking his connections and finances, monitoring his political leanings, and evaluating his mental stamina."

"Mental stamina?" she asked. "How do you evaluate such a thing?"

Sebastian hesitated but could not come up with a valid reason not to elaborate. "By placing obstacles in his path and then observing his reactions."

Her eyebrows rose. "You can't be serious."

"Why is that?" he asked. "To be a successful agent

of the Nexus, one must prove oneself capable of logical thought while under incredible pressure."

"Sounds insidious."

"Yet necessary."

"I shall have to take your word for it." She rubbed her hands down her skirts. "Jeffrey passed your little test, I take it."

"More than passed it, he excelled at that particular stage of the recruitment process."

"How many stages are there to becoming an agent?"

He rolled his shoulders and rested his forearms on the back of the chair next to hers. Being able to discuss his work with her felt good. Oddly liberating and unexpectedly intimate. His gaze wandered over the soft lines of her face. "As many as it takes for us to know."

❧

Catherine caught Sebastian's slow perusal of her features and felt an answering jolt in the vicinity of her chest. She angled her body more fully toward him. "Know what?"

"That the individual is trustworthy." He pushed away from the chair back and prowled around the side, his luminous gaze locked with hers. "That he is English to the core." He stopped in front of her. "That he has a good chance of survival."

She swallowed back her trepidation. There was something about this side of him that intrigued her beyond bearing. His tactics were calculating, merciless. Some would even call them cold and unfeeling. But Catherine saw also their brilliance and a deeper, more underlying quality that drove him to these brutal lengths. He cared—about England and his agents.

"What is it exactly that they must survive, my lord?"

"A power-hungry dictator who wishes the world to bow at his Corsican feet," Sebastian said. "At present, Napoleon Bonaparte's most desperate wish is to destroy France's longtime enemy, England. How will he do this? By closing the continent to British trade, thus destroying us without the mess of bloodshed."

Everything Cochran had told her was a lie. Everything. The Nexus was organized to protect English shores against a French invasion, not to invite them in. And Jeffrey had been in league with the Nexus, not investigating them. Shame filled her heart.

"How could I have been so stupid?"

He sent her a sharp look. "There's nothing stupid about believing in the purity of another's heart. Unfortunately, there are those who would take advantage of such goodness."

Catherine could barely breathe around the constriction in her throat. "When did Jeffrey become a member?"

He stopped before her, and she felt the same sense of being overwhelmed as she did all those days ago in London. This time, however, she better understood the man behind the cool facade. Knew the hero within. The masked vulnerability without. He lowered himself in front of her.

"Sebastian, what of your knee?"

"All the pressure is on my good one. Do not worry, mama hen."

Her lips twitched. "You were saying?"

"About four years ago." He readjusted his weight. "We discussed his inclusion during my last visit to Showbury."

"During the Harrison house party?"

"Yes. How did you know?"

She couldn't hold his gaze. "A guess."

"A very good one." Bending forward, he gripped the arms of her chair. "What brought you to that conclusion?"

Her chest seemed to cave in, pressing against her lungs. She forced herself to face him again. "It was my last glimpse of the man I married. All the times I saw him between then and his death, he was nothing more than an actor playing a part. Badly."

The warmth that had been building behind his steel-gray eyes extinguished, and his supple lips compressed into a thin, resolute line. With one glance, she knew he regretted the consequences of his association with her husband and she also knew he would not apologize for them either. He was a man of action. Once he evaluated the situation and made a decision, he did not look back.

Instead of moving away, he pressed closer. "Do you miss him?"

"Would it matter if I did?"

"No." His eyes remained hard, but his voice grew rough. "But I would like to know, all the same."

She shook her head. "No, Sebastian. I stopped missing him a long time ago."

He brought his hand up to caress the line of her jaw. "Ashcroft served his country well. First as a messenger, then as an intelligence agent. He saved lives, helped avert disasters. He was a hero. Remember that, Catherine. And one day, when Sophie is older, tell her. Tell her how her father helped save England during its bleakest hour."

She knew from experience that such knowledge did not soothe the hurt of missed birthdays and holidays, of not witnessing a daughter's first big catch or her first gallop across the meadow. The Navy had been Catherine's father's life, his one passion above all else, even above his family. All his colorful medals and his crew's effusive praise had done nothing to mend the many breaks in her heart.

But she appreciated what Sebastian was trying to do. Catherine folded her hand over his and kissed his palm, afraid to meet his gaze or express her gratitude. Because if she had done either one, he would have seen her fall in love with him.

Sensing her distress, he framed her other cheek and claimed her mouth. His kiss was passionate, full of volatility. The bone-deep chill that had invaded her body began to thaw, warming beneath his sensual assault. For the briefest of seconds, he let her burrow beneath the iron casing protecting him from harm. Beneath the casing beat the noblest of hearts, the purest of intentions. Beneath the casing she found hope.

Catherine pushed deeper, needing to learn more about this complicated man. But he discerned her attack and nudged her back, closing the small portal.

Lifting his head, he leveled his burning, yet resolute gaze on her. "What do they want?"

"Sebastian, I'm so sorry—"

He placed a finger across her mouth. "There's no need."

"But—"

The pad of his finger smoothed over her lower lip. "Answer me one question."

She nodded, and he drew his hand away. He said nothing for several seconds, seeming to debate the merits of asking his question.

Then, "At any time, did you enjoy my touch?"

Catherine's throat ached for the courage it took to ask such a question. She brushed the backs of her fingers along his unshaven jaw. "Every time, Sebastian. *Every* time."

Beneath her caress, a muscle jumped. She returned her hand to her lap, unwilling to reveal any more of her blossoming feelings. For she knew, despite their shared passion, he would leave. And she would be alone again. This time, however, she knew better than to wait, for this man would not return.

He pressed a kiss to her forehead and rose. At the corner table carrying an array of spirits, he paused. His stillness disconcerted her. "Are you unwell?"

"I'm fine." When he turned back, he asked, "What does Cochran want?"

His expression, his tone, his stance—it was all reminiscent of the day she had visited him at his London town house. That meeting now felt as if it had taken place an eternity ago. Catherine fought to hold back an indelicate shiver.

"A list."

If she thought he was still before, she had been wrong. The man who faced her was hewn of solid marble, not a hair or muscle moved. All warmth was gone. "What sort of list?"

"The one cataloging all trait—agents of the Nexus."

Fury twisted his handsome face into a mask of hatred. He grasped something off the table and propelled it across the chamber; a monstrous shattering of crystal followed. "Bloody Reeves!"

Frowning, Catherine asked, "Reeves?"

But his anger made him deaf to her query. He prowled the length of the chamber, muttering recriminations and casting Reeves to the devil.

Catherine rose and placed the chair between them. She did not really believe the chair could protect her, but the meager barrier gave her a sense of comfort all the same.

He stopped. "Who the hell is Cochran?" White flames licked the outer edges of his steel-gray eyes.

Catherine clenched her teeth. "Supposedly a friend of Jeffrey's. Someone who worked with my husband at the Foreign Office."

His eyes narrowed. "When did Cochran first approach you?"

"In London. The afternoon following our meeting. He caught me outside Grillon's and offered his condolences."

"And offered you a good deal more information, I suspect."

With his mask of indifference back in place, Catherine could no longer read the true intent behind his words. "Yes."

"So," he said, "the Foreign Office official shared some of the sordid details about your husband's death, enough to cast me in a poor light." He paused and lifted a brow in her direction.

She nodded.

"Then he ever so casually mentioned the government's investigation into my last mission, sending further suspicion in my direction."

Catherine closed her eyes, feeling like the absolute gudgeon she was.

"After Cochran established his willingness to share sensitive information, he asked for a favor in return."

Nausea bubbled in the back of her throat. "All I wanted was the truth about my husband's death." She covered her mouth with her hand, certain she was about to be sick.

A large warm palm wrapped around her trembling fingers. He drew them to his lips, kissing their pads. "I'm sorry, Catherine. I should not have allowed my anger free rein. You are innocent in all this."

"My stupidity"—his hand tightened, cutting off her recrimination—"my naïveté knows no bounds, does it?"

"Do not fret." He pressed a gentling kiss upon her lips. "We have all succumbed to such ploys."

She swallowed, wanting more of his reassuring lips. "I find that hard to believe."

"Believe it." He released her hand and moved away. "Did Cochran ever mention a Lord Latymer?"

"No, not that I recall."

He released a frustrated sigh. "Then I would like to know how Cochran found out about Reeves's directive that I provide a list of all my agents, including their true identities."

"Who is Reeves?"

"He's the new Superintendent of the Alien Office." He threw her an inquiring look. "Cochran explained the Alien Office's function?"

"Intelligence gathering?"

"Good enough," he said. "To my knowledge, no

one knew about Reeves's order, besides myself and three of my agents."

"Maybe they let it slip?" she suggested.

"No," he said. "At the time I informed them, I had not committed to the deed."

"And now?" Catherine held her breath, expecting a rebuke.

His gaze flattened. "There is no and will be no catalog of agents. I will take their identities to the grave."

Catherine stared at him with something akin to awe. How does one contain such a noble heart behind a shroud of ice? At great sacrifice to himself, he planned to disregard his superior's order and protect the men and women under his command. The same way he protected his young wards all those years ago. The same way he promised to protect her and Sophie now.

On the cusp of that realization, her awe began to fade and a new sentiment emerged.

Terror.

"If I don't bring Cochran the Nexus, he's going to kill my daughter."

A cold smile graced his lips. "Then let us give him the Nexus."

Twenty

August 18

SATURDAY MORNING DAWNED BRIGHT, MATCHING Sophie's winsome birthday smile. Her daughter's infectious exuberance swept through the household with a velocity that would rival the *ton*'s most determined gossip. By the time the festivities started, Catherine's entire staff was giddy with anticipation and Sophie was near bouncing off the walls.

If Cochran's threat hadn't been hanging over her head and Sebastian's peculiar statement ringing in her ears, Catherine would have enjoyed the day immensely. As it was, she glanced around the parkland like a nervous bird every five minutes, seeing strangers in their midst.

"The gathering is a smashing success, Mrs. Ashcroft." The vicar appeared next to her, juggling a heaping plate while following the children's sack race. "Creating a life-sized version of Castle Dragonthorpe was no small feat."

Catherine agreed. A drawbridge made of burlap, a

moat outlined by timbers, and trellises for turrets took a great deal of ingenuity, but all the effort had been worth her daughter's jubilation. "I'm glad you could come, Mr. Foster," she said. "The day would not have been the same without you."

"Meghan McCarthy's violent death has shaken Showbury's residents," he said. "Some have gone so far as to whisper names for the missing father."

Catherine raised an eyebrow. "And, therefore, the murderer?"

"Yes." He wrestled a melon ball onto his fork. "This is a disturbing turn of events, but not surprising. In our grief, we believe the only way to set our loved one's soul to rest is by punishing those responsible."

Catherine caught sight of the earl strolling along the perimeter—er, moat—of Castle Dragonthorpe's inner bailey. He projected calm and idleness. Few would recognize the occasional narrowing of his eyes or his preference for hovering near her daughter.

"But justice," the vicar continued, "is mankind's tool, not God's, for keeping peace and is society's attempt at soothing the hollow ache of those left behind."

Could the same philosophy be applied to Catherine? Was her effort to track down Jeffrey's killer and bring the man to justice nothing more than an attempt to relieve the never-ending void of loneliness in her heart? Something she had lived with long before his death?

"Forgive me, Mrs. Ashcroft." His kind eyes roamed over her features. "This is not the place to discuss such a dreary topic. Today is about celebrating life and laughter."

She smiled, thankful to be quit of the subject, even though a shadow lingered in her thoughts. "Indeed, Mr. Foster." For what seemed like the hundredth time, her gaze sought out her daughter's location and found her playing quoits with Teddy. "How is your courtship going?"

The vicar's face reddened, then beamed with delight. "Miss Walker has consented to a drive and picnic tomorrow after services."

Catherine placed her hand on his sleeve. "That is good news, Mr. Foster."

"Thank you. I appreciate your kind counsel on the matter."

"Good morning, Vicar. Mrs. Ashcroft," a newcomer interrupted. "How do you fare today?"

Catherine started. Sebastian's voice sounded inches from her ear. Lifting her gaze, she found him staring at her hand resting on Mr. Foster's arm. She eased her fingers away and clasped her hands together.

"I'm doing very well, my lord," the vicar said. "How goes the search for a new steward?"

"Slow, I'm afraid." He scanned the gathering. "If you know of a dependable gentleman with legitimate references and experience, please send him my way."

"As it happens, I heard from an old university chum yesterday," the vicar said. "His employer passed on and the heir is a bit of a scoundrel, or so my friend tells me. Timms is now considering his options. You'll never meet a more honorable man. Such a shame, what's happening, but fortuitous, don't you think?"

"Sounds just the thing, Mr. Foster," Sebastian said. "Please have him come see me."

"Thank you, my lord," the vicar said. "He'll be delighted—"

"My dear Vicar." Catherine's mother sailed into their midst. "I see you have cleared a spot on your plate. Come with me and I'll introduce you to Cook's famous lemon cheesecake."

He hesitated, clearly not interested in giving up his tête-à-tête with the earl.

"I promise you, sir," her mother coaxed. "You shall not be disappointed."

Pasting a vicar-like smile on his face, he said, "Pardon, Mrs. Ashcroft. My lord. I will return in a moment."

"Please do." Catherine followed the duo until her mother began an animated conversation on—she squinted to make out the object of their attention—she knew not what.

Sebastian guided her away from her guests milling about. "You and the vicar were rather cozy."

She sent him a sidelong glance. "I've told you before, he's a dear friend."

"Dear enough to marry?" He must have regretted his query the moment it emerged, for he followed it with a rough command. "Forget it."

"That's not possible." Her daughter's laughter caught her attention. She watched Sophie's next throw and smiled when the shoe hit the iron hob. "Where is this line of questioning coming from, Sebastian?"

A full minute ticked by before he answered. "The vicar mentioned he was contemplating marriage during our ride the other day," he said. "I thought perhaps you were his chosen bride."

His jealousy should have irritated her, but instead,

his gruff explanation charmed her. "No, Sebastian. The good vicar has his sights set on Miss Walker, and she on him. But neither have had the gumption to approach the other."

"I suppose you have been encouraging him to declare himself during your long drives?" he asked.

Fingers of heat spread into her cheeks. "Life's too short to spend it alone and unhappy."

She felt his searing gaze on her, but did not dare meet it. "How is that particular endeavor coming along?"

"They're going on a picnic tomorrow afternoon."

"What of you, Catherine?"

His low, intimate tone pierced her heart. "I don't understand your question."

"What will you do once your mourning has ended? Will you seek a father for your daughter?"

"Eventually," she said. "I am wise enough to realize not all men are like my father and husband. Next time, I will choose more carefully."

"Indeed—" Something caught his eye over her shoulder. "Where is Sophie?"

"She's right over there." Catherine swung around to where her daughter and Teddy were throwing quoits. Her eyes widened when she found nothing but two iron hobs sticking out of the ground and their discarded quoits. "Sebastian," she whispered. "I saw them playing not but a minute ago."

"Calm yourself," he warned. "There are many tempting items in your make-believe castle to draw their attention." He peered over her shoulder and flicked his index finger in a sharp circle. "Let us make a circuit of the area."

"Yes, of course." She accepted his arm. "Cochran

would be a fool to attempt something while so many people are in attendance."

"And yet a crowd can provide the best cover." He glanced down at her. "I mention this not to frighten you, but to keep you from becoming complacent. You must never, ever underestimate your enemy."

Catherine's heart hammered within her chest. She did not like this spying business. Before this was all finished, she was quite certain her heart would never pound again.

They made a full circle around the crowd without one glimpse of a golden-red mop of curls. Her trepidation grew. She had made Sophie promise to stay within sight today, an edict that engendered a great many moans. But Catherine had never considered her daughter would disobey her in this way.

When Sebastian finally drew them to a halt, the muscles in Catherine's throat ached from her effort to hold back the compulsive scream of her daughter's name. She peered up at him. "I will round up several of the adults to scour the area. I don't want to scare the children." The moment she made to pull away, he covered her hand.

"A moment." Rather than searching the area again with a thorough sweep of his gaze, Sebastian's attention jumped from one point to the next.

"Sebastian, please." She pulled at her hand. "I cannot stand this inactivity."

He nodded at someone in the distance, and the tension faded from his taut features. "Come, I believe we missed a hiding spot."

Confused by his odd behavior, Catherine accompanied him across the lawn without a word, although she chafed at his unhurried pace. He stopped next to the dessert table and pointed to a two-inch gap between tablecloths. "Your damsel in distress, madam."

Catherine crouched down and peered into the gap. Sure enough, Sophie and the stable lad, Teddy, sat beneath the table, alternately stuffing chocolate puffs into their mouth and staging battles with pieces from her daughter's Dragonthorpe collection.

"Sophia Adele, may I see you for a moment?"

Round blue eyes peered through the opening.

Catherine crooked her finger.

"Do not kill my gargoyle while I'm gone, Teddy. I'll be vexed." Her daughter scampered out from beneath the table. She brushed an incriminating crumb from her lavender skirts. The half-mourning color was a small concession for her party. "Yes, Mama?"

Catherine grabbed her daughter's hand and led her several feet away. "Did you not promise to stay within sight?"

Sophie glanced back at the table.

"I shall have your full attention, young lady." Catherine waited until her daughter's gaze returned to hers. "Did I not tell you, if you can't see me, I can't see you?"

"But, Mama," Sophie said. "I could see you." She indicated the space between the tablecloths, where Teddy now watched her daughter's scolding with rapt attention. "I saw you chatting with the vicar and strolling with the earl."

Catherine blinked, unable to think of a response to her daughter's six-, or rather, seven-year-old logic. "Do you know the scare you gave me?"

"I'm sorry, Mama." Sophie turned her doleful blue eyes on her. "Please don't be upset."

Cupping the back of her daughter's head, Catherine kissed the vixen's forehead. "I'm not, but allow me to clarify my statement. We must *both* be able to see each other."

Sophie nodded, her gaze going back to the table again.

"None of that, dear," Catherine said. "You have many guests to attend. All of your time cannot be spent with Teddy, no matter how tempting."

"Do you think the earl would mind if Teddy came along to see his horses?"

Catherine glanced back to find Sebastian encouraging the boy from beneath the table. "There's only one way to find out, and that's to ask." She held out her hand when Sophie started to rush over to her two favorite men. "Make your request like a young lady, title and all."

Her daughter smiled. "Thank you, Mama."

She took off, but immediately slowed her breakneck pace to a more sedate stroll. Well, almost sedate. She looked the epitome of sweetness from the waist up. However, her feet were throwing up patches of grass in her wake.

Stopping before Sebastian, Sophie executed a perfect curtsy. "Good afternoon, Lord Somerton. Are you enjoying my birthday celebration?"

He bowed. "Indeed, I am."

She waved her hand toward her friend. "I see you've met Teddy. Did he tell you about his mama?"

Sebastian glanced at Catherine, a glint in his eyes. "I'm afraid not."

Sophie sent her friend a sympathetic look. "His mama is terribly ill."

"I'm sorry to hear that, Teddy."

The stable lad's face flamed. "Thank you, sir."

"He loves horses." Her daughter bent at the waist until Sebastian's attention shifted back to her. "The only horses he sees all day are Guinevere and Gypsy. Sweet creatures, but they cannot compare to a *whole barn full* of horses." She rose up on her toes as if to punctuate her statement, an expectant look lighting her cherub face.

"Hmm." Sebastian rubbed his jaw. "As it happens, I have a whole barn full of horses."

Sophie clapped her hands together, looking from Sebastian to Teddy. "I know."

In a conspiratorial whisper, Sebastian asked, "Do you think your friend would like to join us later this afternoon?"

Her daughter let out an excited squeak. "Teddy, the earl has invited you to see his horses. Maybe he'll let you ride Cira, too."

Catherine raised an eyebrow, but Sebastian kept his gaze on the boy.

Teddy smiled, revealing the beginnings of a new tooth coming in. "Thank you, m'lord."

"Oh, dear me." Sebastian laid an exaggerated hand to his chest, a look of consternation on his handsome face.

Sophie and Teddy shared a worried glance. "What's wrong?" she asked.

"I just recalled something very important. Something that might change your mind about visiting my stables."

Catherine watched her daughter slip her hand into Sebastian's. "Don't worry, sir. Teddy and I will want to see your stables, no matter what."

"Truly?" He looked between two pairs of earnest eyes. "Even if I don't have a red horse?"

Sophie frowned and Teddy looked bewildered. Catherine covered her mouth to hide her smile.

Then Sophie noticed Sebastian's lips twitch. "Oh, Bastian. Horses are nothing to joke about."

"Sophie," Catherine scolded. "You must not be so informal with his lordship."

"I gave her leave to do so." Sebastian sent her daughter a gentle smile. "Didn't I, sprite?"

She giggled. "Yes, Bastian. If I'm a sprite, does that make Teddy a brownie?"

Sebastian, bless him, tousled poor Teddy's hair. "What do you say, lad? Would you like to be a brownie to Miss Sophie's sprite?"

He gave them another gap-toothed grin. "Brownies like barns, don't they, sir?"

"Indeed, they do."

"Then I shall be a brownie."

"And I a sprite."

"And I Bastian."

Three pairs of eyes turned toward Catherine. "What?"

"What shall we call you?" Sophie asked, bouncing with excitement.

"Um… Mama?"

Sophie groaned, Teddy ducked, and Sebastian smiled.

"Let us give your mother's nickname some thought, shall we?" Sebastian suggested. "In the meantime, I believe sprite has a few guests she needs to greet." He glanced at Catherine for confirmation.

"Off you go," she said.

"Come on, Teddy," Sophie said. "Let's see who we can get to bob for oranges."

"Oranges don't float," he protested.

"Precisely, you silly brownie!"

Catherine shook her head, enjoying Sophie's boundless good cheer.

"She is a marvel," Sebastian said.

"Yes." Catherine peered up at him. "You're very patient with her, *Bastian*."

A tinge of color darkened his cheeks, and Catherine's unsteady wall crumbled to the ground.

"Years ago, when my wards were young and grieving over the loss of their parents, I made many mistakes." He met her gaze. "Not knowing if I would be alive or dead from one day to the next, I taught them skills that might one day save their lives, and I ensured they never had to be concerned about finances."

"Where is the fault in your actions, sir?"

"I kept them at arm's length, praising them rarely and hugging them never." He released a shaky breath. "I told myself it was for their own good. So they would never feel the devastating loss of a guardian again."

"In your own way, you were trying to protect them," Catherine said. "No matter how hard we try to do right by our children, we will inevitably get it wrong at times. Take my current circumstances, for instance."

As if they read each other's mind, their gazes sought out Sophie.

"Yes, well," he said. "I lied. To myself. You see,

before joining the Alien Office, I wanted a wife and family. Desperately. But after my mentor's and his wife's brutal murders, I suppressed the need. Keeping the two young deBeaus at a distance was as much for my protection as theirs. In the end, I fell in love with the little terrors anyway. Too bad they will never know."

"Pardon, m'lord. Ma'am." A maid with cropped sable hair and a scarred left cheek held out a tray of oysters nestled in scallop shells. "Care for one?"

Sebastian stiffened. "No, thank you."

"Are you sure, sir?" she asked. "I hear they're a right treat."

Catherine noticed Sebastian's complexion turned a nasty shade of red. Thinking he was upset by the maid's interruption, she said, "Thank you…"

"Belle, ma'am," she said with a curtsy.

"Belle, I should like to try one." She picked up a shell. "My mother is quite fond of these. Please see if she would like one."

"Yes, ma'am." She curtsied again. "Sir."

The moment the maid turned away, Catherine saw Sebastian's eyes narrow on the young woman's back. "My housekeeper must have hired additional staff for today."

"Why do you say that?"

"Besides Belle, I see two other unfamiliar maids and a couple new footmen."

He sent her a sidelong glance. "Care to point them out?"

Feeling ill at ease with his request, Catherine located the older maid weaving through the guests. "The buxom maid striding by my mother."

Steel-gray eyes followed her direction, his lips thinned. "Who else?"

"The distinguished footman with a queue helping Belle fill her tray with more delicacies."

"Go on."

"Near the bevy of young misses is a roguish footman with black-as-night hair eyeing Miranda Walker." The gentleman glanced in their direction before turning back to his companion.

The earl nudged her in the opposite direction. "Any other foreign faces?"

"Only the tall maid, with the black hair and spectacles."

Sebastian stopped and performed a surreptitious scan. "I don't see a black-haired maid."

Catherine followed his lead. "She looked to be taking care of refreshments and cleaning away dirty dishes. I do not see her now." A thought struck her. "You don't think those people work for Cochran, do you?"

"Doubtful, but I will look into it." He resumed their stroll, halting a few feet behind the vicar and her mother. "You concentrate on making Sophie happy. I'll look into the matter of the servants."

"But—"

"Trust me," he said. "I might be a failure in the area of finer feelings. But, when it comes to protecting those under my charge, I am unmatched."

Emotion gripped her chest, and Catherine wanted nothing more than to kiss the man silly. She settled for a hand on his sleeve. "I have not found you lacking in either pursuit, my lord." Something feral and very male entered his expression. Catherine swallowed and retreated with a pat to his arm. "Very well, my lord. See to the mysterious servants and I'll take care of my daughter."

His heavy-lidded gaze did not budge from her face for several heart-pounding seconds. Catherine began to fear he would do something embarrassing—and highly enjoyable—like kiss her.

Then he drew back a step and inclined his head. "Until later."

Catherine forced her gaze to sweep over her guests, rather than follow Sebastian's progress. Had she done otherwise, she would not have been able to mask the yearning burning in her soul.

Arm in arm, Catherine and Sophie strolled down the path leading from the barn to the house. Dusk was on the horizon, signaling the end to a memorable day. Catherine glanced down at her daughter's bent head. "What's the matter, dear?"

She shrugged her narrow shoulders. "I wish Teddy didn't have to do chores."

"Me, too, sweetheart." Catherine hugged her closer. "But that's the deal he struck with Carson so he could spend time with you today. He made a choice, one he seemed more than content with."

"I suppose so."

They entered the house and made their way to the nursery. "It was kind of you to include him on your tour of Lord Somerton's stables."

"Bastian's horses were grand, weren't they, Mama?"

"Very grand."

"Did you see me ride Cira?"

"Indeed, I did. You were quite accomplished, young lady."

Sophie beamed. "I thought about asking Eloisa Walker, but she would have complained about the smell the whole time."

"Then it is good you didn't extend an invitation."

"She might be miffed at me."

Catherine held back a smile. "I'm sure you will have no problem coaxing her out of her pout." She pushed open the nursery door and found Mrs. Clarke pacing inside.

The governess swung around, her eyes red-rimmed and her hair askew.

Oblivious, Sophie ran to her faux governess. "Mrs. Clarke, you should have joined us. So many lovely horses."

The governess rested her hand on Sophie's shoulder. "I'm sorry I missed your outing. Sounds like you had an exciting time."

Sophie's smile diminished. She reached up to trace a fingertip over Mrs. Clarke's blotchy cheek. "Does your head still hurt?"

Fresh tears wobbled in the woman's eyes. "Somewhat. Thank you for asking." She grasped Sophie's hand in both of hers, kissing her fingertip. "Now we must wash the barn from your body."

Her daughter groaned.

"Perhaps we can hold off until tomorrow morning, Mrs. Clarke," Catherine suggested.

Sophie turned wide, hopeful eyes on her governess.

Mrs. Clarke nodded. "As you wish, ma'am." To

Sophie she said, "I have your nightclothes laid out in the other room. Let us get you ready for bed."

"Sophie," Catherine said, "get started without Mrs. Clarke. I need to speak with her for a moment."

Her daughter tore across the chamber and flung herself into Catherine's arms. "Thank you for the best birthday ever."

Tears stung the back of Catherine's eyes. "You're welcome, pumpkin." She kissed her nose. "Now off with you."

Sophie skipped from the room, leaving two teary-eyed women behind.

"Why are you here?" Catherine asked in a quiet voice.

"To watch over your daughter."

"Yes." Catherine clasped her hands together. "That's why Cochran brought you here. What I want to know is why *you* are here."

A haunted expression froze the governess's features. "I don't know what you're talking about."

Catherine shuffled closer. "Don't you?"

The governess shook her head, her lips firming to stop their trembling.

Closer still. "I recognize a mother's fear," Catherine pressed.

Mrs. Clarke's eyes closed briefly. When they opened again, bleakness penetrated their depths. "Please don't."

"Why? There is no one to hear."

A maniacal laugh burst from her lips. "There is *always* someone to hear, Mrs. Ashcroft. Never doubt it." She threw off her grief as if it were a cumbersome mantle. "Now, if you will excuse me. I must attend your daughter." With that pronouncement, the woman marched into the next chamber.

Catherine's gaze cast about the nursery, recalling Sebastian's warning never to underestimate her enemy. Feeling heartsick, she left her enemy behind to tend her daughter. Two doors from her bedchamber, she rounded the corner and came to an abrupt halt.

In the middle of the dimly lit corridor stood Silas, looking more tattered than normal, with his neckcloth missing and an unflattering amount of flesh showing. The area around his mouth glistened in a way that turned Catherine's stomach, and she could see he was holding something behind his back.

"Have you anything for my master?"

Why was he asking now rather than waiting until her return later this evening? Much about Silas tonight seemed stranger than normal. Thank goodness, she and Sebastian had been able to sneak away for a little while to discuss their next steps while Bellamere's stablemaster fielded Sophie's and Teddy's many questions. Recalling Sebastian's instructions, she said, "This afternoon, I found what looked like a catalog of names and locations, but everything appeared to be in some type of code."

"How many traitors are on the list?"

Her heart froze in her chest. They had not discussed numbers. "I didn't count them."

His head tilted to the side and he seemed to be playing with something in his teeth. "What is your best guess, madam?"

What would be a believable number? One that

wouldn't be laughable or too extraordinary, but large enough to give Cochran pause? She released a slow breath. "If I had to guess, I would say between twenty and twenty-five."

He stared at her, unblinking, for several bone-racking seconds. "When can you make delivery?"

"Within the next couple days, I suspect."

"Not sooner?"

"I don't see how," she said. "The list is in his lordship's bedchamber. It's difficult to copy something so well hidden when I'm rarely left alone."

"Then do not copy it. Bring the original."

The longer they spoke, the more agitated he became. In a level voice, she said, "Mr. Cochran's instructions were quite clear, sir. I am not to arouse Lord Somerton's suspicions. If I take the list and he's still cataloging agents, he will warn every member of the Nexus."

As if Silas weren't peculiar-looking enough, his right eye twitched when angered.

"Are we finished here, Mr. Silas?"

The twitching grew worse. He nodded but did not move out of her path. And his hand remained half hidden behind his back.

Catherine lifted her chin and strode forward. "Good night, Mr. Silas."

His arm swung out, and Catherine saw something large and cudgel-like in his hand. She gasped, ducking beneath the cover of her arms, and waited.

Nothing happened.

Then came a disgusting sucking noise. Easing up from her crouched position, she saw the sound was coming from Silas's mouth. He was ripping chunks of meat off a large bone with his jagged teeth. Juices from the succulent piece dripped down his chin and landed on his bare chest.

Bile shot into the back of her throat.

"Your reflexes are much better than his lordship's." He cocked his head to the side. "And you did not wail like the Irish girl."

She pressed her back against the wall. "You're the one?"

It was then Silas did something even more terrifying. He smiled. An awful smile, filled with bits of meat and rotting teeth. *Evil.*

"His lordship interrupted my search."

"What were you looking for?"

"The same as you, madam."

"What of Meghan McCarthy?"

"She had become burdensome to my master." He jerked his head toward the empty corridor. "His lordship awaits."

The conversation concluded, and Catherine was glad of it. Once she had scooted clear of her gaoler, she ran the short distance and slammed her door shut. She knew he would follow, knew he would eventually bed down outside her door. The hour she sought her bed might change from night to night, but Silas's constant guard never faltered.

They had killed Meghan. Did that mean Cochran was the father? It must, but how? He had only arrived a few days ago. Had he been watching her for much longer? Or waiting for Jeffrey to make an appearance? Had he been the one to kill Jeffrey, too? Perhaps his letters were warning Sebastian of Cochran's perfidy. Good Lord, could this situation get any more complicated and dangerous?

She reviewed her brief conversation with Silas. Had the seed she'd planted taken root? Had it burrowed deep into Silas's fertile mind? Could he even now be making his way to Bellamere to steal the nonexistent list of agents? She fought to control her fear for Sebastian. Would he be ready for Cochran's miscreant?

The thought of something happening to Sebastian scorched her soul. So many depended upon him, and England's safety revolved around his continued leadership of a little-known group of spies. Moreover, she would miss him.

She drew in a deep breath and transformed her fear into faith. He was England's greatest spymaster, a man sworn to protect his countrymen and one who'd promised to keep her and Sophie safe. A villainous official and a puny footpad would be no match for Sebastian's lethal mind.

Squaring her shoulders, she clicked the fragile door lock in place, knowing it provided minimal protection. She strode to her dressing table and peered in the looking glass at her hair. The wind had not been kind.

She located the painted porcelain dish, which held her stash of pins. And that's when she noticed the letter. Her name was not written on the front, nor did it contain an address. But the missive sat propped between a bottle of lotion and a tin of powder. She glanced around the chamber. The room was quiet, almost as if it held its breath, waiting for her to assuage her curiosity.

A heavy blanket of dread bore down on her as she reached for the scrap of paper. Unfolding the note, she read the neat but hastily written message. By the time she reached the end, the words were hidden behind a veil of tears and the pressure around her chest threatened to suffocate her.

"*Sebastian.*"

❧

Catherine peered down at the anonymous letter again, her tears making the feminine handwriting blurry and incomprehensible. She stared at the author's name. *Cora-belle.*

Cora. Lord Somerton's ward, or rather former ward. She was here. And sometime during the festivities, she had invaded Catherine's private quarters and used her personal stock of paper to write a devastating letter.

My dear Mrs. Ashcroft,

I risk discovery to bring you the truth about Lord Somerton's care of my brother Ethan and myself. Not only did the earl offer shelter to two grief-stricken orphans, who were no relation to him, he gave us a home, one complete with all the comforts a child could want and all the parental devotion a child might need.

Never once in all the years I lived beneath his guardianship did I doubt his love for me. There are many ways to love another, and all do not require a confession of emotion. Love is in the heart, and I see it shining in his for you.

*If you feel the same, which I believe you do,
seize this moment. He will never give you a day
where you doubt his affection, for his is the truest
of hearts.*

*Warmly, and your new admirer,
Cora-belle*

*PS—Lord Somerton can at times be rather mulish
in his protection of those he loves. Sometimes that
noble quality can lead to sacrificial decisions. If you
need suggestions on how best to knock some sense
into him, I am at your service.*

With trembling fingers, Catherine set Cora's note
down and wondered how her life had become so
complicated so fast. Her love for Sebastian grew with
every encounter, and not even his alleged involvement
in Jeffrey's death had stopped her from plunging in
over her head. How had she managed to attach her
affections to a man even more obsessed with his cause
than either her father or her husband?

A low knock sounded, and Catherine stiffened. She
hastily wiped her eyes and tucked the missive away. At
the door, she asked, "Yes?"

"May I come in, daughter?"

Catherine patted her cheeks and hair and ran her
hands down the front of her dress before unlocking
the door. Brown eyes, not dissimilar from Catherine's
own, rounded at the sight of her daughter's ravaged
face. Her mother rushed forward, slamming the door
closed behind her and enfolding Catherine in her arms.

"Oh, daughter," her mother whispered. "All will be set to rights."

The warmth, the security, and the familiar scent of gardenias in her mother's embrace propelled Catherine back to her adolescence. The traitorous tears came faster. "It's too much."

"No, it's not." Her mother clasped her tighter. "You have a strong spirit, one that will see you through this and many more challenges in the years to come. Do not give in to the fear. Sup from it, draw strength from it. Then vanquish it."

Catherine pulled away, swiping at her face. "Silas admitted to attacking Lord Somerton and killing Meghan McCarthy."

"Dear God."

"There's so much at stake, Mother. One wrong word or one erroneous act, and I could lose my mother and daughter and the man I—" The damning words stuck to the back of her throat.

Keen-witted woman that she was, her mother offered, "The man you love?"

Closing her eyes, Catherine fought back a wave of shame. "Caught in my own tangled web." She drew in a deep breath and stepped away as an unaccountable chill settled in her bones.

"Do not be so harsh on yourself, daughter," her mother admonished. "Given the circumstances, you were left with few choices. As for you falling in love with his lordship," she propped her hands on her hips, "many a male neighbor and traveler has tried to seduce you into their beds over the last few years, with no success. So I suspect there's something rather special about Lord Somerton, or you would have sent him to the devil with all the rest."

Using her fingertips, Catherine placed pressure on each throbbing temple. "For years, I viewed Lord Somerton as a cold, reclusive man with little interest in his country estate."

"And now?" her mother asked.

"Now, I see that he is everything I was certain he wasn't." She thought of his kindnesses toward Sophie, his sense of urgency with the tenants and the various repairs, and his unwavering determination to find Meghan McCarthy. And then there was the way he had ripped away her loneliness with a single, passionate kiss. "Even so," she wrapped her arms around her middle, "I will never go back to my former half-life. For years, I wondered what horrible thing I had done or hadn't done to cause Sophie to lose her father. All those worries and recriminations were for nothing. I suffered years of useless guilt. Never again."

Catherine halted her monologue long enough to draw in a calming breath. "This might sound selfish, but I'm beyond caring. I want a gentleman who will put me—and my daughter—above all else. Someone who will love me and stay by my side, no matter how badly I vex him."

Her mother's smile was a mixture of pride and sorrow. "As you should, daughter."

Catherine did not know how to ease her mother's past regrets. "Mother, we must all begin anew." Catherine squeezed her mother's hand. "Let us put the past to rest."

Her mother peered down at their joined hands,

saying nothing. Then her free hand covered Catherine's. "Yes," she said. "Yes, I do believe you're right." With her normal fortitude, her mother collected herself. "The seed is planted?"

Nodding, Catherine asked, "Did you pass Silas outside my door?"

"No," her mother said. "Nor did I see him lingering outside the nursery."

Silas's unusual behavior and Mrs. Clarke's tear-stained face made Catherine uneasy. "I'm so torn. I need to convey Silas's confession to Lord Somerton, but I also wonder if I should forego visiting him tonight."

"Why is that, dear?"

"Our unwanted guests appear out of sorts, don't you think?"

"Not anymore than normal, but I haven't seen either one since before you left for Bellamere's stables." Her mother glanced at the closed door. "If you stay, you take the risk of agitating Silas. He doesn't seem the type one should provoke."

Catherine recalled the man's twitching eye, awful smile, and vile confessions and decided her mother was correct. "I suppose, though my stomach is not happy about it."

Twenty-one

"YOU CAN'T BE SERIOUS, CHIEF," LORD DANFORTH said. "She picked everyone out?"

Sebastian stared into the empty fire grate, not looking up at the small group of Nexus agents assembled in the drawing room. Had he done so, the mixture of irritation and pride alighting his eyes would have confused them all.

"Everyone but you and Bingham, and that's only because you were both walking the perimeter." Many years ago, Sebastian had hired Bingham, along with Dinks and Jack, to watch over Cora while she was on assignment in France. Bingham acted the coachman, Jack the footman, and Dinks the lady's maid. The quartet had become close, each protecting the others like beloved family members.

"No one ever pays attention to servants," Danforth grumbled.

"I have come to realize Mrs. Ashcroft isn't like most people."

His statement was met with a thick fog of silence. He glanced up then and found four pairs of fascinated eyes on him. Danforth looked more appalled. Lord

Helsford stared without expression. Cora appeared on the verge of happy tears. And Dinks chortled until she snorted.

"I'm doomed." Danforth groaned and slumped back in his chair.

Cora sent her brother a sharp look. "What are you nattering on about?"

"If a woman can steal the chief's heart," Danforth nodded toward Sebastian, "there is no hope for my continued bachelorhood."

"Ethan!" Cora scolded.

Sebastian's muscles coiled into bands of steel. Although Danforth had a tendency to blurt out whatever was on his mind, inappropriately so at times, the man's instincts tended toward genius. Which, in this particular case, did not bode well for Sebastian. "I assure you, my heart is where it should be."

He resumed their former discussion. "In addition to identifying each of you, Mrs. Ashcroft noted an unfamiliar tall, black-haired woman. Anyone else notice her?"

Danforth perked up. "Black hair, you say?"

Nodding, Sebastian asked, "What do you know?"

"Nothing for certain." The viscount's gaze turned inward. "But that description matches the maid who helped nurse me back to good health." His brow clenched together. "Except the tall part. That's not how I would describe her."

"You were also flat on your back," Helsford said, "with a concussion and a number of other injuries hampering your judgment."

"True."

"Let us set aside the black-haired maid for now,"

Sebastian said. "Catherine will be here soon, and I think it best to keep your presence a secret for a while."

"Are you sure?" Cora asked. "She might like knowing help has arrived."

"You're no doubt correct," Sebastian said. "But she's not accustomed to prevarication. Ignorance will protect her while interacting with her gaolers."

Danforth interjected, "What next? Track down Cochran, or wait for him to come to us?"

"Find him," Sebastian said. "He's somewhere close. The three of you, go into the village and ask around."

"Guy and Ethan can interrogate the villagers without me," Cora said. "I should like to stay here and keep watch."

"I don't need you underfoot." *Or nosing into my affaire with Catherine.*

"You won't even know I'm here."

He would know, but let the topic go. To Helsford, he said, "You delivered my message to Reeves?"

"I had to leave it with his clerk Bradford. The superintendent is attending a family crisis at the moment. Bradford expected him to return this afternoon."

"Very well. Report back here tomorrow morning."

As they began filing out of the drawing room, Sebastian halted Danforth. "Stay in Showbury."

The younger man's face hardened. "I learned my lesson well last time, Chief. I will be where you tell me to be." He strode from the room.

Helsford bent to kiss Cora's temple. "Don't do anything foolish—"

She leveled her blue-green eyes on her betrothed, retribution in their depths.

"Until I return," he finished.

She waved her hand toward the door. "Go play nursemaid to my brother, while the chief and I develop a plan to bring down our enemy."

A feminine snort sounded from the back of the room.

"Yes, dear." Helsford winked at the buxom lady's maid. "Behave."

Dinks laughed. "I'll work on it, my lord." She sobered. "Watch over that hothead for us."

"You can be sure of it," Helsford said.

"And that shite-scooping mongrel," she muttered. "Watch over him, too."

Helsford shared a look with Cora. "Is that your way of asking me to give Bingham a kiss for you?"

The maid's face heated. "Bah!" She marched away.

"Do you think they'll ever declare their feelings for one another?" Helsford asked.

"No," Cora said, smiling. "They're having too much fun tormenting each other."

Helsford nodded, then turned to Sebastian. "I'll send word of any developments." After one last long look at Cora, he followed in Danforth's wake.

A prickle along his neck warned Sebastian that he had become the focus of determined feminine attention. He glanced longingly after the other two men.

"Do you love her?" Cora asked in a soft voice.

Having no intention of answering her question—for he didn't know the answer—he sent her a withering glare, which she ignored.

"If you do," she said, "don't lose her to this cause. One lifetime is not enough."

She would know. Of all his agents, Cora would be

most familiar with that particular sentiment. "In case you have forgotten, she is newly widowed and not in a position, nor I doubt inclined, to accept the suit of another man." He speared the crystal decanters a glance.

"Then wait for her."

Sebastian set his jaw, irritated with himself for even engaging in this fruitless conversation. "I have not acted the gentleman with her."

"Start over," Cora pressed. "Court her as you would any potential wife."

Wife. The word caressed the rough edges of his soul. "We are too far beyond courtship."

A charged silence followed his statement, and Sebastian saw the two women share a glance.

"There's nothing for it then, my lord." Dinks smacked her thigh and marched over to stand in front of the decanters filled with amber temptation. "You must seduce her. To do that, you're going to need all your wits."

"You go too far, Dinks."

She braced her hands on broad hips. "You can give me the boot after you woo your lady. Until then…" The maid widened her stance, and her gaze became even more defiant.

"Dinks is right." Cora broke into the pair's visual duel. "Keep Mrs. Ashcroft in bed until she promises you forever. From the looks she was casting your way today, I would say she's already halfway—if not entirely—in love with you."

In an uncharacteristic move, Sebastian tunneled his fingers through his hair. "Even if that were true, Cora, she wouldn't have me."

"Why on earth would you say such a thing?"

"Because her marriage with Ashcroft was nothing short of disastrous, and any union with me would be ten times worse. Not only that, anyone associated with me becomes a target, or worse, leverage." He caught her gaze. "As you well know."

"Dinks," Cora said, "would you give us a moment?"

"Certainly." The lady's maid sent Sebastian a warning glare before hastening from the room.

"She does understand that I pay her wages, right?" Sebastian asked.

"She's worried about you. As am I."

"There's no need." He moved to the opposite side of the room from the brandy.

"More than likely, our enemy has already discerned your affection for Mrs. Ashcroft. There is no safer place for her than by your side."

"Where did you learn to be so ruthless?"

"I was mentored by the very best."

He sighed. "Let us focus our attention on how we will keep the Ashcroft ladies safe until this is all over, shall we?"

"What will you do?" she asked. "When it's over?"

"Return to London."

"And what of Mrs. Ashcroft?"

Her intrusive questions made him think about things he had no wish to think about. Catherine and he had an agreement to end their *affaire* once he returned to the city. Nothing had changed to alter their plans. Nothing. "I suspect she will continue on as before." His stomach cramped into a tight ball.

"Have you never considered giving up the Nexus?" she asked.

Every day since returning to Bellamere. "Why would I surrender my only sense of purpose?"

"You don't mean that."

"Why wouldn't I?" The words emerged harsh. "I have no other interests, no hobbies or expensive peccadillos. I live, eat, breathe, sleep this fight against Napoleon's domination. Someone with my specialized talents is of little use anywhere else."

"I disagree, sir," Cora said, rising. "For I have always known you were meant to be more than a mentor or guardian or even a chief of the Nexus." She gazed upon him with gentle, loving eyes. "You were meant to be a father and a husband."

Twenty-two

CATHERINE RUBBED THE GROWING ACHE IN HER STOMACH. It was stronger now, verging on nausea. At first, she thought the unpleasant sensation was nothing more than nerves. After all, a country mother could only handle so much deceit, death, and threat before falling victim to such feminine frailty. But she was not experiencing a bout of anxiety. No, these symptoms were darker, graver. They bespoke foreboding and danger. *Death*. The warning flashed through her mind, sharp and clear.

She buried her nose in the thin layer of linen covering Sebastian's chest and inhaled. His familiar scent, his silent strength, and his willingness to just hold her for the last hour had done nothing to assuage the dread crawling in her stomach. "I'm sorry," she said, "but I must return home." Unfolding her body, she rose from his lap. "I cannot shake this feeling that something is wrong."

The moment she had arrived, she'd conveyed her conversation with Silas to Sebastian. Although disturbed by the news, he had not been surprised by her gaoler's revelations.

Sebastian pushed out of the cushioned high-back chair to stand beside her. "I have men watching over your family." He slid a large, warm hand around the side of her neck, his thumb smoothed across her cheek.

"The last time I experienced this kind of unrelenting anxiety," she said, "I found Sophie stuck in a tree with a feral dog prowling beneath."

His other hand came up to frame her face and then he kissed her. A long, slow, achingly tender kiss. A kiss that wove soft fingers of longing into the midst of her fear.

Lifting his head, he said, "Then it is a sensation not to be ignored." He moved away and began tucking in the tail of his shirtsleeves.

"What are you doing?"

"Coming with you."

"I thought we were to carry on as before—at least for another day or two."

He grasped her hand and towed her from his bedchamber. "It's always best not to draw undue attention, that is true. However, your gaolers cannot fault me for seeing you home."

Fifteen minutes later, they guided their horses down the path connecting their two properties. With unerring accuracy, Sebastian guided them along the same route she'd taken since the onset of their *affaire*. He even selected the narrow deer path she preferred, rather than forging down the wider track that skimmed along the edge of a thirty-foot ridge. In the daytime, she enjoyed the view such a path provided. At night, she liked something a little more stable. "Have you been following me home?"

"What gave you that impression?"

Did the man never provide a direct answer? "Your familiarity with a route others would pass by without notice."

"I might have ventured along this path a time or two."

She narrowed her eyes on his back. "Still don't trust me with your secrets, my lord?"

He threw her a heavy-lidded glance over his shoulder. "The same could be said of you."

"What do you mean?" she asked. "I have told you every detail of Cochran's plan—at least, what I know of it."

He whipped his big, black horse about, making Gypsy toss her head in annoyance. "I'm not speaking of Cochran's plan." His blue-gray eyes caressed her features with a thoroughness that left her breathless and exposed.

She lowered her gaze to Gypsy's mane, afraid he saw too much. "Pray enlighten me, sir."

Silence reigned through the dense woodland for several uncomfortable seconds. Then he said, "Some secrets are best left unrevealed, don't you think? Enlightenment can sometimes complicate an uncomplicated situation."

He definitely saw too much. The back of her throat ached with unshed tears. Had she really allowed herself to hope? To think that their time together had burrowed beneath his skin and taken hold, as it had hers? *Stupid, stupid, lonely widow.*

"Wise as always, my lord." She squared her shoulders and then met his gaze. "Perhaps we should carry on."

He hesitated but a moment before turning toward

Winter's Hollow again. If Sebastian's pace was somewhat faster than before, Catherine dared not remark upon it. One reminder of their agreement in a five-minute time span was more than enough.

They spent the rest of their journey in contemplative silence, a circumstance both painful and welcome. Once they reached the edge of her garden, they dismounted and tied off the horses. Grasping her hand, he led her along the garden wall, pausing several times to listen. Then he circled around to the east side of the manor. All the while, his gaze never stopped moving, never stopped searching. The closer he maneuvered them to their destination, the more focused he became.

Rather than continuing on to the front entrance, he stopped at the corner, pressing them up against the rough stone of the manor. "What's wrong?" she asked.

He squeezed her hand in warning and then peered around the corner. When he shifted back, his gaze sought hers. "Do you trust me?"

The planes of his face appeared cast in granite and his beautiful eyes had transformed into spheres of ice. She nodded, afraid to speak.

He lifted their clasped hands and kissed the tips of her fingers. "You mentioned once that Silas greets you in the hall each night."

"Yes."

"You must find out if he's there."

"Where will you be?"

"My men are not at their posts," he said in a calm voice. "I must try to locate them."

Her heart bashed against the cage of her chest. The

dread she'd been carrying intensified to a crushing degree. *Sophie*. She pushed away from the stone wall. Sebastian dragged her back and placed his index finger over her protesting lips.

Then he directed his gaze to the curtain of darkness. In a voice barely above a whisper, he said, "Raven, to me."

Catherine's eyes widened when a short-haired woman wearing exotic, silken breeches emerged from the shadows.

The young woman stopped beside them. "Chief. Mrs. Ashcroft."

"Did you see any signs of them?" he asked the newcomer.

"No, sir."

Without conscious thought, Catherine leaned into Sebastian's body. The scar curving around the woman's left cheek triggered a vague memory, but her mind wanted to focus on nothing but getting to Sophie and her mother. "Sebastian, please—"

"Catherine," he said. "This is my former ward, Cora. She will accompany you inside while I check on things out here. You may trust her as you trust me."

Everything came together in a flash of images. The maid serving oysters, the servants she didn't recognize at her daughter's party, the heart-wrenching note scribed by Cora-belle. The Nexus had come.

To Cora, he said, "One of her gaolers might be awaiting you just inside. Dispose of him if you must; however, your mission is to locate the child and grandmother."

"Yes, sir."

"If I do not return in ten minutes, go to Helsford and get the women to safety. Understood?"

The younger woman's lips compressed, but she nodded her agreement.

Sebastian's thumb swiped over the ridges of Catherine's knuckles before nudging her out of the shadows. "Go."

"But—"

"Go, Cat," he said again. "Listen to Cora."

"Come, Mrs. Ashcroft," Cora said in a gentle, yet firm voice. "Let us make sure your family is well."

The landscape of Catherine's world shifted and tilted in so many directions and with such velocity that she found herself following a stranger, who wore a contraption around her midsection housing an assortment of lethal weaponry, without complaint. Accustomed to making her own decisions, she would have found her current dilemma laughable if it wasn't all so terrifying.

Before rounding the corner, Catherine glanced back to find Sebastian's luminescent eyes on her. The situation was reminiscent of their time in the woods while searching for Meghan McCarthy. A shiver tracked down her spine.

Drawing in a deep breath, she followed *Raven* into God-knew-what.

❧

The moment Catherine disappeared from view, Sebastian forced his clenched fist open, releasing some of the tension of his decision to part ways with her. With Danforth and Helsford in the village, it was left to him to secure their perimeter. After Cora's recent encounter with the French, he did not worry about her ability to protect Catherine. She was as capable as any of his male agents, though he would have preferred not to have involved her, especially so soon after the difficulties of her last mission.

He found Jack and Bingham behind the gardener's shed—bound, gagged, and unconscious. After a bit of shaking, Jack came to and staggered to his feet. However, nothing Sebastian did roused the older Bingham.

"Jack," Sebastian said. "Can you make your way to the village? Helsford and Danforth are there."

The young Irishman ran a hand around the back of his neck, angling his head this way and that. "Aye, m'lord." He stared down at his comrade. "What of old Bingham?"

"He received a bad knock to the head. For now, he's safe."

Jack ripped off his coat and placed it beneath the older man's head.

"What happened?"

"Can't say, m'lord. One minute I was walking toward Bingham to see if he had any news, and the next, I was waking up to you rattling my head."

Frustration coiled through Sebastian. "How long ago were you attacked?"

"What's the time?"

"Half past ten."

"Not more than twenty minutes ago."

Sebastian stilled, his gaze seeking the high angles of the manor's roof. "Bring Danforth and Helsford now." He didn't wait for Jack's acknowledgment before turning toward the house.

Toward Catherine's terror-filled scream.

❧

Later, Catherine would not recall her flight from the ground floor to the third-floor nursery. Silas's absence at the door combined with Sebastian's missing men confirmed the sensations she'd been battling all evening. Sophie was in danger. And Catherine had not been here to protect her baby girl.

Somewhere along the way their panicked flight roused her mother, who was now trailing in their wake. Once they reached the nursery's closed door, Cora motioned for Catherine and her mother to move aside. The agent drew a wicked knife from the intriguing sash around her middle. She turned the handle and stepped back, using her fingertips to slowly open the door.

Cora's gaze met Catherine's across the short distance and she raised a staying finger. Catherine nodded and held her breath as the agent slipped into the too-silent room. She had no intention of lingering in the corridor while the other woman put her life in danger. After three full seconds, she inched her body around the open doorway until she found herself facing Castle Dragonthorpe. Her mother's shoulder bumped into hers.

The two of them stood side by side, shaking with fear but determined to save their girl, the one who brought sunshine into their lives each and every day.

Castle Dragonthorpe yawned before them,

occupying half the common room. The other half consisted of a school desk, a small bookcase, and an assortment of more feminine toys littering the floor. Two doors framed the common room, the right one an entrance to her daughter's bedchamber and the left one spilling into the nurse's small chamber, which was currently occupied by Sophie's faux governess.

Cora was nowhere in sight.

Foregoing the nurse's chamber, Catherine veered right, her mother at her heels.

"Mrs. Ashcroft," Cora yelled from Sophie's room. "Come quickly."

Blood fired through her veins. Catherine barreled across the short distance and skidded to a halt inside her daughter's bedchamber. "What?"

An answer was unnecessary, for the pool of blood at her daughter's bedside said it all. Terror gurgled up into the back of her throat, and Catherine released it in one long never-ending breath.

Twenty-three

TEDDY CLOSED THE BARN DOOR, EXHAUSTED TO THE bone. Guinevere and Gypsy had made a right mess out of their stalls while he was away. And if that wasn't enough, one of the sheep had managed to wedge its head in between the rungs of an old cartwheel, forcing Teddy to chase the bleating animal all around the barnyard. He hadn't been gentle when he popped the wheel off the blighter's head.

Lifting his arms high above his shoulders, he stretched his aching muscles before turning toward the dark, shadow-ridden lane. He didn't care much for this part, although given the same choice—play with Sophie Ashcroft or finish his chores on time—he would make the same decision again. Being the focus of her pretty smile all day was worth every hair-raising step he was about to take.

Not for the first time, Teddy regretted his family's *reduced circumstances*, as his mother liked to call their lack of funds. According to his parents, they once lived in a grand house like Winter's Hollow and had scads of servants seeing to their every need. Teddy recalled only small glimpses of their former life, yet it was enough to make him yearn for more than their single-room cottage and meager table fare.

Especially now that his mama was sick. Money would pay for a doctor and medicine to make her better. Money would allow them to hire servants to see to her comfort while he and Papa were at work. Money would mean he could go home tonight and melt into a plump, warm bed, rather than having to fix dinner for his papa and care for his mama.

Night sounds closed in around him, growing louder with every meter he distanced himself from the barn. The sunny day had given way to a partly cloudy night, and at times, Teddy could barely see the hard-packed road beneath his feet. Hunching his shoulders, he shoved his hands in his pockets and wrapped his fingers around the wooden piece Sophie had given him. He drew comfort from the small, solid piece of Dragonthorpe. Even still, he picked up his pace, not daring to look left or right for fear of encountering a pair of bright eyes.

Had it not been for the distinctive jingle of a horse's harness, Teddy might have toddled right into the back of the motionless carriage. As it was, he'd stopped not six feet away. Fear flashed like a frigid breeze across his flesh before plunging beneath the surface to lock around his pounding heart.

Some instinct urged him to hide. Ducking low, he scrabbled for the knee-high weeds along the side of the lane and crouched there. From this position, he could make out the carriage's black-as-night panels and carved trimmings. Four matching bay horses stood quietly at the lead, their driver faced forward in the same state of readiness.

Readiness for what?

Teddy glanced down the lane, from where he had just come, but the lack of moonlight prevented him from making anything out. The silent wait did funny things to his body. Sweat slicked down his back and his stomach gurgled. With each passing second, the gurgling grew in intensity, an unpleasant sensation that would normally have sent him running for the nearest privy. But he dared not move, even though he was in danger of soiling himself. Something didn't feel right about the carriage sitting on the dark lane, with no lamplight.

With Sophie's papa gone, there was no one to protect her but him. Teddy recalled the new people staying at her house. People she refused to talk about but always watched with a wary eye. No one knew them, and they seemed to just show up one day. When he asked Carson about the new people, the groomsman had told him to mind the shite and not the goings-on at the big house.

Teddy began to squirm, and his face flushed with heat. When he thought he would have to rush into the woods, the air around him stirred and a hint of foul odor assaulted his senses. Out of the darkness emerged the most hideous creature, one he'd encountered several times in the last sennight.

Silas.

Teddy's eyes narrowed. The skeletal man's body looked larger than normal, misshapen. Teddy hunkered down as the man drew near. The large, deformed lump at his shoulder materialized into a body. Sophie's body.

She dangled over the man's shoulder, unmoving. Teddy nearly gave his hiding spot away at the sight of his friend. She did not struggle or scream or curse her captor to perdition. She simply hung there.

Silas tapped on the carriage door, and Teddy's heart stopped in shock when the window curtain parted.

A man inside said, "I see the governess held up her end of the bargain."

"Yes, sir," Silas said.

"And the governess?"

"Taken care of, as you instructed."

"My message?"

"Delivered."

"Very good, Silas." The carriage door opened. "Place the girl on the bench and let us be off."

After Silas completed his task, he shut the door and climbed up into the driver's box. Once he was settled, the coachman flicked the reins and the carriage lurched forward.

Teddy rose from his crouched position and glanced toward Winter's Hollow. He heard no sounds of rescue. Swinging his gaze back to Sophie, his knees almost buckled when the ambling carriage disappeared behind a wall of impenetrable black.

With one last look toward the big house, Teddy took off and he did not slow until his fingertips touched the metal rail of the carriage's luggage boot. Having climbed rickety ladders all his life, it took little effort for him to maneuver himself onto the small ledge.

He folded his arms around his raised knees and winced when he felt something sharp prick his hip.

Reaching into his pocket, he pulled out the wooden archer Sophie had given him. The carved piece stood with his legs splayed, one hand holding a bow and the other drawing back an arrow. He had been drawn to this figure from the first moment he saw it standing atop Dragonthorpe's parapet, a brave soldier protecting his princess with nothing more than a bit of iron and willow.

At the crossroads, the carriage veered toward London and Teddy squeezed his eyes shut, burying his face into his upraised knees. He prayed his mama and papa would be all right without him.

Twenty-four

"DAUGHTER," CATHERINE'S MOTHER SAID IN A HARSH voice. "The blood is not Sophie's. Look, child. *Look.*"

Catherine blinked hard, her narrowed vision slowly expanding outward to include the governess's body, with Cora hunched at her side. "Is she—"

"No." Cora's voice was grim, and the look she cast Catherine conveyed it was only a matter of time.

Catherine's gaze slashed to the four corners of the bedchamber. "Where's Sophie?"

Cora nodded toward Mrs. Clarke. "Perhaps she can tell us."

Her mother tore a sheet off the bed and knelt on the other side of the governess. She looked at Cora. "Since my daughter is not trying to claw your eyes out, I take it you are a friend."

The agent nodded. "Cora deBeau."

"Evelyn Shaw," her mother said. "Remove Mrs. Clarke's hands, if you will."

After Cora pried the injured woman's bloody hands away, Catherine's mother pressed the bed sheet to the oozing wounds at her stomach and lower back.

The governess cried out and tried to curl into a ball. "None of that now," her mother said. "We must stop the bleeding."

Catherine dropped to her knees to assist, even though precious seconds ticked away.

"S-sorry." Mrs. Clarke fumbled for Catherine's hand. "Had no choice—" A wet, rattling cough seized her and spittle, thick with blood, sprayed the floor and splattered their clasped hands. "My son." Her voice grew weaker and a single tear curled over her nose. "*Giles.*"

Earlier today, Catherine had sensed a kinship with this woman, but no amount of coaxing would lure her to share a confidence. Now she knew why, and felt a stab of guilt for her shabby treatment of this suffering mother. "Mrs. Clarke, where are they taking my daughter?"

"My son. Find him. London boys' home." She coughed again.

"Mrs. Clarke, please—"

"The bleeding won't stop," her mother said. "You must try not to cough, Mrs. Clarke."

More tears streamed over the bridge of the governess's nose. "Tell Giles I l-love him, tell him I wanted to do what was right—" Another wave of coughing, this one far worse than the last, halted her confession. When she finished, she could barely lift her eyelids. "His father—danger…" Her dying body sagged onto the floor like an inflammable air balloon losing its heat. The dead woman's grip on Catherine's hand loosened.

Pounding feet sounded in the outer room a moment before Sebastian stormed into the small chamber, his eyes wild and his hair disheveled. Catherine's vision blurred at the mere sight of him. Relief like nothing she'd ever known poured into her limbs.

"Sebastian," she said through trembling lips. "They took Sophie."

He stepped forward, and Catherine flew into his outstretched arms. They curled around her, holding her close. Between whispered promises to find their girl, he kissed her eyes, lips, cheeks, anywhere he could reach. She wanted to believe him, wanted to trust that everything would be set to rights. But thoughts of Meghan McCarthy intruded, and it was only a matter of time before her active imagination replaced the carpenter's daughter's death mask with her daughter's sweet face.

Her stomach heaved, and she jerked out of Sebastian's arms.

He touched her shoulder. "Catherine—"

"Please don't," she whispered, fighting back the nausea.

Cora moved between them. "Chief, I found this by the woman's body."

Sebastian tore his gaze away from Catherine's quaking back to find Cora holding out a blood-spotted letter. He accepted the missive, ignoring his too-perceptive agent's gaze. "Mrs. Clarke?"

"Dead, sir."

"Let us remove to the outer chamber."

He waited for the women to file out, disappointed when Catherine kept her eyes downcast.

"Did the governess provide any clues to Cochran's destination?"

"No," Cora said. "She spoke only of her son and of

regrets. Given the fact that we found her alive, Cochran can't be that far ahead. London, do you think?"

"Would be a logical assumption," Sebastian said, reading Cochran's letter. "According to Jack, they have twenty—thirty minutes' lead on us."

"What of Bingham?" Cora asked.

"Alive, but badly injured."

"Do you need me to fetch Guy and Ethan?"

"Jack's on it," Sebastian said. "But we must bring Bingham inside to have his injuries looked after."

"Mother," Catherine said, "I'm sure the servants are hovering nearby. Can you ask Edward and a few other male servants to bring in Bingham?"

"Yes, of course." Her mother looked relieved to have something to do.

"May I assist, Mrs. Shaw?" Cora asked.

"By all means. I welcome the help."

"What does Cochran's letter say?" Catherine asked.

Sebastian refolded the paper. "He wants an exchange."

"What sort of an exchange?"

Tension rippled along the muscles in Sebastian's shoulders. He did not want to hurt or frighten Catherine any more than she already was, but he could see no other way around telling her the truth.

Catherine's mother, sensing what was to come, stepped to her daughter's side and wrapped an arm around her waist.

"Sebastian," Catherine said. "What does Cochran want? The list of agents?"

He nodded. "In exchange for your daughter's life."

"Dear God." Catherine turned into her mother's embrace.

Sebastian's jaw clenched, wanting to be the one she sought for comfort. But after his insensitive remark on the path, he understood why she would not want to invest any more emotion into an *affair* with an end date. "*Bloody stupid bastard*," he said beneath his breath.

Cora stared up at him with understanding shining in her eyes. "Does Cochran's letter say anything else?"

"For us to stay put, that he will send more instructions, and to keep the authorities out of it."

Cora raised a brow. "Is that all?"

"I cannot wait so long," Catherine said, swiping at her cheeks. "Mother, please see to Bingham."

"What are you planning, daughter?"

"I'm going after Sophie."

"Don't be ridiculous—"

"Chief, do something—"

"No, you're not," Sebastian said.

Determined brown eyes met his. "You can't stop me."

If she only knew the many ways he could stop her, she would run from the chamber and never look back. "Very well, Catherine. But we ride hard and we ride fast. With any luck, Cochran's using a carriage, thinking he had hours before anyone would notice your daughter's absence."

"I'll come with you," Cora said.

"No," Sebastian said. "Assist Mrs. Shaw with Bingham and have the others follow when they return."

"But—"

"No buts." Sebastian could see the toll this situation was taking on her. Cora hadn't fully recovered from her near-death experience in a French dungeon. Being thrown in the midst of another lethal mission so soon after the last would not help with the healing process. "I can take care of Cochran and his fiendish assistant."

He strode away before his agent could argue further, grasping Catherine's hand on his way by.

Twenty-five

"WHOA!" THE DRIVER YELLED.

Teddy had enough of a warning to brace himself before the front of the carriage bucked high into the air and came crashing back to the ground. Horses screamed, wood splintered, men cursed. Teddy rubbed his bruised bottom.

The carriage door flew open. "Driver, what the hell happened?"

"Pardon, Mr. Cochran," the driver said. "A large branch in the road. With this godforsaken blackness, I didn't see it in time."

Teddy heard a loud click.

"Silas, take a look."

"Yes, sir."

Bracing his feet wide, Teddy levered himself up enough to peer through the small window at the back of the passenger compartment. Inside, he found the shadowy silhouette of Sophie sprawled on the far seat, still in her nightdress. She appeared unharmed, but tousled.

The carriage tilted to the side and then the door

closed softly. Teddy ducked back down, holding on to Sophie's wooden archer with all his might. A scuffling noise to his left made his ears perk up.

"Put your weapon down, Mr. Cochran," a new voice said. "We have your man."

The newcomer's statement caused a moment of silence. Then Cochran demanded, "Who's there? Show yourself."

"Name's Declan McCarthy. Now drop your pistol and stand clear of the carriage."

Teddy's eyes rounded. What was Meghan's papa doing out here?

"McCarthy," Cochran mused. "Little Meghan's father, I presume?"

"That's right, you bastard. You'll pay for what you did to my wee Meghan."

While McCarthy spoke, Teddy followed the path of the man's voice, which seemed to be moving closer to Cochran's side of the carriage. The carpenter wanted to kill the gentleman who'd kidnapped Sophie. Did he even know she was inside? If he shot Cochran, he might miss and hit Sophie. Teddy rubbed his aching chest.

Then the soft thud of hooves against hard-packed earth caught his attention. He shifted his gaze to the right and the painful beating of his heart stopped cold. At the side of the road, he spotted a phantom in a long black cape astride an even blacker horse. The rider edged closer, and Teddy pressed his back into the paneling, his eyes growing larger the closer the phantom came. The rider halted and lifted one gloved finger to his lips in an age-old signal for silence. At least, Teddy assumed it was the phantom's mouth.

The large cowl hid the rider's face, revealing nothing but a dark, gaping maw.

"Come now, McCarthy," Cochran said. "Don't the Irish reproduce like vermin? Surely, you have another child to take the chit's place."

Teddy could hear more clicking of metal coming from the passenger compartment. The phantom's presence kept him rooted in place.

"The only vermin here is you," McCarthy roared. "Why did you have to kill her? You could have gone away and never returned."

"And allow the baggage to snivel my name into Mrs. Ashcroft's ears?" Cochran's voice turned cold. "You should thank me; two less peasant mouths to feed."

"Bastard," McCarthy roared. "She wasn't a peasant, she was my daughter!"

"McCarthy, no," someone cautioned.

Teddy recognized the butcher's voice.

"Yes, calm yourself," Cochran said, unruffled.

"I won't tell you again," McCarthy said between harsh breaths. "Drop your weapon and step away from the carriage."

"Tell me one thing first."

Teddy swiveled around when he heard another noise, this time closer. Two men in ragged clothing were inching their way toward the carriage. With their dirty faces, they were near invisible. But Teddy saw them. One was serious and intent. The other flashed Teddy a white smile followed with a wink.

"What?" McCarthy demanded.

"A simple matter of clarification," Cochran said. "How did you know I would be on this road at this time?"

"I received a note from someone named Specter. The message said my Meghan's murderer would be fleeing back to London tonight. Seems my new friend was right."

Teddy glanced at the caped rider.

"I see," Cochran said. "You placed a great deal of faith in a stranger's note."

"Saw no harm in checking things out. Time for conversing is over."

A shot exploded from inside the carriage, and Teddy covered his head with his arms. The carriage door wrenched open and then he heard the most awful words.

"Stay back," Cochran warned, "or I'll kill the girl."

No longer silent, the night came alive. Masculine voices from all directions hissed curses upon Cochran's head. Teddy peeked over his arms in time to see the phantom motioning instructions to the two men before melting into the shadows.

Teddy rolled to his knees but froze when Cochran backed into view. He held Sophie against him, her arms and legs dangling like a doll's and her head rocking back and forth. Sweat bubbled on Teddy's brow and skated down his sides. Another step back and Cochran would find his hiding place. He glanced at the two ragged men drawing closer.

"Put the Ashcroft girl down," McCarthy demanded. "You've no call to bring her into this."

"I think having her at my side evens things out nicely." Cochran whirled around, baring his back to Teddy.

But not before Teddy saw Sophie's eyes flutter open. Heartened, he gripped his wooden archer tighter and prayed for a heroic plan to come to mind. Nothing surfaced, for his mind was too frozen with fear. If all went wrong, he could lose his friend. His brow scrunched into an angry vee. He couldn't let that happen.

In the distance, Teddy heard a steady roll of thunder. Cochran heard it, too, and glanced up the road. For an instant, fear slackened the gentleman's features before they transformed into a slab of hatred.

"I require a horse." Cochran faced his unseen foes. "Now."

Teddy heard the sound of feet wading through tall grasses. When McCarthy spoke next, his voice seemed to be within reaching distance.

"You'll have it," McCarthy said. "Let the girl go."

Sophie spotted Teddy then, and he glimpsed her determination, the fire burning in her blue eyes. A new terror gripped Teddy as the thunder grew louder.

"Bring the horse and I'll deposit her a mile down the road."

No! Teddy held his breath while waiting for McCarthy's answer. Cochran would take off on that horse with Sophie and he would never see her again.

Getting his feet underneath him, Teddy waited for Cochran to turn toward the thunder, which seemed to be right on them now. The two ragged young men were shaking their heads and waving him off. Teddy ignored them, catapulting himself onto the scoundrel's back. Teddy slammed the archer's wooden arrow into the man's neck, causing Cochran's grip on Sophie to loosen. She took the opportunity to squiggle down far enough to sink her teeth into his arm, forcing a roar to rip from Cochran's injured throat. He dropped her, and Teddy went sailing through the air. His head struck the road, sending shards of pain through his skull.

Teddy heard a feminine scream and a man's yell a moment before a large black horse trampled his prone body.

Twenty-six

SEBASTIAN PUSHED REAPER, AND THE OTHERS, TO greater speeds. Charging through the night placed them all in peril, but overcoming Cochran's carriage before he gained the city was paramount. The clouds loosened their hold to reveal a waxing moon. Light sprayed over the road, and Sebastian peered into the distance. The outline of a carriage at the far end of the road materialized, and his pulse leaped with hope.

He glanced over his left shoulder to find Catherine riding low over Gypsy's neck and Helsford, Danforth, and Jack at her back. Jack had caught up with the two agents in the village mere seconds after Helsford's informant had passed on precious intelligence about Cochran's intended flight with Sophie. Once again, Helsford's informant had provided accurate and timely information in support of their cause. One day, Sebastian would meet their mysterious savior and offer him a job.

"Carriage up ahead." He caught Catherine's gaze. "Remember my instructions."

She nodded, a determined look in her eye.

He had to trust that she would allow him to manage the situation without her interference. But for good measure, he sliced a meaningful glare at Danforth, who nodded.

They gained on Cochran much faster than Sebastian had anticipated. He could see now that the carriage was stopped in the middle of the lane and a man stood next to it. The man must have heard their approach, for he angled around and—

"Oh, dear Lord," Catherine cried.

Cochran held Sophie against him, her arms and legs swung lifelessly from her body. The backs of Sebastian's eyes burned at the sight. From this distance, they appeared too late, but if that were the case, the girl would be of no further use to the man and he would not be holding her in such a defensive manner.

Sophie's kidnapper whipped around, yelling at someone beyond the tree line. Sebastian saw no one, but a movement at the back of the carriage captured his attention. A small boy leveraged himself into a crouched position on the luggage boot.

Teddy. Two children in harm's way. Ice glazed Sebastian's spine and sweat dampened his palms.

His gaze narrowed on the boy, who had his hand raised in an attack position. Sebastian could not detect a weapon, but Teddy was definitely preparing to do something rash.

"Don't do it," Sebastian demanded in a harsh whisper. He gave Reaper all the lead he wanted, and his mount burst forward in an amazing display of power.

The boy picked that moment to launch himself onto Cochran's back.

The night exploded into a cacophony of screams and curses.

~⁂~

"*Teddy!*" Catherine yelled. She couldn't believe what she was seeing. The stable lad had launched himself onto the back of a grown man, who would as soon kill the boy as look at him. Infuriated and writhing in pain, Cochran dropped Sophie and wrenched the boy off his back, throwing him across the road like a bucket of yesterday's slop.

Right into their path.

"Watch out," Sebastian warned.

Out of nowhere, a big black horse appeared carrying a cloaked figure. The rider maneuvered his mount over the stable lad, shielding him from their approach.

Sebastian jerked his horse to the right and Catherine pulled Gypsy's reins to the left; the three men behind followed suit.

"Danforth, to Catherine. Jack, the boy," Sebastian directed, after they cleared that particular danger. Helsford followed Sebastian into the fray.

Catherine scrambled off her horse and stood paralyzed as she watched Sebastian dismount and draw a pistol from the back of his waistband. Sophie was on the ground, kicking at Cochran as he attempted to recapture her. From a distance, Catherine heard Danforth calling her, but she couldn't obey his entreaty for her to come away. The two people she loved most in the world were fighting for their lives.

"Cochran, stand down," Sebastian said, leveling the pistol at his head.

Desperate now, Cochran smacked away Sophie's legs and scooped her up.

"You killed Teddy, you beast!" Sophie cried. "How could you?" She no longer dangled passively in Cochran's arms. She fought like a wildcat.

Catherine was equal parts proud and terrified. She wrenched free of Danforth's hold and ran forward.

"Get back, Catherine." Sebastian's harsh command stopped her in her tracks. His eyes blazed with a luminescent vengeance that froze her heart.

From behind the battling duo emerged Declan McCarthy and several men from the village, including the vicar, who ran over to assist Jack with Teddy. Two of the men held Silas between them.

With her daughter acting the she-cat, Cochran appeared to Catherine almost relieved when Sebastian stowed his pistol and then plucked Sophie off her cursing and bleeding captor. Her sweet girl scratched at the air, determined to do the man more damage.

McCarthy sank a fist into Cochran's stomach, then kneed him in the face when the man bent forward. He knocked the man to the ground and forced his arms behind his back. Helsford pulled a length of rope from his saddle and tied Cochran's wrists and ankles.

With both men subdued, Catherine ran forward. Even though Sebastian tried to shelter Sophie's curious eyes from McCarthy's attack on Cochran, her daughter observed far too much.

"Sophie." Catherine held out her arms. "Come to Mama."

Fierce blue eyes turned her way. From one second

to the next, the fight went out of her daughter and her eyes filled with tears. "Mama."

Sebastian handed her daughter over, and Catherine's pulse quickened when the girl's small frame began to quake. "I have you now, pumpkin. Everything's fine." Catherine smoothed her hand over Sophie's back in wide, calming circles. Sebastian also placed a hand on Sophie's back while he angled around until he stood face-to-face with her daughter. "Brave little sprite, why the tears? You vanquished the enemy with nary a bruise."

Sophie reared back and settled liquid blue eyes on him. An instant later, she bounded up and wrapped her thin arms around his neck. "Bastian," she said. "You saved me."

With Sophie half in Catherine's arms and half in Sebastian's arms, he stood awkwardly for a few seconds before finally giving in and embracing them both. Catherine closed her eyes and absorbed the moment. It was likely the last hug she would ever receive from him.

"Ah, that's so precious, Somerton," Cochran said. "Weren't you supposed to protect the Ashcroft ladies, rather than seduce them?"

The muscles in Sebastian's arm rippled against her waist, and she heard Helsford order Cochran to be quiet right before the prisoner grunted in pain.

❧

Sebastian ignored the ice raking down his spine long enough to finish his conversation with Sophie. "No, sprite. Your brownie friend must take all the credit for your rescue."

Pushing off his shoulders, Sophie said, "But Teddy's dead." Tears leaked from her eyes.

Sebastian glanced over to where a small group had formed around the boy. The cloaked savior had disappeared, as had the two young men who were approaching the carriage before Sebastian stormed into the fray. From here, he could not see if the boy was coming to, or if Cochran had managed to do the unthinkable.

"Miss Sophie," Declan McCarthy said.

She peered over her shoulder at the carpenter.

"I believe this belongs to your brave knight." He held out a carved figure of a man holding a bow and arrow.

Sophie accepted the piece. "I gave this to him." She glanced up at McCarthy, her pride evident. "Did you see Teddy jab the arrow into the bad man's neck?"

"Yes, miss," McCarthy said. "He's a courageous lad. You must be a very good friend."

"Mama," Sophie said. "I must go see Teddy."

Catherine glanced at Sebastian, and that's when he realized he still held them close. Stepping away, he said, "Get them both out of here, Catherine. Please."

She nodded. "Be careful."

"You may depend upon it."

She strode away, toward the fallen boy, glancing back when she set Sophie down. The incredible pressure around his chest did not relent until he saw Teddy wobble into a sitting position.

The carpenter's normally wary eyes burned with purpose. "I'll take care of that mewling coward who killed my Meghan."

"You know?"

"Aye, m'lord," McCarthy said. "I received a note that the men who killed my girl were fleeing tonight. The murdering bastard admitted his crime right before you arrived." His hand balled into a fist. "Time to make him suffer."

Understanding the man's pain, Sebastian gentled his voice. "I can't let you do that."

McCarthy's jaw stiffened. "Don't try to stop me, m'lord."

Sophie's kidnapper laughed. "Get in line, Irish. Somerton's not going to let a dead girl stand in the way of protecting his precious Nexus."

"Quiet." Helsford ground the heel of his boot into the traitor's back.

"Danforth. Mr. Foster," Sebastian called.

The agent and vicar were at his side in an instant. "Yes, sir?"

"How's our intrepid hero?"

"He'll be fine," the vicar said. "The lump on his head will cause him some pain for a while."

"Danforth, we need that carriage for Catherine and the children. And we need the men from the village out of here. Now." To the vicar, he said, "Make sure the men have everything they need when they get back to Showbury."

"Will do, sir." The vicar strode off.

Sebastian faced the angry carpenter.

McCarthy's green eyes burned with a mixture of grief and hatred. "I'll have justice for my Meghan and her wee babe."

"Yes, you will," Sebastian said. "But not until after I extract some information."

"For this Nexus." McCarthy's lip curled in disgust.

"No." The lie fell smoothly from Sebastian's lips. "Cochran speaks only to confuse you. His one hope of surviving this situation is to pit us against each other and only then might he have a chance at escaping."

The carpenter's hands balled into massive fists.

"McCarthy, I need the carriage free and operable. Can you and the other men make that happen? I want to get Mrs. Ashcroft and the children away from this place." And he wanted to give the man something else to focus on.

The men spent the next ten minutes readying the carriage, then Catherine bundled the two children inside. Sebastian frowned when he noticed Catherine and Danforth engaged in a heated exchange. Then the viscount threw his arms up and grumbled something about stubborn women.

Mr. Foster climbed into the driver's box, ushering Cochran's coachman into the hands of two of the villagers. The carriage lurched forward, escorted by an unhappy McCarthy, the rest of the villagers, and Jack riding at the back. Catherine stood at the side of the road, watching the conveyance lumber out of sight.

"Mr. Foster, wait." Sebastian rushed forward, but the vicar ignored his command and continued on toward Showbury. "What are you doing, Catherine?"

"What does it look like?" she asked in a calm voice. "I'm staying."

Warmth seeped into Sebastian's heart, followed quickly by an ungovernable fear for her safety. "It's too dangerous."

"For you, as well."

"This could become unpleasant, Catherine. I don't want you exposed to this." Nor did he want her to witness his darker side, the one most detested for its ruthlessness.

"I will not watch the bad parts, Sebastian," she said. "Understand that I'm not leaving you." She cleared her throat. "I mean, I'm not leaving you here to sort out Jeffrey's mess."

I'm not leaving you. A wild instinct, ominous and possessive, assailed his senses, overwhelming in its strength.

"Chief, perhaps we should finish this," Helsford said.

"The carriage is gone," she said. "And I'm not walking back alone."

"Dammit, Catherine. You have no business here."

"I have as much right to be here as the rest of you." Her gaze landed on Cochran. "He threatened my baby girl."

She had placed him in an untenable situation. How could he protect her *and* conduct a thorough interrogation of his prisoner?

Cochran laughed. "What's the matter, Somerton? Afraid your mistress won't like what she sees?"

Sebastian ignored him. Pointing toward the shadowed tree line, he said, "Stand over there. Do not go near either prisoner, no matter what. Understood?"

"Yes, *Chief.*"

He waited for her to comply before heading back to the circle of men. "Pick him up."

Helsford pulled Cochran to his feet. With his wrists and ankles bound by the same rope, the prisoner hobbled about until he gained his balance.

"Tell me who you're working for," Sebastian said.

Cochran smiled. "Why would I need to take orders from anyone?"

"Because you're not intelligent enough to master-mind this elaborate a plan."

Cochran's gaze sliced to Silas, who stood passively in Danforth's grip. "Intelligent enough to locate and silence your nosey agent."

Catherine's sharp intake of breath speared through their circle.

"Was it Latymer?" Danforth demanded.

Cochran's gaze landed on Silas again. He said nothing.

Sebastian nodded to Helsford, who knocked Cochran's feet out from underneath him. The prisoner landed on his face with his bound hands behind him. Helsford grabbed the rope connecting Cochran's hands to his feet and set a boot to the middle of the man's back. Then he pulled on the rope like a bowstring, wrenching the prisoner's arms and legs into an unnatural angle. Cochran cried out.

"I believe Danforth asked you a question," Sebastian said.

"Go to hell," Cochran said through gritted teeth.

The rope tautened.

"Care to try again?"

"*Yes*," Cochran ground out. "I reported to Latymer."

Sebastian released a satisfied breath. "What was your agreement with the former under-superintendent?"

"To retrieve a list of your agents."

"In exchange for?"

More silence.

The rope tautened.

"Latymer discrediting you," Cochran gasped. "I've answered your questions. Now call off your dog."

"How would you benefit from my disgrace?"

Cochran glared up at him. "I would have taken your place."

Danforth barked out a laugh. "You? Chief? Please tell me you aren't serious."

"If not for someone named Specter muddling in my affairs, I would have been the new chief of the Nexus by tomorrow's end. Some of the greatest minds in England would have been at my disposal."

"Get him up," Sebastian said to Helsford. "What made you think Reeves would appoint you as chief, rather than one of my agents?"

"Latymer still has powerful friends in the Foreign Office," Cochran said.

In a lightning-swift maneuver, one Sebastian had never witnessed before, Silas somersaulted out of his captors' grip and snatched a pistol from Danforth's waistband. Using his weapon, he motioned for a fuming Danforth to step back and then leveled the barrel at Sebastian. The look on the man's face could only be described as gleeful.

"*No.*"

Sebastian glanced back to see Catherine scrambling out from the cover of a tree, her fiery gaze on Silas. "Catherine, no!" He had wanted to know what it would feel like to have a champion in a wife. This was as close as he would ever come to knowing the feeling—and he liked the sensation. A lot—until the terror took hold. "You promised, remember?" He waited for her to acknowledge him before pouring all the love that had been building in his heart over the last sennight into his gaze.

Tears filled her eyes. "*Sebastian*."

"Stay put, love." Then his smile faded. Taking advantage of the distraction, Sebastian inched his hand toward his weapon.

The little man tsked. "Kindly raise your hands, my lord."

Sebastian weighed his options. With Silas's weapon pointed at his chest, he had none. He lifted his arms in the air.

"Silas," Cochran said. "Come remove these bindings."

"In a moment, sir."

"What do you mean 'in a moment'?" Cochran tried to wrench free of Helsford's hold.

Silas's watery eyes settled back on Sebastian. "I am saddened by this turn of events," he said in perfect French. "The widow has been a worthy adversary, as have you. We shall meet again."

Before Sebastian could work through the man's cryptic remark, Silas swept his weapon toward Helsford and fired.

"No—" Sebastian dove toward his agent in a futile attempt to block the bullet, but it was not Helsford's body that bucked against the impact.

Cochran's neck jolted back and his body froze for an instant before melting in Helsford's arms. Then his head rolled forward, revealing the bullet's entrance, his death told by a single track of scarlet liquid.

With a fluid sweep of his arm, Sebastian grabbed his gun, twisted his body around to face Cochran's murderer, and pulled the trigger. Sebastian's bullet cleaved into Silas's forehead at the same time another lead ball from behind blasted into the man's back.

"Get down!" Sebastian yelled as he dove to the ground. "Helsford, to Catherine." He didn't have to look to make sure his agent followed his direction—the man was trained to do so without question. He watched Silas's body collapse in a heap, dead before his face hit the hard-packed road.

"Who's there?" Sebastian's gaze flicked from one corner of the darkness to the next. "Show yourself."

"It would be my pleasure, Lord Somerton," a new voice said. "As soon as you lower your weapons."

Sebastian glanced from Danforth to Helsford; both agents shrugged their shoulders. "I'll have your name, sir."

"Reeves. John Reeves, Superintendent of the Alien Office."

Twenty-seven

"IF YOU THREE WOMEN DON'T STOP PACING," DANFORTH said from his location near the drawing room window, "you're going to give me a megrim."

Catherine halted behind one of Sebastian's burgundy damask chairs, clutching the back with her cold, clammy hands. Cora and Dinks continued their assault on the expensive carpet, pausing only long enough to throw Danforth a leave-me-be look.

"No sign of them yet?" Catherine would never forget the steel coating Sebastian's blue-gray eyes when he forced her to return with the viscount while he, Helsford, and Reeves dealt with the aftermath of Cochran's failed abduction.

Danforth sighed, having fielded the same question no less than a dozen times since they had returned to Bellamere an hour ago. "They could be coming down the drive right now, for all I know. This blasted darkness has been both a blessing and a damned curse."

"If you don't mind, Miss Cora," Dinks said, "I'll look in on the wee ones. This waiting has my nerves stretched thin."

"Of course," Cora said. "Why don't you make sure Bingham is still abed? I caught him trying to limp off toward the stables not long after we arrived."

The maid's eyes narrowed toward the open door. "Did he, now?"

"Thank you, Dinks," Catherine said. "I doubt Mother has left the children's side, but I'm sure she's curious if there have been any new developments."

Dinks picked up the tea tray and turned to leave. "I'll have a fresh pot brought around."

Catherine noted Cora's sly smile. "Something amusing, Miss deBeau?"

"Do call me Cora. I detest such formality amongst friends."

Glancing between brother and sister, Catherine said, "We are friends?"

The other woman lifted a sable-colored brow. "Are you finished plotting against Somerton?"

Danforth paused in his surveillance of the front drive to await her answer.

Heat rushed into Catherine's cheeks. "Of course. I hold no ill will toward Lord Somerton." She strengthened her voice. "I did what I had to do in order to save my daughter. And I would do it again."

Brother and sister shared a satisfied look and then two sets of blue-green eyes settled on her. Cora said, "You will make a nice addition to our circle."

Catherine's nails scored the tight weave of the upholstered chair. "It is kind of you to say so. But in a few days, the lot of you will return to London, and I will settle back into country life here in Showbury."

Danforth made a choking sound and pivoted back

to the window. Cora scowled at her brother. "Why don't you head down the lane to meet the others?"

"Believe me, sister," he said. "I would like nothing better, given the new direction of this conversation. Not sure why I was relegated to women-sitting, rather than Helsford. All the same, I prefer my head attached to my shoulders."

Catherine frowned. "What do you mean, sir?"

Cora answered, "He means Somerton will lop it off if he leaves us—or rather you—unattended."

A soft knock drew their attention to the open door. Mrs. Fox said, "Pardon, the interruption. I have a warm pot of tea."

"Come in—" Cora said.

"Please bring it in—" Catherine said at the same time.

Catherine's gaze cut to Sebastian's former ward, a fresh wave of humiliation burned its way up her neck and into her cheeks. "My apologies, I forgot myself."

Cora smiled. "Mrs. Fox, please set the tea tray on the table next to Mrs. Ashcroft. She can do the honors." After the housekeeper withdrew, she nodded toward the tea. "I hope you don't mind."

"Not at all." Catherine appreciated the distraction. It would give her something to do with her hands besides worrying a hole in the chair's upholstery.

"None for me," Danforth said. "I will raid Somerton's stash over there."

Catherine lifted her gaze to Cora. "Sugar?"

"No, thank you," she said. "A spot of cream only."

Once they had their respective drinks, Catherine and Cora perched on matching chairs while Danforth kept watch.

"Catherine," Cora said after a short silence. "Your life in Showbury will be much altered now. Surely, you realize that."

"I have no doubt the events of the last fortnight will haunt my thoughts for some time," Catherine said. "But I don't see how that fact will affect my living here."

A low groan sounded from the window. "Ladies, I am going to walk the perimeter." Danforth lanced his sister with a severe look. "Stay put, or I will haunt you—headless and all."

"You ceased intimidating me when I was twelve, brother," Cora said. "Save your threats for your elusive cloaked savior."

His lips thinned. "Can you not do as I ask just this once?"

Cora laughed. "This coming from the King of Rogues? From a man who takes the solitary path more often than not?"

From the thunderous look on the viscount's face, Catherine thought he might do his sister bodily harm. Instead, he jabbed his finger in the air. "You're Helsford's problem now." Then he stormed from the room.

"Rather lacking, as comebacks go, wouldn't you say?" Cora asked in an amused voice.

"Should he be left to his own devices?"

"Do not let our sparring upset you," Cora said. "It's our way." She set her teacup down. "Do you love him? Somerton, I mean."

Catherine could do little more than stare. Like Sebastian, Cora dipped and swayed from one topic to the next, making it impossible to anticipate the woman's next question.

"You think me too bold?" Cora asked. "I don't blame you. It is no one's business but your own."

"Thank you."

Cora sent her an admonishing look. "I ask only because I want for Somerton what I have with Guy. As agents, we've devoted our lives to this fight against Napoleon, never taking for ourselves. Somerton more so than the rest of us. Until now, I never knew the sacrifice mattered to him."

Shock jolted her heart into an uncomfortable rhythm. "Surely, you're not suggesting that Lord Somerton holds any meaningful affection for me." Then she recalled the fleeting expression that crossed his face when he thought Silas was about to kill him. Catherine swallowed back the lump of joy.

"You are surprised by the notion?"

"I am *appalled* by the notion."

That stiffened the younger woman's back. "I can't think why you would be."

Catherine's unease with their conversation grew with each word uttered. "Did Lord Somerton explain the *full* nature of our association?"

Intelligence gleamed behind the woman's sharp gaze as she assessed Catherine's words, then the sharpness softened into comprehension and, even worse, empathy.

"Believe me, when I tell you," Cora said, "if there is one man in all of England who would understand your motives, it is Somerton. He might even be more drawn to you because of your warrior instincts."

"You do not understand. I deceived him in the worst possible way."

"Did he not deceive you by keeping the manner of your husband's death to himself?"

Catherine stood. "It's not the same. I made love to him to obtain a list!"

"Of suspected traitors?"

Catherine turned her burning eyes on her.

"To save your daughter?"

Her breathing became more difficult.

"Do you not think England's greatest spymaster would do the same in your stead?" Cora rose and moved to stand in front of her. "No need to answer, for I will. He would. That, and a whole lot worse."

"Our association has been built on suspicion and betrayal," Catherine said. "A poor beginning."

"One does not *make love* to obtain information," Cora pointed out. "One does something altogether less pleasurable."

"You sound as if you speak from experience." Not for the first time, Catherine wondered how the agent came by the scar on her cheek.

"I do." A shadow crossed Cora's face. "And that experience tells me the two of you have much more to build on than the awful circumstances that brought you together."

A disturbance from the entry hall caught their attention and they grappled for each other's hands in a show of feminine support. They rushed to the door, but when Catherine made to open it, Cora placed her palm against the oak panel and directed her unsettling gaze on her. "Give him a chance to love you."

The pressure around her chest tightened, and Catherine's pulse roared in her ears. Overcoming the reason that brought them together was only one of their many hurdles, the biggest being Sebastian's role with the Nexus. That role would take him away from her for long periods of time, during which she would constantly worry for his return. Constantly be waiting.

Catherine turned the latch, prompting Cora to remove her hand. She stepped through the portal and pivoted toward the commotion. There, at the far end of the corridor, where it emptied into the entry hall, stood Sebastian, looking disheveled and dangerous. The sight of him sent a tide of relief through her body, and she released a *whoosh* of air.

Give him a chance to love you.

As if he sensed her presence, his gaze caught hers, and held. Something primitive marred his handsome features, and he stepped forward as if pulled by the strength of her gaze. Then Cora squeezed past Catherine and headed straight for her betrothed. The small disruption was enough to sever her visual bond with Sebastian.

He retreated beneath the guise of cold civility he wore so splendidly, and Catherine nudged the loose brick in her wall back into place.

Sebastian's heart nearly exploded with relief to find Catherine hale and looking more beautiful than anyone had a right to after such a harrowing experience. Confronted with losing her daughter, she had exhibited great courage—and foolishness—in running Cochran to ground. Thank God, the children had been clear of the area when the shooting began. As for Catherine, he could only be grateful that she had listened to him when it counted most. If something had happened to her and Sophie...

An image of his mentor's wife's dead body flooded his vision. The horror the man must have faced haunted Sebastian every time he gazed upon Catherine. Knowing one's wife was about to be murdered and being helpless to do anything was a nightmare Sebastian had sworn he would never experience.

But he'd come close tonight. Not with a wife, but with a little girl who had somehow attached herself to his heart. As had her mother.

Ice crackled, fusing together, inch by inch, until it slowly encased him inside a protective shell. Only he knew, far too well, that one kiss from Catherine would shatter the fragile barrier, leaving him exposed to a crushing torment.

She must have sensed his withdrawal, for her expression molded itself into one of indifference. Clasping her hands at her waist, she retreated from view.

"Let us move to the study," Cora said, clinging to Helsford.

Sebastian followed behind Danforth, Reeves, and the inseparable pair, mentally preparing himself for the next few hours. They had much to discuss, and unfortunately, he would have to pretend that he did not wish to whisk Catherine away to a private chamber.

Not thinking, Sebastian strode to the side table holding an assortment of crystal decanters. He poured brandy for the men and sherry for the women. When he made to tip back his first glass, he caught Catherine's concerned look out of the corner of his eye before she hastily averted her gaze.

Something unpleasant swelled in his gut. The sensation grew worse when his nose caught its first whiff of the amber liquid's rustic fruity blend, followed swiftly by the sharp sting of alcohol. Lowering his hand, he returned the squat glass to the side table and took up a familiar position near the fireplace.

"Superintendent Reeves," Cora said, "what brings you to Showbury? At such a propitious moment?"

If the Foreign Office official was bothered by Cora's suspicious tone, he did not show it. "Lord Somerton's letter."

Sebastian's agents turned as one to him. "At no time did our evidence point to Reeves, even though he was the logical choice," he said. "But I knew Cochran was getting his information from within the Foreign Office. So, I took a leap of faith."

"After a few inquiries and several threats," Reeves said, "I found Cochran's source. My clerk, Bradford. A man I trusted."

"Does Cochran even work at the Foreign Office, sir?" Catherine asked.

"Yes, ma'am," Reeves said. "He's a minor clerk to the under-secretary of the Foreign Office. In Bradford's defense, he did not realize the information he confided to Cochran was being used for such ill purpose. The man's ambitious nature led him to risky choices. I daresay he hoped Cochran would provide a suitable reference when the time came."

"And the investigation against Lord Somerton?" Helsford asked.

"Dropped."

The room's occupants breathed a collective sigh of

relief. Catherine ducked her head and closed her eyes. Sebastian watched her mouth move over silent words.

Tearing his gaze away, he said, "Thank you, sir."

"It is I who should thank you," Reeves said. "Although you were not fond of my decision to place you on leave, you appeared to understand." His gaze roamed the room at large. "And my apologies to all of you—especially Mrs. Ashcroft and her family—for the role my clerk played in this injurious plot. You cannot know how aggrieved I am at your suffering."

"Thank you, Mr. Reeves," Catherine said. "But you are not to blame. If anyone owes us an apology, it is Frederick Cochran, and he is dead. So, we will pick up the pieces of our lives and carry on, good sir."

"You are too gracious, I assure you, ma'am," Reeves said, with a bow. "But I thank you, all the same."

"Three dead bodies in a small village like Showbury are bound to attract some notice." Danforth sank deeper into his chair. "Not good for the Nexus."

"Leave the bodies to me." Sebastian kept his gaze ahead.

"As I do not fully comprehend what 'leave the bodies to me' means," Catherine said, "I would like to make arrangements for Mrs. Clarke to have a proper burial."

Sebastian straightened and gave her his full attention. "You wish to look after a woman in league with the man who threatened your daughter's life?"

She lifted her chin, meeting his gaze. "I do."

"Care to expound, madam?"

"She was a mother."

Sebastian studied her resolute gaze, her squared

shoulders, and her clasped hands. "I take it the two of you found something in common."

Her nod was somewhat shaky. "Before she died, she spoke of her son, Giles." She stared down at her hands for a moment, struggling with emotion. Then she raised her head, her pretty brown eyes full of misery. "He's in London, at a boys' home somewhere, to ensure his mother's cooperation. Mrs. Clarke did what she had to do to protect him."

As she had with her daughter, as he would with her and Sophie.

"We will find him," Sebastian assured her, recalling the name *Abbingale Home* from Ashcroft's missing letter. His gaze settled on Danforth, who nodded his understanding. With luck, Abbingale would provide the link they needed to locate Latymer. A scene flashed through his mind. "Silas, before he was killed, spoke fluent French."

"Perhaps others besides the Frenchman Valère have been working Latymer's marionette strings," Reeves said.

Helsford, who stood behind Cora, smoothed his hand over her sable locks. She grasped his fingers and kissed their tips. The sight sent an answering pang of longing through Sebastian, and his gaze sought Catherine's, but she was also watching the display of affection.

"Where do we go from here?" Danforth asked.

Sebastian rubbed his temple, feeling the events of the day depleting his strength. "You can begin making inquiries into homes for orphans. Start with Abbingale Home." He dropped his hand. "Helsford, see if your informant can track down Latymer."

"Yes, sir," Helsford said.

"What of me?" Cora asked.

"You are on leave until after the first of the year."

"What?"

"If you push me," Sebastian said in the hardest voice he could muster, "I will make it permanent."

Cora's body vibrated with anger, but she said nothing.

"Enjoy your respite, runt," her brother said. "Go home and play with that thing you call a kitten. If that doesn't excite you enough, I should like to have a nephew. Or a niece, if you must."

"Ethan," Cora attempted to rise, but Helsford grabbed her shoulders, "do you recall our conversation about your head getting lopped off?"

Danforth held a large bolster across his body like a shield. "No need for violence, sister. Just trying to offer you my support."

Helsford broke in. "Shall we report back to you here? Or London?"

The silence that pervaded the study rubbed Sebastian's nerves raw, as did the avid stares of everyone in the room. Everyone but one, that was. He felt Catherine's disinterest more keenly than any probing gaze.

"London," he said. "It is past time for my return."

"Well," Catherine said, rising. "Since there is nothing left for me to do here, I shall collect Sophie and be off."

Sebastian's stomach knotted, yet he could not bring himself to dissuade her.

"Catherine, you must stay the night." Cora sent Sebastian a cross look. "We cannot be certain the danger has passed."

"For me, it has," Catherine said. "Cochran and Silas are dead, and Lord Somerton is aware of my ruse. My unique services are of no further use to anyone. Now, if you'll excuse me—"

"Bastian! You're back." A whirlwind of fluttering furbelows and bouncing curls charged into the room and slammed into Sebastian. Thin arms enfolded his middle, and Sophie buried her face into the soft fabric of his waistcoat.

Stunned by the child's enthusiastic greeting, Sebastian stood rigidly in the center of the study, with his arms aloft. He glanced at Catherine for guidance and found her eyes misted with tears. Then she lifted her watery gaze up to his, and Sebastian felt his heart rip in half.

Sophie peered up at him. "What took you so long, Bastian? Ethan said you would be along soon, but that was *hours* ago."

He rested a hand on top of her head. "Ethan, is it?"

She gave him a broad grin, one that conveyed she already knew how to wrap a man around her little finger. Then her smile dimmed. "Did you take the bad men to the con-*stable*?"

Sebastian froze, his gaze seeking Catherine's again. This time, she nodded.

"Constable, pumpkin."

"Didn't I say that, Mama?"

Sebastian crouched down. "You don't ever have to worry about the bad men again."

She leaned into him and toyed with his collar. "Do you promise?"

He tapped his finger beneath her chin. "Promise."

"Brilliant! That's what I told, Mama. That you would always protect us." Her voice lowered into a stage whisper. "She was crying when she returned, and I wanted to make her feel better."

"You were quite right to do so."

She shook her head and tears cracked her voice. "She cried harder, Bastian."

Sebastian clenched his teeth so tight that he was certain they would shatter from the pressure. He fought to keep his attention centered on Sophie and not her mother, because if he saw the truth of the girl's words on her mother's face his control would crumble to the ground. "We will have to convince her, won't we?"

Sophie's head bobbed. In a normal voice, she proclaimed, "Teddy has a big bump on his head."

Sebastian blinked at her change of topic. "A badge of courage."

"When my head hurts, Guinevere always makes it feel better." Her gaze turned earnest. "Imagine what a whole stable full of horses could do for Teddy's pain."

He chuckled. "Indeed, sprite. You should talk to Ethan about visiting them tomorrow morning. He loves showing off my stables." In typical Danforth fashion, he was more interested in the swirling contents of his glass than the poignant conversation. "Isn't that right, *Ethan*?"

"What?" The viscount glanced between Sebastian to Sophie. "Uh, yes. That's correct."

"Oh, Ethan!" Sophie skipped across the room and crawled up into Danforth's lap. "Teddy will be so happy."

From the look on Danforth's face, one would think

that an enormous spider was crawling across his legs.
Slouched down in his chair, Danforth was nose-to-
nose with the girl as she nattered on about all the
horses she'd seen earlier that day. The viscount sent
Sebastian a distressed look, making it impossible for
Sebastian to contain his smile.

Sebastian gave in to the impulse and glanced at
Catherine. The smile she gave him was warm and
appreciative, but coated with a brittle edge. She would
survive this just as she had survived her father's death
and her husband's murder, standing against a village full
of opportunistic shopkeepers and matrons who sought
to place Ashcroft's abandonment on her shoulders.

She would survive the end of their *affaire*, as would
he. One minute at a time, one day at a time, one
month at a time. Because surviving was what they
both did, no matter the personal sacrifice.

"Sophie." Catherine held out her hand. "Allow Lord
Danforth to catch his breath. It's time for us to go."

Cora stepped forward. "Please reconsider. There's
plenty of room."

"I don't think it's a good idea—"

"Cora's right," Sebastian heard himself say. "You're
welcome to stay. The cloud cover remains thick,
making for a treacherous journey."

Sophie vibrated with excitement. "Oh, please,
Mama. Can we stay with Bastian?"

Catherine's face softened. "Would you like that?"

"Yes!"

"Very well," she said. "But you must turn in early.
You've had a busy day."

Sophie nodded her agreement. "I'll get lots of

sleep, so Ethan and I can help Jasper feed the horses in the morning.

Danforth groaned and murmured, "God, help me."

Twenty-eight

IN HER BORROWED DRESSING GOWN, CATHERINE PACED the length of her bedchamber, knowing she would enjoy little sleep while beneath Sebastian's roof. She had made a mistake in accepting his invitation to stay. Such temptation so close at hand was far stronger than her meager will. She wanted one more night in his embrace, one more evening where she felt womanly and strong and cherished. One more evening to love him.

Catherine threw back her head and stared at the ceiling. How? How had she managed to fall in love with a man burdened with every trait she despised? Why couldn't she have found a nice gentleman like Mr. Foster? Someone who would spend his entire life in service to the residents of Showbury and be happy about it. Gentle. Predictable. *Boring*.

She released a huge sigh while her gaze traveled around the rose and lemon bedchamber. So different from the countess's cream and gold silk-draped chamber. And a good deal safer. But the more modest-sized room made her feel caged and restless. She strode to the door leading out to a small balcony and thrust it open. A gentle summer breeze whipped through her loose hair and caressed her burning cheeks. The air was redolent with the lush scent of roses.

The clouds had finally moved on, leaving behind an ebony sky sprinkled with diamonds. Two hours ago, one would never have known such perfection rode above the thick veil of evil. Meghan McCarthy's youthful face surfaced in her mind's eye, and Catherine clenched her teeth against the sadness. Through no fault of her own, the young woman had become embroiled in the machinations of ambitious, greedy men.

Sebastian and the others had speculated that a disguised Cochran had made secret trips into Showbury, looking for clues to Jeffrey's whereabouts and learning the landscape. Somewhere along the way, Meghan had caught Cochran's eye.

Catherine leaned against the iron railing, absorbing the innocence of Sebastian's moon-kissed gardens. Her gaze touched on every hedge, every blooming flower, every gnarled limb. When she reached the sunken garden, a man emerged from beneath the canopy of a small, multi-stemmed tree, his face uplifted, his gaze luminescent and focused on her. *Sebastian.*

Catherine's fingers curled around the top railing, the metal cool and solid. Her heart thumped an erratic tattoo in her ears, but not loud enough to drown out the single word echoing in her mind. *Go. Go. Go!*

Not stopping to think, to consider the consequences, she swung around and rushed through the bedchamber, having no care for her dishabille and bare feet. She stormed through the mansion as if outrunning logic and good sense. She ran until her lungs heaved and her muscles ached. She ran until she came face-to-face with her heaven and her hell. "*Sebastian.*"

He gave her no time to catch her breath. He framed her face in the cradle of his hands and closed his mouth over hers. She curled her arms around his back and met his fierceness with a passion that bordered on desperation. He tasted of warmed sugar and of green tea and mint. He tasted of home.

She broke off for a much-needed breath. "Sebastian."

"Mmm-hmm." His magical lips continued their assault down her throat.

"I don't want you to go."

He froze, and Catherine winced. Where had those words come from? She had intended to beg him to make love to her, not declare such fruitless yearnings. "I'm sorry. I-I shouldn't have said—" She swallowed back the damning words and stared at his chest in mortification, waiting for him to deliver his painful reminder.

Sebastian curled his finger beneath her chin and nudged her face up. "It occurs to me that this is Saturday."

What an odd thing to say when she'd just made a fool of herself. "Yes, what of it?"

"That's four days until Wednesday."

"Now that we have established that you know the days of the week and their proper placement, perhaps you could tell me why that's important *now*.

"The timing is important, my impatient one, because it means I'm not going anywhere for four days."

"But you told Lord Helsford to report to you in London."

He nodded. "After Wednesday."

Vexing man. "I don't understand the significance of this time frame."

"You wound me, madam," he said. "The end date of our *affaire* approaches. Does that fact not hold some importance in your heart?"

Catherine studied his tender expression and the playful curve to his mouth. Something had changed in him during the short time they had been apart. Something significant.

"What are you about, sir?"

His lips twitched. "Whatever can you mean, dear lady? The notion that you may have forgotten our pleasurable arrangement calls for some distress on my part, don't you think?"

Her eyes narrowed in warning. "I have not forgotten our arrangement, as you well know. Hearing that you intend to stay for a while longer pleases me a great deal. But I wonder for what purpose?"

The playful amusement left his face. "For the pleasure of each other's company, of course."

"That reason is no longer enough." Her admission hovered in the air between them. They had been through too much, tiptoed around too many issues not to speak plainly now. "I have gone and complicated this situation even more by falling in love with you."

"Catherine, I—"

She set a finger over his lips. "I know you care for me, Sebastian. And I also understand intimate relations amongst your set are commonplace. That our time together was nothing more than a pleasant diversion for you during your banishment."

He pulled her finger away. "I admit that was the case in the beginning."

"I'm not casting judgment. Lord knows I have no right to after what I've done."

He skimmed the side of his finger along her temple. "You are a mother. You did what you had to."

"Perhaps," she said. "Perhaps not. One always has options."

"Does that mean you wanted to share my bed?"

For far longer than you shall ever know, my dear sweet lord. "You sound surprised."

"Relieved, more like," he said. "A man is no different from a woman in this regard. We want to be desired for ourselves and not for what one can gain from an association with us."

The vulnerable quality to his statement made her throat ache. "My point in all this is to release you from our arrangement."

His countenance darkened. "What if I don't wish to be released?"

"Sebastian, it would not be wise for you to stay." She squeezed his hand. "Surely, you see that."

A muscle in his jaw jumped. "I don't."

She pushed out of his arms and paced away. The stubborn man was going to make her splay open her soul in all its foolish glory. "If you leave now, there's a slight chance that I might survive this *affaire*." Catherine raised her gaze to his, tears welling in her eyes. "Stay, and I am l-lost."

"Cat," he said thickly, taking a step toward her.

Unable to speak, she shook her head. One touch from him and she would gladly plunge into the abyss, for which only heartache lay at the end.

"Will you answer one question?" he asked.

She moistened her dry lips. "Of course."

"If I resigned my position as chief, would you have me?"

Her heart fluttered. "Have you?"

"As a husband?"

"You would do that?" she asked, startled. "Give up the Nexus—for me?"

"Without hesitation."

"But why, Sebastian? Why would you give up a cause that you have devoted your life to?" Her eyes narrowed. "I hope not because of some bothersome gentleman's code. My honor does not need protecting."

"No." The rich timbre of his voice prickled her skin. "Nothing so inconvenient as protecting your honor."

"Then why?"

"Because I love you and want nothing more than to spend my days with you and your managing daughter."

The tears spilled over her lids and streamed down her cheeks. "Truly?"

He smiled. "Truly."

"I deceived you in the worst possible way."

"Not the worst way, Catherine. Believe me." He smoothed his thumb over her damp cheek. "You exhibited great courage during a dangerous situation. A quality to be admired, not judged."

"Cora knows you well."

His lips thinned. "Does she?"

Catherine slid her hand up his chest. "I didn't dare

believe her when she said you'd understand why I did what I did."

"I hadn't realized my agent had become a damned matchmaker."

"She wants you to have what she and Lord Helsford have."

"You may spare me the Raven's wisdom," he said. "I shall have to put up with her gloating looks for years as it is."

Catherine toyed with a pleat on the shoulder of his shirtsleeves. "Sebastian, I don't want you to give up the Nexus. They need you. As does England."

The muscle beneath her fingers stiffened. "My position requires me to be away for long periods of time and often without notice."

Past hurts crowded into her mind. "Yes, well. I won't lie and say that condition won't be difficult. A few assurances on your part might be necessary."

He cocked his head to the side. "What sort of assurances?"

Catherine tried twice to force the words out, but they remained lodged behind a lump in the back of her throat.

He combed his fingers through her hair, soothing her like one would a distressed animal. "Don't lose your nerve now, my love." The tenderness in his gaze made the lump grow larger.

"That you'll always put us—Sophie and me—first."

"Done."

She raised a brow. "Just like that?"

"Yes," he said. "Perhaps you need something more tangible?"

Catherine could do nothing more than stare like a young miss right out of the schoolroom.

"Reeves offered me the under-superintendent position." He fanned her hair over her shoulders. "I would be required to stay in London—no jaunts to the continent, no covert missions. My responsibilities would include coordinating the Nexus's efforts with those of the Foreign and Home Offices."

"Does this position interest you?" Catherine tried to keep the budding hope from her tone.

"Oh, yes." He kissed her cheek, the corner of her mouth. "It would allow me to get started."

Her breaths came in short bursts. "Started on what?"

"A family."

Warmth encased her heart. "I believe such a task requires a wife."

"Indeed, it does." He whispered the words near her ear a moment before his lips closed around her earlobe.

Tingles raced down her spine, and she arched her lower body into his hardness.

"I believe one will become available next summer, after a certain mourning period has elapsed."

He worshipped her throat with slow, openmouthed kisses. Stopping only long enough to say, "Perfect. I have much to settle in the intervening months."

"Like locating Lord Latymer?"

"Yes," he said. "Before this incident, he was nothing more than a French pawn, for reasons I still don't understand. Now he's an active participant, which makes him a great deal more dangerous."

"Who will replace you as chief?"

"A good question," he said. "Helsford, Cora, and

Danforth are the most experienced of my agents. All three are trustworthy, intelligent, and strong."

"Whatever choice you make will be the right one." She could see the decision troubled him, so she redirected their conversation back to a topic of great importance to her. "You will visit us often?"

"No."

"No?"

He kissed her forehead. "I will have no need to visit, because you and Sophie will be with me."

"In London?"

"Yes, or Bellamere. Or Winter's Hollow. We can divide our time between the city and the country. But no matter where we settle, we'll be together. So much so, you will become sick of me and beg a reprieve."

She snaked her arms around his neck, more happy than she'd been in years. More complete. "Never, my lord."

"That's what I was hoping you would say." He pulled her closer. "Now, have I ever told you about the delights to be found in this particular section of the garden?"

He backed her into the shadows until the ground beneath their feet softened and the sweet scent of freshly shorn grass reached her nose. Then slowly, inexorably, he lowered her to the velvety carpet and proceeded to show her how a spymaster loves his lady: Above all else.

In case you missed it, here's an
excerpt from Tracey Devlyn's debut

A Lady's Revenge

Available now from Sourcebooks Casablanca

⤜❦⤛

1804

Near Honfleur, France

GUY TREVELYAN, EARL OF HELSFORD, STOPPED SHORT
at the sharp smell of burning flesh. The caustic odor
melded with the dungeon's thick, moldy air, stinging
his eyes and seizing his lungs. His watery gaze slashed to
the cell's open door, and he cocked his head, listening.

There.

A sudden scrape of metal against metal. A faint
sizzling sound followed by a muffled scream.

He stepped forward to put an end to the prisoner's
obvious suffering but was yanked back and forced up
against the dungeon's cold stone wall, a solid forearm
pressed against the base of his throat.

Danforth.

Guy thrust his knee into the bastard's stomach,
enjoying the sound of air hissing between his assailant's lips, but the man didn't release his hold. Nearly
the same size as Guy, the Viscount Danforth wasn't

an easy man to dislodge. Guy knew that fact well. For many years they had tested each other's strength.

"What the hell is wrong with you?" the viscount whispered near his ear. "We're here for the Raven. No one else."

Guy stared into Danforth's shadowed face, surprised and thankful for his friend's quick reflexes. What would have happened had he stormed into the cell to save a prisoner he knew nothing about, against odds he hadn't taken time to calculate? Something in the prisoner's cry of pain struck deep into his gut. His reaction had been swift and instinctual, more in line with Danforth's reckless tendencies than his own carefully considered decisions.

"Leave off," Guy hissed, furious with himself. He pushed against Danforth's hold, and the other man's arm dropped away.

He had to concentrate on their assignment, or none of them would leave this French nightmare alive. The mission: retrieve the Raven, a female spy credited with saving hundreds of British lives by infiltrating the newly appointed emperor's intimate circle and relaying information back to the Alien Office.

Guy shook his head, unable to fathom the courage needed to pull off such an ill-fated assignment. The ever-changing landscape of the French government ensured no one was safe—not the former king, the *Ancien Régime*, the bourgeoisie, or the commoner. And, most especially, not an English secret service agent.

Although Napoleon's manipulation of the weak and floundering Consulate stabilized a country on the brink of civil destruction, the revered general-turned-dictator wasn't content to reign over just one country. He wanted to rule all of Europe, possibly the entire world. And, if his enemies didn't unite under one solid coalition soon, he might achieve his goal.

Another muffled, gut-twisting cry from the cell drew his attention. He clenched his teeth, staring at the faint light spilling out of the room, alert for movement or any signs of what he might find within.

Sweet Jesus, he hoped the individual being tortured by one of Valère's henchmen wasn't the Raven. In his years with the Alien Office, he had witnessed a lot of disturbing scenes, some of his creation. But to witness the mangled countenance of a woman… The notion struck too close to the fear that had boiled in his chest for months—*years*—giving him no respite.

On second thought, he hoped the prisoner was the Raven. Then he wouldn't have to make the decision to leave the poor, unfortunate soul behind, and they could get the hell out of this underground crypt posthaste.

"Are you well?" Danforth asked, eyeing him as if he didn't recognize his oldest friend.

Guy shoved away from the stone wall, shrugging off the chill that had settled like ice in his bones. Devil take it, what did the chief of the Alien Office expect him to do? Walk up to the prisoner and say, "Hello, are you the Raven? No? What a shame. Well, have a nice evening." Only one person knew what the agent looked like, and Somerton did not offer up those details before ushering them off to France. *Why?* he wondered for the thousandth time. It was an answer he intended to find as soon as they got back to London, assuming they survived this mission.

"I'm fine." He jabbed his thumb over his shoulder. "Now cease with the mothering and get behind me."

He barely noticed the fist connecting with his arm, having already braced himself for Danforth's retaliation. Some things never change. Inching toward the cell door, he tilted his head and concentrated on the low rumble of voices until he was close enough to make out individual words.

"Why do you force me to be so cruel?" a plaintive voice from inside the chamber asked. The Frenchman spoke slowly, as if talking to a child, which allowed Guy to quickly translate the man's unctuous words. The gaoler continued, "All you have to do is provide my master with the information he seeks."

A chain rattled. "Go to the devil, Boucher," a guttural voice whispered.

Guy's jaw hardened. The prisoner's words were so low and distorted that it was impossible to distinguish the speaker's gender. Every second they spent trying to solve the prisoner's identity was a second closer to discovery.

The interrogator let out a deep, exaggerated sigh. "The branding iron seems to have lost its effect on you. Let me see if I have something more persuasive."

An animallike growl preceded the prisoner's broken whisper. "Your black soul will burn for this."

Boucher chuckled low, controlled. "But not tonight, little spy. As you have come to discover, I do not have the same aversion to seeing you suffer as my master does."

Something eerily familiar about the prisoner's voice caught Guy's attention. His gaze sliced back to

Danforth to find puzzlement etched deeply between his friend's brows.

Guy turned back, the ferocity of his heartbeat pumping in his ears. His stomach churned with the certain knowledge that what he found in this room of despair would change his life forever. He steadied his hand against the rough surface of the dungeon wall, leaned forward to peer into the cell, and was struck by a sudden wave of fetid air. The smell was so foul that it sucked the breath from his lungs, and he nearly coughed to expel the sickening taste from his mouth and throat.

The cell was twice the size of the others they had searched. Heaps of filthy straw littered the floor caked with human waste and God knew what else. Several strategically placed candles illuminated a small, circular area, leaving the room's corners steeped in darkness. In the center stood a long wooden table with a young man strapped to its surface by thick iron manacles.

A young man. Disappointment spiraled through him. He glanced at Danforth and shook his head, and then evaluated their situation. The corridor beyond the candlelit chamber loomed like a great, impenetrable abyss.

The intelligence Danforth had seduced from Valère's maid suggested the chateau's dungeon held twelve cells. If the maid's information was correct, that left four more chambers to search. Would they, like all the others, be strangely empty?

Guy narrowed his gaze, fighting to see something—anything—down the darkened passage. It yawned eerily silent. Too damned silent. The lack of movement, guards, and other prisoners scraped his nerves raw. That and the realization they would not be able to slide past the nearby cell without drawing attention from its occupants.

Dammit.

He ignored Danforth's warning tap on his shoulder and peered into the young man's cell again. The prisoner's filthy legs and arms splayed in a perfect X across the table's bloodstained surface. A few feet away, with his back to the prisoner, stood a slender man dressed in the clothes of a gentleman, his unusual white-capped head bent in concentration over an assortment of spine-chilling instruments. *Boucher.*

Guy watched the man assess each device with the careful attention of an enraptured lover, masterfully prolonging the young man's terror. Give a victim long enough, and he'll create plenty of painful scenes in his own mind that the interrogator need only touch his weapon to the prisoner's skin to elicit a full, babbling confession.

He couldn't walk away from the poor soul struggling on the table, nor could he cold-bloodedly put an end to his misery. The young man was a countryman, not his enemy, and he would never leave one of his own in Valère's hands.

With great care, he withdrew a six-inch hunting knife from his boot. He heard Danforth curse softly, violently, behind him, and then a rustle of movement. His hand shot out to stay his friend, and a short struggle ensued. Their roles now reversed, Guy whispered in Danforth's ear, "There's no way around, and I'm not leaving him here."

"We don't have time—"

"I'm. Not. Leaving. Him."

After a moment, Danforth gave a sharp nod and settled into the rear support position once more, anger dripping off him in waves.

He couldn't blame his friend for wanting to press on. Evil penetrated every crack and hollow of this place. Even with his vast experience with the darker side of human nature, Guy felt trapped and edgy and unusually desperate.

Guy shifted his attention to the prisoner just as the young man's head swiveled toward the open doorway. Bleakness and terror etched his swollen, blood-encrusted face, but something more blazed behind the young man's steady gaze—strength, fortitude, and a hint of hope.

He was a fighter, a warrior entombed in a rapidly weakening young man's body. A rush of fury mixed with a healthy dose of respect surged through Guy. How did one so young get involved with the likes of Valère?

The prisoner's chest rose high with each deep, agonized breath. As his torturer intended, the young man knew Boucher's next attempt at pulling information from him would be far worse than the last.

Candlelight flickered over his youthful features. When the prisoner focused in on Guy's position, his terrified blue-green eyes—or eye, as one was little more than a bloated slit—opened wide.

Guy's heart jolted, fearing the young man would call out. With an index finger to his lips, he motioned for the prisoner to remain quiet.

Familiarity washed over Guy again. His gaze cleaved to the prisoner's; his focus sharpened.

Blue-green eyes. An unusual color Guy had seen only once before. His muscles contracted. A wave of frigid heat swept across every inch of his skin, and nausea twisted in his gut.

He knew those eyes.

The young man wasn't a man at all. But a goddamned woman.

Cora.

Acknowledgments

A huge thanks to my amazing editor, Deb Werksman, and my patient agent, Donald Maass, for believing in my stories and me and for helping me make them shine.

Much love to my husband, Tim Curtin. You are my rock, my love, and my sunshine. Thanks for enduring the rigors of my sophomore book and for keeping me supplied with Slim Jims, Starbucks, and pasta puttanesca. On top of all that, you're a fabulous beta reader, too!

Sending a shout-out to my awesome publicist, Beth Pehlke. Thanks for all your support and for making my releases seamless and fun. Heartfelt thanks to the rest of the Sourcebooks team—Skye Agnew, Susie Benton, Cat Clyne, and my incredible cover designer, Aleta Rafton. A special thanks to Danielle Jackson.

Big hugs to my critique partners Adrienne Giordano, Kelsey Browning, Theresa Stevens, and Tara Kingston. You are the best, most amazing buds a girl could have. Thanks for always being there for me.

This acknowledgment would not be complete if I did not express my gratitude to my friend and fellow author Dyanne Davis. Enormous thanks to you (and Bill!) for spotlighting local writers at Bolingbrook Community Television. It's always a pleasure to be your guest. You're an incredible advocate for the romance genre and to writers at every level.

And to readers, librarians, and booksellers everywhere—thank you, thank you, thank you!!

When You Give a Duke a Diamond

by Shana Galen

———— ❧ ————

He had a perfectly orderly life...

William, the sixth Duke of Pelham, enjoys his punctual, securely structured life. Orderly and predictable—that's the way he likes it. But he's in the public eye, and the scandal sheets will make up anything to sell papers. When the gossips link him to Juliette, one of the most beautiful and celebrated courtesans in London, chaos doesn't begin to describe what happens next...

Until she came along...

Juliette is nicknamed the Duchess of Dalliance, and has the cream of the nobility at her beck and call. It's seriously disruptive to have the duke who's the biggest catch on the Marriage Mart scaring her other suitors away. Then she discovers William's darkest secret and decides what he needs in his life is the kind of excitement only she can provide...

———— ❧ ————

For more Shana Galen, visit:

www.sourcebooks.com

Waking Up with a Rake

Connie Mason and Mia Marlowe

The fate of England's monarchy is in the hands of three notorious rakes.

To prevent three royal dukes from marrying their way onto the throne, heroic, selfless agents for the crown will be dispatched…to seduce the dukes' intended brides. These wickedly debauched rakes will rumple sheets and cause a scandal. But they just might fall into their own trap…

After he's blamed for a botched assignment during the war, former cavalry officer Rhys Warrick turns his back on "honor." He spends his nights in brothels doing his best to live down to the expectations of his disapproving family. But one last mission could restore the reputation he's so thoroughly sullied. All he has to do is seduce and ruin Miss Olivia Symon and his military record will be cleared. For a man with Rhys' reputation, ravishing the delectably innocent miss should be easy. But Olivia's honesty and bold curiosity stir more than Rhys' desire. Suddenly the heart he thought he left on the battlefield is about to surrender…

For more Connie Mason and Mia Marlowe, visit

www.sourcebooks.com

How to Tame a Willful Wife

by Christy English

How to Tame a Willful Wife:

1. Forbid her from riding astride
2. Hide her dueling sword
3. Burn all her breeches and buy her silk drawers
4. Frisk her for hidden daggers
5. Don't get distracted while frisking her for hidden daggers…

Anthony Carrington, Earl of Ravensbrook, expects a biddable bride. A man of fiery passion tempered by the rigors of war into steely self-control, he demands obedience from his troops and his future wife. Regardless of how fetching she looks in breeches.

Promised to the Earl of Plump Pockets by her impoverished father, Caroline Montague is no simpering miss. She rides a war stallion named Hercules, fights with a blade, and can best most men with both bow and rifle. She finds Anthony autocratic, domineering, and… ridiculously handsome.

It's a duel of wit and wills in this charming retelling of *The Taming of the Shrew*. But the question is…who's taming whom?

For more Christy English, visit:

www.sourcebooks.com

Once Again a Bride

by Jane Ashford

She couldn't be more alone

Widowhood has freed Charlotte Wylde from a demoralizing and miserable marriage. But when her husband's intriguing nephew and heir arrives to take over the estate, Charlotte discovers she's unsafe in her own home…

He could be her only hope… or her next victim

Alec Wylde was shocked by his uncle's untimely death, and even more shocked to encounter his uncle's beautiful young widow. Now clouds of suspicion are gathering, and charges of murder hover over Charlotte's head.

Alec and Charlotte's initial distrust of each other intensifies as they uncover devastating family secrets, and hovering underneath it all is a mutual attraction that could lead them to disaster…

Readers and reviewers are charmed by Jane Ashford:

"Charm, intrigue, humor, and just the right touch of danger."—RT Book Reviews

For more Jane Ashford, visit:

www.sourcebooks.com

About the Author

Tracey Devlyn writes historical romantic thrillers (translation: a slightly more grievous journey toward the heroine's happy ending). She's a co-founder of Romance University, a group blog dedicated to readers and writers of romance, and Lady Jane's Salon-Naperville, Chicagoland's exciting new reading salon devoted to romantic fiction.

An Illinois native, Tracey spends her evenings harassing her once-in-a-lifetime husband and her weekends torturing her characters. For more information on Tracey, including her Internet haunts, contest updates, and details on her upcoming novels, please visit her website at www.TraceyDevlyn.com.